"What the hell?" asked La Forge,

leaning to either side of the console tower to see that the same information appeared to be broadcasting on the adjacent workstations. "Something's got this thing's attention."

Worf pointed to one of the screens. "This is an indication similar to what was displayed when the tactical system detected the *Enterprise*."

"Yeah," the engineer said, "but I canceled that alert." Then his communicator chirped.

"Chen to Commander La Forge! The defensive systems are coming online, on their own!"

Stepping closer to the console, Worf glowered at the collection of monitors. "I thought you said those processes were deactivated."

"This is my fault, sir!" replied Chen. *"We thought we'd found an override for one of the other protected systems, but I must've entered the code wrong, because it looks like the computer's invoking some kind of override. I don't know, maybe there's another security code or something else that's needed that we don't have."*

La Forge, studying the new readings, felt his pulse beginning to race and anxiety welling up within him. "Damn it. Whatever caused it, this thing is getting ready for a fight."

STAR TREK
THE NEXT GENERATION®

ARMAGEDDON'S ARROW

DAYTON WARD

Based upon
Star Trek® and
Star Trek: The Next Generation
created by Gene Roddenberry

POCKET BOOKS
New York   London   Toronto   Sydney   New Delhi

Pocket Books
An Imprint of Simon & Schuster, Inc.
1230 Avenue of the Americas
New York, NY 10020

This book is a work of fiction. Any references to historical events, real people, or real places are used fictitiously. Other names, characters, places, and events are products of the author's imagination, and any resemblance to actual events or places or persons, living or dead, is entirely coincidental.

First Pocket Books paperback edition June 2015

POCKET and colophon are registered trademarks of Simon & Schuster, Inc.

For information about special discounts for bulk purchases, please contact Simon & Schuster Special Sales at 1-866-506-1949 or business@simonandschuster.com.

The Simon & Schuster Speakers Bureau can bring authors to your live event. For more information or to book an event, contact the Simon & Schuster Speakers Bureau at 1-866-248-3049 or visit our website at www.simonspeakers.com.

Manufactured in the United States of America

10 9 8 7 6 5 4 3 2

ISBN 978-1-4767-8269-0
ISBN 978-1-4767-8270-6 (ebook)

For Michi, Addison, and Erin,
who remind me every day what really matters.

HISTORIAN'S NOTE

This story takes place in early January 2386, approximately seven years after the *U.S.S. Enterprise*-E's confrontation with the Romulan Praetor Shinzon (*Star Trek Nemesis*) and just over two months after Kellessar zh'Tarash is elected President of the United Federation of Planets following the assassination of Nanietta Bacco (*Star Trek: The Fall–Peaceable Kingdoms*).

THEN

1

Centered on the targeting screen and highlighted by the pulsing blue reticule, the moon seemed small and insignificant. It hung alone before a backdrop of utter blackness, reflecting the rays of the Canborek sun as though sending out a beckoning signal. It possessed no atmosphere to provide even minimal protection from uncounted generations of punishment it had suffered in the form of violent impacts from meteorites and other objects traversing the Canborek system. Even from the ship's current distance, the evidence of this abuse was clearly visible, with uncounted craters marring the bulk of the moon's surface. Other terrain features—mountains and canyons—also were observable.

"Targeting telemetry is locked in," reported Bnira, the crew's weapons specialist. Shifting in her seat, she turned so that she could look down from her station at Jodis. "Primary weapon will be at full power in less than three *linzatu*."

Glancing up at his shipmate and close friend, Jodis nodded at the report. "Very well." Once the antiproton particle cannon reached full power, it would require only another *linzat* or two to carry out what in stark reality was little more than a test of the ship's capabilities. Only after this trial run was completed would the true mission begin. Even the ship seemed to know this, as Jodis could feel the reverberations coursing through his console, the deck plating beneath his feet, and every surface of the cramped cockpit as power from nonessential systems was channeled to feed the vessel's mammoth armaments. The *Poklori gil dara* was a ship created for a single purpose, and everything and everyone aboard was here for no other reason than to support that goal: win a war, now and for all time.

As Bnira turned back to her station, Jodis heard her grunting and muttering a string of vulgarities as though to herself. "Is something wrong?" he asked.

"I think these restraints are trying to kill me," Bnira replied. "I need to adjust them." As with everyone else operating stations on the command deck, she was held in her seat by a harness to prevent her from floating out of her chair. Each seat had been custom designed and molded to fit its intended occupant to maximize protection, and this included the integrated restraint system worn across the body. "It feels like it was set for Ehondar."

Jodis could not help a small laugh as he thought of the *Poklori gil dara*'s diminutive engineer, who at this moment was overseeing all onboard systems from his workspace several decks below the cockpit. The accomplished technical specialist was of slim build and modest height, presenting the appearance of an adolescent. Only the deep lines in his dark, weary face betrayed his true age.

As for the special seats and their restraints—including those plaguing Bnira—they were necessary, as no gravity plating had been installed in the cockpit, thereby allowing the ship's designers to take full advantage of the space. The command deck's eight workstations—one for each member of the crew—were positioned along the bulkheads as well as what would be the cramped chamber's floor and ceiling. While Jodis's station faced forward, Bnira's consoles were mounted above him and to his left.

The other stations, each dedicated to the oversight of major systems, were vacant, as the rest of the crew had moved to the engineering spaces deep in the bowels of the ship. Behind Jodis, a pressure hatch led to a narrow tunnel that connected the command deck to the rest of the vessel's interior compartments. The hatch was locked, and the cockpit could be jettisoned to act as an emergency escape pod in the event of catastrophic damage to the rest of the ship.

"Add it to the list," Jodis suggested, doing his best to suppress another laugh at his friend's expense. "We will address it later."

Despite the numerous cycles he and his crew had spent training for this mission, all of that preparation had taken place using simulations and mock-ups of the *Poklori gil dara*'s systems and work areas, while the ship's construction continued during that same period beneath a shroud of near-total secrecy. Consequently, Jodis and his team had spent only a minimal amount of time aboard the vessel. It had not taken long for the crew to discover that not everything was the same as it had been represented in their simulators. While the vital systems and other major features were performing within acceptable parameters, Jodis and the others had found a string of minor discrepancies that did not detract from the ship's operational status despite being inconvenient or simply irritating to varying degrees. Some of the computer software had not been properly installed, requiring adjustments and other modifications to bring it up to specifications. Even the targeting scanner had required realignment before it could be used, making it one of the first problems to be remedied once Jodis and his crew boarded the ship. As for Bnira's seat straps, they were but the latest addition to a growing roster of annoyances, but they could be corrected. Such trivial tasks would just have to wait for a more appropriate time.

Ignoring the weapons technician's complaints, Jodis returned his attention to the targeting scanner and the moon displayed upon it. The sunlight playing across its drab, battered topography offered the momentary illusion that this was not an inert astral body but instead a planet like the one it orbited. It was a cradle of life to be protected rather than destroyed. While that was true in a minimal sense, the moon never would be able to sustain a civilization on its own. It was a resource, exploited by the people of its host world for the diverse array of mineral ores, and to that end was home to a handful of military outposts and mining facilities scattered across its surface. Orbiting Copan, the Canborek system's third planet, the moon had been claimed generations earlier by the Golvonek, the powerful civilization from the neighboring world, Uphrel. It had taken far less time for the moon to become yet another key point of contention in the ongoing war between the Golvonek and Jodis's people, the Raqilan.

The war.

It was a conflict which had raged since long before Jodis's birth and been the focal point of reality his entire life. Nearly all of Raqilan civilization had been affected by the generations-long struggle between Uphrel and his own planet, Henlona. The resources of both worlds had been all but depleted, necessitating expansion to the other planets and moons orbiting the Canborek sun. Though supplying the ongoing war effort was of prime importance, of course, there also was simple survival to consider, as even if hostilities ceased today, it still would take uncounted generations to recover from the war's effects. It was uncertain if either planet would be capable of sustaining their respective populations, but government and science leaders on Henlona already were developing plans for larger, permanent space-based habitats as well as colonizing the system's remaining planets. Though such information typically was not shared with the civilian populace, Jodis knew that according to the most dire predictions, if drastic action was not taken, the planet of his birth would be incapable of sustaining life in less than five generations.

Perhaps, Jodis mused. *Perhaps not.*

"At last report," he said after a moment, "there still were personnel on one of the outposts who had not yet evacuated the moon."

Without turning from her station, Bnira replied, "We have not received any new status updates. Our observation satellites recorded all but one of the transports assigned to bases on the moon lifting off and heading away on trajectories which should return them to Uphrel." After a moment, she craned her neck to once more look down at him. "Our orders have not changed."

"I am aware of that," Jodis snapped. Looking away from the targeting scanner, he paused to study the moon through the curved transparent barrier forming the command deck's forward observation port. Though he tried to resist it, he still felt a momentary hesitation grip him. It was true that the moon was a legitimate military target, and advance warning of their impending attack had been communicated to the highest echelons of the Golvonek civilian government and the leadership of their military forces. By now, both parties were aware of the *Poklori gil dara* and the simple fact that nothing in their remaining arsenal was a match for the mammoth warship. Still, given their principal, ultimate objective, was this demonstration of the vessel's power truly necessary?

Yes, Jodis reminded himself. Setting aside the moon's value to Golvonek so far as its location and wealth of resources, the truth was that the ship's primary particle beam weapon had not yet been tested. Such trials had been all but impossible, given the *Poklori gil dara*'s sheer size and the capabilities its design boasted, along with the unquestioned need to keep the massive vessel's existence a secret until it could be launched. As with everything else, Jodis and his crew had been forced to train using computer simulations that utilized algorithms and other data to hypothesize the scope of the cannon's power and effects. Now, however, the time for practice and pretending was past, and there was no hiding the ship from the Golvonek. No other options remained to him except to follow his orders.

It is time.

An alert tone sounded from above him, and Bnira announced, "Weapon is at full power."

"Stand by to fire," Jodis ordered. With his selection as commander of the *Poklori gil dara* and all the preparation required for their mission, it had been many cycles since he had last seen actual combat. The familiar sensations of anticipation were awakening every nerve in his body. He shifted in his seat, feeling his muscles tensing. With one last look at his targeting scanner, Jodis pushed himself into his seat and braced for whatever was to come.

"Execute."

His order was followed by Bnira pressing the appropriate control on her console, and in response, lights and indicators across the small command deck flickered as power was drawn from every shipboard system and fed to the particle cannon. Even the vessel's immense engines wavered for a moment in reaction to the new demands being made of them. Then, all of that was lost amid the fury of the *Poklori gil dara* establishing its reason for being.

Jodis threw a hand up to protect his eyes as the cannon fired, a great, broad beam of brilliant, pulsing red-orange light erupting from the port which was the vessel's prow. The effects inside the ship were immediate as the bulkheads groaned in unison with the howl of energy surging forth from the weapon's power generator. Despite the array of thrusters installed all along the hull—all of them controlled by the onboard computer to maintain the ship's position—Jodis's stomach told him they were being pushed backward from the force of the unleashed energy.

"Maintain fire!" he shouted over the increasing din, and stared through the forward viewing port as the beam crossed the void separating the *Poklori gil dara* from its target. It struck the moon's surface, and Jodis saw the impact as the energy pierced the pale, arid soil. A ring of dirt and debris pushed outward in an expanding circle. Cracks—deep, dark fissures illuminated with the same golden hue as the beam itself—appeared at the point of contact, expanding and widening with each passing moment. As the cannon continued to drive its focused antiproton stream into the dead satellite's core, Jodis felt his jaw slacken while watching immense portions of the moon beginning to separate.

"Cease fire," he ordered, his gaze riveted to the viewing port and the horrific scene unfolding before him. The moon was continuing to come apart, enormous sections pushed away by the force of the particle cannon. A haze of debris surrounded everything, cascading in all directions in a growing cloud.

From above him, he heard the astonishment in Bnira's voice. "That is unbelievable. I know the simulations taught us what to expect, but that is still the most incredible thing I have ever seen."

Jodis ignored her comments, his attention instead fixed on his own instruments and status indicators. An instant later, a collision warning pierced the air of the confined command deck.

"Scans are registering the expected shock wave!" he called out. "Full power to forward defenses." Reaching for his console, he activated the ship's internal communications system. "This is Jodis. Brace for impact!" As with the cannon, the *Poklori gil dara*'s protective force fields had not been tested under actual combat conditions. Though all indicators showed the generators for that system were functioning as projected, there was only one way to gauge their effectiveness.

Jodis gripped his seat's armrests just as an unseen force slammed into the vessel. Though the force of the impact was far less than he had anticipated, it still was enough to trigger another wave of alarms as he felt himself jostled in his seat, his body straining against his harness. All around him, monitors and status indicators flashed and blinked, and Jodis heard the steady thrum of the engines waver as the ship struggled to withstand the onslaught.

"Force fields are holding!" Bnira called out, her anxiety palpable as it laced her words. "But there are power fluctuations across the ship."

The wave was subsiding, a fact Jodis could verify from instrumentation as well as his own body and ship. Outside the viewing port, he could see the expanding debris cloud steadying as maneuvering thrusters worked to retain the ship's present position. A quick glance to the targeting scanner confirmed what he already suspected. "Engaging our withdrawal course heading," he said, his hands moving to the helm controls on the console.

"Jodis," said a new voice, filtering through the internal communications system, *"this is Ehondar. We are registering several shipwide overloads and circuit faults. None of them appear to be serious, but they will take time to repair."*

Before Jodis could respond to the engineer, a new alert tone sounded from the targeting scanner, and he saw that the computer-generated readout now depicted several new contacts. Thirteen red indicators had appeared at the lower edge of the screen and now were moving toward its center and the larger green icon representing the *Poklori gil dara*.

"Incoming Golvonek ships," Bnira said, turning once more in her seat. "According to the readings, it appears to be an entire attack squadron."

A Golvonek military response was not an unexpected development, of course. The enemy would be marshalling ships for deployment the instant their deep space scanners detected the *Poklori gil dara*. That action would only be accelerated once it became evident that the massive ship was the source of the threat communicated to the Uphrel planetary government and the moon that until moments ago had orbited the planet Copan. In fact, Jodis was surprised it had taken the Golvonek military leadership this long to send out any sort of reaction force. They now were on their way, and Jodis knew the commanders of the ships approaching them would not be swayed even by the demonstration of immense power which had just been provided.

"An entire attack squadron," Jodis said, his gaze fixed on the targeting scanner. Though computer training scenarios had shown the *Poklori gil dara* as more than capable of fighting multiple enemy ships, the mammoth vessel's effectiveness was impacted as the number of opponents increased. Simulated engagements against a full squadron of Golvonek combat ships had been inconclusive, with the enemy contingent winning nearly as many of those fictitious encounters as it lost. In simpler terms, there was no way to be certain that the approaching armada could be defeated.

"Prepare to cover our withdrawal," Jodis said before keying the control to open the communications channel. "Repairs will have to wait, Ehondar. Enemy ships on attack course. Stand by for defensive action."

2

Ehondar stared at the array of monitors and indicators filling the engineering space's primary operations cluster, which now was conveying far too many warnings and other troublesome status reports for his liking. Positioned at the center of the raised platform that ran the length of the immense chamber, the workstation was a five-sided tower, with each side featuring identical consoles, screens, gauges, and numeric readouts. The same information was communicated on each of the tower's sides, so that anyone working at any other station in the room, no matter where they were situated, could glean information regarding the current status of every major shipboard system. What the cluster now told him was troublesome, to say the least.

The drone of the engines was increasing as the ship changed to its new course and began to accelerate. Ehondar knew that up on the command deck, Jodis and Bnira were executing a strategic retreat. What now was required was a concerted effort on the part of the entire crew if they were to mitigate the effects of the pending attack long enough to make their final escape.

"Route power to secondary distribution network," Ehondar called out, removing the headset that he had worn to protect his hearing from the cacophony generated by the firing of the *Poklori gil dara*'s primary weapon. The engineering area, including the operations deck and like the rest of the ship's habitable crew spaces, had been constructed around the massive cylinder housing the antiproton particle cannon which was the vessel's singular reason for being. Though the ferocity of the weapon's harnessed energies could be felt throughout the entire ship, the effect was most pronounced here.

Experience and the tremor in the deck and bulkheads informed Ehondar before the cluster's status monitors that the ship was making the shift to faster-than-light speed. Overhead lighting flickered, and a noticeable warbling in the hum of the engines accompanied the transition.

"Pulse drive engaged," Ehondar reported as he moved to the closest of the tower's consoles, noting from the status readings that the faster-than-light engine was performing above specifications. A review of another monitor showed that the ship was proceeding away from the Canborek system, on a circular course which—if all went according to plan—would in time return the *Poklori gil dara* to the point from which it had departed.

In a manner of speaking, Ehondar reminded himself as he reached for the workstation. The rows of controls and switches, as with every console aboard the ship, were arranged in a manner that allowed ease of use by any member of the crew. The design scheme, developed by Ehondar and a team of technical specialists during the vessel's construction, eschewed conventional aesthetics in favor of a sleek, simple approach that could be utilized on any workstation anywhere on the ship. This facilitated rapid cross-training and allowed any member of the crew to assume the duties of a colleague with minimal transition delays.

In response to the commands he entered to the console, Ehondar heard the drone of the ship's main power plant as energy was redirected away from damaged conduits to backup systems. The redundancy was one of many protective measures incorporated into the vessel's design as a means of aiding the crew to make repairs without the benefit of a dedicated facility or other support base. This made perfect sense, given the mission for which the mammoth ship had been created, and the likelihood that once deployed to carry out that assignment, there would be no one to whom Jodis and his crew could turn for help.

Assuming we survive the next few linzatu, Ehondar mused.

"Have you seen the tactical scans?" a voice asked from behind him, and he turned to see Dlyren, his assistant engineer who also was trained to assist Bnira on the command deck with the ship's weapons and defense systems. "An entire Golvonek attack squadron is pursuing us."

Forcing a smile, Ehondar turned from the operations cluster. "You worry too much. This ship is bigger and stronger than anything the Golvonek can send against us. Besides, Jodis is a military commander without peer. Our enemies are doomed. They simply do not yet know it."

Unlike the younger Raqilan, Ehondar had been involved with most of the *Poklori gil dara*'s early design and a fair portion of its actual construction. While Jodis and the rest of the crew had been immersed in their training regimens in preparation for this mission, Ehondar had worked with engineers throughout the building process, educating himself about every facet of the vessel from its basic framework to each of its onboard systems. There was precious little crammed into this ship of which he was not aware, let alone eminently qualified to operate. Aside from the Raqilan civilian and military leaders who had ordered the ship's creation and those who had worked to realize its creation, Ehondar was the one individual most knowledgeable about the *Poklori gil dara* and everything it carried. It was this particular expertise that made him question whether the vessel might well find itself outmatched in any prolonged skirmish with a fully armed Golvonek attack squadron.

If fortune is with us, we will soon be away from here.

Another indicator flashed on the operations cluster's status display, telling Ehondar that more power was being called to the ship's defensive systems. The shields, though impressive, as they had protected the *Poklori gil dara* from the effects of the shock wave following the moon's destruction, still had suffered from the stresses inflicted upon them. The generators responsible for feeding power to the shields were still operational, but now they were being pressed into further service before Ehondar and his team could inspect them. If he had any single regret about the mission he and his crewmates were undertaking, it was that despite all their training and other preparations, the truth was that the ship and those tasked with piloting and caring for it had been rushed to duty without the benefit of a proper, final acceptance exercise. Key systems remained untested, including some of the critical equipment that the crew in very short order would be entrusting with their very lives.

Can one not say that about everything else around us?

Setting aside the errant thought, Ehondar once more eyed the status monitors. He reached for the console, each of his right hand's three long fingers moving to manipulate separate controls to shift the information being presented. One of the screens now offered a readout from the vessel's tactical scanners, mimicking the same data the engineer knew Jodis and Bnira were receiving on the command deck.

"Routing to the secondary distribution network is complete," Dlyren reported. "Force field generators are once again at full power."

Ehondar nodded in approval before pressing a control to open a communications channel. "Neline and Rilajor, what is the status of the suspension cradles?"

There was a lag before Neline, the *Poklori gil dara*'s medical specialist, replied, *"Our preparations are nearly complete, but there may be a problem. The shock wave damaged one of the computer's memory crystals."* Her voice faded for a *linzat* as she moved away from the communications port to say something Ehondar could not hear, though the annoyance and earnestness in her tone was evident as she issued instructions to her assistant before returning her attention to him. *"I have replaced the crystal from reserve storage, but now I must update the procedures overseeing the suspension and revival process. The auxiliary storage modules were not properly revised with the most current procedures prior to our departure."*

Grunting in frustration, Ehondar rubbed the skin on the top of his smooth head. That oversight was one of many which had plagued the ship since its departure, though this one, at least, could be explained by the secretive nature of the mission Jodis and his crew had been given. Final determinations and instructions regarding the *Poklori gil dara*'s projected course and target of its pending mission had been protected almost until the moment of the vessel's departure, necessitating a flurry of rushed updates to the computer to incorporate newly disseminated information. Most of the required revisions could be dealt with at a more opportune time, but those affecting the suspension cradles were of particular concern.

Time. The single word burned in his mind. *We needed more time.* Both he and Jodis had requested sufficient opportunity to make these sorts of final adjustments. Given the mission and its parameters, time seemed the one luxury that could be afforded. Much to Ehondar's disappointment and utter lack of surprise, Raqilan senior military leadership had disagreed with the recommendations, for reasons surpassing understanding.

"Acknowledged," Ehondar replied into the open channel, catching himself before he could append a string of vile oaths. "Keep me informed," he instead said, before tapping the communications control to terminate the connection.

"Ehondar," said Dlyren, and the engineer turned to see his protégé moving to the operations cluster. Dlyren pressed a series of controls, and Ehondar watched as the data stream on another of the monitors shifted. "These readings indicate that the chronopulse drive will not be ready before the attack squadron engages us."

"We are not helpless," Ehondar said, allowing a hint of irritation to punctuate his reply. "Our weapons are more than sufficient to repel their attack long enough to make the transition."

"But what of the calculations?" Dlyren pressed. "They require constant refinement, particularly if we are under way at the time of transition."

Ehondar nodded. "I understand the variables, and the risks." Still, Dlyren had raised a valid observation. Temporal displacement was a dangerous exercise, even when all possible safety precautions were observed. Having borne witness to the experiments conducted with automated drones as the technology was perfected, Ehondar had seen both successes and failures as the test craft were pushed mere *linzatu* into the future and retrieved for study. Those had been controlled trials, with limited parameters and posing very little danger. What the *Poklori gil dara* was about to undertake, however, was another matter altogether, and the suspension cradles were a vital part of the process. Without them, the crew—at least as far as all of the scientist and engineers who had worked to perfect the chronopulse drive had come to believe— would not survive the displacement.

"Tend to your duties," Ehondar said, gesturing for Dlyren to return to his station. "We all have much to do if this outlandish venture is to succeed."

All around them, the ship shuddered as though rocked by an enormous impact. Ehondar sensed the fluctuations in the gravity plating beneath his feet and lunged for his console to steady himself. Dlyren mimicked his actions, and Ehondar saw the expression of worry on the younger Raqilan's face as the entire engineering space echoed with the whine of the engines, an objection echoed by the very frame of the ship itself.

"The pulse drive is offline!" Dlyren shouted above the new chorus of alarms which had begun wailing throughout the chamber.

"Assess damage!" Ehondar snapped, his fingers already moving across his console as he worked to ascertain the ship's status. As before, an alarming number of indicators were flashing. Grunting in irritation, he slammed his hand down upon the control to activate the communications channel.

"Jodis! We have lost the pulse drive!"

Were he to ignore the information relayed to him by his console and his engineer, Jodis might almost believe that the ship was suffering no ill effects from the assault being waged against it. However, his instrumentation was providing a much different interpretation of current events.

"Can you restore the drive?" Jodis asked, still digesting Ehondar's report.

"Not while we are fighting the Golvonek," the engineer replied. *"I need power reserves that are being routed to defenses."*

Jodis nodded, having anticipated the answer. "Divert all efforts to readying the chronopulse drive. We will continue to repel the attack." The Golvonek attack squadron had wasted no time engaging the *Poklori gil dara*, with each of the thirteen ships breaking off and launching independent, simultaneous strikes. Most of the initial volleys had been absorbed by the vessel's protective force fields, but the squadron had pressed its assault and now it was beginning to tally hits that were inflicting legitimate damage.

"Force fields are wavering near the rear coolant exchange manifolds," Bnira said. There was obvious worry in her voice, but that was the only outward sign of her growing unease. Glancing up, Jodis saw that the alert indicators on her console bathed the skin of her smooth head in a wash of blinking colors. She was keeping her focus on her own station, her hands moving across the rows of controls with purpose and determination. "And we took another strike near the weapons port at that location. The port is offline."

Jodis already was aware of this latest damage to the ship, thanks to various status indicators flashing on his own console. The shields were a concern, of course, but so too was the weapons port. Aside from the antiproton cannon, which was its principle offensive armament, the *Poklori gil dara* also carried conventional particle weapons mounted all along its outer hull. With the oversized vessel unable to carry out the sorts of evasive tactics on which smaller craft relied during combat, those ports provided the ship with its chief means of defense. Losing any one weapon opened up a gap in the protective field of fire, allowing perceptive opponents to capitalize on the perimeter breach and perhaps inflict more harm to that undefended area.

The hum of the ship's engines dropped in pitch as Bnira once more engaged weapons. Studying the targeting scanner, Jodis saw the fifth of what originally had been thirteen icons denoting Golvonek ships turn and move away from the others. "Another hit!"

"Yes," Bnira replied. "Its forward shields are down, and scans show damage to its forward weapons ports." A *linzat* later she added, "The ship is retreating."

"Increasing to maximum speed," Jodis said, tapping the controls necessary to call for the much-needed acceleration. On the scanner, he saw the larger avatar representing the *Poklori gil dara* moving away from the eight remaining Golvonek ships, but the diminished squadron was falling into formation in pursuit. Beneath his hands, his console trembled yet again, communicating yet another strike from enemy weapons against the shields.

"Shields at the rear manifolds are offline," Bnira reported. "Any further strikes there will likely damage the hull plating."

Even the ablative armor covering the ship's exterior would not be able to withstand prolonged abuse from the Golvonek weapons. The vessel's sheer size saw to it that there was no place for it to hide, and outrunning the attack squadron without the pulse drive would be impossible. The only option remaining to Jodis and his crew was to continue mounting whatever defense they could muster and buy time for Ehondar and his engineers to finalize their hurried preparations.

Remembering a ploy he had learned while serving on an escort ship earlier in his career that had been assigned to one of the Raqilan fleet's larger and far less-maneuverable fighter transport vessels, Jodis keyed a new set of commands to the directional thrusters. "I am initiating a roll," he said, for Bnira's benefit. "That should help protect the vulnerable section. Program the remaining weapons ports to compensate and engage automated tracking. Full defensive fire patterns." He hoped that the intensified barrage of fire from the ship's array of weapons ports would at least keep the remaining Golvonek ships occupied for the next few precious *linzatu*.

"Acknowledged," Bnira replied. "I do not believe this will protect us for very long."

"It will not need to," Jodis countered. "If we do not make the jump, it will not matter." Shifting his gaze from his instruments to the viewing port, he was able to see how the Golvonek ships were reacting to the roll maneuver. They were altering their attack vectors in a bid to focus their weapons at points along the *Poklori gil dara*'s hull that now were moving even as the vessel itself continued to accelerate on its new course heading. "We are now at maximum velocity. Are the calculations for the chronopulse drive ready?"

"Ehondar reported that Rilajor and Gagil were still making adjustments," Bnira said, referring to the two members of the engineering team tasked with overseeing the care of the still-untested chronopulse drive.

Engaging the controls which would allow the onboard computer to pilot the ship while compensating for the feeble defensive maneuvers he had enacted, Jodis once more opened the communications channel, this time setting it so that his message was broadcast throughout the ship. "This is Jodis. Secure your stations and report to the suspension cradles."

Without waiting for any responses, he released the harness holding him into his seat. "It is time," he said, gesturing for Bnira to follow him from the command deck. He used the cockpit's weightless environment to propel himself into the connecting tunnel, feeling the first tendrils of gravity seize hold of him as he reached for the conduit's access ladder.

Reaching for rungs on the ladder was enough to push him through the constricted passage, by which time the effects of the normal gravity plating had taken hold. Jodis emerged headfirst, rising from the open port in the deck plating and up onto the main passageway which ran from front to rear the length of the ship's habitable areas. He offered a hand to Bnira as she climbed from the tunnel before both of them began running down the larger corridor. Only once was Jodis thrown off balance as another barrage from one or more of the Golvonek ships impacted against the *Poklori gil dara*'s hull. He stumbled and nearly fell to the deck, but he managed to maintain his footing as he and Bnira pressed forward.

They arrived in the suspension chamber, and Jodis saw that three of the room's eight peculiar cradles already were occupied by members of his crew. Dlyren, Gagil, and Waeno were settling into their suspension cradles, which looked like nothing more than compact beds tucked into transparent cylinders.

Looking to Neline, who was overseeing everyone's preparations, Jodis asked, "You have completed your updates to the computer for the cradles?"

The medical specialist replied, "The suspension and revival procedures are now set, but I did not have time to run a complete test of the configurations. However, none of those settings were altered before the damage, so the risk should be minimal."

Bnira said, "Or, at least no more severe than anything else."

"Correct. The remaining calculations have also been programmed." Neline was speaking in rapid, clipped tones that conveyed the urgency of the situation. "Once we are in suspension, the ship will nullify forward acceleration and execute the chronopulse jump."

"And what if the Golvonek lock on to us before the jump?" asked Bnira as she unfastened the closures on her flight suit and stepped out of the garment. Now nude, she held her arms away from her body as Neline's assistant, Rilajor, began applying small sensors at key points along her bare skin.

"Then our journey will be a short one," said Neline before turning to Jodis, who also had disrobed, and affixing similar sensors to his body.

Behind Neline, Ehondar turned from a workstation along the room's far bulkhead, which Jodis could see was being used to maintain constant vigil on the ship's status. "Another shield generator has gone offline, as have three more weapons ports. We are running out of time."

Jodis ordered everyone to finalize their preparations for entering the suspension cradles, then stood in silence as Neline completed the process of applying the sensors to his skin. He felt the throes of the ship around him as—guided by the onboard computer—it fought to keep its attackers at bay and give him and his crew sufficient time to complete these final tasks.

Once she was finished, the medical specialist waved him to his own cylinder before she and Rilajor began readying themselves, but Jodis took the brief opportunity to scan the status monitors Ehondar had left active on the nearby workstation. The reports were worrisome, but there now was nothing he could do to affect the situation. Regardless of the outcome, he and his crew were committed to their current course of action.

"Jodis, it is time," said Bnira from behind him, and he turned to face her. There was nothing more they could do, except trust the ship and its computer to carry out the tasks for which they had been created. Chief among those responsibilities was the care and safety of the crew that soon would trust their lives to this collection of machines.

Reaching for her hand, Jodis pulled Bnira close enough so that he could stroke the side of her face. She smiled, mimicking the gesture. Their relationship had evolved far beyond the tenets of commander and crew owing to the long periods spent ensconced in rigorous training. The strict need for secrecy had seen to it that the eight members of the *Poklori gil dara*'s crew were forced to work and live only with one another, so it was natural that bonds would form. Though counselors had warned of the dangers of such affairs, Jodis and the others paid such cautions no heed. After all, they had no one else.

"I hope yours is the first face I see upon waking," Bnira said.

Jodis smiled. "I look forward to that."

At another console, Neline, nude and with a set of sensors now affixed to her own body, touched several controls in rapid succession before moving from the station and to her own suspension cradle. A mechanical voice began reciting a numeric sequence in descending order.

Lying prone in his own cradle, Jodis watched as the transparent cylinder closed and sealed around him before a slight hiss echoed within the closed compartment as the programmed sequence of cryogenic vapors was introduced. Beyond the clear barrier, the now muffled voice of the computer was continuing its countdown. He turned his head and saw the rest of his crew, each of them ensconced in their own cradles, their interiors clouding up with the gases and other compounds necessary to induce hibernation.

A tremendous jolt rocked the entire ship, eliciting a host of new alarms and other warnings from the workstations positioned around the room, but by now Jodis could only lie motionless and wait. Outside his cradle, the computer counted down the few remaining *linzatu*, and as the inescapable tendrils of induced suspension embraced him, his final thoughts turned to the mission that still lay ahead of them.

There will be no war.

NOW

3

"You want to know the problem with going somewhere no one's ever been? It takes so damned long to get there."

Sitting at a table near one of the forward viewing ports of the *Enterprise*'s crew lounge, Lieutenant T'Ryssa Chen smiled as she watched her dining companion, Lieutenant Commander Taurik, look up from his breakfast of mixed fruits and regard her with the Vulcan equivalent of a perplexed expression, which consisted of him cocking his right eyebrow. For a moment, Chen was certain she had prompted a lecture on the nature of vast interstellar distances and the limited capabilities of modern vessels to traverse such expanses. Instead, Taurik's reply was far more understated.

"Indeed."

His response only made Chen's grin widen. "That's it? 'Indeed'? I lob an easy setup like that, and all you give me is 'Indeed'? You're not even trying."

Despite his self-discipline, she still saw the faintest tease of a smile tug at the corners of Taurik's mouth. "I saw no reason to refute your statement. Though colloquially stated, your observation is valid." Then, as if remembering his role in whatever game she seemed bound to involve him in on this occasion, he added, "I should think that you in particular would be excited at the potential our mission carries."

Here we go, Chen mused, claiming victory. "Me in particular?"

Taurik nodded. "You are a contact specialist. With few exceptions, our assignments since your arrival aboard the *Enterprise* have not provided you with many opportunities to perform the duties for which you were trained. Our current mission promises to offer at least some prospects for making first contact with new civilizations." He returned his attention to his meal, but only for a moment before adding, "I am happy for you, T'Ryssa."

"You're *happy*?" Chen caught herself, realizing her voice had raised in volume enough to attract glances from crew members at nearby tables. For his part, Taurik seemed unperturbed by her near outburst. "*You're* happy?" she pressed. "You've been hanging around me too much."

Without hesitation, the engineer replied, "It is not unreasonable to hypothesize that prolonged contact with you may be inflicting as yet unidentified effects on my thought processes, emotional reactions, and responses to various external stimuli."

Chen bobbed her eyebrows. "Tell me more about the various external stimuli."

After glancing around them as though confirming that no one was overhearing their conversation, Taurik leaned closer. "No, I do not believe that I will."

"Then I'll just have to come up with my own." Chen eyed him with no small amount of mischief.

Taurik used his fork to spear a piece of yellow-orange fruit she could not identify. "I suspect that your imagination will provide no small number of possibilities," he said, before bringing the fruit to his mouth. He punctuated the remark with another lifting of his eyebrow, a simple gesture that threatened to send Chen into a fit of uncontrollable laughter.

Teasing and—occasionally—even flirting with the Vulcan engineer had long ago become one of her favorite hobbies, though it really had become fun only after Taurik began playing along. Despite the composed façade and rigid emotional discipline expected of anyone possessing their joint heritage, and which Chen herself tended to eschew, he harbored a gentle and even shrewd sense of humor and wit. She found those traits appealing, even alluring, and it was but one of many reasons she had come to admire him in the time they had known each other. This remained true even after their brief, clumsy attempt at a more intimate relationship before settling into a comfortable, mutually respectful friendship.

"Why are you smiling?"

It took Chen a moment to realize Taurik was talking to her, and that she had allowed herself to become lost in a host of pleasing memories. Feeling her cheeks warm in embarrassment, she reached for the glass of water next to her plate.

"Oh, nothing," she said before sipping her water.

"According to Commander La Forge," Taurik said, changing the subject, "you are assigned to engineering today."

"Looks that way," Chen replied. "I volunteered to run level one diagnostics on the shuttlecraft and install software upgrades to their onboard computers. According to Commander La Forge, it's time for it to be done, and will probably take a few days to complete." She shrugged. "Fine by me. At least it's something constructive to do." Waving toward the forward viewing ports and the kaleidoscopic maelstrom of stars streaking past as the *Enterprise* pushed through space at high warp speed, she added, "At least until we get where we're going, anyway."

For Chen, the prospect of the *Enterprise*'s chief engineer assigning her to several duty shifts' worth of meaningful if not glamorous work was not an issue. She long ago had grown accustomed to such realities, given the obvious lack of need for a contact specialist during the bulk of her tenure aboard ship. Choosing to view the situation as a chance to expand her skills and experience in a variety of areas and disciplines, Chen had volunteered to assist any department that requested additional personnel, for whatever tasks that might entail. Since arriving on the *Enterprise*, she had acquired hands-on training in nearly every major system, from the main computer to the warp drive and everything in between.

She had received plenty of opportunities, as only on rare occasions had her specific job role and accompanying training and skills been called into action. Such was the case, she knew, with contact specialists on any number of starships, as much of Starfleet's resources in the wake of the final Borg Invasion of the Alpha Quadrant focused on rebuilding efforts on worlds across the Federation. To that end, Captain Picard and the *Enterprise* had been assigned a variety of missions during the ensuing three years that had called upon everything from the captain's diplomatic expertise to the military capabilities of the starship itself, particularly with the rise of the Typhon Pact and the rapid spread of its influence. Though casting itself as an "alternative" for nonaligned worlds seeking the security to be found in a larger community, the unlikely alliance of six interstellar powers—the Romulans, Gorn, Tholians, Breen, Tzenkethi, and the Kinshaya—had since its forming caused no end of strife for the Federation.

One of the Pact's earliest victories had come from stealing top-secret schematics for slipstream drive technology from the Utopia Planitia Fleet Yards. Although the damage from that theft ultimately had been mitigated, it showed that the Pact was not a rival to be underestimated or trusted. Later, the Tholians' cast Starfleet and the Federation as willing to stand by and allow the Andorians to suffer extinction rather than offer classified data that might save their endangered civilization. This had resulted in Andor's unsettling—though temporary— secession from the Federation, which it had helped found more than two centuries earlier.

In and around these and other events, Captain Picard and the *Enterprise* had undertaken a handful of missions that dealt in one manner or another with the Pact or other issues plaguing the Federation, including the assassination of President Nanietta Bacco and the hunt for her killers. Following the exposing and arrest of those responsible for the heinous act, including no less than Ishan Anjar, the Bajoran official selected to serve as president pro tempore until a special election could be held to choose Bacco's successor, there remained numerous issues requiring attention. Searching for anyone else who may have played a role in Bacco's murder, as well as the ongoing concerns raised by the Typhon Pact, along with continuing the process of healing the rift between the worlds of the Federation and her allies, were just a few of the challenges faced by the new president, Kellessar zh'Tarash, and Starfleet.

And yet, here we are, heading for the far end of nowhere.

The *Enterprise* had spent weeks traveling at high warp, with the most exciting part of the transit for Chen being the deployment of subspace buoys that would aid in communicating with Starfleet Command. Now the starship was closing on the first of the star systems it was assigned to explore in this region beyond Federation territory, which until now had only been reconnoitered by automated survey drones. According to data collected by the probes, the system—designated as System 3955 in the stellar cartography database—contained two planets capable of sustaining life, as well as indications of intelligent, even advanced civilizations on both worlds. If they possessed faster-than-light propulsion technology, then chances were good that Captain Picard would initiate first contact procedures. This meant that Chen would be assigned to any away team sent to the surface to meet with representatives of whatever government or authorized body was honored to be the first to greet visitors to their world from beyond the stars. Chen could feel anticipation mounting at the prospect.

"You appear preoccupied," Taurik said, and when Chen looked up from her breakfast, she saw him studying her. How long had she been lost in thought? A glance to Taurik's plate told her that it had been at least a few moments, as the Vulcan had finished his meal.

"I'm sorry," Chen replied. "I was just thinking again how it feels so odd for us to be out here when there's still so much to do back home." In truth, not a single day had passed since the *Enterprise*'s departure from Earth that she did not ponder their new assignment, and whether the ship, its crew, and in particular its captain were not better utilized elsewhere. Following the arrest of Ishan Anjar, Picard had notified Admirals Leonard James Akaar and William Riker of his concerns with Starfleet's role as an instrument of Federation policy, and how more martial endeavors—though necessary—had threatened to supplant its primary charter of exploration and the expansion of knowledge. To the surprise of many, Picard had returned to the *Enterprise* not to announce his retirement or promotion and reassignment, but with orders directing the ship to a new region of space. After a few brief delays, owing mostly to requests from Admiral Riker for the *Enterprise* to assist in tasks requiring the special expertise of its captain and crew, the starship had departed the familiar cradle of Federation space in search of the unknown.

"There are those who would say that the ideals upon which the Federation and Starfleet were founded have been tested," Taurik said, "and that our ability and even willingness to honor those principles has fallen short. I believe that dispatching ships to undertake missions such as the one assigned to the *Enterprise*, along with the other initiatives President zh'Tarash has set into motion, will do much to dispel such perceptions."

Chen nodded. She had entertained similar thoughts, and it was comforting to hear Taurik give voice to them. If a buttoned-down, ever-logical Vulcan could see the good in what they were doing, then it had to be the correct course, right?

I guess we'll find out.

The lounge's casual atmosphere was interrupted by the familiar sound of an alert, and indicators mounted around the room began flashing in time to the new signal. Both Chen and Taurik, along with everyone around them, straightened in their seats and all of the various conversations died as a high-pitched tone was piped through the ship's internal communications system.

"*This is the first officer,*" said the voice of Commander Worf over the intercom. "*The ship is now on yellow alert. This is not a drill. All personnel report to your stations. Captain Picard and senior staff officers, please report to the bridge. Lieutenant Chen, report to the bridge.*"

Hearing her name, Chen frowned. "Me?"

"That is what the commander said," Taurik replied.

She tapped her combadge. "Chen to bridge. I'm on my way, Commander." As Taurik rose from his seat, she added, "I guess I'm on my way to the bridge."

"I am going to engineering," replied the Vulcan.

As they moved toward the door, falling in with the rest of the officers and other crew members making their way from the lounge to their duty stations, Taurik said, "Perhaps this means the captain will have need of a contact specialist."

Forcing a smile, Chen shrugged. "And I was so looking forward to upgrading the shuttlecraft."

4

Standing at the center of the *Enterprise* bridge, his arms folded across his chest, Captain Jean-Luc Picard studied the as yet unidentified object now displayed before him on the main viewscreen. That it was a vessel was obvious, given its smooth surface, straight lines, and sharp angles. Even from this distance, the image—as conveyed by long-range sensors—was clear enough that Picard could see seams where hull plates, shifting in color from gray to varying shades of amethyst, had been joined to the vessel's enormous frame. Long and narrow, and possessing flared sections of curved hull segments extending outward from its tapered core, it resembled a wedge of sorts. Beginning with a giant, bell-shaped aft section, it narrowed almost to a point at its opposite end. An assortment of ports, hatches, protrusions, and other attachments festooned its hull on all sides. Weapons placements and what likely were maneuvering thrusters also were evident, positioned at regular intervals from bow to stern, including a massive circular port at the very front of the ship. The craft appeared to be devoid of external light sources, its depiction made possible thanks to the *Enterprise* sensors and the main computer's imaging software, and it was clear that the gargantuan vessel was adrift.

"Long-range sensors first detected the vessel less than ten minutes ago," said Commander Worf from where he stood before his seat next to Picard's command chair. "We attempted to hail it on all frequencies, but we've received no response. No signs of propulsion are evident, and so far we've registered no life-form readings." The first officer paused, and Picard noted the small gleam in the Klingon's eyes. "I thought you might find it interesting, sir."

Picard smiled. "Something of an understatement, Number One." Returning his gaze to the apparent derelict, he asked, "Have you completed your initial sensor sweep?" His attention now was focused on the numerous scorch marks, impacts, and breaks scattered across the ship's hull, all evidence that the vessel had seen some form of combat.

From where she sat at one of the science stations along the bridge's starboard bulkhead, Lieutenant Dina Elfiki replied, "Yes, sir. Most of our scans are being disrupted, possibly from an unknown substance or material used in the vessel's construction. The hull plates are a composite of what appears to be neutronium along with several other minerals we've never encountered." After a moment, the science officer added, "We'll know more after we get closer. For now, though, sensors are still picking up minor power readings. If I had to guess just based on the energy signature, I'd say it's some form of backup system."

"It's definitely adrift," said Lieutenant Aneta Šmrhová, the *Enterprise*'s chief of security. "I'm not detecting any signs of propulsion." Standing at her station behind Picard's left shoulder, she tapped her console several times before adding, "So far, there's no indication that it's reacting to our presence."

"Conn, adjust our course and speed for intercept," Picard ordered.

Seated at the flight controller's station, Ensign Allison Scagliotti replied, "Aye, sir."

"Sir," Šmrhová said, "we've collected enough data to put together a preliminary tactical view."

"On-screen."

In response to Picard's order, the viewscreen changed to a computer-generated representation of the unidentified vessel, now depicted as a wire-frame model, which began a horizontal clockwise rotation. Once the technical diagram had completed a full circle, it lifted so that Picard now saw what he presumed to be a dorsal view of the craft, looking as though down at the top of its hull. The model then rotated from this new angle for a complete circle, before the presentation reset and began again, providing the captain with a complete view of the entire ship—at least as translated by the main computer from telemetry received by the *Enterprise*'s sensor array.

"No sign of active weapons or other defenses?" Picard asked.

"Nothing I can detect, sir," answered the security chief. As though anticipating his next question, she added, "The battle damage, if that's what it is, looks to be approximately one hundred twenty years old. Most of it appears to have been inflicted by some kind of particle beam weaponry, but it's not matching anything we've seen before. There also are penetration points along the hull suggesting something like an energy torpedo, but not as advanced as ours."

"We're approaching the ship now, Captain," reported Scagliotti.

"Bring us out of warp, Ensign," Worf ordered. "Shields up." When Picard cast a wry look in his direction, the Klingon did not flinch. "One can never be too careful, sir."

Picard nodded. "Agreed." To Elfiki, he said, "Give us back normal view."

The image on the main viewscreen shifted again, this time to show red-blue streaks of light receding to distant pinpoints peppering the total blackness of interstellar space as the object of their curiosity careened into view. As before, it was a foreboding vessel, spinning in rather lazy fashion on its long axis, dark and angular like a fighting blade. *No*, Picard decided. To him, the ship resembled the sharpened head of a massive spear.

"It reminds me of a Tholian ship," Worf said.

"We're well away from their territory," Picard replied, "even if we took into account how fluid their borders tend to be." That said, the first officer's observation was not entirely without merit, for the gargantuan ship did indeed possess a strong resemblance to the far smaller yet still wedge-shaped vessels favored by the Tholian Assembly. "Lieutenant Šmrhová? Any similarities with Tholian technology?"

The security chief said, "No obvious ones, sir. I mean, besides the general shape. Its internal power systems are completely different from anything we'd expect to find aboard a Tholian vessel."

Behind him, Picard heard the sound of doors parting at the rear of the bridge, which was immediately followed by the voice of his chief engineer.

"Wow," was Commander Geordi La Forge's initial comment, but it was enough to make Picard turn from the viewscreen in time to see the awestruck expression on the other man's face as he emerged from the turbolift. "Would you look at that?"

"We have," Picard said, unable to suppress a mild grin. "Welcome to the party, Mister La Forge."

"Thanks for inviting me, sir," the commander replied, stepping to the engineering station at the rear of the bridge. Arriving with him was T'Ryssa Chen, who moved from the turbolift to stand next to Šmrhová.

"Reporting as ordered, Captain," she said.

Picard nodded. "I thought you should have a look at this too, as it might well be the first representative technology from a species indigenous to this region." Looking to Elfiki, he said, "Lieutenant, what more can you tell us?"

Elfiki replied, "It measures in excess of twenty-seven hundred meters in length, and nearly eight hundred meters at its widest point. Our scans are able to partially penetrate the hull plating, but the readings are muddled. I'm having to modulate our sensors." She frowned, shaking her head. "Judging by the size of those engine exhaust ports, whatever drives that thing is likely pretty impressive."

La Forge said, "Despite our limited scans, I'm still seeing what looks to be a rudimentary form of warp drive. If I had to guess, I'd say its top speed was about warp two or two point five, so somewhere between first and second generation, and probably not good for much beyond flights between planets in the same system." He frowned, nodding toward the viewscreen. "Of course, that makes you wonder what it's doing way out here."

"Drifting, mostly," Šmrhová replied. "I've tried backtracking its course to determine a point of origin. I can't make a conclusive determination, sir, but its trajectory suggests that it came from the star system we're approaching."

Picard considered the possibility. "Sensor data collected by the survey drones that mapped this area indicated advanced life-forms."

Looking up from her station, Chen said, "I've read those reports, sir. They didn't mention anything about warp capability. This may be a relatively new technological breakthrough for them."

"My thoughts exactly, Lieutenant." Picard offered a small smile. "If that's the case, then you may be busy quite soon." Turning back to the screen, he said in a louder voice, "It looks as though the rest of us have a bit of a mystery to solve."

The captain, for one, welcomed the diversion that—for the moment, at least—appeared to be benign. Following a rendezvous at Starbase 24 in which the *Enterprise* had received a final consignment of supplies as well as its chief medical officer and his wife, Doctor Beverly Crusher, returning from her temporary assignment at Deep Space 9, the starship had set out for parts all but unknown. Weeks of travel from the heart of Federation space had yielded precious little about which to be excited. That much had been expected from the transit to "the Odyssean Pass," which Picard believed was so named in a poetic whimsy by the Starfleet cartographer reviewing data from the first unmanned survey probes to chart the region. On two-dimensional star charts, the Pass was an area between two branches of Federation territory that skirted the far boundary of space claimed by the Romulan Empire, extending beyond its borders away from Federation, Klingon, and Romulan territory. That the Pass represented one of the few directions in which the Romulans were capable of expanding was not lost on anyone, particularly Picard, who more than once had considered the ramifications should the Federation run afoul of the Empire with respect to any future border disputes.

"Is there a chance that ship belongs to any of our

friends from these parts?" Chen asked. Looking over his shoulder at the young lieutenant, Picard noted her wry expression and discerned her meaning.

"If you mean the Romulans," said Šmrhová, "I doubt it. There's nothing in that ship's construction or metallurgy that's even remotely similar to anything the Empire might have."

And yet, Picard decided, there was something about this vessel's elongated, conical silhouette that somehow was familiar. "How long until we intercept it?"

"Just under an hour at our present speed, sir," replied Glinn Ravel Dygan, the young Cardassian officer manning the ops station to Chen's left. Aboard the *Enterprise* thanks to an officer exchange program between Starfleet and the Cardassian military, the glinn had requested his assignment to be extended so that he could stay with the ship during its new mission to the Odyssean Pass.

Dygan almost had not made the journey, owing to concerns and pressures over which he had no control. The fallout stemming from President Bacco's murder and the revelation that a group of Cardassians representing an extremist group calling themselves the "True Way" had been behind the assassination with the aid of none other than President Ishan Anjar and his chief of staff, Galif jav Velk, was affecting diplomatic relations between the Federation and the Cardassian Union. Though the alliance had suffered in the wake of the tragic events and the search for the responsible parties, newly elected President zh'Tarash remained confident that the bonds of friendship and respect that had been forged after so many years of distrust and conflict could withstand even the horrific truths that had been dragged from the shadows into the light.

This, Picard knew, was due in no small part to the efforts and determination of Elim Garak, Castellan for the Cardassian Union, with whom the captain also had formed his own unique bond. One of the many initiatives Garak had put into motion after consultation with the new Federation president was the expansion of programs such as the one that had brought Ravel Dygan to the *Enterprise.*

"Captain," La Forge said, "I think I've managed to tune the sensors to give us a slightly better picture." He frowned. "Whatever that thing's made of is doing a fine job blocking most of our scans, but I'm at least able to push through the hull to a degree. I can't rule out other power sources that might be shielded, but Lieutenant Elfiki's right. There's a huge power generation system in there, and it's not like anything I've ever seen."

The engineer was cut off by Šmrhová, who called out, "Captain, sensors are reading a massive power surge from the ship. I'm picking up indications of a handful of systems coming online."

"What sort of systems?" Picard asked. "Can you identify?"

Rather than a reply from the security chief, the abrupt wailing of the red alert klaxon answered his question. He turned to the viewscreen to see a series of harsh orange lights flaring to life at regular intervals down the length of the alien ship's hull.

"I think it's reacting to our scans, Captain," Šmrhová said. "I'm reading sensors of its own, scanning in all directions, including ours."

"Full power to the deflector shields," Worf ordered. "Stand by phasers."

"Shut off the alarm," Picard added. His attention fixed on the viewscreen, he saw numerous weapons ports activating as the *Enterprise* continued its flyby, the particle weapons beginning to swivel in their mounts. "Conn, move us away. I want some maneuvering room."

Šmrhová's voice rose. "Weapons are coming online! They're targeting us!"

"Lock phasers on those ports and stand by to fire," Picard ordered.

From her science station, Elfiki said, "Captain, its defensive shield generators are powering up. If you're going to fire, you'd better do it now."

"Too late!" warned Šmrhová.

An instant later the first strike impacted against the *Enterprise*'s shields. With Ensign Scagliotti guiding the ship on an evasive course away from the larger vessel, the result was only a glancing blow, but still enough to make the deck quiver beneath Picard's feet. As the surface of the derelict passed by on the viewscreen, Picard saw that lights along its hull were beginning to fade.

"What's happening?" Worf asked.

"More power fluctuations, sir," replied Šmrhová. "As fast as they came up, they're dropping off. I can't explain it." Glancing at another readout, she added, "No damage reported from the attack, Captain."

Picard turned from the viewscreen to regard the security chief. "Can you tell us why the attack stopped?" He saw her eyes narrow as she continued to study the incoming streams of sensor data.

"There seems to have been some kind of failure in their power distribution network, sir. I can't pinpoint the source."

"But you registered no life-form readings," Picard said, "so either someone's over there who doesn't register on our sensors or this is some form of automation."

Šmrhová asked, "And if this ship's been drifting out here as long as we think it has, maybe some of its systems have fallen into disrepair?"

"Perhaps," said the captain. On the viewscreen, the entire vessel was once again visible, and all of the lighting and other indications of life which it had displayed mere moments ago had disappeared. "What do your readings show now, Lieutenant?"

"Everything looks to be back to what it was when we first arrived, sir. At this point, all I can guess is that it has some kind of automated system designed to detect and react to approaching ships. Not a very friendly way to greet visitors."

Worf countered, "Such a response would be consistent with a military vessel."

"About that," said La Forge from where he sat at the engineering station. "Captain, you should take a look at this." Waiting until Picard and Worf joined him, the engineer began tapping a sequence of controls on the console's illuminated surface. A rough schematic of the derelict craft appeared on one of the station's display screens, and La Forge gestured to it, indicating a massive cylindrical construct running the length of the ship and ending at the bulbous projection that Picard recognized as the massive port at the craft's bow.

"From what I can tell, the bulk of the energy produced by this power plant is for this," La Forge said. "And it's definitely not an engine."

Worf grunted. "A weapon."

"Looks that way," the engineer replied. "A massive

particle beam cannon. It's heavily shielded, so we won't know too much about its construction or what it actually fires unless or until we can get a closer look, but it's pretty much the central component around which the rest of the ship was constructed. This is—or rather, was—a combat vessel of some kind, Captain."

"A weapons platform, with elementary warp capability?" Picard asked.

"It may have been intended as a first-strike option against another planet in the same solar system," Worf offered.

Considering that possibility, Picard said, "That would suggest an interplanetary conflict between two or more worlds. Nothing in the survey probes' sensor data suggested anything of that nature."

"How long's it been since we sent anyone or anything out here?" La Forge asked. "A lot can happen."

"Indeed," Picard said. "The first attempts to explore the region were more than a century ago, but those were civilian colony ships, without Starfleet support, and none of them made it out this far. I remember reading about them back when I was on the *Stargazer*." It was during his time as captain of that vessel that he had become acquainted with the first new information from surveys into the Odyssean Pass. The name had caught his attention as he sifted through the volumes of reports sent from Starfleet Command and with which he was expected to familiarize himself. Picard had begun reading the transcripts of data collected by the automated drones sent into the newly charted region, and he had been surprised to learn of the earlier exploration and colonization attempts. "All contact with those ships was lost, so no one knows what happened." Over the ensuing decades, interstellar political shifts and other priorities eventually saw to it that exploring the area was relegated to a low priority, then eventually to no priority at all.

Until now.

Picard's diverse interests in everything from exploration and archeology to the simple allure of an unsolved mystery were but a few of the factors that had led to his fascination with the Pass. Those same curiosities had driven him to accept the *Enterprise*'s current assignment. If he had known it would take all these years after he first read those early reports for someone to be given the enviable task of exploring the region, and that he would be the one so nominated to lead such an expedition, he might have lobbied harder for the assignment.

"Is there any possibility that this vessel could have been constructed by those colonists, or their descendants?" Worf asked.

La Forge shook his head. "I doubt it." He waved once more to the schematic on the display monitor. "There's nothing in this thing that's similar to any technology the crew of a civilian colony ship would have at their disposal." Then, the engineer shrugged. "On the other hand, if they came across someone else's technology, or came into contact with a more advanced civilization and collaborated with them? I suppose it's possible."

"But we've detected no traces of either colony ship," Picard said. "Of course, we've no way of knowing if we're even following their original course." He stepped back from the station, drawing a deep breath. "It's quite a mystery, isn't it?"

"I'll say," replied La Forge. "Well, except for getting shot at, of course."

"There may be other unknown dangers," Worf said. "I would advise caution if we are to investigate further, Captain."

The chief engineer grinned. "Party pooper."

"Captain," said Elfiki, turning from her station, "I've found something else you might want to see."

"The mystery deepens," Picard said, moving along with Worf to join the science officer. "What is it, Lieutenant?"

"I couldn't believe it when I first saw the readings, sir," Elfiki said, her fingers moving across her console. She finished entering commands and a new image appeared on one of her station's monitors, and when Picard read the information scrolling on the screen, his eyes widened in surprise.

"Chronitons? Are you certain?"

Elfiki nodded. "I checked it three times to be sure, sir. They're faint, but there."

"Time travel," Worf said.

"That, or it came into contact with some sort of temporal anomaly," replied the Egyptian lieutenant. "From what I was able to determine, whatever encounter they had with any temporal displacement or other phenomenon happened around one hundred twenty years ago." She paused, sighing. "For all we can tell right now, that ship could be carrying time travel technology."

Picard said, "One hundred twenty years? That's the same age as the battle damage Lieutenant Šmrhová detected." He studied the readings displayed on the screen. "So, this ship either encountered a spatial anomaly that left behind residual chroniton particles, or else it traveled to a point over a century ago from an as yet unknown moment in time."

La Forge smirked. "If you were looking for something interesting to alleviate the boredom, this should do it."

"And then some," Picard said. He turned from the station, his gaze returning to the image of the gigantic derelict centered on the main viewscreen. "If it did travel through time, did it come from the past or the future? Are we dealing with a potential disruption of our timeline?" It would not be the first time the *Enterprise* had faced such a possibility, and it was not something Picard was eager to do again. The risks inherent in such activities and the hazards they posed to the accidental or even purposeful altering of history—theirs or anyone else's—were too grave to dismiss.

Of course, just the simple act of encountering the alien ship might well be sufficient to cause such damage. For all he knew, everything that was to occur from this point forward would only serve to worsen that divergence.

Let's not get ahead of ourselves.

"Maintain yellow alert for the time being," Picard said after a moment, "and hold our position at the limit of our weapons range." Almost as an afterthought, he added, "Keep attempting to hail the ship until further notice."

"So we're going to take a closer look?" La Forge asked, and there was no mistaking the anticipation in the engineer's voice.

Picard nodded. "It's definitely an intriguing puzzle, and I'll admit it's gotten my attention. Mister Worf, you and the commander assemble an away team and make your preparations. If we get no further reaction from the ship, then we'll take it from there."

The mystery deepens.

5

———

"Time travel? You're sure?"

Inspecting the contents of the engineer's tool kit he was packing to take with him, Geordi La Forge looked up from where he had placed the kit on the desk to see Doctor Tamala Harstad lounging on the bed they shared in what had become their joint quarters. She was smiling at him, watching as he completed his packing.

"That's the current theory," La Forge said, eyeing one of the hydrospanners he had brought with him from engineering and deciding he preferred the comparable tool from his personal kit. "The sensor readings are inconclusive, so the only way to be sure is to go over there and have a look around."

"Even after the thing shot at us?" Harstad asked.

La Forge shrugged. "Only the one time, and now sensors say the thing's gone back to sleep, or whatever it is that it's doing. We'll be careful."

"You're not worried that the transporters won't work?" Harstad asked.

"It's not the first time we've had to use a shuttle to get somewhere." La Forge had just read the updated information from Lieutenant Elfiki, which indicated that the mammoth vessel's heavy ablative hull plating was sufficient to block transporter beams. While the need to utilize shuttlecraft to make the transit from the *Enterprise* to the alien ship added a layer of complexity to the away team operation, La Forge was not concerned. Sensors had revealed the presence of a landing bay, and scans of the mechanisms controlling the access hatch were enough to tell him that gaining entry to the ship should not pose much difficulty. What did continue to trouble him was the possibility of the derelict awakening again from its slumber. Facing off against one of the vessel's particle cannons with a shuttlecraft was not something he was eager to attempt.

"I'm more interested in what we'll find once we're inside," he said, pushing aside the worrisome thoughts. Closing the tool kit, he placed it inside the satchel he planned to carry. "Even this close, that thing's hull is still playing hell with our sensors." From the *Enterprise*'s current distance, its sensors should be more than able to scan through the vessel's heavy armor plating, but instead they continued to have only limited success. Despite this difficulty, the science officer had managed to provide at least one new revelation. "But now that we know there are people over there, this just got a whole lot more interesting."

Elfiki had reported indistinct life signs emanating from within the vessel, and the science officer had only been able to do that after reconfiguring and tuning the sensors to such a degree that the scans now being conducted were limited, very focused attempts. As such, her work had become more time-consuming and even tedious, and new information would be coming at a far slower rate.

Shifting her position on the bed so that she now rested on her right hip as she continued to watch him pack, Harstad asked, "How many people?"

"The readings are too muddled to be sure," La Forge replied. "A handful, at most."

"That's all? Seems like an awfully small crew for a ship that size."

La Forge shrugged. "Assuming it's even the crew. From what Elfiki's been able to tell, most of the onboard systems are automated, overseen from several key points throughout the ship. If that's true, and the computer's sophisticated enough, you wouldn't need a large crew." He paused, frowning. "What's weird is that Elfiki said she hadn't been able to detect any sort of atmosphere or active environmental control systems."

"Some kind of hibernation?" Harstad's eyes widened. "Maybe it's a sleeper ship?"

"With a giant cannon?" La Forge shook his head. "Makes you wonder about the priorities of whoever built the thing. Anyway, no atmosphere means we have to suit up." He smiled. "Worf's really not happy about that."

"I thought you hated working in those EV suits, too?"

"Maybe hate's too strong a word," La Forge replied. "I just don't like the constriction when you're trying to work. Now, Worf? *He* hates them."

Pushing herself to a sitting position, Harstad moved so that her legs now hung off the side of the bed. "But what about the people over there? Are you taking someone from the medical staff to check them out?"

"Are you volunteering?" Closing his satchel, La Forge laid it on its side and reached for the tricorder sitting near the computer terminal on his desk.

"Why not?" She reached for his free hand and pulled him closer to her. "I mean, hibernation itself is nothing new. We've been using it for one reason or another for over three hundred years, and we cover the technology and its effects on various species in medical school, but this is different. Sleeper ships are the kind of thing you read about in history classes at the Academy. I mean, the idea of sealing yourself in a coffin while your ship gets thrown into the void and hopefully finds its way to where it's supposed to go, and waking up after however many years to see a new world you'll call home? There's just something amazing about that kind of adventure."

"I'm okay with the way we get around now," La Forge countered, though he did so with a small grin. "How many sleeper ships did Earth send out in the early days? How many were lost? How many *people* were lost? The odds really weren't in their favor back then."

Harstad reached up to poke him in the stomach. "And yet they went anyway." She gestured around her. "Sure, the way we travel has improved by orders of magnitude, but there's still risk involved, and yet here we are, coming all the way out here to see what we can find."

For the first time, La Forge chuckled. "You're really into this, aren't you?"

"What do you mean?"

"Only that this is a side of you I haven't seen before. I like it." Of course, learning about her various interests and passions was an ongoing process and had been so throughout their on-again, off-again relationship over the past three years, but things had sped up in the wake of their decision to share quarters. Living together had been her idea, put forth while they had enjoyed shore leave prior to the *Enterprise*'s departure for the Odyssean Pass. La Forge had been surprised at the suggestion but, much to his own relief, was comfortable with the idea. The choice of who was to move in with whom was an easy one, as, prior to the ship's current assignment, Harstad had shared quarters with another lieutenant from the science division, while he lived alone in the larger accommodations befitting his rank and position. Though Starfleet regulations varied with respect to billeting aboard starships, commanders of

vessels on long-term missions were allowed a wide degree
of latitude when it came to overseeing such matters, and
Captain Picard had raised no objections.

"Why are you smiling?" Harstad asked.

La Forge laughed. "I was just thinking of the captain's
face when I asked him about us moving in together.
You'd think after serving with the man for more than
twenty years that I'd be able to anticipate his response to
any question, but there are times he still manages to surprise me."

How far we've come, La Forge thought, recalling a time
when Jean-Luc Picard wanted little or nothing to do with
children and considered romantic relationships something
of an impediment to what he perceived as his true calling: commanding a starship. Marriage and fatherhood, it
seemed, along with everything that had transpired across
the Federation during the past several years, had done
much to provide the captain with a vastly different perspective.

"I remember the first time I came aboard the *Enterprise*," La Forge said after a moment. "The old *Enterprise*,
I mean. I was a junior-grade lieutenant, and Admiral
Riker—he was a commander then—and I were transfer-
ring from the *Hood*, and I had my first meeting with Captain Picard in his ready room." He smiled at the memory
of his younger self, nervous and trying not to fidget as
he stood before Jean-Luc Picard, captain of the newly
commissioned *Galaxy*-class *U.S.S. Enterprise*. Already a
Starfleet legend, Picard was an imposing man who seemed
to tower over him despite his modest height. "It wasn't
the first time we'd met, but this was different. Now I'd
be serving under him." Picard's reputation as a stickler
for efficiency and for rules and regulations no matter how

minor or seemingly insignificant preceded him. It also was well known that the seasoned starship commander set a high bar for excellence, particularly for his junior officers. "Still, I knew from that first moment that my tour on the *Enterprise* was going to be something special." He shrugged. "The name carries that level of expectation, you know."

"Why do you think every cadet at the Academy still lists the *Enterprise* as their preferred first posting after they graduate?" Harstad asked. "And you've been a big part of that for a long time." She paused, her eyes narrowing as she studied him. "You don't have any regrets, do you?"

La Forge frowned. "Me? Regrets?" It was not the first time he had pondered such a question. "There was a while where I wondered if I'd made a career mistake, staying on the *Enterprise* as long as I have, but the truth is that I'm happy here, doing what I love to do, and working with people I consider family." He squeezed her hand. "And I certainly don't regret the time we've spent together." Leaning forward, he kissed her, their lips pressing as she arched her back to meet him. Her other hand found his arm and he felt her pulling him toward her, and for a moment he forgot everything but the two of them, here and now.

Their moment was brief, however, and interrupted by the sound of the ship's intercom.

"Worf to Commander La Forge," said the voice of the *Enterprise*'s first officer. *"Report to the main shuttlebay."*

Pulling her mouth from his, Harstad eyed him with no small hint of mischief. "His timing is horrible."

"I'll be sure to tell him you said that."

"Before or after you ask about someone from the medical staff going on the away team?"

Right, La Forge reminded himself as he tapped his combadge. "La Forge here. I'm on my way, Worf."

"Acknowledged."

Once the communication link was severed, La Forge returned his attention to Harstad. "Let Worf and the security team have a look around over there first, okay? Just to make sure it's safe for the rest of us? Besides, I'd like to see about making sure the ship doesn't wake up and start shooting again."

She maintained a grip on both of his hands. "Fair enough, but you be careful over there, all right?"

"I'm always careful."

Offering a mock snort, Harstad pushed herself back on the bed. "I've read your record, Commander. Trouble has a knack for finding you."

"It's the *Enterprise*, remember?" La Forge said, moving to retrieve his satchel and tricorder. "Like I said, the name carries that extra level of expectation." Smiling at her one last time, he headed for the door. "See you in a little while."

"Hey, La Forge."

"Yeah?" Pausing at the now open door, he turned to see her eyeing him with an expression that seemed to convey love, concern, and so much more.

"I mean it. Be careful. I don't want to have to find another roommate."

"Me neither."

It had been at least a few years since T'Ryssa Chen was required to wear an environment suit, and her feeling about such exercises remained unchanged: she hated it, particularly now that her helmet was sealed and she had no way to scratch her nose.

"Are you okay?" asked Lieutenant Dina Elfiki, her voice muffled and filtered through her helmet's communications receiver. Like Chen and everyone else aboard the *Jefferies*, the science officer was wearing an EV suit, or "standard extravehicular work garment," as it was known in Starfleet nomenclature. Elfiki sat across from her in the shuttlecraft's passenger area, studying her through their helmets' faceplates.

"I'm fine, thanks," Chen replied. "It's just the usual aversion to being hermetically sealed inside one of these things. I'll be okay once we start moving around."

Elfiki nodded. "Same here. I never like wearing these suits either, but it's this or we hold our breath the whole time."

"I always feel like a fish in a bowl," said Lieutenant Rennan Konya from where he sat next to Chen. The deputy chief of security, along with Lieutenant Kirsten Cruzen, had been selected to accompany the away team as its security detail.

Sitting next to Elfiki, Cruzen added, "I always feel like a vacuum-packed field ration."

"Spend enough time in one of these," Konya said, smiling through his faceplate, "and you'll start to smell like one, too."

Without missing a beat, Cruzen replied, "You manage that even without the suit." Her remark elicited good-natured chuckles from Konya as well as Chen and Elfiki. For the first time since the team had boarded the shuttlecraft, Chen turned to Konya.

"I'm glad you're coming with us."

"Your first real first-contact mission in forever?" The Betazoid smiled, though Chen thought he might be forcing it, if only a bit. "I wouldn't miss it for anything."

"Is everybody going to give me grief over that?" Chen asked. "It's not my fault it's taken this long."

"You should've joined security," Cruzen offered. "It's never boring, that's for sure."

Chen nodded. "Maybe I'll start training for that once this mission's over."

"I'll dig out the holodeck training programs when we get back," Konya said, and again, Chen wondered if he might be trying too hard to affect a relaxed air, with the two of them sitting next to each other inside the shuttle's cramped passenger compartment. Despite the confining EV suit, she reached up and patted him on the arm.

"Deal."

Though she had come to terms with the way her romantic relationship with him had ended in abrupt fashion a few years earlier, the truth was that awkwardness had clouded most of their interactions since then. She had been hurt by Konya's sudden decision to stop seeing her but had come to realize that his actions were part of a larger process of healing and coming to terms with the guilt and other traumatic feelings haunting him in the aftermath of the final Borg Invasion. He had been plagued by the shame he believed he deserved for surviving that brief yet costly conflict and had withdrawn from nearly everyone and everything around him. She knew that he still occasionally visited with Doctor Hegol Den, the *Enterprise*'s counselor, though those sessions had tapered off in recent years. As for their friendship, Konya had been the first to make overtures, though the spark that they had shared in the beginning was conspicuous in its absence. Though she still harbored feelings for him, Chen knew that he had to figure out for himself what was best for him, and if she could be a strong supportive friend as he sought those answers, that was enough.

From where he sat next to Commander La Forge in the shuttle's cockpit, Commander Worf said, "*Enterprise, we are approaching the landing bay.*"

"*Acknowledged,*" replied the voice of Captain Picard. "*There's been no apparent reaction to your presence.*"

After a brief pause, Lieutenant Aneta Šmrhová said over the connection, "*Power readings remain at minimal levels, Commander, and there are no signs of weapons or defenses coming online. So far, everything's quiet.*"

"Good to know," Chen said, the memory of the alien ship's brief attack on the *Enterprise* still fresh in everyone's minds. Leaning forward in her seat, the Vulcan was able to look through the open hatchway separating the shuttle's passenger compartment and cockpit. Her vantage point afforded her a view through the forward port, which now was filled with the gray and purple plates of the alien vessel's hull. The ship appeared to be rotating to starboard as Worf maneuvered the *Jefferies* and aligned the shuttlecraft with the larger vessel's landing bay access hatch.

"That is one big damned ship," Cruzen said.

"No kidding." Chen had seen images of the entire craft on the bridge viewscreen as well as the computer terminal in her quarters as she prepared to join the away team, but those depictions had not conveyed the craft's sheer size. From the shuttle's current distance, the seams between hull plates were clearly visible, along with other features like maneuvering thrusters and weapons ports. The weapons, Chen decided, were particularly large.

"All right, everybody," La Forge said as the *Jefferies* pivoted and came to station keeping at what had to be a distance of less than a hundred meters. "We're in position." Beyond the viewing port, Chen saw the immense hatch which, if the chief engineer was right, would lead to the landing bay and the rest of the colossal ship.

"Are you certain this will work?" Worf asked.

Even wearing his EV suit, the chief engineer still was able to manage a shrug. "Beats me. I've scanned the hatch-locking mechanism, and it seems to work with a magnetic seal not all that different from our own airlock systems. It uses a harmonic transceiver to control access, so it should just be a matter of transmitting the right frequency. The computer's given me several combinations to try, so let's see what happens."

His gloved hands moving across his console, La Forge entered a lengthy string of instructions. With all members of the away team sharing the same active communications channel, Chen and the others listened as La Forge murmured and muttered under his breath while transmitting different signal patterns. After nearly two full minutes, he sat back in his seat.

"I think that's it."

In response to his statement, several recessed lights positioned around the large hatch flared to life, one of them directing a harsh beam of brilliant white illumination through the shuttlecraft's viewing port. Chen raised her hand to deflect the glare, and in doing so saw that the hatch was beginning to open. The heavy door split into eight sections that pulled away from the entry's center and receding into slots that formed the port's threshold.

"Open Sesame," La Forge said, and Chen saw Worf look at him with a confused expression. "That's what Data would say if he were here."

The Klingon grunted. "I highly doubt it."

"You weren't there."

"Where?"

"Wait. You were there." La Forge held up a hand. "Never mind. It's a long story."

Beyond the viewing port, the hatch had cycled open, revealing a chamber that was more than large enough to accommodate the shuttlecraft. No one said anything, and Chen realized after a moment that she was holding her breath as she waited to see if the alien craft took some form of umbrage at their intrusion.

It did not.

For now, anyway, Chen mused.

"There are two smaller ships inside the bay," La Forge reported after the hatch finished opening, "but there's plenty of room for us. *Enterprise*, except for the hatch, our sensors are showing no other changes in response to our presence."

"*We read that, too*," replied Picard over the open frequency. "*The life-form readings Lieutenant Elfiki detected have not changed, either. Proceed at your discretion, Number One.*"

"Understood," Worf said.

The Klingon guided the *Jefferies* through the open entry with a deft hand, and within moments the shuttlecraft was settling onto the bay's metal deck. Working together, Worf and La Forge secured the shuttle's systems and powered down its engine. Reaching over his head, Lieutenant Konya tapped a control that brightened the illumination inside the passenger area.

"How do you want to proceed, Commander?" asked the deputy security chief as he rose from his seat.

Stepping from the cockpit into the shuttle's rear compartment, Worf replied, "We will reconnoiter the landing bay first and verify that it is secure. Once that is accomplished, we will proceed to the source of the life-form readings Lieutenant Elfiki identified."

"Keep this channel open at all times," Picard ordered, *"and enable your helmet visual feeds. At the first sign of trouble, I want you out of there."*

"Aye, sir," said the first officer, and the away team members each checked their individual suit controls to ensure their communications systems were transmitting both audio and visual signals back to the *Enterprise*.

"We're receiving your signals," said Picard. *"Good hunting."*

His phaser in his right hand, Worf moved to the hatch and pressed the control to open it. Without waiting for an order, Konya and Cruzen—each of them carrying phaser rifles Konya had retrieved from the shuttle's weapons locker—fell in behind him. As Worf stepped through the hatch and down to the deck, the pair of security officers followed suit, moving to either side of him, their rifles up and aimed ahead of them. Chen felt a sudden knot twist in her gut, and her grip tightened around the phaser pistol in her hand.

"Let's go," La Forge said, his engineer's satchel slung over his right shoulder and across his chest. He led Chen and Elfiki through the open hatch and out onto the landing bay.

As she dropped to the deck, Chen pressed the control pad on her left thigh that engaged her boots' magnetic grip, and she felt the bottom of her foot press against the metal plating. Walking in a microgravity environment with an EV suit was a simple enough matter, though a bit more labor intensive than normal movement. Still, training and experience saw to it that she was moving with relative comfort after just a few steps. She followed La Forge as the chief engineer made his way toward the bay's still open hatch, beyond which lay open space and, in the distance, the *Enterprise*.

"Now that I've got at least one of the proper sequences," La Forge said, his voice echoing in her helmet as he held up his tricorder and aimed it in the general direction of the entryway, "we should have a pretty easy time moving through the ship." He pressed a control on his tricorder, though Chen heard no sound emitted from the device thanks to the vacuum surrounding them. However, a second later the massive door began to close.

"Geordi," Chen heard Worf say over the open channel, and at the same time she noticed that it was getting easier to see around her. The shadows cloaking the bay were retreating as overhead lighting increased in intensity, provided by lengths of what to Chen looked like luminescent strands running along creases in the ceiling panels.

"What was that?" La Forge asked, turning away from the hatch. "Did somebody trip something?"

Worf replied, "Negative. No one has touched anything."

Beyond the first officer, Chen saw that Konya and Cruzen had taken up defensive positions near the *Jefferies* and now were sweeping the chamber, their phaser rifles tracking wherever they searched for potential threats. On the other side of the bay, the two other craft now were plainly visible, each of them half again as large as their own shuttlecraft and possessing low, sleek profiles that suggested to Chen that they were ships intended for combat.

"Number One," Picard said over the open frequency, *"we're detecting a modest increase in energy levels over there. They seem localized to your immediate vicinity."*

"I think I know what this is," said Elfiki, waving with her free hand and indicating her tricorder. "This looks like it might be an automated response. Our accessing the system controlling the landing bay hatch seems to have triggered a protocol to restore the internal environment, at least in this area of the ship. I'm picking up indications of life-support systems coming online, including whatever it is that they use to achieve artificial gravity."

Scanning her own tricorder, Chen nodded in agreement. "I think she's right, sir. There's a definite increase in power levels, but only in this compartment as well as one of the connecting corridors. As for the atmosphere, it's Class-M. Once everything's up and running, we should be able to move around without our suits."

"You're saying the onboard computer rolled out a welcome mat for us?" La Forge asked.

"That was nice of it," Cruzen said.

Elfiki said, "Well, likely not for us, but obviously the computer is programmed to respond to changes in whatever it considers to be the ship's current status."

"What about those life-forms Elfiki found?" Konya asked. "Could they be behind this?"

"There's only one way to find out," Worf replied.

6

Nothing is ever as simple as it first appears to be.

How many times, Picard wondered to himself, had he pondered that thought, or some variation, as he sat on the bridge of his ship while people he commanded marched off into the unknown and perhaps harm's way? Far too many, he conceded. Protocol often called for a commanding officer to stand or sit idle as other men and women carried out hazardous missions, sometimes at the cost of their very lives. As a younger man, Picard had been uncomfortable with the idea of sending others into danger while he remained behind, but age, experience, and even wisdom had made him realize that the rules existed for good reasons, even if there were times when he did not agree with them.

Now was one of those times.

Rising from his command chair at the center of the *Enterprise* bridge, he stepped forward until he stood between the conn and ops positions. "Lieutenant Šmrhová, any changes in your readings?"

Behind him, the security chief replied, "Nothing beyond what we're already detecting sir. Minor increases in power emissions, and what looks to be life-support systems powering up in isolated areas, but nothing like we saw before. To be honest, sir, the pattern of the increases doesn't make any sense to me."

Picard frowned. "What do you mean?"

"The areas that are coming online aren't really connected in any way that I can see," Šmrhová replied. After a moment, during which Picard heard her tapping controls on her station, she added, "If I didn't know better, I'd say it was a random sampling, which doesn't make any practical sense, given that the life-form readings are all grouped together. In fact, the compartment where we detected life signs isn't receiving any of this."

Recalling the theories La Forge had offered to explain the odd readings, Picard said, "If the life-forms are in some form of hibernation, is it possible there's a malfunction of sorts, and it's impacting whatever's happening now?"

"It's as good a guess as any, sir."

Picard regarded the main viewscreen, which had been configured so that the display's top two-thirds depicted an image of the enormous alien craft. The screen's remaining portion now was split into six equal sections, each relaying the visual feed from the helmets of the away team. Worf's and La Forge's feeds were on either end of the group, bracketing the remaining officers. Given how the team was ordered as it made its way deeper into the derelict ship, most of the feeds showed little more than the back of the person in front of the helmet transmitting the picture. Only Worf, who currently was leading the team, offered a view of the large, straight corridor the team now traversed. The passageway was itself unremarkable, at least from Picard's vantage point, being a utilitarian affair adorned with all manner of control panels, gauges, and conduits as well as the occasional sealed hatch or what appeared to be something like ladder rungs disappearing above the ceiling or beneath the deck to other levels.

"I can't believe I didn't notice this before," said the voice of Geordi La Forge over the open communications channel. *"There's no dust on anything. I mean, anywhere. Just*

looking around, it's like somebody cleaned up the place five minutes before we got here."

T'Ryssa Chen replied, *"Some kind of automated cleaning apparatus or heavy-duty air filtration system?"*

"Maybe," said La Forge, *"but it'd have to be pretty robust to stay active for a century or more with no regular maintenance schedule."*

Another voice, this one belonging to Lieutenant Rennan Konya, added, *"So, either they build things really well wherever this ship is from, or else somebody's on board and apparently ignoring all our attempts to communicate. That's comforting."*

"Where are they in relation to the life signs we detected?" Picard asked.

Šmrhová said, "Less than one hundred meters, sir. At their present rate of progress, they should be there in eight to ten minutes."

"And you're certain there are no other onboard reactions to their presence?"

"None that I've been able to detect, sir."

The report did little to placate Picard's unease, which had remained elevated after the alien ship's initial response to the *Enterprise*'s presence. The feeling had taken a sharp upswing with the away team's departure and the derelict's reaction to the shuttlecraft *Jefferies*'s arrival in its landing bay. Did the gargantuan vessel have intruder control systems? Had its crew simply deployed crude but dangerous or even potentially lethal booby traps to thwart unwanted visitors? The ship had been out here a long time, after all, and even if the *Enterprise* was the first vessel to encounter it, surely its builders or masters had, given its apparent primary purpose, foreseen the possibility of trespassers?

"Geordi, look at this," said the voice of Worf over the

intercom. On the viewscreen, Picard saw the visual feed from the first officer's helmet swing left, coming to rest on one of the several control consoles the away team had passed during their transit from the landing bay, but which was markedly different from its counterparts. *"This station is active."*

"It sure is," replied La Forge, and his own helmet's feed now also was transmitting images of the operating console.

"Are you able to access it?" asked the captain.

"Maybe. It'll take some time to understand the interface, but from what I'm seeing, this console has full access to the onboard computer and every system across the ship. If we can establish a link with the Enterprise, *the universal translator can get to work."*

Sitting at the ops station, Glinn Ravel Dygan said, "That seems odd." When Picard turned to regard the young Cardassian, he added, "I mean from a security standpoint, sir. A console in an indiscreet location such as a common corridor, available to anyone and allowing access to the ship's most sensitive systems, does not seem like a prudent design."

"On the other hand," countered Šmrhová, "if we're talking about a small crew and a ship that runs largely on automation, it makes more sense for anyone to be able to access any critical system from anywhere."

Dygan seemed to contemplate the security chief's hypothesis for a moment before nodding. "An excellent point, Lieutenant, and one I had not considered."

"Enterprise, *are you seeing this?"* La Forge asked. On the viewscreen, Picard saw that the engineer was still studying the workstation, which now featured an active display depicting a technical schematic. Picard recognized it as a section of the alien craft, with a focus on its internal systems. *"I think we can put to rest any idea of this not being a combat ship, and I mean that in the truest sense. If I'm reading this right, nearly every onboard system is designed to prioritize weapons and defenses, with the main particle cannon taking precedence over everything else. This thing is essentially the cannon with an engine attached, and some support systems to help it get to whatever it's supposed to blow up next."*

Lieutenant Elfiki added, *"The computer's decision-support software is incredible, and the entire system looks to be heavily encrypted. It'll take days to sift through."*

"There'll be plenty of time for that," Picard said. "Number One, once Commander La Forge has set up the data link to the *Enterprise*, proceed to the source of the life-form readings."

"Acknowledged," replied the Klingon.

Turning from the screen, Picard said to Šmrhová, "Lieutenant, alert engineering about Mister La Forge's plan. I want Commander Taurik to oversee the operation and guard against any infiltration of our computer by anything over there."

The security chief nodded. "Aye, sir."

Though he allowed himself a small sigh, Picard forced himself to maintain his composure. As always, one of the most frustrating parts about sending an away team on a mission was the waiting.

Waiting for what, exactly?

"Worf, we're here."

Standing behind the Klingon in the large passageway, La Forge indicated with his tricorder an oversized, sealed hatch set into the bulkhead. The door, like much they had encountered so far during their exploration of the alien ship, was composed of unpolished, unpainted metal. A string of characters rendered in an indecipherable script was etched into the hatch's smooth surface, and above the door was yet another luminescent strand providing dim illumination to this part of the corridor.

"I think this says something about suspension," La Forge said, studying his tricorder. "Could mean hibernation." Not for the first time, he willed the universal translation protocols currently being employed by the *Enterprise*'s main computer to work faster as they continued their process of interpreting the unknown language of the ship's builders and possible inhabitants.

"You got it right, Commander," said the voice of Lieutenant Šmrhová over the open channel. *"The computer confirms that the label reads 'Suspension,' along with some kind of code it thinks might be a room or compartment number."*

"How's the computer coming with the rest of the translation?" La Forge asked.

The security chief replied, *"Still working, but the database it's building is already pretty large. The translation matrix found thirty-eight distinct languages represented in the ship's computer files. A few of those were really interesting, and by that I mean odd, like they didn't belong with the rest. Within an hour, you should be able to interact with any of the onboard systems."*

"And talk to anybody we meet?" Chen asked.

"That's the plan, Lieutenant."

La Forge said, "Well, there's still the security lockouts and decryption. Baby steps, but for now we'll have to muddle through as best we can." Moving so that he stood before the closed door and the control panel set into the adjacent bulkhead, he held up his tricorder and keyed one of the harmonic sequences he had assembled, similar to the one he had used to open the landing bay's external hatch. This time it took him three attempts before he found a sequence that worked. An indicator on the control panel flared a bright yellow and there was an audible click as magnetic seals were disengaged.

"You're getting pretty good at that, Commander," said Lieutenant Cruzen from where she stood at the rear of the group, positioned so that she could keep watch down the length of corridor they had already traversed.

The hatch opened, receding into the door's frame until it was flush with surrounding bulkheads before sliding upward and out of sight. Beyond was a room perhaps thirty meters deep and half as wide, a guess La Forge confirmed with a quick scan of his tricorder. Like the corridor, the room was adorned with more of the lighting strips, running the length of the walls as well as across the ceiling. One bulkhead was crowded with control stations similar to those the team already had encountered, but the chamber's most striking feature was the eight cylindrical objects, each nestled within a frame secured to the deck plating.

"Oh, wow," said the engineer. "Look at this." He was about to enter the room when he was stopped by a hand on his shoulder. It was Worf, who said nothing as he moved around La Forge, phaser held out before him, and stepped through the doorway. After taking a few seconds to examine the room's interior, the Klingon gestured with his free hand.

"All clear."

La Forge led the rest of the team into the room, and Konya and Cruzen took up positions just inside the door, leaving the others to spread out and examine the consoles and, of course, the eight tubes. Each of the cylinders was composed of a transparent material, and as he inspected the closest specimen, La Forge saw that its interior was coated by a thick layering of frost. The frames in which the cylinders rested featured their own control panels and arrays of status monitors, with indicators flashing in rhythmic sequences while the occasional stream of data in the now familiar yet still unreadable alien text scrolled across compact screens. Even through his helmet, he heard the steady hum of equipment stored within the frame and likely the undersides of the cylinders, as well.

"Definitely a form of cryogenic suspension," said Elfiki as she stepped closer to examine one of the cylinders. "These don't look too different from the sort of suspended animation capsules that were developed on Earth in the late twentieth and early twenty-first centuries, like those used in the first pre-warp sleeper ships."

"Their reliability was about the same as these, too," Chen said. She was standing between a pair of the tubes, and La Forge saw that those two cylinders, like four of the remaining six, were dark and lacked the frost permeating the interior of their companions.

"Left to the mercy of a machine," Worf said, disapproval evident in his voice. "A deplorable way to die."

Still standing with Cruzen near the door, Konya said, "Damned right."

La Forge stepped closer to one of the active units, and through the layer of ice crystals on the inside of the otherwise transparent shell, his ocular implants allowed him to see the humanoid figure encased within. Unclothed, the hibernating subject had no visible body hair, and its smooth skull was larger than that of a normal human, with an elongated crown. Its eyes were closed, flanking a shallow crease with a single opening that suggested a nasal passage. He noted the ridges on the sides of its head that covered small openings he took to be auditory organs. Prominent ridges connecting its neck to its torso reminded La Forge of Cardassian physiology, though in this case the alien's skin was smooth, sporting a pigmentation that suggested wine, or perhaps lavender, and its musculature was on par with a human male in prime physical condition. Several dark patches were affixed to the subject's skin and La Forge saw that they each contained some form of compact circuitry or technology.

"They all have small sensors attached at various points to their bodies," Elfiki said. "Some sort of biomed tech, I'm guessing."

La Forge nodded. "I was thinking the same thing."

"From what I can tell," the science officer continued, "we have one male and one female. I don't know about the . . . the six who didn't make it. As for the two survivors, their life readings are very low, likely owing to the cryogenic process, but without a basis for comparison I have no way to know what's 'normal' for these people."

Chen asked, "Can they be revived?"

"That may not be prudent," Worf warned. "We know nothing about them. Bringing them out of hibernation could be a risk."

Nodding, La Forge replied, "Plus, we don't know anything about their physiology or environmental needs."

"Their atmosphere looks to be compatible with ours," Elfiki said, "but there are other considerations. Hopefully we can gain access to any relevant medical information, and see where that takes us. If our scans are right and they've been in hibernation for over a hundred years, we don't know what kind of debilitating effect the process has had on their bodies." She held up her tricorder. "My scans show no significant atrophy of muscles, bone, or tissue, but they may still be too weak to walk or even sit up once they're revived."

La Forge gestured to the closest of the cylinders. "We don't even know how to bring them out of hibernation, anyway, but the process has to be accessible via their ship's computer. Something had to be programmed to wake up these people at some point."

"Number One," said Captain Picard over the comm frequency, *"I've already alerted Doctor Crusher that her services will be needed over there. She's assembling a medical team to accompany her, and we'll be dispatching another shuttlecraft in short order. Notify Lieutenant Šmrhová if you have any other personnel or equipment needs."*

Worf replied, "Aye, sir. I would like to continue our investigation. We still have not reached anything resembling a bridge or engineering."

"Or any of the systems overseeing the giant cannon," added La Forge, "but from what I've seen so far, there's definitely enough to keep us busy for quite a while." He glanced down at the transparent cylinder and its slumbering occupant. "Hopefully, these guys can help us fill in the blanks."

And let's hope we don't hate what they tell us.

7

Stepping through the doors leading to the *Enterprise*'s childcare center, Picard found it odd that he might consider this room to be more relaxing than the bridge. However, it was precisely that feeling which came over him as he stood near the door and took in the scene around him.

"Captain," said Hailan Casmir, the center's primary supervisor, as he rose from the chair behind his desk to greet Picard with a warm smile. "It's good to see you, sir." An Argelian, Casmir never seemed to lack for an upbeat attitude and even good humor. Picard had enjoyed his company from the first time they had met, when Casmir's wife, Lieutenant Taro Trinell, came aboard the *Enterprise* as a new member of the engineering department. A civilian, he wore a loose-fitting, cobalt blue tunic over dark gray pants. His blond hair was long and fell to his shoulders, and he favored a trimmed beard that reminded Picard of his friend and former first officer, William Riker.

"It's good to see you, too, Hailan," Picard said.

"I understand things are getting interesting aboard that ship over there."

Picard nodded. "Indeed. We're only just scratching the surface, it seems." It did not surprise him that news about the away team's progress aboard the mysterious alien vessel already was spreading through the ship. After weeks of uneventful travel just to get to the Odyssean Pass, any break in the routine was going to attract everyone's attention. "While I can do without the firefights," Casmir said, "it's times like these that I wish I was a member of the crew so that I could go and have a look around for myself."

"Perhaps we can arrange an internship of sorts." Picard offered a small, sly grin. "I'm sure Mister Worf can find a suitable place for a man of your many talents. For the moment, though, we need you here."

He divided his attention between Casmir and the handful of children who were visible in the center's main room. The oldest looked to be about the same age as his own son, with the others perhaps younger by a year or so at most. None of the three infants belonging to members of his crew was present, and Picard knew that any of the babies placed in the center's charge would be sequestered in a separate room with their own caregiver. Of the children Picard could see, they appeared occupied with books, games, padds, or other activities that—for the moment, at least—had harnessed their attention. For however long it lasted, the childcare center was an oasis of peace and quiet.

"How did they react to our earlier bit of trouble?" he asked.

"Surprisingly well, actually," replied the Argelian. "Children are amazingly resilient, Captain. We as adults and parents tend to be too zealous to protect them, and we often underestimate their ability to respond and adapt to new situations, even those that might be stressful or frightening. They were alarmed for a few moments, of course, but as you can see they've returned to their normal routine. We can learn a lot from our children, you know."

"I do, indeed," Picard said. With a small sigh, he shook his head. "I don't know how you manage to do it."

Casmir asked, "Do what?" Noting where the captain was looking, the Argelian added, "Years of practice, Captain. Argelians often tend toward large families, and I was one of the older children in my family. I learned at an early age how to help my parents look after my younger siblings." He gestured toward the kids he now oversaw. "Compared to my brothers and sisters, these children are . . . what do humans call them? Angels."

The remark drew a light chuckle from Picard. "Regardless, you've done a remarkable job here, for which I'm grateful." Recalling something he had read in one of the department reports routed to him by Commander Worf, he said, "I saw your request to schedule more holodeck time for the children."

"Yes," Casmir said. "I've been working with some of the science departments to expand the curriculum in geology, astronomy, stellar cartography, and so on. We can simulate different planetary environments, and program virtual tours of star systems and other spatial phenomena."

"I've already asked Commander Worf to look into it," Picard said, "but I'm sure we can make arrangements. René in particular might enjoy the astronomy material." The captain had been intrigued by the proposal from the first time he had read Casmir's report. He remembered the countless nights he had spent sitting under one of the trees on the family vineyards in France, staring up at the night sky for hours, making do with a telescope and his own eyes as he imagined traveling among the stars. Holodeck technology could be brought to bear to provide his son and the other *Enterprise* children with all manner of breathtaking interactive simulations that would rival even his own fevered childhood imagination. "And if you decide to add any courses on archeology," Picard added, "I might be interested in participating with him, as well."

Smiling, the Argelian nodded. "As a matter of fact, I've been considering such a course, and you were the first person I thought of. I'm well aware of your fondness for the subject. Perhaps you might consider offering the children your own insights?"

"Me? Teach the children?" Picard asked.

Casmir's eyes narrowed. "You're a natural mentor, Captain. They look up to you. Having you along for one of their classes would be a tremendous treat for them."

"Doctor Crusher put you up to this, didn't she?"

"I can neither confirm nor deny your wife's complicity in this scheme, sir."

Laughing again, Picard nodded in approval. "Well played. I'll consider your suggestion." He paused before adding in a lower voice, "Perhaps I may even enjoy myself."

I can hear Marie laughing from here.

What would his sister-in-law, widow of his deceased older brother, Robert, and mother of his own beloved late nephew, young René, say about him now? Upon hearing that he, of all people, would soon have a son of his own, Marie Picard had repeatedly assured him that he would make a wonderful father. She cited as her evidence his interactions with her son and how the two had bonded over their mutual love of space, the questions it posed, and the answers which could only be found among the stars. Picard had mourned the passing of his brother, who had died in a fire nearly fifteen years earlier at the family home on Earth, but he had been devastated upon hearing that dear René also had been lost.

Their deaths had weighed on him for years afterward, and he often wondered if his desire to honor their memory by giving their names to his and Beverly's son had been motivated by guilt at what he had missed by not spending more time with them. At first he had avoided home due to his strained relationship with Robert, but even after the two had closed the gulf separating them, duty continued to keep Picard away from Earth for long periods—or had it? Looking back on the missions given to him during his final years in command of the *Enterprise*-D, he had wondered if his presence really had been required for every assignment. No small number of those tasks could have been handled with ease by Will Riker, who by that point had more than proven himself to be a highly capable starship commander. Should Picard have left his ship in Riker's hands more often, knowing that he could trust his first officer to mind the store and allow him increased opportunities to visit his family?

Stop it, he scolded himself. *You can't change the past.*

He looked around the room once more. "Has Doctor Crusher come to visit René?"

Casmir nodded toward one of the center's satellite rooms. "She's with him now, in the computer lab. I understand she's heading over to the alien ship."

"Yes," Picard replied. "The vessel's crew is in a state of cryogenic hibernation, and the onboard computer seems to be having difficulty awakening them. Hopefully, Doctor Crusher and her team can assist in that endeavor."

"I wish them luck, Captain." Casmir looked like he might be about to say something else, but a beep from his desktop computer terminal caught his attention. "If you'll excuse me, sir."

"By all means. Thank you, Hailan." As the supervisor returned to his desk, Picard stepped toward the center's computer learning lab. Six workstations were arrayed around the room, each featuring a computer terminal. None of the stations were in use, though inside he did find Beverly Crusher and their son, René Jacques Robert Francois Picard. She was sitting in one of the chairs, and René stood next to her, his expression one of confusion and concern.

"It's just for a little while," Beverly was saying, holding the boy's hand. "I'll be back before you know it."

René, his eyes wide and moist, replied, "But you were gone so long before." Picard noted how his lower lip trembled, but otherwise the boy was doing a commendable job maintaining his composure.

"That was different," Beverly said, only then realizing that Picard had entered the room. She smiled at his arrival. Upon noticing his father, René stood a bit straighter, though he still appeared sullen.

"Hello, Papa," he said, accenting the second syllable as he had done since first learning to speak the word. No matter the stresses of the day, hearing his son call him by that name never failed to make Picard smile.

"You look sad," he said, dropping to one knee so that his face was closer to René's. "What's the matter?"

"Mommy's leaving again."

Despite the boy's demonstrated intelligence and maturity, Picard had to remind himself that he still was only four years old and tended to see the world around him not in degrees but rather absolutes. His mother was here, and soon she would be gone. René understood at a rudimentary level the concept of time and measuring its passage, though he, like most other children, tended to view it more often in terms of "now" and "forever."

"Not for long, though," Picard said. This would—if all went according to plan—be little more than a routine excursion, and not at all like the separation René and he had endured while Beverly had served as the interim chief medical officer at Deep Space 9, an assignment preceded by the mission she had undertaken to a distant world which once had been the home to several slave labor camps during the Cardassian Occupation of Bajor. Her journey to that planet, Jevalan, had been part of the larger effort to expose the truth behind the assassination of President Bacco and the role her replacement, Ishan Anjar, had played in the commission of that heinous act. For young René, the separation from his mother—the longest they had been apart since his birth—had been difficult, though the frequent conversations over subspace had helped to alleviate his missing her.

They helped me, as well.

Returning his gaze to her, René gripped his mother's hand in both of his. "Can I go with you?"

"I wish you could," Beverly said, "but I'll just be working the whole time, and it wouldn't be any fun."

"If it's not fun, then why are you going?"

Picard resisted the urge to laugh. "That's a fair question. I think what your mother means is that while it might be fun for grown-ups, it would probably be boring for children."

"Do you want to know a secret?" Beverly asked, reaching with her free hand to sweep back a lock of René's auburn hair that had fallen across his forehead. "Your father can't come with me, either, even though he wants to and thinks it would be fun."

Nodding, Picard added, "She's right, you know." In some ways, exploring the alien vessel would be fun; an exhilarating experience such as those that fueled the imaginations of children, Academy cadets, and seasoned officers alike. "I have to stay here and work. Maybe you could keep me company?"

His young eyes narrowing, René regarded him with a quizzical expression. "But you'll be on the bridge. Children aren't allowed up there."

From the corner of his eye, Picard saw Beverly put a hand to her mouth in an effort to stifle a giggle. As though waiting until she was sure she had composed herself, she laid her free hand on Picard's shoulder.

"You should really talk to someone about that, Captain."

"I'll get right on it." His standing order that the bridge and other sensitive areas of the ship were off-limits to all but authorized personnel was in accordance with standard Starfleet procedure and also a holdover from his earliest days as captain of the *Enterprise*-D, the first vessel he had commanded which had allowed for civilians as part of the ship's company. There had been many more non-Starfleet members back in those days, and certainly far more children, and he had conjured all manner of disastrous scenarios involving someone's toddler accidentally blowing up the warp core or transporting a friend into deep space. He had known then that most of those situations likely would never arrive, though Beverly's first son, Wesley, had on occasion tested the limits of his patience and imagination.

The *Enterprise*-E had not been designed with children and civilians as a primary consideration, and as a consequence many of his crew who had families from whom they did not want to endure prolonged separation had sought reassignment to other ships or starbases. Over time and with the evolution of the ship's role in the years since Picard had first taken command of the vessel, accommodations had been made as members of his current crew had children of their own. Then, of course, René had come along, requiring not only a reconfiguration of Picard and Beverly's living arrangements but also a decision regarding whether they would even remain on the *Enterprise*. During its last layover at McKinley Station and prior to its departure for the Odyssean Pass, the starship had undergone several upgrades and interior renovations, including an enhancement of the captain's quarters, which he, Beverly, and René shared. The rooms to either side of his suite had been reconfigured so that all three compartments now were joined, resulting in a more expansive living space than the largest apartment he had ever occupied while living on Earth.

Still holding his mother's hand, René asked, "How long will you be gone? When will you be coming back?"

Beverly replied, "Not long, but I may not make it back before your bedtime. If that happens, your father will have to tuck you in."

This actually seemed to make the boy happy, and he turned his attention once more to Picard. "Will you read me more of that storybook?"

"Indeed I will," Picard said, already looking forward to returning to the novel he and René had been enjoying the previous evening. "I've been waiting all day to read it."

Offering a mock frown, Beverly asked, "And which book is this?"

"The one with the aliens who crashed on Earth a long time ago," René replied, growing excited as he offered his description. "It's a big secret, and everybody's looking for them and worried that more aliens will come, but there are these people who are nice and who are trying to help them get away."

Beverly shook her head, but her smile betrayed her. "Just the perfect thing to fill a young boy's head before going to sleep." Eyeing Picard, she added, "I suppose it's better than Dixon Hill."

"That's tomorrow night," Picard said.

The whistle of the ship's intercom system filled the computer lab, followed by a voice the captain recognized as belonging to Doctor Tropp, the *Enterprise*'s assistant chief medical officer. *"Sickbay to Doctor Crusher."*

Beverly tapped her combadge, which chirped as it activated. "Crusher here. Go ahead."

"Doctor Harstad wanted you to know that your team's preparations are complete, and they're ready to depart whenever you are."

"Excellent," Beverly replied. Checking a chronometer on the closest of the computer workstations, she added, "Let them know I'll be ready to leave within the hour. Meet me in the shuttlebay at seventeen hundred hours."

"Acknowledged. Tropp out."

The connection closed, and Beverly leaned closer to René, cradling his face in her hands. "Time for me to go, little man, but I'll be home as soon as I can. I promise."

As though anticipating that the private meeting was coming to a close, Hailan Casmir appeared in the doorway leading from the computer lab. "All right, René. It's time to continue our afternoon lessons."

"Can I have a snack?" the boy asked, his mood and attention shifting on a whim as only children could accomplish.

Casmir nodded. "I think we can arrange that." He extended his hand and René stepped around his mother, though he did pause before allowing the Argelian to lead him from the room.

"Bye, Mama," he said, before kissing her on the cheek.

Watching him leave with Casmir, Picard waited until both were out of earshot before asking, "Are you all right?"

"Yes," Beverly replied, before drawing a deep breath and pushing herself from the chair. "It's just like going to work any other day, right?"

Picard said, "To us, yes."

"I know it's silly, and it's not like I haven't been through this before, but still."

"Well, you just do what he says, and come back soon." Picard reached out and placed a hand on her shoulder. "And be careful over there."

"I'll have Worf and an entire security team with me," Crusher countered. "I'll be fine, but it could take some time to figure out how to revive the crew."

Recalling the latest reports offered by Worf and La Forge, which detailed the status of the alien vessel's various onboard systems, Picard said, "Assuming you can do it without harming them. If you can't do it there, we'll discuss options for transporting them back here."

"One thing at a time," Beverly said. Then, she gave him a playful poke in the arm. "You're really going to read him that silly book tonight?"

"Absolutely," Picard said. "I can't wait to see what happens next."

8

T'Ryssa Chen loved zero gravity.

There was a unique freedom to floating and moving around in weightlessness. Even swimming, another activity she had come to love, was not a proper comparison. Though she had experienced low- or null-gravity environments on infrequent occasions during her childhood, it was not until her enrollment in Starfleet Academy that she realized it was something to be enjoyed.

"I swear, you're just like a kid sometimes," said Dina Elfiki as she followed behind Chen, who at the moment was amusing herself by putting her body into a twisting roll as she drifted through the narrow, weightless tunnel.

"I can't help it," Chen replied, following Cruzen as the security officer led the way up the tunnel to the cockpit, and maneuvering without effort through the null-gravity space. "I always have fun in zero-*g*. It's like flying." She and the science officer had ventured along with Lieutenant Kirsten Cruzen to investigate what appeared to be the mammoth ship's bridge. After nearly four hours aboard the alien ship, gravity and environmental control systems now were online in several of the vessel's habitable areas. While the atmospheric requirements of the ship's passengers seemed largely compatible with most of the humanoids on the *Enterprise* crew, Elfiki had determined that the oxygen content here was more similar to Vulcan than Earth. Therefore, Commander Worf had authorized the inoculation of the entire team with tri-ox compound from the shuttle-craft's medical kit to compensate for the disparity. This allowed the away team to dispense with their EV gear while moving about. Chen, like the rest of the away team, was dressed in the gray, single-piece form-fitting garments typically worn underneath the heavier suits, which bore no rank insignia or other accessories save their combadges as well as the phasers and tricorders they carried in holsters on their hips.

Scans had revealed that certain areas—including most of the tunnels and passageways linking the ship's different decks—were deliberately designed without artificial gravity systems. Chief among those, it turned out, was the bridge and most of the tunnel connecting that compartment with the main passageway running the length of the ship. For her own part, Chen was having a ball with the whole setup.

Ahead of her, Cruzen said, "I can't say I hate it, but I don't love it, either. Mostly it's just a pain in the ass."

Chen could not agree. Even at the Academy, where other students had dreaded those exercises, she looked forward to them and even scheduled additional after-hours training time in zero-*g* simulators. She also took advantage of holodeck programs that re-created early spacecraft from Earth, Vulcan, and other planets, which had been constructed and flung toward the stars long before their respective homeworlds discovered artificial grav-ity technology. Her favorite simulations of this type were the first flights from Earth, in which she would portray one of the astronauts journeying in small, fragile ships to make those initial, hazardous landings on Luna. It was a period of human history which had always fascinated her, and though she had read numerous books and seen historical recordings recounting those missions, Chen still wondered what must have gone through the minds of the men who made those original flights while trusting their lives to machines and technology which were little more than a child's toys by modern standards.

Cruzen emerged from the connecting tunnel, reaching for handholds as she twisted her body up and away from the opening so that Chen and Elfiki could follow her. Chen pushed her way into the cockpit and oriented herself, noting how the eight workstations had been arranged around the compact space, taking advantage of the bulkheads and ceiling.

"Interesting layout," Elfiki said as she pulled herself out of the tunnel. "Maybe we can get Captain Picard to reconfigure our bridge this way." Using one foot to give herself a slight push, the science officer sailed toward the cockpit's forward canopy and the workstation positioned in front of it. "Some of the monitors and other indicators are active and operating at minimum power levels. It mostly looks like current system status updates, that sort of thing." She retrieved her tricorder from the holster on her hip and activated it, the sound of its warbling echoing in the restricted compartment. "Just like that console we found before, all of these workstations appear designed to access any shipboard system."

"I know that we've figured the ship incorporates an enormous amount of automation," Cruzen said, having maneuvered herself so that she was resting against a seat at the station adjacent to the one Elfiki was studying. "But this is something else."

Elfiki nodded. "I don't know what the builders had in mind so far as letting the onboard computer run the show while the crew was in hibernation. The fact that it's been doing just that for over a hundred years, and that's after the ship took what looks to be a serious beating, is some damned fine engineering."

"I can't wait to see what Commander La Forge finds," said Chen, using her free hand to push away from the console to the right of the forward-facing position and float across the cockpit to the adjacent seat. Her tricorder continued to scan the unfamiliar controls, only a few of which now made sense thanks to the *Enterprise* computer's ongoing efforts to build a language database for the universal translation protocols. "You know he's probably having the time of his life down there." The chief engineer, along with Worf and Rennan Konya, had decided to make their way to whatever passed for the engineering section closer to the massive ship's far end. "The propulsion and weapons systems alone are probably jaw-dropping."

Cruzen said, "What I want to know about is the time travel. Where the hell did this thing come from, and did it really jump from there back a hundred years or more? If so, why? That's the mystery that has my attention."

"I should've known that if I hung around long enough," Chen replied, "we'd find a way to get mixed up with time travel. Ours, or somebody else's."

One of her preferred leisure activities since being assigned to the *Enterprise* was reviewing the logs of its previous missions, which of course were the sorts of things one heard about from official news sources as well as Academy curriculum. Several missions—not just those of the current starship but also its predecessors—had involved exposure to various temporal anomalies or beings who traveled through time. While many details of those encounters remained classified, enough information had escaped redaction to make an engrossing study for many a hopeful cadet. Indeed, there were numerous stories and tall tales shared by senior cadets alleging that the simple matter of naming a new vessel "*Enterprise*" brought with it the jinx of being plagued by all manner of time-based trickery, and that the Federation's Department of Temporal Investigations even had a special group, "Section 1701," dedicated to nothing more than dealing with the fallout of these encounters. While there was no evidence to prove such assertions and Chen had always rejected such fanciful gossip, there was no denying that the current *Enterprise* and those which had come before it had endured their share of odd experiences, with time itself as much as anything else.

"Assuming we're right and this ship did travel through time," Chen said, "you don't suppose DTI will come all the way out here to investigate, do you?"

Shrugging, Elfiki replied, "Who knows? If those people are anything, they're unpredictable."

"Maybe they're on their way here and they'll be here yesterday," Chen said.

Cruzen groaned. "You're not allowed to make jokes for the rest of this mission. I'm going to ask the captain to make it official when we get back."

Having maneuvered herself into one of the seats, Elfiki was using her tricorder to scan the console's interface. "The translation protocols are making some decent headway," she said after a moment. "I should be able to get started on some decryption protocols soon, and hopefully then we can access their computer's database." Guided by her tricorder and the information it was processing both from its own scans as well as data sent back to it from the *Enterprise*, the science officer began pressing controls and moving her fingers across touch-sensitive panels in a sequence which to Chen seemed almost arbitrary, but after a few moments Elfiki looked as though she had been working the console all her life.

"Well, Commander La Forge was right," Elfiki said. "A lot of the files I'm finding are protected by security lockouts, but there's still enough here to confirm what we were thinking from the beginning. This ship has one purpose, and it's to blow up stuff."

"What kind of stuff?" Cruzen asked.

Instead of replying, the science officer brushed her fingers across one of the console's flat surfaces. In response to her movements, the screen at the center of her workstation activated, depicting what Chen saw was a moon or planetoid.

"I found this recording in one of the unsecured files," Elfiki explained. "From what I can tell, it's one of the last entries in the database. According to notes appended to the footage, this is a test of the primary particle weapon." She pressed another control, and an instant later the moon was consumed by a wide, bright beam of white fire which surged forward to strike it. The assault continued as a wave of energy washed over the moon's surface, and with all three officers watching in stunned silence, the planetoid broke apart.

"Dear god," said Cruzen, her voice all but a whisper.

Elfiki halted the playback and the screen went dark. "I'm still sifting through files, but pretty much everything about this ship is—or was—a secret, and it was built to be a first-strike weapon."

"You mean a last-strike weapon, right?" Chen asked.

Shrugging, the science officer replied, "That's another way to look at it. The people who built it call themselves

Raqilan, and two of them are sleeping belowdecks, and from what I've been able to pull out of the computer, they're at war with another race called the Golvonek. They live on different planets within the same solar system."

"Like the one we were heading for when we changed course to come check out this ship?" Cruzen asked.

Elfiki nodded. "Looks that way." She tapped controls on her tricorder. "I need to start sending this data back to the *Enterprise*. Captain Picard's going to want to see it."

"I'm going to have a look at some of the other systems," Chen said, maneuvering her way to one of the other workstations and settling herself into its seat. It took her a moment to figure out the chair's restraint system but in short order she had secured herself in place. Using her tricorder, she accessed the information the away team had collected and shared pertaining to the computer interfaces. After studying the data and comparing it against what she was seeing on the console before her, she tapped her combadge. "Chen to Commander La Forge."

"La Forge here."

"Sir, I'm attempting to access some of the ship's automated systems, but a lot of them appear to be protected by encrypted security lockouts."

There was a pause before the chief engineer replied, *"We're still finding our way around down here, Lieutenant. We found a master control console in the engineering compartment, and we're using it to reactivate some systems. I'm trying to do things in a logical sequence, but it's slow going as we figure it out a step at a time."*

"Maybe I can help," Chen replied. With the tricorder data to guide her, she began making tentative taps on the console. In response to her efforts, some of the station's indicators flickered to life. "I think I've found a startup sequence, sir."

A tone from one of the consoles which to this point had sat dormant caught their attention, and Elfiki was the first to maneuver across the weightless cockpit. Chen shifted in her chair and saw the science officer scanning the workstation with her tricorder. "These controls oversee the ship's weapons and defenses, including their version of sensors and a targeting array, and what looks to be some kind of early warning system." As she relayed her report, the other stations began activating around them, each console and its host of monitors, status controls, and interfaces activating and executing what Chen figured to be their respective startup sequences.

The entire cockpit was coming to life.

"Commander, are you seeing this? We're starting to see some serious activity up here."

Standing at the five-sided tower that was the centerpiece of the alien ship's engineering space, with its collections of display monitors, status indicators, and clusters of controls, Geordi La Forge grimaced as he heard T'Ryssa Chen's report and realized what had happened. In front of him, the family of monitors was giving him updates fed to it from all across the colossal vessel as various onboard systems reported being up and running. Initiating the restart protocols had been almost too easy, thanks to the sophisticated software which allowed the ship's computer to run with near total independence.

"That's my fault, Lieutenant," he said. "I didn't expect it to happen as fast or go as far as it did, or else I would've warned you beforehand. With that sequence you activated, you should be seeing most of the stations up there coming online."

"They're back, all right," Chen said. *"It's like what*

happened before. The tactical scanners are cycling through a whole process to ascertain the ship's current position and whether there are any threats. They've once again registered the Enterprise *as a vessel within the defensive system's pre-determined protective sphere, identity unknown and possibly dangerous, but I'm not seeing anything that indicates weapons or shields are being activated."*

La Forge nodded. So far, his plan for bringing up the various systems was proceeding without any problems. "We've found a way to keep those systems out of commission for the time being. We don't need a repeat of what happened before, and we sure as hell don't want that particle cannon turning itself on."

"Good thinking," replied Chen.

Studying the array of status monitors on the closest of the five workstations positioned around the central tower, La Forge nodded in approval. "I think we're done pushing buttons for the time being. Lieutenant Elfiki, take a scan of the workstations up there, but don't touch anything else. I want to see what kind of data they're accessing, and compare it to what's going on down here."

"Aye, sir," replied the science officer. *"Elfiki out."*

The connection was broken, leaving Worf and La Forge to continue their inspection of the alien systems. Peeking and peering into the compartment's every nook and cranny had been an eye-opening experience for the chief engineer, to say the least. The area of the room in which they stood, which in reality was little more than a section of deck plating mounted on a support frame above the main floor and accessible via a trio of slender ladders, looked to be the main point from which engineers and other mechanical specialists oversaw the ship's various systems. The chamber itself was spacious, essentially a massive tube dominated by the cylindrical structure occupying its center. La Forge knew that the conduit was itself a protective shell encasing the power plant for the primary particle weapon, which like the hull of the ship itself seemed impervious to his tricorder scans.

"Without tearing this thing apart, we're not going to get a good look inside," he said. "Until then, I have no idea how it was built, or what materials they used, nothing." Turning to face the collections of workstations, La Forge blew out his breath. "This setup is brilliant. Whoever designed these interfaces knew what they were doing. The computer's doing all the heavy lifting behind the scenes, but you can control to what extent from any one of these stations. If sections of the ship are cut off for whatever reason, the crew's not stuck having to figure out workarounds. It's really something."

"What if the computer fails?" Worf asked.

"There's a backup," La Forge said, pointing to one of the monitors. "A protected archive that's identical to the one currently running the show. It's updated at regular intervals with the latest information from every onboard system, but it's a one-way transaction. The secondary core is shielded against attack or disruption as a consequence of being linked to the main system. Even if the entire computer network crashed, the backup can be in place and running everything in a matter of hours."

Worf grunted, folding his arms across his broad chest. "And what if *that* system fails?"

"Then I figure the crew has a hell of a lot more to worry about," replied the chief engineer. "Still, for all the effort they put into the computer and automation systems, the ship itself still took quite a beating from somebody." For the second time since he and Worf had entered the massive engineering area, La Forge looked at the console monitors which were providing a current list of damage assessments as collated by the ship's computer. "Their warp drive, such as it is, is offline, as are a few of their shield generators and weapons systems, but most of it looks like it can be repaired without too much trouble. There are also a lot of non-critical systems which suffered damage to one degree or another." He gestured toward one of the other monitors. "And then there's this."

Depicted on the screen was a computer-generated schematic of a power-generating mechanism that shared some similarities to the alien ship's warp core, though it had taken La Forge time to confirm that despite the tremendous energies it appeared capable of producing, the engine was not linked to anything resembling a propulsion system.

"My tricorder shows that this thing has the largest concentration of residual chronitons on the entire ship. I have absolutely no idea how it's supposed to work, but I've seen enough to convince me this is a temporal displacement device." A few of the lingering energy signatures reminded him of what he had scanned more than a decade earlier from the Borg ship which the *Enterprise* had chased through time to twenty-first-century Earth. He had compiled enough information during that encounter to aid him in re-creating what the Borg sphere had done, allowing the starship to return to its own time. Agents from the Department of Temporal Investigations had interviewed him for nearly two full days following that incident, anxious to know everything he had learned and whether the technique La Forge had improvised could easily be repeated. Though the data he had collected had been stricken from the *Enterprise*'s main computer and deemed classified by Starfleet, he remembered enough that he was confident he could—in a pinch—re-create the process.

Not that I'm in any hurry to do that.

Worf, ever the skeptic, scowled as he studied the screen. "Does it still work?"

Shrugging, the engineer replied, "I guess the only real way to know would be to fire it up and see where it takes us. Want me to do that?"

"I would rather you didn't. That never seems to work out very well."

La Forge smirked. "Yeah, tell me about it. If I'm reading these diagnostics correctly, this thing is dead. Whatever damage was inflicted on the ship just prior to its jump resulted in a series of power spikes and cascading failures. A number of systems were fried, and I'm not picking up any power readings leading to or from this component. The computer's logged several areas of critical damage that would have to be addressed before we could even attempt to reactivate it." Tapping the screen, he added, "It could take weeks or months for us to get that far."

"We need to inform the captain about this," Worf said. "If this *is* from the future, then it's a possible danger to the timeline."

"Yeah," La Forge replied, nodding in agreement. He was certain that Captain Picard would order no action taken against the supposed time travel engine, or whatever the hell this ship harbored. Instead, he would send a report back to Starfleet Command and the Department of Temporal Investigations and request their counsel. However, the *Enterprise* was a long way from home or help, which of course begged another question.

"If this is some kind of time ship," La Forge said, "don't you think somebody would come looking for it? Or maybe they already did, or will, but years in the future? Maybe they're already here? Or, what if our coming aboard the ship and poking around has already done something to change future history?"

"You enjoyed the temporal mechanics courses at the Academy," Worf replied. It was not a question.

Smiling, La Forge nodded. "Oh, yes."

Before the Klingon could respond, monitors on the workstation flared to life, and indicators began flashing in hectic sequences. Streams of telemetry rendered in the still mostly untranslated text began a horizontal scroll across the different screens.

"What the hell?" asked La Forge, leaning to either side of the console tower to see that the same information appeared to be broadcasting on the adjacent workstations. "Something's got this thing's attention."

Worf pointed to one of the screens. "This is an indication similar to what was displayed when the tactical system detected the *Enterprise*."

"Yeah," the engineer said, "but I canceled that alert." Then his communicator chirped.

"Chen to Commander La Forge! The defensive systems are coming online, on their own!"

Stepping closer to the console, Worf glowered at the collection of monitors. "I thought you said those processes were deactivated."

"This is my fault, sir!" replied Chen. *"We thought we'd found an override for one of the other protected systems, but I must've entered the code wrong, because it looks like the com-*

puter's invoking some kind of override. I don't know, maybe there's another security code or something else that's needed that we don't have."

La Forge, studying the new readings, felt his pulse beginning to race and anxiety welling up within him. "Damn it. Whatever caused it, this thing is getting ready for a fight."

9

Picard emerged from his ready room onto the *Enterprise* bridge, directing his gaze to the main viewscreen and the image of the alien vessel displayed upon it. Although the red alert signal which had sounded mere seconds earlier had already been muted, silent alarms continued to flash at different consoles. To a person, each of the crew members on duty were hunched over their workstations, hands moving at a rapid pace across their instruments.

"Report."

Lieutenant Šmrhová, standing at the tactical station, replied, "Its weapons and defensive shields have come online again, sir. Our shields are up."

"The onboard computer has activated some sort of secondary protocol," said Worf over the open communications channel. *"Commander La Forge believed he had disabled the tactical systems, but an override process has been triggered. We are attempting to deactivate it."*

Šmrhová called out, "Captain! We're being targeted!"

The warning was all she had the chance to utter before the ship was rocked by an unseen impact. The deck trembled beneath Picard's feet despite artificial gravity and inertial damping systems, and he was forced to steady himself by gripping the back of the ops officer's chair.

"Faur, evasive course," he ordered, but the young flight controller was already entering the necessary commands to her console, and on the main viewscreen the image of the alien ship rolled toward the display's upper right corner as the *Enterprise* began maneuvering away from it. Despite quick reaction from Lieutenant Faur, the starship shuddered once more around them as the *Enterprise*'s deflector shields absorbed another attack.

"Shields down to seventy-eight percent," Šmrhová said.

Pushing himself away from the ops station and back to his own seat, Picard said, "Keep us facing the ship and divert power from the rear shields forward as we pull back." He dropped into the command chair, scanning the compact status displays set into its arms and noting the rapid stream of data as damage reports began arriving.

"Can you disable the weapons ports without risk to the away team?"

Šmrhová replied, "I'm not sure, sir."

"*Captain!*" shouted La Forge. "*The primary weapon's been activated. Its power-up sequence is slower, but you don't want to be here when it's ready to fire.*" The chief engineer's report was punctuated by a third strike against the shields, followed within seconds by another attack. With each new barrage, Picard felt the ship tremble with increasing intensity, and he knew that its defenses would not withstand prolonged abuse.

"Shields down to fifty-two percent," Šmrhová said. "We're being targeted by multiple ports, Captain."

"Lock phasers on those weapons and return fire."

Wasting no time, Šmrhová unleashed a barrage of phaser volleys, each shot aimed with pinpoint precision thanks to the aid of the *Enterprise*'s fire control systems.

On the viewscreen, the alien ship was visible once again, now a target as the phaser strikes impacted against its own defensive screens.

"Their shields aren't as good as ours," Šmrhová said, "but they're still hampering our counterattacks."

"Continue firing." Picard gripped the arms of his chair, bracing himself as yet another attack plowed into the shields. Now the overhead lighting around the bridge was wavering in tandem with the strikes. "Give us some maneuvering room, Faur. Šmrhová, tell engineering to route power from all non-essential systems to the shields." Raising his voice for the benefit of the intercom, he added, "Commander La Forge, find a way to disable those systems."

"Working on it, Captain!"

Another pair of volleys rammed the shields, accompanied by a new alarm wailing for attention. It was quickly silenced, but Picard knew the cause even before Šmrhová offered a report.

"Shields are down!"

Left with no choice, Picard ordered, "Faur, get us out of here."

"Their shields are down, sir," Šmrhová reported, "and three of the weapons ports are destroyed. There's a gap in their field of fire we can use."

"Feed that information to the conn, and continue targeting the ports in proximity," Picard said, with no small amount of relief. "Mister La Forge, is that ship able to maneuver?"

The chief engineer replied, *"Negative. Its shields are still offline, but I can't rule out the computer pulling another trick out of its hat."*

"You can thank Lieutenant Šmrhová for that," said Picard. "Pull out whatever you have to, Geordi, but I want that ship immobilized."

"On it, sir."

Rising from his chair, Picard stepped forward until he stood between Lieutenant Faur and Glinn Ravel Dygan at the ops station. "Damage reports?"

"Still coming in," Šmrhová said. "So far, it's mostly overloads, but our shield generators took the brunt of it. Commander Taurik is inspecting the damage now." She paused, checking other readings on her console, before adding, "The alien ship's stopped firing, sir."

"Mister La Forge?" Picard prompted.

"I think we got it, Captain," replied the engineer. *"The computer's still active, but I was able to find a lockout for the tactical systems. We had to feed it a fake security code, something the crew likely would have to do."*

To Picard's surprise, T'Ryssa Chen's voice came on the line. *"I'm the one who's responsible, sir. When I started activating various systems, the computer interpreted it as someone attempting an unauthorized access—which we were doing, really—and instituted protective measures. Nothing like that appeared on any of our scans or searches of the computer's database. All I can figure is that they're buried in one of the files we haven't decrypted yet."* There was a pause, and when Chen spoke again her voice was tinged with guilt. *"I'm sorry, sir."*

"Engineering is already addressing the damage," Picard said.

La Forge said, *"I can be back there in fifteen minutes to start on the repairs."*

"No," the captain countered. "I want you to remain there until we're certain that ship's computer doesn't have any other traps waiting to be triggered. Once that's done,

Mister Taurik can replace you over there." Though he was irritated at what had just taken place, Picard found it difficult to fault La Forge or Chen. There simply were too many unknowns surrounding the mysterious derelict. Now that they had all seen what the vessel was capable of doing if left to its own devices, Picard was disinclined to leave anything to chance. "I know you're trying to be careful, Geordi, but if it's a choice between preserving what you find and letting it take some other course of action on its own, do whatever you must to keep that from happening."

"*Understood, sir. We're holding off activating anything else until we get a complete picture over here. I've got Elfiki and Chen up on the bridge, continuing to work at decrypting the protected files, and Doctor Crusher and her team are examining the crew.*"

Picard released a small sigh. "That should keep us busy for a little while, I think."

T'Ryssa Chen had hoped that immersing herself in work might soften her irritation, but as time passed—ten hours, four of them devoted to a restless and ultimately futile attempt at sleep—she realized her annoyance with herself showed no signs of ebbing.

"Damn it."

Looking up from the console which had been the focal point of her attention since taking over for Commander La Forge after he returned to the *Enterprise*, Chen reached up to rub her temples. Even with the Vulcan aspects of her physiology, she was starting to feel the effects of the long hours spent here aboard the derelict, her lack of sleep, and the stresses of dealing with the unfamiliar systems. How long had she been here today, anyway? A glance to the chronometer on her tricorder told her that she and the rest of the away team had been here for nearly five hours on this, their second day investigating the alien ship.

"Are you all right, Lieutenant?"

Even Worf's deep voice was muted by the omnipresent hum of the alien ship's massive power plant. Turning from the console, Chen looked up to see the *Enterprise*'s first officer regarding her with concern—the Klingon equivalent of concern, anyway.

"I'm just tired, sir," she replied. She leaned back in the curved seat which, despite its odd construction, was rather comfortable. "I've been staring at these screens too long."

"Perhaps," Worf said, "but that is not all. You are still angry with yourself."

Chen nodded. "Oh, yeah. I'll probably be angry with myself for a while yet."

"You blame yourself for the attack on the *Enterprise*."

"Damned right I do." Chen paused, blowing out her breath. "I'm sorry, sir. It's just that I'm the one who decided to start poking around with the computer, instead of following Commander La Forge's lead and restoring systems in the order he was using. I figured we could help Doctor Crusher to revive the crew, and learn something about how this ship was put together. I know I didn't press the buttons that fired those weapons, but I obviously did something wrong, and the computer reacted to my tinkering around just the way it was supposed to. It acted to protect the ship from intrusion. It protected itself from *us*."

Crossing his arms, Worf stood like a statue, studying her with his typical implaccable expression. "Is there anything you did that should have alerted you to the potential for trouble?"

"Based on the readings we were getting?" Chen rubbed the bridge of her nose. "I honestly don't see how, but that doesn't mean I couldn't. It just means that I *didn't*."

The price for her not seeing the potential trouble could have been much higher than what already had been paid. Her imagination had been taunting her with what might have happened had the brief yet intense skirmish managed to inflict greater harm to the *Enterprise*. What if someone had died? How would she have been able to face Captain Picard and her shipmates, or even look at herself in a mirror?

Thankfully, the damage was minor, if widespread. Upon returning to the *Enterprise* after judging that the mysterious ship's computer system posed no new danger, Commander La Forge had gone straight to engineering to find that repairs were well under way and proceeding at a steady pace ahead of even his assistant chief engineer's estimates. The starship's damaged deflector shield generators remained the most daunting task, but even those were expected to be restored to full operational capabilities before the start of the next duty shift. Despite her own intention to pitch in for the remainder of the work, Chen had been overruled—albeit in gentle fashion—by Worf, with the first officer directing her to her quarters for a mandatory rest period before returning to the alien vessel. Despite the Klingon's directive, she had lain awake in her bed, staring up at the overhead and contemplating her role in the events of the past hours.

Incompetent and *useless. Not bad for day's work.*

"I was here with Commander La Forge when you interfaced with the computer," Worf said, "and I saw nothing you did that was wilfully negligent. Neither did Commander La Forge, or Lieutenant Elfiki or anyone else."

The words did little to assuage Chen's feelings. "I know I shouldn't be beating myself up about this, sir, at least not this much." She shook her head. "It took me a long time to realize that I'm happy on the *Enterprise*, and I really don't want to be anywhere else, or doing anything else. And then, there I am, standing there while my ship and all the people I care about are being shot at by weapons I helped activate." Sensing Worf preparing to respond, she held up her hand. "I know, sir. I didn't actually do that, but come on. It's a matter of semantics, right?" She sighed. "I just feel like I let Captain Picard down. Hell, I feel like I let everyone down."

Worf said nothing, though his gaze did not shift from her, and after a moment she was beginning to feel uneasy. Then, finally, he broke the silence.

"Do you remember when you were first assigned to the *Enterprise*?"

"Like it was yesterday." There were times when Chen marveled at just how much time had passed since her arrival aboard the Federation flagship, itself a premiere, coveted posting by junior officers throughout Starfleet. The starship carried with it a history and pedigree that was required reading at the Academy. Even before that, its name had been the source of stories and even legends dating back centuries, to well before humans had launched themselves to the stars but instead traversed the oceans of the world they called home.

"Do you remember what I told you with respect to learning?" Worf asked.

Chen smiled. "Yes, sir. You said to never be afraid of

making a mistake. Instead, we should learn from it, and never make the same mistake twice."

"Actually, I believe it may have been Commander La Forge who said that last part."

"Could be."

Pushing herself to her feet, Chen nodded and attempted a smile. "Thank you, Commander. It helps to be able to talk it out, you know? Talking's always helped me relieve stress."

"I feel the same way after fighting," replied the Klingon.

The deadpan response caught Chen off guard, and she could not help the unrestrained laugh that forced its way up from her belly and echoed off the surrounding bulkheads. "Oh, wow, did I need that." She was wiping a single tear from the corner of her eye when her communicator chirped.

"Crusher to Lieutenant Chen."

"Chen here," replied the Vulcan. "What can I do for you, Doctor?"

"We've made some progress with our scans of the aliens, and we think we have an idea on how best to revive them, but we could use some more help understanding their equipment."

"On my way. Chen out." Closing her eyes, she drew a deep breath, releasing it slowly and enjoying the calming sensation that washed over her. After a moment, she nodded, more to herself than Worf or anyone else.

"All right. Back to work." When the Klingon nodded, Chen smiled again. "And I'll be sure not to make the same mistake twice."

10

—————

Staring at the hibernating aliens, Chen decided that she was envious of anyone who could sleep for more than five hours, let alone a century.

"I think I need to give this cryogenic suspension thing a try," she said, stepping around one of the transparent cylinders encasing the derelict vessel's two surviving Raqilan crew members. "Imagine being able to sleep all the way out here from Earth, and all the work details I could've skipped."

"Don't think I haven't thought about it," replied Doctor Beverly Crusher from where she stood along with Lieutenant Dina Elfiki at the row of workstations which had been identified as overseeing the hibernating crew. "If you believe I enjoyed catching up on all the overdue crew physicals, then I have a beach resort on Ferenginar I wouldn't mind selling you."

Raising her eyebrow to a degree that would make any proper Vulcan proud, Chen offered the doctor a mock frown. "I've been to Ferenginar. I think I'll pass."

Crusher turned from her review of the monitors and leaned against the console. "Right now, just about any sort of leave sounds good. I don't remember the last real, substantial time off I had. And no, an uneventful, weeks-long cruise at high warp with no pit stops doesn't count."

"Beats getting shot at," said Elfiki, dividing her attention between the status screens and her tricorder.

Nodding, Crusher replied, "Okay, I'll give you that."

Her tricorder still in hand, Chen gestured with the device toward the closest of the hibernation cylinders. "I'm familiar with the stasis technology we employ, and I've read about its use during the early days of interplanetary and interstellar travel, but this is like nothing I've ever seen. According to my readings, there's almost no evidence of muscle atrophy or other deterioration that you'd expect to find after long-term cryogenic suspension."

"It's quite something, isn't it?" Pushing herself from the console, Crusher moved to stand so that the cylinder was between her and Chen, then ran her hand across its smooth surface. "Of course, if this ship is from the future, it would make sense for its technology to be more advanced, at least in some areas."

"Even if it came from the past," Elfiki countered, "that would still track. Different civilizations achieve different technological milestones at varying rates, of course, and not always in an order of progression that makes sense."

With a knowing grin, Chen said, "This is starting to sound like one of those sociological lectures at the Academy. We tend to assume that a society will make advances in a linear fashion similar to how it was achieved on Earth or Vulcan: flight, space travel, interstellar flight, and so on, with other technology being discovered or developed along the way as a means of furthering the primary goal of being able to push ever outward from our home planet."

Elfiki giggled. "I see you attended at least one of Professor Palmieri's guest seminars."

"I actually went to all of them." Chen had of course enjoyed those sessions, a series of talks which had peppered the course syllabus during her xenosociology and cultural studies training. The seminars and the ideas put forth by the prominent experts in these fields had only fueled her interest in these subjects and pushed her further down the path she eventually had taken toward becoming a contact specialist.

"Maybe something caused their development of faster-than-light travel to stall out," Crusher said, enjoying the discussion, "so they put a greater focus on improving their cryogenics technology." She patted the cylinder with its slumbering alien occupant. "Still, I expect there'll be some initial disorientation and vertigo, but in theory they should be able to just walk out of here." Sighing, she added, "Assuming we can figure out how to get them out of these things, of course."

The examination of the Raqilan vessel's cryogenics systems had consumed a considerable portion of the past two days. Doctors Crusher and Harstad, along with two other members of the medical staff, had worked alongside Elfiki as the science officer struggled to coax information from the ship's computers. The *Enterprise* computer's universal translation processors had successfully constructed a linguistic database for communicating with the other ship and—in theory, at least—its crew, but Elfiki along with La Forge had run into obstacle after obstacle within the unfamiliar system framework.

Tapping the console which had all but consumed her attention over the past several hours, Elfiki said, "I've isolated the protected sectors that contain all of the software for the cryogenics systems, but the level of encryption is at least as high if not more so than other processes we've already managed to crack." She sighed. "Whoever designed this thing knew what they were doing when it came to computer security, and they went to great lengths to make sure anybody who wasn't supposed to be mucking around in there stayed out."

"If you're having trouble, that's saying something," Chen said. It was common knowledge that Dina Elfiki was more talented with computer systems than was implied even by her A6 computer expert classification, and she was rivalled by no one among the *Enterprise* crew. Even Commander Taurik, whose own computer skills were formidable, had acknowledged her superior ability.

Elfiki shook her head, "It's not about ability. I can see what this thing is doing, but without a key, or a way to figure out how to forge our own key, there's no way to decode the protection schemes. We can do it, but it just takes time." Shrugging, she added, "More time than I expected, is all."

"What can we do?" Crusher asked. "I'm no computer wizard, but I've managed to fumble my way through a problem or two."

"Same here," Chen said. Though she was confident in her own expertise, she knew Elfiki outclassed her, as well. "Maybe some new eyes will help."

The science officer replied, "At this point, I'll try anything, but first I want some coffee." After pausing to stretch her back muscles, she said, "Doctor, I'm making a run to the shuttle. Can I bring you anything?"

Chen held up her hand. "You take a break. I'll get it." After taking what turned out to be lunch orders and making a mental note to ask Commander La Forge about getting a portable replicator so as to avoid making trips of this sort, she started the long trek back to the landing bay where the *Jefferies* waited.

Thankfully, the walk separating her from the shuttle-craft was anything but boring, due to the ship itself and everything its designers had seen fit to cram into it. Despite its obvious practical aesthetic—and what in her opinion had to be a conscious decision on the part of its builders to forgo anything resembling comfort or visual style—the vessel's interior still harbored a certain beauty Chen could appreciate. Everything, from the bulkheads and deck plating to the workstations and every other component and contraption the away team had encountered since first coming aboard, begged for her attention. Form and function had come together with a grace that was intriguing, and as she progressed through the long central corridor Chen imagined herself as a member of this vessel's crew. What would it have been like, shepherding a craft of such immense power, and for what purpose? If the ship truly was intended as a sort of ultimate weapon, what did that say about the people charged with piloting it to its target and perhaps causing the destruction of entire worlds?

"Hey, slow down."

The voice came from behind her, startling Chen and causing her to turn to look over her shoulder. Walking behind her, just over an arm's length away and moving with what had to have been utter stealth, was Rennan Konya. How had she not heard him?

Seeing her look of surprise, Konya held up a hand. "Sorry. I didn't mean to startle you. I called after you twice, but I guess you didn't hear me."

"What?" Chen shook her head. "Wow. I was . . . hell, I don't know. Daydreaming, I guess."

Moving so that he could walk beside her, Konya smiled. "Probably not the best idea, you know."

"You said the ship's safe, right?" Chen asked, with a hint of teasing in her words. "Didn't you and the security detail conduct a full sweep?"

Unperturbed by her gentle taunt, the security officer

shrugged. "Sure, but you never know. Anyway, you probably shouldn't go anywhere alone, just to be safe."

"Is that why you followed me?" Chen asked, continuing her playful tone. "Just to keep me safe?"

"That's my job."

Chen giggled. "Overachiever." They walked for almost three dozen paces before she said, "Okay, Rennan. What's really going on?"

"What?" Konya asked. "Can't a guy go to get a sandwich with the girl he brushed off without there being anything more to it?"

The brazen remark caught Chen off guard. "You said it. I didn't," she snapped, unable to stop the retort from escaping her lips. The instant the words were spoken, she felt herself blushing in embarrassment. "I'm sorry. That was uncalled for."

Konya shook his head. "No, Trys, it wasn't. I deserved that, and a lot more, if we're being honest with each other."

Stopping in the middle of the corridor, the last of her footsteps echoing along the metal deck plates, Chen turned to face the Betazoid. "Come on, Rennan. You're never this coy. What's this about?"

"You know when we were in the shuttle the other day, on our way over here for the first time?" Konya sighed. "It occurred to me while we were talking that I never apologized to you."

"Sure you did," Chen countered, almost talking over him.

"No, I didn't." Crossing his arms, Konya cast his gaze toward the deck, taking a moment to examine his boots. She watched him until he apparently forced himself to look up at her once again. "I mean, we started talking again. You know, after I did what I did, and you were very supportive of me during that time I was . . . working things out, but I never actually said the words. So, I'm saying them now: I'm sorry. I'm sorry for how I treated you, Trys, and how I made you feel."

Reaching out, Chen placed a hand on his forearm. "It's okay. I can't say I understood what you were dealing with, but I get that you had to work it out on your own, and that it takes as long as it needs to take." She squeezed his arm. "I'm just glad we're still friends."

Konya smiled. "Part of me working out my issues is recognizing that people around me want to help, or are trying to help, or are just doing their best to give me the space I need to do things myself. I know it's hard to be that kind of friend, let alone anything more, and I didn't make it any easier for you. For that, I'm sorry."

There was no mistaking the pain and remorse in Konya's eyes. Chen had seen this haunted look before, on numerous occasions since her relationship with him had deteriorated in the period after the Borg Invasion. There was no denying that even now, five years after the horrific events of that last assault on the Federation by the relentless cybernetic race, Rennan Konya still carried within him the guilt he felt at the choices he had faced and orders he had been forced to issue, several of which had led to the deaths of shipmates and friends. It was obvious that he had made tremendous progress, and bit by bit was coming to terms with his feelings. Chen knew he would never truly rid himself of his inner turmoil, but he at least seemed to have found a way to live with it and keep it at bay, and the change in his demeanor, especially in recent months, had been palpable. Much of his old humor and warmth had returned, and he smiled more. She had always liked his smile.

"Apology accepted," Chen said. Then, before she comprehended what she was doing, she stepped closer to Konya, her other hand reaching up around his neck and pulling his face toward hers. Their lips touched and her eyes closed, and she felt him pressing against her. She pulled back after a moment, seeing the surprise in his eyes, but there was no disapproval or displeasure. Even as she extracted herself from their embrace, she saw him offer a small, sly grin.

"Maybe we can continue this discussion later," he suggested.

"Yeah," Chen replied. "We should probably get back to work. Besides, I'm supposed to be getting lunch for everybody." Clearing her throat, she brushed at the front of her uniform, noting with no small amount of amusement that Konya was mimicking her movments. Looking at him, she saw his features communicating a hint of empathy as he regarded her.

"This mission's not exactly what you were hoping for, is it?"

Chen resisted the impulse to express a sigh of disappointment. "If Doctor Crusher can't bring the crew out of hibernation, all we'll have is the ship's computer. That's more Dina's or Commander La Forge's area of expertise, and they won't have any real need for a contact specialist."

"I seem to recall you having no small amount of computer skills, yourself," Konya countered. "Come to think of it, I'm fairly certain I remember you and your talents getting us all out of at least a crisis or two."

Chen felt her cheeks warming in response to the praise. "I've gotten lucky a few times, but I don't have anything on Dina, or Taurik, or a dozen people I could name off the top of my head." The challenge of coaxing answers and other secrets from the derelict's computer was interesting, of that there could be no doubt.

"But talking to a computer isn't exactly what you were counting on, right?" asked Konya.

Chen shrugged. "Let's just say that it doesn't arouse the same level of intense curiosity that might come from talking directly to our friends sleeping upstairs."

Needless to say, she was rooting for Doctor Crusher.

11

"Bridge to Captain Picard."

Sitting in the recliner in his small study with a book propped in his lap, Picard glanced at the chronometer. It was less than two hours before the start of alpha shift, and only ninety minutes since Beverly had awakened so that she along with Commanders Worf and La Forge and their away team might get an early start on their ongoing survey of the alien vessel, which now was into its third day. Unable to sleep with her away, Picard had attempted to lose himself in the pages of a book. Through the open door leading to his son's bedroom, he could hear the sounds of soft breathing. Satisfied that neither the intercom signal nor Commander Aiden Lynley's voice had roused René from slumber, he said in a soft tone, "Picard here."

"I apologize for disturbing you sir," replied the gamma shift watch officer, *"but long-range sensors have detected the approach of two vessels on an intercept course. They're traveling at warp one point four, outbound from System 3955."*

"Do you have a visual on them?"

"Yes, sir. Already routing a feed to you."

Setting aside the book, Picard reached for the computer terminal on his desk and pressed its activation control. The image on the interface's screen shifted from a Federation logo to show a pair of vessels, traveling together but in a loose formation. The ships were of near-identical design, each looking like a wedge with a squat, wide contour that gave him the impression of blades slicing through whatever obstacle appeared in their paths. Dark hull plating and a lack of exterior lighting almost made the ships disappear into the dark curtain of open space behind them. Only the computer's imaging processor, working from the information it received from the *Enterprise*'s sensors, allowed the vessels to be seen with such detail. Instinct told Picard that these ships were military in nature.

"Can you trace their course back to a point of origin?" Picard asked, reaching up to rub his chin.

Lynley said, *"We're not able to pinpoint an exact starting point, sir, as their approach was partially masked by the sun, but given what we know of the system, it has to be either the second or third planet."*

"What about their weapons or defenses?"

"Sensors are picking up particle beam weapons, but no deflector shield technology. It's more like an ablative armor, similar to the weapon ship but not nearly as durable. Still, if both of the ships ganged up on us, or called for some friends to help them, we might have a problem, but that's a tall order. Their propulsion is basically first-generation warp drive, sir. Assuming they did come from one of the system's two habitable planets, at this distance it would take nearly seven hours for reinforcements to arrive." After a moment, Lynley added, *"They've also got sensor technology, but it's not as sophisticated as ours. Still, I'm guessing they're looking us over and probably a little worried about what they're seeing."*

"I can imagine," Picard said. If the approaching vessels' sensors were advanced enough to scan the *Enterprise*, then their crews already knew that the starship outclassed their own craft in capability. He hoped that would be enough to forestall any ill-advised acts of aggression. "Estimated time to intercept?"

"Three hours forty-three minutes at their present speed, sir."

Nodding in approval, Picard ordered, "Maintain yellow alert, Commander. Weapons offline until further notice, but keep the shields up." The shield generators had only been restored to full functionality within the last few hours, and he was still leery in the wake of the unexpected attack from the derelict and its overly zealous automation system that had incapacitated them in the first place. "I'm on my way."

After contacting the specialist on duty in the ship's childcare center and requesting assistance, Picard took a moment to look in on René, who still had not stirred. While it was not unusual for both him and Beverly to be away from their quarters at odd hours, he still felt a pang of guilt at having to call for someone to look after their son when circumstances required him to be elsewhere. That, and he knew he might not be here when the boy awakened, thus depriving Picard of their habitual shared breakfast.

Duty calls.

The early hour, at least so far as the ship's clocks and schedule were concerned, saw to it that he encountered no one on the way from his quarters to the bridge, where he found Commander Aiden Lynley standing at one of the tactical stations behind the captain's chair. Lynley had been a tactical officer earlier in his career, and it was not uncommon to find the watch officer operating any of the bridge consoles during his duty rotation, as he tended to use the often-quiet hours of gamma shift to maintain his training and certifications in various areas of starship operations.

"Good morning, sir," Lynley said, nodding in greeting as Picard stepped out of the turbolift. "Sensors show there's been no change in the ships' course or speed, and they're running right about at their maximum velocity. They're still heading in our general direction, and they've definitely attempted to scan us with whatever they have that passes for sensor technology."

Picard moved to stand just behind the ops and conn stations. "Open a hailing frequency. Let's see if they're interested in talking." He waited, counting off the seconds he knew were required for the standard signal to be transmitted and received. What were the captains of the approaching vessels thinking as they considered their options for responding to what was hoped to be a request for peaceful communication?

"We're getting a reply, sir," Lynley reported after a moment. "The language is consistent with one of the thirty-eight we found represented in the alien ship's computer records."

Now things are getting interesting, Picard thought. Were these people looking for their lost ship? If so, why now? Had the *Enterprise*'s arrival on the outskirts of the system been detected? Those were questions requiring answers, to be sure, but despite them, Picard felt a familiar rush of enthusiasm already coursing through him. It had been some time since he had made first contact with a heretofore unknown species, and though he had done so on nearly thirty previous occasions, the thrill of carrying out one of the most anticipated and cherished duties of a starship commander never failed to excite him.

"On screen, Commander."

In response to his order, the image shifted from that of the approaching ships to what appeared to be a female humanoid. A long mane of stark white hair framed a slim face with a high forehead and prominent cheekbones tapering down to an almost pointed jaw. Brilliant emerald eyes peered out at Picard from beneath a protuberant brow that curved along the sides of her yellow-green face to disappear beneath the hair on the sides of her head. She wore a wine-colored one-piece garment that featured ornate embroidery on the sleeves and around the neck, and appeared tailored to fit her slender frame to an exacting degree.

Behind her was what looked to be a command center or bridge with a half-dozen consoles visible, each facing toward the viewscreen and manned by a female or male of similar physiology. Hair color varied, and two of the personnel, a female and a male, had no hair at all. They all wore matching uniforms, with the only distinction from person to person being the amount and patterns of the embroidery on their sleeves. As for the female who was their apparent leader, her expression was unreadable, her eyes fixed on him from across the void separating them.

"Greetings," he said, stepping closer to the viewscreen. "I am Captain Jean-Luc Picard, commanding the *Starship Enterprise* and representing the United Federation of Planets. We have come on a mission of peaceful exploration and are honored to make your acquaintance."

"I am Mynlara, Fleet Legate of the Golvonek Protective Directorate, and commanding the expeditionary vessel Calkurizar. *It is I who am honored to meet you today, Captain."* She paused, her expression softening. *"We have heard stories of great civilizations living far away among the distant stars, and it is the dream of many a Golvonek child to journey from our home system in the hopes of meeting such people."*

Despite his poised demeanor, Picard could not help allowing a small smile. "Our exploration of this region includes visiting what I presume is your home system, and investigating the inhabited worlds to see whether we might make formal contact with your government. It is the mission of my people to search for intelligent life wherever it may reside in the galaxy, in the hopes of opening a dialogue and perhaps forming a lasting and mutually beneficial friendship. The Federation is a cooperative of nearly two hundred worlds and civilizations, but we are always hoping to meet and welcome new friends."

It was obvious to him that Mynlara, like him, was a veteran leader and accustomed to maintaining her bearing in all manner of situations, but he still saw the flicker of surprise in her eyes as she listened to his descriptions. She had every reason to be astounded by the information she had just received. Based on their demonstrated technology, there would have been almost no chance of traveling to worlds in another solar system, let alone one possessing a civilization similar to her own, and now to confront someone claiming to speak for nearly two hundred such planets? Picard believed she could be forgiven any momentary lapses in composure.

Of course, all of this would be true had the *Enterprise* encountered the *Calkurizar* within the boundaries of System 3955. That Mynlara had seen fit to venture into the interstellar void suggested another purpose, doubtless related to the mammoth vessel drifting beyond his own vessel's port bow. For the moment—and setting aside the possible time travel component affecting the current situation—Picard decided that honesty was the prudent course.

"Fleet Legate, while en route to your system, we detected the presence of a rather large spacecraft drifting in open space. Our initial scans of the vessel indicated that most of its power systems were inactive, though we did detect life-forms aboard. I sent a team to the ship to investigate and see if we could be of assistance." Though he knew the answer to the question he was about to pose, he asked it anyway. "Do you know anything about this vessel?"

On the screen, Mynlara appeared to be contemplating her own options, though to her credit her delay before responding was but a single brief moment. *We only became aware of its presence a short time ago. One of our outlying early warning stations detected an energy signature as well as a communications signal.*" She paused, as though once more considering how to proceed, before adding, *"Our scans indicate it is rather large. So large, in fact, that it actually masked your own ship's presence until we drew closer."* Her lips pressed together, as though she realized she had offered more information than intended. Had she offered an inadvertent admission about her vessel's sensor capabilities?

Setting aside that thought, Picard replied, "The ship's size is indeed impressive, though it appears to possess a very small crew. My team found eight individuals, all in a state of cryogenic suspension. Unfortunately, six of them died while in hibernation. The other two remain in stasis, and my chief medical officer is attempting to revive them." Then, playing another hunch, he said, "Perhaps you can assist us in identifying the crew and even ascertaining where they're from. I can tell you that based on visual evidence, they do not appear to be representatives of your world." Without waiting for an answer, he looked over his shoulder to Lynley. "Commander, retrieve an image of one of the crew members from the away team's tricorder data and transmit it to the Golvonek vessels."

"Aye, sir," replied the watch officer. A moment later, he looked up from his console as the main viewscreen shifted to include an inset image of one of the hibernating aliens from the derelict.

To Mynlara, Picard said, "Do you recognize this species, Fleet Legate?" Even as he asked the question, he saw the recognition in her eyes. Her posture straightened, and her voice took on a more official tone as her gaze locked once more with his.

"Captain, I must now inform you that I am obligated to take custody of that vessel, as it is a military craft in service to the Raqilan, with whom we are currently at war."

Picard had expected such a response and decided that remaining truthful still was the best way to proceed. "I have only recently learned of this conflict between your worlds. It is not our wish to interfere in your affairs, or to take sides. However, my people are aboard that vessel in the hopes of assisting its crew."

"That is my duty to perform, Captain," Mynlara countered. *"The Raqilan aboard that ship will be taken into custody, after which they will be processed and classified as prisoners of war."*

Picard knew that he had to step with care. Even setting aside the Prime Directive considerations forbidding Starfleet officers from interfering in a sovereign nation's internal politics or other societal or technological development, the obvious challenge now facing him was how to remain diplomatic—and detached—from what obviously was a sensitive situation between the Golvonek and Raqilan people.

"I have no intention of opposing or circumventing your laws, Fleet Legate," Picard said, stepping closer to the screen. "However, as I informed you, the ship's crew remains in hibernation, and my medical officer informs me that reviving them would be a time-consuming and perhaps even dangerous task. With that in mind, I offer our assistance in bringing them out of stasis." He could almost hear the proverbial wheels turning in Mynlara's mind as she considered his overture, no doubt attempting to see the proposal from all possible angles and determine what advantages she might gain from agreement. Would she appeal to him—and by extension, the Federation—to ally with her people? Perhaps she sought a tactical advantage by somehow capturing the *Enterprise.*

That was highly unlikely, Picard decided.

"Your offer is most generous, Captain," Mynlara said after a moment. *"On behalf of my people, I accept, but I ask that you refrain from any further action aboard that ship until our arrival."*

"Very well," Picard said. To Lynley and for Mynlara's benefit, he said, "Notify Commander Worf that the away team is to return to the *Enterprise* immediately."

"Thank you, Captain." Perhaps emboldened that her request had been granted without resistance, she added in a slightly more forceful tone, *"I must also warn you that any attempt to prevent me from carrying out my duty would not . . . further whatever peaceful mission you hope to accomplish here."*

Picard replied, "There is no need to posture. We are visitors here, and we will do our best to abide by your wishes. I look forward to meeting you in person, Fleet Legate. Picard out."

The connection was severed, and the image on the viewscreen returned to that of the drifting alien vessels. Turning to Lynley, Picard asked, "Mister Lynley, is the away team en route back to the *Enterprise?*"

"Most of them are preparing to beam back, sir," replied the commander. After the initial away team investigation and as a means of overcoming the interference with transporter beams caused by the alien ship's hull, Commander La Forge had deployed a portable transporter pad in the vessel's landing bay and linked it to the *Enterprise* using site-to-site interlocking. Now personnel and equipment could be moved back and forth without the need to rely on shuttles, though Picard had ordered at least one craft to remain on site so long as members of the crew were working over there.

"Captain," Lynley said a moment later, and Picard saw that he was uncomfortable having to relay that report. "Commander Worf and Doctor Crusher are standing by to speak with you."

Gesturing for him to open the channel, the captain announced, "Picard here. What's your status, Number One?" Expecting to hear his first officer, he was surprised when his wife's voice burst from the intercom.

"Crusher here, Captain. We can't leave. My team and I have discovered how to initiate the process for bringing the crew out of hibernation. It takes time and the computer oversees most of it, but one of Geordi's engineers had to help us reroute part of the systems that were damaged."

Already knowing where her explanation was going, Picard said, "You're saying part of the automated oversight process was included in that damage?"

"That's right," Crusher replied. *"It can still watch over most of the procedure, but this whole thing works in stages. If the computer misses the administration of required medications and other treatments at the proper intervals throughout the process, it could kill the crew. I can't stand by and let that happen, Jean-Luc."*

Of course you can't, Picard mused, at once proud of his wife's devotion to her patients and her duty while also irritated by her impeccable if unfortunate timing. "How long will the process take?"

"Right now, we're estimating about two hours. It could be longer, depending on whatever we have to deal with as the process continues."

Behind him, Lynley said, "Captain, the Golvonek ships won't arrive until after the doctor is finished."

There was no other choice, Picard knew. For better or worse, they were committed. "Very well, Doctor. Remain on station, with only the essential members of your medical team. Mister Worf?"

"Worf here, Captain."

"You, Lieutenant Konya, and the security details from both teams are to remain with Doctor Crusher and whoever she needs to carry out the procedure. Commander La Forge and everyone else are to return to the ship immediately."

"Acknowledged. Worf out."

The channel was closed, leaving Picard to stare in silence at the colossal Raqilan vessel. Now, at least, some of the questions had been answered.

Other questions, like the ship itself, beckoned.

12

———

"The Raqilan call it '*Poklori gil dara*,' which more or less translates to '*Armageddon's Arrow*.' Basically, this ship is meant to end their war with one hell of a knockout punch."

At the head of the curved table that ran the length of the *Enterprise*'s observation lounge, Picard sat in his high-backed chair with his hands resting in his lap studying—along with Lieutenants Šmrhová and Elfiki—the computer-generated technical readout of the Raqilan ship displayed on the room's central viewscreen. The diagram rotated in place, offering views of the vessel from multiple angles. Standing next to the screen, Lieutenant T'Ryssa Chen paused after delivering her report, awaiting further instructions.

"*Armageddon's Arrow,*" Picard repeated, almost to himself. "Rather dramatic, wouldn't you say?"

Chen sighed. "Maybe if the ship didn't live up to its name, but this one does, and then some." She tapped the image and the screen froze, after which she touched the image of the ship itself and the schematic zoomed in. The vessel's outer layers separated and pulled away, exposing the massive cylinder that was its core.

"This particle cannon can outclass just about anything we might throw against it. The antiproton beam it generates, as we've already seen from the ship's computer records, is more than capable of taking out planet-sized targets."

Nodding, Picard recalled the data file sent to him by Lieutenant Elfiki and demonstrating the weapon's tremendous power. Only on rare occasions had he seen a weapon of such ability, and rarer still had he seen the effects. Even the Borg, with all the technology at their disposal thanks to their assimilation of races across the galaxy, thankfully had never acquired something of this magnitude.

And thankfully, they never will.

"So these people, the Raqilan," Šmrhová said, "they built this thing to . . . what? Destroy the Golvonek homeworld?"

"It looks that way, sir," Elfiki said. "According to the historical records we found in the ship's computer, they haven't liked each other pretty much since their first meeting, which took place a little over a century ago. Both planets progressed independently of each other, and their level of technological advancement is within a few generations of each other. In some ways, they're very similar to the Onarans and the Brekkians in the Delos system, or even Romulus and Remus." She shrugged. "Anyway, both worlds developed rudimentary space travel capabilities within a generation or so of each other, and started sending out probes and small ships to their worlds' respective moons and later the system's other planets."

Chen added, "By the looks of things, that first meeting didn't go very well. The records on the *Arrow* do a pretty good job of downplaying things, Captain, and of course they paint the Raqilan in the best possible light, but it looks to me as though they were the aggressors. Once the war finally got going, most of the engagements looked to have been initiated by them, with Golvonek forces fighting largely defensive actions." She shrugged. "Yes, there were occasions when the Golvonek went on the offensive, but based just on the data available, I'd argue they were counterattacks or preemptive strikes intended to upset a pending action by the Raqilan. On the other hand, the primary goal of the Raqilan was overwhelming, decisive victory at all costs."

"This probably explains their comparable advances in space flight as well as developing warp capability," said Šmrhová. "As we all know, war has a tendency to speed up the research and development of new technologies."

Stepping away from the viewscreen, Chen returned to her seat at the conference table. "And that seems to have driven the tempo of their war. After going at it pretty hot and heavy for several years, things calmed down and both sides went back to their respective corners, if you'll pardon the expression. Though there was no permanent peace treaty, both governments apparently were able to negotiate a ceasefire that lasted for a few decades. Then, things took another bad turn and hostilities started up again. Before they discovered warp drive, both sides had already been establishing satellites, space stations, and outposts on the system's outlying planets and moons. They spent years establishing footholds on new territory, exploiting whatever resources they could find, and so on. Warp drive is a relatively new advancement for them, only within the last couple of decades, and it looks to be restricted for military use."

"So, of course they're using it to renew and extend their attacks," Picard said.

Chen replied, "To a degree, yes sir. The planets are hundreds of millions of kilometers apart, so it could take months to get between them. Before warp drive, attacks against either homeworld were rare, but they tended to inflict a lot of damage." She shrugged. "With warp drive, the same attacks could occur within minutes, and that's the way it went for years afterward."

"Is the conflict resource-motivated?" Šmrhová asked.

Elfiki replied, "It may not have started out that way, but that's what it seems to be now." She raised her hands, holding them apart. "The two planets orbit the Canborek sun almost opposite to each other. The Golvonek world, Uphrel, is about thirty million kilometers closer to the star than Henlona. The climate on Uphrel is closer to Earth, while Henlona is more like Mars. The current, terraformed Mars, that is. The atmospheric makeups aren't identical, but they're within ranges that make both worlds viable for either side." Frowning, the science officer leaned forward in her chair. "Or, they will be, up until a century or so from now."

Šmrhová asked, "Time travel?"

Instead of Elfiki, Chen replied, "Right. According to the computer records, the *Arrow* traveled through time from a point approximately ninety-four years in the future, back to approximately one hundred twenty-two years ago. We're still refining the translations, so we don't have exact departure and arrival points yet."

"So the Raqilan military must have constructed this vessel with the intention of traveling back in time to a point before the war began," Picard said.

"Exactly," replied Chen. "In the decades to come, the war's effects on both planets will be devastating. As the conflict drags on, resources for ships and weapons powerful enough to make the trip between the two planets will get harder to come by, and direct attacks will start to taper off in frequency. Eventually, the war is again reduced to little more than occasional skirmishes, with both sides turning their attentions more and more to claiming additional resources across the rest of the solar system." She shook her head. "But the damage will have been done. Orbital bombardments will have long-term environmental consequences. The Golvonek will get the worst part of that deal; in the long run, there won't be any real winners." Pausing, Chen looked over her shoulder at the vessel schematic still displayed on the viewscreen. "I guess they figured they could launch the mother of all preemptive strikes, and possibly avoid the worst of the war's effects."

Rubbing the bridge of his nose, Picard allowed himself a small sigh of exasperation. Temporal mechanics, despite the intriguing possibilities and theories bandied about for centuries from learned scholars, wild conspiracy theorists, and representatives from organizations such as the Federation's Department of Temporal Investigations, had never been one of his favored subjects. Fate and circumstance had seen to it that he and the *Enterprise* had encountered their share of various time-bending anomalies, agents, and other oddities, and they were not experiences he was keen to revisit. In particular, he had no desire to deal with any variation of the scenario that had befallen Earth on at least one occasion, thanks to the machinations of the Borg. The parasitic race had attempted to use time itself as a weapon, traveling back to a point before Earth had made its first contact with beings from another world. Left unchecked, humanity would have been assimilated into the Collective more than two centuries before his birth. It was only through happenstance and good fortune that Picard and the *Enterprise* were able to follow the Borg ship back through time and thwart that effort.

"Their plan was to come back and what?" Šmrhová

asked. "Blow up the Golvonek homeworld? That seems a bit extreme, doesn't it?"

Elfiki added, "And that's before we get into the ethical considerations of preemptive attacks."

"History is filled with first strikes carried out for the right reasons," Šmrhová countered. "While I suppose one could make the argument for launching an attack to prevent an assault you know is coming, that's not what this seems to entail."

Chen said, "I suppose it depends on how you look at it." She gestured to the screen and the ship depicted on it. "Even though that thing comes from the future, the Raqilan and the Golvonek *are* at war right now."

Frowning, Šmrhová rested her hand on the conference table. "While I'm not one of them, there are people who'd argue that falls within the acceptable parameters of a justified action."

"Actually, it isn't," Picard said. "Lieutenant Elfiki, there's an element to this equation we haven't yet discussed."

The science officer replied, "That's right, sir. The *Arrow*'s original destination was a point in time one hundred twenty-one years in the past. According to what I've been able to dig out of their computer, the crew was supposed to have been revived shortly after their arrival, but it looks like some key onboard systems were damaged during a skirmish the ship encountered just prior to their time jump."

"They were being attacked by Golvonek ships right up to the last second," Chen said. "The Golvonek learned about the *Arrow* soon after its launch, though I don't think they knew—or will know—about its true mission when they sent ships out to meet it."

"As a consequence of that attack," Elfiki added, "whatever damage was sustained prevented the computer from initiating the revival procedures, so the crew has remained in hibernation all this time."

Šmrhová said, "They jumped back to a point before the war even started."

"It's worse than that," Chen replied. "Their target was a point in time before the two races even met." When no one said anything in immediate response, the young lieutenant added, "Does that sound familiar to anyone besides me?"

Picard rested his head on the back of his chair. "Indeed it does. Except for the time travel element, it's the Xindi all over again."

"But time travel even played a part in that, sir," Chen said. "Or, at least something like it. It's not like we ever got a straight answer about any of that."

Nodding as he recalled more details from memory, the captain said, "Correct, Lieutenant." Even before enrolling in Starfleet Academy, he was familiar with the Xindi attacks on Earth during the mid-twenty-second century. An alliance of five distinct advanced species that all had evolved on the same planet, the Xindi had come to believe that the Federation would—in centuries to come—be responsible for the destruction of their homeworld. Convinced of this threat by parties from another alien race that possessed the ability to examine the course of future history across multiple timelines, the Xindi set about constructing a massive weapon with the intention of destroying Earth. Their intentions had only become known after they opted to deploy a prototype version of the weapon against the planet, and the results of even that limited attack had been considerable.

"Except it looks as though these guys were smart enough not to tip their hand too early," said Šmrhová. "The Xindi screwed up by attacking Earth with a prototype version of their super weapon. If they'd run their test on some other planet, we'd never have known they were coming until it was too late." She paused, frowning. "Perhaps *test* isn't the appropriate word."

As a teenager, Picard had read the historical narratives of the catastrophic incident in which more than seven million people had been killed in a matter of minutes, and he recalled having thoughts similar to those expressed by Šmrhová. Why had the Xindi squandered their advantage of total surprise in such heinous fashion? He did not remember a suitable explanation ever being given, beyond the simple belief that the Xindi believed humans incapable of determining the identity of their attackers. While Picard knew that some form of investigation had revealed the truth behind the perpetrators, he suspected there was more to that story than was contained in the official records. Any information pertaining to how the Xindi came to know about future events would be classified and closely guarded, restricted only to DTI personnel and a very small circle of senior Federation and Starfleet officials. Rumors persisted that some form of time travel on the part of Starfleet officers two centuries earlier may even have played a role in the eventual foiling of the Xindi plot, but none of that had ever been confirmed, denied, or even entertained as a possibility by anyone in a position to know what really happened.

"We know the Raqilan tested the weapon before their time jump," Elfiki said. "They recorded the results of the particle cannon fired at a moon being used by Golvonek forces as a forward military base. Raqilan leaders warned their counterparts on Uphrel that the attack was coming and gave them time to evacuate, which when you think about it is pretty strange, considering the *Arrow*'s ultimate mission."

Chen, her elbows resting on the conference table, replied, "Maybe not. We know that both sides continuously pursued diplomatic solutions throughout the war's duration. They were doing it when the ship was launched, and if I read the dates right on the records I reviewed, they're in the midst of such negotiations right now. I've been able to determine that in this time frame, there haven't been any significant engagements for nearly eighteen years."

Picard shook his head. "And then one side felt compelled to build something like this." In short order, and despite whatever steps he did to prevent or even mitigate their involvement, he and the *Enterprise* would find themselves in the midst of this decades-old struggle between two worlds. How best to deal with the situation, particularly in light of the information he possessed about the future of both these civilizations?

"Lieutenant Elfiki," he said after a moment, "the moon that was destroyed in the future. Were you able to ascertain its location in this time period?"

"Yes, sir," replied the science officer. "It's there, all right, but our long-range scans show no definite signs of habitation." She shrugged. "Interference from an asteroid field between the system's fifth and sixth planets is playing hell with our sensors. The only way to get good readings would be to move into the system." Gesturing toward the screen, she added, "I can do some further digging in their computer records to see about determining when the Golvonek established a presence there."

Waving away the suggestion, Picard said, "Perhaps

Lieutenant Chen can research that later. The information may come in handy if and when we have to deal with officials from either planet." He was not sure just yet how useful such knowledge might be, but he believed that in this case, with so many unknowns still facing them, it was prudent to put forth every effort to be prepared, if indeed that was even possible in this instance.

"Captain," Chen said, swiveling her chair to face him, "what do we do about the Golvonek? Fleet Legate Mynlara is coming to take possession of the *Arrow* and custody of its crew. Since she said they're considered prisoners of war, she's almost certainly going to interrogate them. What do we do if they find out about the ship's mission and that it came from the future?"

Clasping his hands and resting them in his lap, Picard replied, "I honestly don't know at this point, Lieutenant. To say this is a fluid situation would be an understatement of enormous proportions." Though he already had agreed to Mynlara's request to remove his people from the ship, Doctor Crusher's efforts to revive the crew from their cryogenic stasis had reached a point that required her constant supervision. His attempts to update the Golvonek fleet legate had been received, but no response had been offered, and now Picard was worried that tensions between him and Mynlara would be prematurely heightened before they engaged in their first meaningful dialogue. Even that, he knew, would present something of a challenge, as the *Enterprise* most definitely was in uncharted territory here. Starfleet regulations did cover various scenarios relating to time travel and other situations involving temporal manipulation, but he recalled no specific language pertaining to which might help him with the situation he and his crew now faced.

Even with the wide latitude afforded to starship captains to interpret existing orders and rules so that they might make correct if unorthodox decisions when dealing with unprecedented events and circumstances, Picard knew he would still have to answer for any choices he made here today. Being judged for his actions did not concern him as much as ensuring he did not—despite the most noble of intentions—do irrevocable harm to the Golvonek or the Raqilan.

"The Prime Directive is our point of departure here," Picard said, "and we will simply have to use our best judgment as we react to the unfolding situation. Lieutenant Chen, I'll want you to observe our first formal meeting with Fleet Legate Mynlara as well as whoever ends up being the first Raqilan representative."

"What if that turns out to be the hibernating crew?" Šmrhová asked.

The captain nodded. "Then we shall tread carefully." That would be the rule of the day, with the Raqilan crew members as well as the Golvonek vessels, which were drawing ever closer with each passing moment. Picard did not need to check the chronometer displayed upon one of the screens set into the observation lounge's forward bulkhead to know just how many minutes remained until the Golvonek ships arrived. Eighty-six minutes and an odd number of seconds separated him from his first face-to-face meeting with Fleet Legate Mynlara. Would this introduction bring with it the promise of friendship, or something else?

They all would know in eighty-six minutes.

The chime of the ship's intercom system beeped for

attention and was followed by the voice of Commander Aiden Lynley. *"Bridge to Captain Picard."*

"Picard here. What is it, Mister Lynley?"

"Commander Worf wanted you to be advised of Doctor Crusher's progress, sir. They think they're just about ready to bring the Raqilan crew out of hibernation."

13

———◆———

As a doctor, the notion of holding another person's life in one's hands was far from a figurative concept, and something Beverly Crusher kept foremost in her mind whenever duty, circumstances, or even fate put her in the position of caring for a patient. It did not matter whether that patient was a member of her crew, a total stranger, a friend, or an enemy. All that was important was the life before her and her responsibility to safeguard it and to do no harm.

Such thoughts, in rather scattershot fashion, raced along with dozens of others through Crusher's mind as she sat at the expansive workstation inside the chamber housing the hibernation cylinders, scrutinizing the display monitors arrayed before her along with the portable computer interface provided to her by Lieutenant Dina Elfiki. Thanks to the science officer's efforts as well as those of the *Enterprise*'s main computer, Crusher now was able to use the new protocol to understand and interact with the litany of information being provided by the Raqilan vessel's own systems.

"So far, so good," she said, turning from the console to face the row of hibernation chambers. "The revival protocols look to be operating as intended."

Standing near the closest of the transparent cylinders, holding her tricorder and studying its readout, Doctor Tamala Harstad reached up with her free hand and wiped perspiration from her forehead. "Here's hoping it doesn't take too much longer. It's starting to feel like a dry sauna in here."

"I know," Crusher replied. Like Harstad, she already had undone her collar and shrugged out of her jumpsuit uniform's upper half, tying it around her waist before rolling up the sleeves of her blue undershirt. The heightened activity from the equipment in this compartment over the past hour had resulted in an increase in the room's temperature, which already was warmer than the neighboring sections. Crusher suspected that was a deliberate attempt to make the room as comfortable as possible for the crew when they emerged from hibernation.

Not so great for those of us waiting around for something to happen. Would it have been easier to transport the slumbering Raqilan to the *Enterprise* so that she could oversee their revival with her own equipment and within the familiar environs of her sickbay? That had been Crusher's initial plan, but she encountered her first obstacle upon inspecting the hibernation cylinders and being unable to find a means by which the mechanisms sustaining the crew's cryogenic state could be removed for transport. Unwilling to chance endangering the sleeping aliens, that left her no alternative but to monitor the process aboard the Raqilan vessel. She had later come to the realization that carrying out the revival here also would be of benefit to the crew from a psychological perspective, as they would awaken in recognizable surroundings.

To that end, Crusher had elected to remain here in spite of the captain's order for the away team to return to the *Enterprise*. After explaining the situation to her husband, she had kept Harstad in addition to one of her medical technicians, Ellwood Neil, and two nurses, Lieutenants Amavia and Mimouni, on hand to assist her after sending the rest of her team back to the starship. Standing just outside the door leading from the compartment were Lieutenant Rennan Konya and Ensign Bryan Regnis, whom Commander Worf had assigned to the medical team for the duration of their stay aboard the alien vessel. Once the Raqilan were out of their cylinders, Crusher and her team would escort them to the medical facility, which they had prepared as best they could to receive the revived crew members.

"The tubes' internal atmosphere and temperatures are stabilizing," said Harstad, her attention once more on her tricorder and the status gauges on the side of the hibernation unit. "Respiration and heart rates are all rising. They should be breathing on their own in a few minutes."

Crusher nodded. "I guess all we can do now is wait." Thorough examinations of the cylinders had yielded no obvious external means of opening them. Even with the computer overseeing all aspects of the hibernation process, it seemed to her an odd and even dangerous design choice not to have some evident form of manual intervention. At this point, for better or worse, the revival procedure was in the hands of the alien computer.

"I've never been good at waiting," Harstad said, stepping away from the cylinder and moving toward its adjacent companion. "I always feel so useless, standing around while a machine does all the work."

Nodding in agreement, Crusher replied, "I know exactly what you mean." Even in the most routine treatment of her patients, she disliked having to rely solely on the ministrations of equipment and other automated processes. She had come by this attitude as a child, learning it from her grandmother, who, while not a physician herself, had become something of a healer late in life. Forced by tragic circumstance to learn a variety of rudimentary medical techniques while struggling with young Beverly to survive a disastrous epidemic that had befallen the Federation colony on Arvada III, Felicia Howard—dear sweet Nana—had passed that knowledge on to her granddaughter, along with an uncompromising stance on how best to treat the patients under her care. The lessons took firm hold as they endured that crisis, and they did not diminish with the passage of time.

She had never forgotten one of the first guest symposiums she had attended at the beginning of her medical training, when similar views were espoused. The doctor who had hosted the seminar, himself a veteran of both civilian practice and service as a Starfleet medical officer with nearly a century of experience to his name, had paced back and forth before the rows of young, wide-eyed, and even naïve students for nearly three hours. He did not discuss the latest medical advances or technology, or the most efficient ways of carrying out a particular surgical procedure or treating peculiar injuries of the sort the cadets might encounter over the course of their careers. Instead, he had spent his time offering a range of opinions regarding the ethics of those who chose to study and practice medicine, and though somewhat aged and appearing to carry the weight of the galaxy on his stooping shoulders, there was no denying the passion that still burned in the elder physician's eyes and perhaps his very soul.

"We as doctors are always told that we hold life in our hands," he told the cadets. "Sure, it's true enough. I mean, we're supposed to save lives, right? It's dramatic and makes you sound like a damned hero. If that's what you're after, then you're in the wrong line of work, and you should get up and go tell someone in the front office that you want to be something else when you grow up. If you're here to be a doctor, then be a damned doctor. That doesn't mean waiting for the blasted machines to tell you what to do. No computer or gadget will ever be a substitute for a well-trained doctor who gives a damn about their patient. How many damns is that, anyway? I'm only allowed so many during these damned lectures."

Crusher smiled at the memory of the raucous laughter his comments elicited. Though she would attend many more classes, symposiums, and lectures during her training, few of those sessions stuck with her with the same intensity, all the more because the cantankerous yet endearing old physician's views so closely mirrored the values Nana had instilled within her.

"Doctor Crusher."

Startled from what she realized had been a momentary mental drift, Crusher looked up to see Harstad moving closer to the first hibernation cylinder. "What is it?" she asked, just as alert indicators began beeping on the workstation behind her. Turning to study the portable computer interface, she saw several status markers shifting from yellow to green, programmed to do so when the monitoring devices detected that the slumbering Raqilan's respiration and pulse had increased to normal levels.

"This is it," she said, pushing away from the workstation. She along with Harstad and the rest of her team positioned themselves so that they could reach any of the cylinders and assist its occupant. Crusher had just moved next to the closest of the tubes when she heard a series of clicks, as though internal locking mechanisms were being disengaged. Inside the tube, the gases and ice crystals that had obscured the Raqilan it hosted had all but disappeared, and Crusher now could see the alien's eyes moving beneath closed lids, and his chest rising and falling with each deep breath. She flinched when a metallic snap echoed in the room, accompanied by a hiss of escaping air as the cylinder's transparent shield opened. It slid in its mounting from left to right, retracting into the base supporting the tube and leaving the Raqilan nude and exposed in his cradle.

Tricorder in hand, Crusher moved closer and waved the device over the alien, watching the unit's readings for any signs of concern. "From what I can tell, all readings are normal." She glanced up at the other cylinders, none of which had opened.

"If he's the leader," Harstad said, "his tube may be programmed to open first." The doctor shrugged. "Just a guess."

Crusher nodded. "As good as anything I've got." Satisfied that the Raqilan appeared to be in no danger as a consequence of his revival, she stepped closer, studying his face. His eyes had not yet opened, and he removed still.

"Can you hear me?" she asked, her voice soft, but the Raqilan did not respond or offer any other indication he had heard or understood her. "You've been asleep for a very long time, but I promise you that you're safe."

His eyes opened, wide and alert, with an abruptness that made Crusher start to pull away from the tube, but she was still close enough to be in reach of the Raqilan's right hand, which shot upward from its resting position on the bed and clamped around her left wrist.

"Doctor Crusher!" Harstad snapped, lunging around the head of the adjacent cylinder and reaching for the Raqilan's arm.

"Don't hurt him!" Crusher warned, pulling against the alien's grip. The Raqilan was using his other hand to push himself to a sitting position. His expression was unreadable as she felt him pulling her toward him.

The high-pitched report of a phaser whined in the room as a bright orange beam struck the Raqilan in the chest. As the pulse of energy washed over him, he uttered his first sounds—surprise—before his body went limp. Crusher was able to catch him before he slumped backward, cradling him as she laid him down on the bed.

"I only stunned him," said Ensign Regnis, aiming the phaser in his right hand at the prone alien. Eyeing Crusher, the security officer asked, "Are you all right, Doctor?"

She replied, "I'm fine, thanks." A moment's scan with her tricorder was enough to alleviate her concerns that the phaser beam might have caused any adverse effects. To Harstad she said, "He's fine, but prepare sedatives for his friend. We'll administer those as soon as her tube opens, then transport them both to the medical facility."

"Yes, Doctor," said Harstad, even as Nurses Mimouni and Amavia were moving toward the field medical kit they had brought with them from the *Enterprise*.

Shaking her head in dismay, Crusher said, "I guess I can understand the reaction, but that doesn't make it any easier."

"I wouldn't be too hard on him, Doctor," Konya said. "If they're military, then he probably acted as much on instinct as anything else. Once he wakes up and has a chance to collect himself, he'll hopefully realize we're not here to hurt him."

Ensign Regnis asked, "Maybe not us, but what about the Golvonek?"

"Well, there's that," replied Konya with a small shrug.

None of that concerned Crusher. Her first priority for now was treating her patients. Despite suspecting that seeing to their physical issues would be only a part of their overall treatment, she had hoped to engender an atmosphere of trust to assist in their revival. Their lives would become complicated enough once the Golvonek arrived, but she was confident in Jean-Luc's ability to manage what promised to be a fluid situation.

Crusher could only hope that the Golvonek, and indeed the newly awakened Raqilan, felt the same way.

14

"Pressure's equalized and the exterior docking hatch is secure, sir. We can head in whenever you're ready."

Nodding at the report from Lieutenant Kirsten Cruzen as the security officer pressed the control to open the interior hatch leading into the *Arrow*'s landing bay, Picard watched the reinforced door cycle open before she and another member of the *Enterprise*'s security detail, Lieutenant T'Sona, stepped through the portal and into the spacious chamber. The first thing Picard saw as he followed them into the bay was the newly arrived transport craft, its engines or other power systems still whining as the ship rested near the massive exterior hatch.

"Captain," said Worf, his voice low, "as first officer, I must state for the record that I am concerned with your decision to meet the Golvonek here, rather than on the *Enterprise*."

"I'd expect nothing less, Number One, and your concerns are duly noted." The last communication Picard had shared with Fleet Legate Mynlara had been short and formal, at least with respect to her responses as he had again explained the situation with the hibernating Raqilan and the need for Doctor Crusher and her medical team to watch over the revival process. Now that the Raqilan had emerged from their cryogenic suspension and were resting in the *Arrow*'s medical facility, Picard—conscious of the potential Prime Directive minefield he was traversing, to say nothing of the possible threats to future history—had advised his wife to keep their interactions with her patients to the minimum required for medical purposes. Otherwise, she was to avoid direct discussion with them until the Golvonek's arrival.

The hiss of escaping air filtered across the landing bay, and Picard saw that a hatch on the side of the transport craft was beginning to open. In his peripheral vision, he noticed Cruzen and T'Sona moving to flank him and Worf.

"Here we go," said Cruzen. Ordered to keep their phasers holstered, the security officers stood with their hands clasped behind their backs. Worf also was armed, but Picard had opted to eschew carrying a weapon for this meeting, unwilling to communicate the wrong message to Mynlara for this, their first official meeting.

He said nothing in response to Cruzen's remark, his attention fixed on the Golvonek transport as he detected movement inside the open hatch, from which now protruded a short, narrow ramp leading down to the landing bay's deck. A figure appeared in the entryway, and Picard recognized Fleet Legate Mynlara as the first person to disembark. She was followed by four additional Golvonek, who like her wore maroon bodysuits with varying degrees of embroidery on their sleeves. Though she appeared to carry no weapons, each of her four escorts wore what could only be sidearms in holsters strapped to their chests. The moment Mynlara's gaze found his, her features seemed to soften and she quickened her pace, with her entourage fanning out to either side as she walked toward the center of the immense chamber.

"Captain Picard," she said when they were but steps apart. Arms at her sides, she bowed her head, and he forced himself not to react when she reached out to take his left hand in both of hers before raising it so that his palm rested for a brief moment on her forehead. "On behalf of the people of Uphrel, it is my honor to stand with you this day."

Doing his best to mimic her greeting and placing the palm of her left hand on his forehead, Picard noted how her yellow-green skin was cool to the touch. "Fleet Legate Mynlara, the privilege is mine to stand with you this day representing the United Federation of Planets. You honor us with your welcome, and I sincerely hope that our meeting is but the beginning of a long, rewarding friendship between our peoples."

Mynlara nodded, her expression brightening. "That is my fervent hope, as well. That someone would travel from distant stars to visit us is but one of the dreams that fire many youthful imaginations. While we obviously have knowledge of life on other worlds, we always believed that the vastness of space would ensure our isolation. I certainly never thought I would live to see such a meeting, let alone participate in one." She paused, her expression turning thoughtful. "How is it that we are able to understand one another?"

"It's called a universal translator," Picard explained. "Essentially, our ship's computer has been studying the data files stored aboard this vessel in order to interpret the native languages and build a database which it can then use in collaboration with our communications systems. By the time you and I spoke while you were en route here, our computer had constructed a comprehensive language database it could reference during all our subsequent interactions."

For the first time, the Golvonek officer emitted what Picard took to be a laugh. "I will not even pretend that

I comprehend any of what you just described, Captain."

Though her demeanor was warm, he still sensed an underlying tension. No doubt she harbored at least some small fear that all might not be what it seemed. Perhaps her perception was guided by the knowledge or at least suspicion that her two ships, impressive though they may be by Golvonek and even Raqilan standards, would be bested by the *Enterprise* if the situation devolved to a point that an altercation was the only option. Then there was the *Arrow*, which carried more than enough power to destroy his ship and the Golvonek vessels.

Mynlara introduced her second-in-command, a male Golvonek named Vedapir who held the rank of "foctine," and the rest of her party. As he introduced her to Worf and his security detail, Picard noted Mynlara's fascination with Worf and T'Sona.

"You truly represent a number of different worlds, Captain."

"Indeed. I am a human, and my home planet is called Earth. Commander Worf is a Klingon, a proud warrior race. The Federation and the Klingon Empire once were bitter enemies, but we now are allies, and Mister Worf is one of the finest officers with whom it's been my honor to serve. I implicitly trust him with my very life. And Lieutenant T'Sona is from the planet Vulcan. Representatives from her world were the first to travel to my homeworld and make their presence known, and our two civilizations have been allies for centuries."

Once Mynlara had introduced her own escorts, Picard said, "Fleet Legate, I know that you probably have any number of questions about us, and I'm happy to answer to the best of my ability. We also have questions, not just about your people but the Raqilan, as well."

"What I know of the Raqilan comes from our history texts," Mynlara replied, "and my experience fighting against them." Her tone lost some of its warmth. "In truth, Captain, I have never even seen a Raqilan face-to-face. Such meetings are . . . rare."

Nodding in understanding, Picard realized that the hostilities between the Golvonek and the Raqilan seemed to possess at least some of the same characteristics as the twenty-second-century Earth-Romulan War. No ground battles were fought, even on planets or moons which had been disputed during the conflict, and according to official records no meeting had ever had taken place between a human and Romulan. Indeed, according to those same accounts, the first true meeting had taken place more than a century later. Picard had always found that hard to swallow, believing as many amateur and professional historians did that such a far-reaching conflict had to have included head-on confrontations by at least some of the people who had waged those battles.

Suppressing an urge to comment on the nature of a war in which the identity of one's enemy is kept in shadow, Picard said, "The two Raqilan aboard this vessel are currently in the care of my chief medical officer."

"They have been revived?" Mynlara asked. "I was not aware that the process had progressed to that point."

Picard replied, "It happened rather quickly. We are still endeavoring to understand this ship's onboard systems, and my people have proceeded with extreme care so as not to damage anything, to say nothing of wishing to avoid harming the Raqilan. However, I have ordered that the crew not be disturbed, pending your arrival." He still was uncomfortable with the fact that he and his people appeared to have walked into the middle of the decades-long conflict between the Raqilan and the Golvonek, and that was before taking into consideration the complication presented by the *Arrow* and its mission.

"This ship and its crew are now my responsibility, Captain," Mynlara said. "I trust this will not be an issue?"

Shaking his head, Picard replied, "Certainly not, although I am concerned with the health of the Raqilan crew members. My medical officer informs me that their recovery may be hindered by the lingering effects of their prolonged hibernation."

"I must confess to some confusion on this point. While I understand the basic concept of placing someone into . . . hibernation . . . I was not aware that such technology had advanced to common use by the Raqilan." Mynlara glanced around the landing bay. "Of course, this vessel, if it also was developed by the Raqilan, comes as something of a surprise, as well. Our best intelligence reports do not indicate such a ship even being constructed. My superiors will be most interested in studying it and questioning its crew."

Doing his best to sidestep, at least for a time, questions about the *Arrow*, Picard said, "You mentioned before that the crew would be considered prisoners of war. Does that mean that they're entitled to certain rights and protections?"

Mynlara replied, "Of course. Though very few prisoners have been taken by either side, at least during my tenure in the Protective Directorate, we have very strict laws and other guidelines regarding the treatment of such persons. They will be questioned, of course, but they will not be mistreated."

"A far better fate for them than if the circumstances

were reversed," said one of her escorts, and the fleet legate did not attempt to hide the glare of disapproval she cast in his direction. Duly chastened, the male Golvonek officer bowed his head and said nothing else.

Returning her attention to Picard, Mynlara said, "Though we are at war, Captain, we are not without principles. The crew will be well treated. Now, please take me to them."

Turning at the opening of the medical facility's main door, Crusher suppressed a smile. Jean-Luc was accompanied not only by Worf and a security detail but also several Golvonek. Having been briefed on the captain's interactions with the commander of the approaching alien vessels, it took her just a few seconds to realize that these were Golvonek military officers.

"Fleet Legate Mynlara," Picard said after everyone had entered the room, "please allow me to introduce my chief medical officer, Doctor Beverly Crusher. She has been overseeing the Raqilan's revival." Turning to the doctor, he asked, "I trust your patients are doing well?"

Crusher replied, "Their metabolic functions have all stabilized, Captain, and they're currently resting in what I suppose is a patient recovery area."

"Fleet Legate Mynlara has requested to see them," Picard said. "Will doing so interfere with your efforts?"

"I can't really call them our efforts, Captain." She gestured to the workstations and other equipment crammed into the room. "Most of the hard work is being handled by the ship's computer. This facility is fitted with something similar to our biobeds. There are a dozen of them in what I'm calling the patient ward, and while the technology is different from our own, of course, thanks to the translation matrix we're able to interpret most of the readings, though I'm still leaning pretty heavily on our own computer interface." The doctor paused, drawing a breath before proceeding into what she knew might quickly become a sensitive topic. "As I said, the Raqilan are resting, but they're still sedated following an incident after their revival. Though we've found no indications of any problems which might stem from their prolonged hibernation, I'd request that they be given sufficient time to fully recover before subjecting them to anything too strenuous."

She emphasized the last word while studying Jean-Luc's face, but her husband's features betrayed nothing. As expected, he was maintaining a professional demeanor in the presence of the Golvonek, not just for the sake of proper protocol but also—she knew—as something of a simple security measure. The practice had been born out of a brief discussion that had taken place at the outset of their marriage with respect to how they would interact in front of the crew. Jean-Luc had been a stickler for rules, regulations, and decorum since she had first met him all those years ago, but Crusher had witnessed the measured softening of the rigid, often unwavering façade he had fashioned at the start of his Starfleet career. Loath as he might be to admit it to anyone—save a handful of close, trusted friends—he had become a happier, more content person during his tenure as captain of the *Enterprise*, even before he and Crusher had finally allowed their true feelings for each other to guide them toward an even richer, more fulfilling life together.

Of course, now Jean-Luc's concern likely revolved around another aspect of that brief conversation he had shared with her, about not wanting to alert strangers such as Mynlara and her escorts that Crusher and he shared a relationship beyond that of doctor and captain. As Worf had stated it in his usual blunt fashion, it was a poor tactic to offer such personal and potentially exploitive information to someone who had not yet achieved a level of trust.

Good old Worf, she mused. *I can always count on you to keep me paranoid.*

"It is not my intention to disturb them, Doctor," Mynlara said, her tone crisp and formal, "but I have a duty to ascertain the crew's condition and determine whether they can answer questions regarding this vessel and their mission."

Feeling her ire rising, Crusher replied, "If you're talking about interrogation, I'm afraid I cannot allow anything which might harm their recovery."

"Doctor," Picard said, and she noted the unspoken warning in his eyes. "Let's at least allow Fleet Legate Mynlara to ascertain for herself your patients' conditions, so that she might prepare a report for her superiors."

Mynlara nodded. "Thank you, Captain."

"Very well," Crusher said after a moment. "Please follow me." She started for the patient ward, but upon noticing Mynlara's entourage following behind her, she raised a hand. "I'd ask your security detail to wait here. The Raqilan are restrained and sedated."

After appearing to consider this for a moment, Mynlara turned and gestured toward a tall Golvonek male whose sleeves sported more decorative braiding than that of his companions save her own. "Savon, you and the others stay here. I will be fine."

In turn, Picard said to Worf, "Number One, you also can remain here."

Though he bristled at the order, the Klingon offered a single, terse nod. "Aye, sir."

Satisfied, Crusher led Picard and the Golvonek officer into the adjoining room. Unlike the medical facility's main compartment and indeed most other sections of the colossal vessel she had seen, the patient ward was not crammed to overflowing with computer stations and other equipment. A modest work area situated along the room's forward bulkhead contained a computer console and a series of display monitors, which Commander La Forge and his team of engineers had determined were intended to communicate information from the equipment mounted at the head of each of the ward's twelve patient beds. The setup was similar to what was available to her on the *Enterprise*, though there were obvious gaps in the technology. As for the beds, two of them were occupied, each hosting one of the Raqilan crew who now were restrained by portable medical force fields retrieved from the shuttlecraft by Lieutenant Konya and the security detail. The illumination in the room had been reduced, highlighting the displays from the different monitors and computer screens.

"As you can see," Crusher said, indicating the beds with a wave of her hand, "the patients are resting as comfortably as we can make them. They appear to have suffered no ill effects from their hibernation." She pointed to the Raqilan male sleeping in the closest of the beds. "However, we were forced to stun this one. He was the first to wake up, and I'm afraid we startled him."

Mynlara asked, "How long were they in this hibernation?"

Pausing, Crusher looked to Picard, who shook his head with such subtlety that only she would have noticed it.

"We're not certain," she answered. While it was not technically a lie, it was close enough that it made her uncomfortable, even though she understood the need to withhold such information at this time. "We're still learning how to navigate the onboard computer system, and although our translation protocols are good, even they have their limits."

"Perhaps the Raqilan will be able to provide that information themselves," Mynlara said. "Have you determined which of them is the leader?"

Crusher pointed to the closer of her patients, who still lay unmoving on the bed. "No, but we suspect he might be. He apparently was supposed to be revived ahead of the others."

Stepping closer, her hands clasped behind her back, Mynlara said after a moment, "Are you able to wake him?"

Once more glancing to her husband, Crusher was not surprised to see him nod in approval at the request. "Yes," she replied. "I can do that." To Tamala Harstad, she said, "Doctor, please administer four cc's of formazine."

Seconds after Harstad pressed a hypospray to the sleeping Raqilan's neck and injected the mild stimulant, his eyes began to flutter. When he opened them, he spent several seconds blinking as though to clear his vision. He moved his head until his gaze fixed on Crusher, at which point he flinched and only then seemed to realize that he was bound to the bed by the invisible force field.

"Please," she said, holding up both hands to show that she meant no harm, "I won't hurt you. We're trying to help you."

"Who are you?" the Raqilan asked, his voice low and weak, and he punctuated his question with an audible clearing of his throat. "What are you?"

"I'm a doctor," Crusher retorted, "and right now I'm

looking after you and your crew." In a softer tone, she added, "My name is Doctor Crusher. We found your ship adrift in space and your crew in hibernation. From what we were able to tell, your ship suffered extensive damage, which likely interfered with your onboard computer's ability to revive you. We were able to repair or minimize some of the damage, which is why we're talking now. Do you feel all right? Are you in any pain?"

The Raqilan's features remained fixed as he listened to her explanation, but after a moment he replied, "I am experiencing no pain." He strained against the force field holding him to the bed, but remained held in place. "However, I do not appreciate being bound like a prisoner aboard my own vessel."

Moving so that he stood beside her, Jean-Luc said, "That was my doing. I'm Captain Picard, commander of the ship that found you. I regret the restraints, but when you were first awakened, you attacked Doctor Crusher. You were sedated, for your protection as well as ours."

"I have no memory of that." The Raqilan blinked several more times, and his expression changed as though he was attempting to recall the incident. He appeared to give up the attempt after a moment and instead lifted his head to look around the room. When he saw the other Raqilan lying atop an adjacent bed, he said, "There were eight of us. Where are the others?"

"Unfortunately," Jean-Luc replied, "six of your hibernation chambers malfunctioned at some point prior to our finding you. Those members of your crew did not survive."

For the first time, the Raqilan offered an emotional response, his eyes closing and his lips pressing together as he absorbed this new information. Then, he drew a deep breath before returning his attention to the captain. "I will want to see them."

"Of course," said Jean-Luc.

"And I want us freed from these beds."

Before the captain could reply, Mynlara stepped around Crusher so that the Raqilan could see her. "All reasonable requests will be accommodated in time, but first there are other matters to attend. I am Fleet Legate Mynlara of the Golvonek Protective Directorate. This vessel and its crew are now in my custody. In accordance with the protocols of engagement agreed upon by our respective governments, I hereby inform you that you are bound as prisoners of war and will be treated in accordance with the directives as outlined in the covenant. Do you understand your current status as I have described it to you?"

Crusher forced herself not to react as the Raqilan directed accusatory glares to Jean-Luc and then her before his gaze locked on Mynlara.

"I understand," he said, his voice tight.

Apparently satisfied, the Golvonek officer asked, "What is your name?" When the Raqilan hesitated, she added, "Proper identification is mandated by the covenant, so that we can notify your government of your capture."

With a questioning look at Jean-Luc, Crusher mouthed the words, "Now what?" but her husband said nothing. Did he not realize the danger of allowing this line of questioning to continue? She opened her mouth to say something but stopped when she felt his hand on hers. When she looked at him again, she saw him shaking his head.

"My name is Jodis," said the Raqilan. "Spra Jodis

Neradin, commander of the combat vessel *Poklori gil dara*, in service to the Raqilan Military Forces." He paused, once more glaring at Crusher and Picard. "I see the Golvonek have acquired some new allies."

Stepping closer, Jean-Luc replied, "You misunderstand. We have not allied ourselves with the Golvonek, or the Raqilan, for that matter. We are explorers, and we've only recently arrived in your star system. We've only just become aware of the conflict between your two peoples."

Though Crusher thought he might be confused with this explanation, Jodis seemed to take it well enough. Then his expression darkened.

"There is much that does not make sense here. How long have we been asleep?"

Heeding her husband's earlier warning, Crusher swallowed a nervous lump before answering, "We're still trying to determine that." With a glance to her husband, she added, "But our initial calculations indicate you've been in hibernation for far longer than intended."

"Doctor," said Jean-Luc, and she heard the caution in his voice.

"What was your mission?" Mynlara asked. When Jodis did not answer, she pressed with, "What is the purpose of this vessel? Where was it constructed? How did you get the materials to build it? It is astounding that you were able to keep it a secret from us. I must admit to being duly impressed. Our scientists and engineers will be most interested in examining its every detail."

"This ship's mission is the same as that of every vessel in service to my people," Jodis said, his tone one of disdain. "Fight. Destroy Golvonek ships. Break your will to continue this war."

Mynlara stepped toward the bed, pointing an accusatory finger at Jodis. "The Raqilan started this war. It is your people who could not accept the simple idea that there are others who exist in this galaxy and that not all of them subscribe to your beliefs. You were not content to live in peace and allow others to do the same. Instead, you brought death and destruction to both our worlds, and for what? Because we are different?"

Glowering at her, Jodis replied, "It no longer matters why the war began, or who is to blame. All our hands are stained with blood, and none of us are above contempt or fault. We and our children will bear the burden of what we have done, unless the entire obscenity can be erased. That is what we were sent here to do. Indeed, we were sent to make sure it never happens at all." Unable to move his arms, he instead gestured with his head to indicate the room around him. "This ship was designed with a single purpose: make sure the war between our people never happens."

"What sort of nonsense are you spouting?" Mynlara asked. "From where were you sent? How are you supposed to undo a hundred cycles of brutal warfare that has all but destroyed both our worlds?"

Jodis shook his head, eyeing her with unfettered scorn. "I do not blame you for your lack of understanding, for I too once harbored similar thoughts, but now your words have proven that what was once only theory is now in fact reality. It was decided long ago that the only way to stop this war is to prevent it from happening at all. That is why the blood and sweat of uncounted Raqilan were sacrificed over uncounted cycles to build this ship, and it is the mission I was sent to complete." When Mynlara said nothing in response, Jodis sneered. "Of course you do not comprehend my meaning, but you will. I come from our future, Fleet Legate, where the war has raged for nearly two hundred cycles, and our inability to find peace has committed whatever generations might survive us to eventual extinction."

"That's enough," Crusher said, putting up her hand so that Mynlara could not move any closer to Jodis. "There will be time for this later, but right now, I want my patients to rest."

"They are not your patients," Mynlara retorted, still scowling in response to the Raqilan's comments. "They are my prisoners, even if this one has taken complete leave of his sanity."

Ignoring her, Jodis instead turned his attention to Crusher. "I see it in your eyes. You know that I speak the truth, as do you, Captain Picard." He looked once more to Mynlara. "It's already too late. Enjoy your time as our captors," he snapped, all but spitting the words. "I promise you that your hold on us will be fleeting."

15

Standing in the corridor outside the medical facility, Picard waited in silence as Mynlara composed herself. Though she had maintained her composure in the patient ward while confronting Jodis, it was obvious that the Raqilan's comments had affected her. She paced back and forth several steps, and Picard noted how her hands clenched and relaxed as she walked. After several moments, with the captain and Worf watching and as her own escorts stood nearby and awaited instructions, the fleet legate seemed to have regained her bearing.

"Vedapir," she said, shifting her attention to the tall Golvonek male she had introduced as her second-in-command. "I want security officers stationed here immediately. We are taking the Raqilan prisoners into custody. For now, they are to remain confined in the medical treatment area." As though sensing Picard's eyes on her, she added, "Do not interfere with the newcomers' work to care for the prisoners, but I want regular reports on their current status."

"Understood, Fleet Legate," replied Vedapir. Turning his own gaze to Picard and Worf, he asked, "What about you?"

Mynlara scowled. "If the newcomers wanted to hurt us, they could have done so before now. I will be fine. Attend your duties, Foctine Vedapir."

His posture straightening, Vedapir nodded. "Yes,

Fleet Legate," he said before turning and heading off to carry out his assignment. Once he was gone, Mynlara turned back to Picard.

"I apologize, Captain," she said after a moment. "I confess that I am still coming to terms with what we were told in there. I . . ." The words trailed off and she cast her gaze to the deck before drawing a deep breath. "As I said before, I have never actually met a Raqilan. I was not adequately prepared for that meeting."

Picard replied, "No apology is necessary, Fleet Legate."

Following Jodis's outburst, Crusher had asserted her authority and banished from the room everyone who was not a patient or a member of the medical team. Mynlara was so caught off guard by the ferocity of the Raqilan's comments that she had not protested when Picard ushered her from the patient ward and out of the medical facility.

"Your doctor is quite intimidating," said the Golvonek officer.

"You have no idea." Picard could not resist the smile that accompanied his reply.

Scowling, Mynlara shook her head. "I do not understand his remarks." She waved her hand to indicate the corridor and, presumably, the rest of the *Arrow*. "He and his crew and this vessel come from the future? How is that possible?" When Picard said nothing, she leveled a finger at him. "He said you knew he spoke the truth. What does that mean? Are you in league with him?"

"No," Picard answered, his tone firm. "As I've told you all along, we only just discovered the ship adrift in space a few days ago. We are only just beginning to understand its technology."

"But you were aware of this claim of his," Mynlara

said. "This outlandish assertion of his that he has traveled from the future to destroy us."

Knowing that the time for obfuscation had passed, Picard replied, "Not because of anything Jodis communicated to us. We have learned that traveling through time leaves residual signs, in the form of particles we call chronitons. Our past experiences with such phenomena have allowed us to develop technology to detect these particles and determine if something or someone has experienced a temporal event."

Mynlara's eyes widened in undisguised surprise. "Have *you* traveled through time?"

"Yes," Worf said, "but I do not recommend it."

Picard punctuated the Klingon's reply with a small smile, which did little to alleviate the fleet legate's obvious concern and uncertainty. "It's not something to be undertaken lightly, and the risks of altering history are not to be underestimated."

"But that's what Jodis and this ship intended to do." Mynlara had begun to pace again. "Their goal was to travel from the future and do what, exactly? Destroy Uphrel at a point before the war takes such a grave toll on both our worlds?"

Though he had wrestled with himself over how much information to convey to her, Picard realized that to continue evading her questions served no purpose. Thanks to Jodis, Mynlara and her people already knew something of the truth, and it was up to them how to proceed with the knowledge they now possessed. To engender trust, Picard had no option but to be honest and as straightforward as he was able.

"From what we've been able to ascertain based on a review of the ship's onboard computer," he said, "we believe the mission given to Jodis and his crew was to travel back to a point before your war began. If we're correctly understanding the data we've found, the ship was attacked by Golvonek forces prior to its time jump from the future. That attack resulted in damage to various systems, including what we believe is the mechanism required for time travel. When the ship arrived at its destination point, the crew was not revived but instead remained in hibernation until my ship found it adrift."

Mynlara closed her eyes for a moment as though weighing the enormity of what she had just heard. "So, you are saying that it was only fortunate happenstance which saved my planet from annihilation nearly eighty cycles before I was born."

"That's our best guess, yes," Picard replied.

The weight of worlds seemed to descend upon her shoulders. "I have to report this to my superiors, but I cannot see how this will not affect the ongoing peace discussions."

"How long have these negotiations been taking place?" Picard asked.

Frowning, Mynlara said, "The current sessions have been ongoing for nearly two cycles now. They start and stop at irregular intervals, based on the mood of various participants. Great progress will be made, but then something trivial derails the agreements reached to that point, and both sides regroup before starting again." She stared at him, her eyes narrowing. "I am a military officer, sworn to obey all proper directives from my superiors and the civilian leadership that oversees us. However, it is frustrating to watch politicians bandy about as though their actions—or lack of actions—have no consequences to those bound by their decisions."

"Such a system, while perhaps inconvenient at times, is far preferable to most alternatives," Picard replied. Even the Raqilan, who appeared to be the aggressors in their conflict with the Golvonek, seemed to understand the virtues of a civilian government's authority over its military, as evidenced by diplomats endeavoring to find some kind of workable resolution to end the war. "If both sides are committed to the peace process, then hope remains."

Mynlara replied, "There are those who do not believe that both sides—at least, not everyone on both sides—really want peace. We know that some Raqilan leaders, civilian and military alike, do not want to stop until they have wiped out our ability to defend ourselves. Perhaps they even mean to subjugate us, though it is rare to hear talk of such things. For the moment, at least, the most extreme voices seem only to be calling for conquest, but such opinions appear to be in the minority. The Golvonek are not entirely without blame either, as there are those among my government who call for increasing the intensity of our attacks against Raqilan forces. It is not enough for them merely to defend our interests. In their minds, we must take the fight to Henlona with ever greater ferocity." Once more, she shook her head. "I do not know that my people, after all this time, have the will to support such a campaign, but what are we to do?"

She again indicated the massive vessel around them. "What will happen when my superiors learn of this ship and the power it wields? Assuming they believe this story that it came from the future to destroy us, what does it say about us that in that time to come, we are *still* at war with the Raqilan? I fear such knowledge will serve only to break my people's spirit."

"It does not have to be that way," said Worf. "If there

is one thing our experience with time travel has taught us, it is that the future is not set. It can be altered. Many times, that is a very dangerous proposition, but there are times I would argue that such ability can be used for good."

Picard added, "Indeed. Think about it, Mynlara: instead of this being a symbol of hopelessness, your people can use it to rally support for a change. Perhaps the Raqilan people, upon seeing what the future has in store for them, will also be compelled to seek another solution."

"Do you really think that's possible?" Mynlara asked.

"I most certainly do."

Releasing another exasperated sigh, the Golvonek officer said, "They are not likely to listen to one such as me, but I believe such an argument could be made by a third party. Someone who stands apart from our conflict."

"You're asking me to address your world's leaders?" Were this any other first contact scenario, such an act would not be unusual. Like any starship captain, Picard was empowered to represent Starfleet and the Federation as their ambassador in such situations, and so in that regard he was at ease with such a prospect. However, Picard could imagine hearing the complaints from agents of the Department of Temporal Investigations even across the expanse of light-years as he considered what they undoubtedly would consider a deliberate meddling with possible future events.

To hell with them, he mused. *I live in the here and now, I refuse to be bound by predestination, and I refuse to stand by and allow others to be so enslaved. Not if there's anything I can do to prevent it.*

"If I agree to speak to your superiors," he said after a moment, "you must know I am required to do the same for the Raqilan. I cannot take sides in your conflict, and I cannot commit the Federation to such action. We must remain neutral, but I am willing to explain this situation as well as I'm able, to leaders from both sides."

"I understand," Mynlara replied. "Perhaps our leaders can be convinced to let you address the peace delegations." Her expression changed. "But there is much to do before we reach that point."

Picard asked, "What do you intend to do with Jodis and his crew?"

"They are still prisoners of war, Captain," replied the fleet legate. "For now, duty requires that I continue to treat them as such, just as it demands that I make preparations to transfer this vessel to one of our facilities. I must notify my superiors of our current situation and receive further instructions." She nodded to Worf before adding, "If you will excuse me, Captain."

"By all means," replied Picard.

After she had left two members of her security detail outside the medical facility, Mynlara departed, presumably returning to her transport craft in the landing bay.

Once she was out of earshot, Picard gestured for Worf to follow him up the passageway, away from the Golvonek guards.

"This is a most complicated situation," said Worf in a low voice.

With a wry grin, Picard replied, "Number One, I see that the years have not yet taken their toll on your gift for understatement."

Worf crossed his arms. "Do you think addressing the Raqilan and Golvonek leaders will accomplish anything?"

"It certainly can't hurt," Picard said. "A formal first meeting with representatives from one or both sides would likely have occurred if we'd continued our investigation into the system. Now that we're aware of their situation, our only course if we wish to establish relations is dealing with both planets." The captain just hoped that the gathering of leaders representing both worlds would allow him to demonstrate that there was an entire universe out there, waiting for them to resolve their own differences and embrace the hand of friendship which had been extended across the stars. While the Prime Directive allowed him to make such overtures to planets that had progressed to faster-than-light travel capabilities, there still existed a number of stipulations he was required to observe when meeting with representatives of less technologically progressed civilizations. In fact, Picard was treading in one of the gray areas where theory and procedure often failed to anticipate some twist or gap provided by reality. It was in situations like these that the experience and judgment of a starship commander became ever vital.

Behind him, the door to the medical facility opened and Crusher emerged. "Captain," she said, presumably for the benefit of the Golvonek security officers still keeping vigil, "may I see you a moment?"

Entering the room once more, Picard and Worf waited as she closed the door before turning to them.

"Jodis wants to talk to you."

Cocking an eyebrow, Picard replied, "Really? Did he say why?"

Beverly shook her head. "Only that he wanted to talk to you without Mynlara or any of her people present."

After directing Lieutenants Cruzen and T'Sona to watch the door, Picard moved into the patient ward, where Jodis still lay immoblized on his bed.

"I apologize for the restraints," he said, moving to stand next to the Raqilan.

"It is I who apologize for making them necessary, Captain." Pausing, he eyed Picard for a moment before adding, "As a child, I used to enjoy stories about traveling to distant worlds and meeting the people who lived there." He turned his head enough to look past Picard and study Worf. "None of those stories featured people like you, though. Still, when I was a boy, I used to wonder what my ancestors imagined about such people, before they and the Golvonek met." He snorted. "Most of those stories seemed so far-fetched. Then again, stories about time travel were fanciful, as well."

Picard replied, "And yet, here you are, having traveled through time. We know what your mission is, or at least what it was supposed to be." When Jodis said nothing, the captain continued, "My people have managed to access your computer data and determined that you've been in hibernation for a very long time. You failed to awaken after your ship made the jump from the future, and therefore you've missed your objective. The war began and continued while you slept, Jodis."

"I know," the Raqilan finally said. "Your doctor was kind enough to show me information from our computer. The war has raged for nearly one hundred cycles. My people and the Golvonek have already inflicted enough destruction on each other that it will take generations to repair, but all is not yet lost. There's still a chance."

"A chance for what?" Picard asked. "To carry out your original mission? That's rather unlikely. You're a prisoner. Even as we speak, Fleet Legate Mynlara is preparing to have this vessel moved to one of her military bases so that it can be studied. Don't you see what that means?

Even if you were freed to carry out your mission in some manner, your ship's temporal displacement equipment has been damaged beyond repair. You're stuck here, Jodis."

"That was always a reality we faced, Captain," Jodis said. "We trained with that knowledge for many cycles, knowing that if we survived our mission, we would be forced to build new lives for ourselves on the world we saved."

Picard was not so easily swayed. "The Golvonek may, in time, learn all the secrets of the advanced technology this ship carries. They may be able to adapt its weapons for use against *your* people."

Jodis said, "That does not have to happen. You can help me."

"Out of the question," Picard countered. "I will not be an accomplice to genocide."

"So what do you propose?"

"Peace."

To Picard's total lack of surprise, Jodis laughed. "Are all of your people possessed with the gift of humor, Captain?"

Undeterred, Picard pressed his point. "At this moment, the leaders from both your worlds are trying to negotiate a peace treaty. I've been asked to address them. This vessel's very existence should be a deterrent. It should be the impetus to motivate your leaders to find a lasting solution and end this war, before greater damage is done to both planets. There's still time, Jodis."

"Even if we do manage to find a way for them to embrace peace," said the Raqilan, "what about the future? How do we know this entire cycle will not simply repeat itself?"

Picard frowned. "Are you saying your people—or the Golvonek—are incapable of anything other than war?"

"No," Jodis said. "What I am saying is that someone, somewhere, will always find a *reason* for war. It does not even need to be a legitimate reason, but rather simply one which can be made to appear legitimate, and which can recruit supporters to its cause. That is easier if one has the weapons to wage such conflict, the will to use them, and no one to stand in their way." He paused, looking around. "This entire vessel is such a weapon, built to demonstrate for all time our military superiority. The power this ship holds is intoxicating, Captain, and no matter which side controls it, someone will become hopelessly enraptured by what it represents."

"So, we'll destroy it," Picard suggested, "or at least render it incapable of harm."

Once again, Jodis laughed. "Do you not understand, Captain? My people are already building this ship, *now*, in *this* time period. It will take dozens of cycles to complete, but the work is under way. Eventually, Mynlara or one of her superiors will realize this, and it will not matter if you destroy this vessel. Eventually, they will have access to another one."

Temporal mechanics, Picard reminded himself. *It always finds a way to complicate everything, doesn't it?*

16

"I don't think I've had this much homework since I graduated from the Academy."

Swiveling her seat away from the workstation that had been the focal point of her existence for nearly four hours since first entering the *Enterprise*'s main computer lab, T'Ryssa Chen rose from the chair and reached for the ceiling, reveling in the stretching of muscles in her back, shoulders, and neck. She groaned in relief before commencing a series of torso twist exercises.

"You should try this. It feels great."

From where he sat at an adjacent station, Taurik replied, "I am in excellent physical condition, and as such I am not easily prone to muscle strain and fatigue." He turned from the console and its set of six different display monitors that he had configured so that each provided him with its own distinct, continuous scroll of data. Folding his hands, he placed them in his lap. "In addition to maintaining a proper posture while sitting or standing for long periods, I also employ a variety of ergonomic exercises which work to mitigate discomfort."

"You're doing some of them right now, aren't you?"

"Indeed I am, and have been since we began this assignment."

Chen smiled. "Of course you have."

"It seemed logical, given the time and effort we are likely to expend on this endeavor," Taurik replied. "Analysis of data stored within an unfamiliar computer system is often time-consuming, as well as mentally taxing, even with the tools at our disposal."

"You know I love it when you talk like that, don't you?"

The engineer replied, "I am aware that you take amusement in a great many things which do not typically invoke similar responses in others."

"So, you're saying I'm special?" Chen asked, casting an impish grin in his direction.

"That you are a unique individual has never been a matter for debate."

With dramatic flair, Chen placed the back of her right hand on her forehead and closed her eyes. "Oh, Taurik. You always know just what to say to sweep a girl off her feet." His sole capitulation to her gentle baiting was the raising of his right eyebrow before returning his attention to his workstation, eliciting from her a small giggle.

"All right, I can take a hint," she said. "Back to work."

With a large percentage of the data stored in the *Arrow*'s onboard computer databases now transferred to work space in the *Enterprise*'s main computer lab, Commander La Forge and Lieutenant Elfiki had tasked Taurik with breaking through the encryption protecting the bulk of the information. Elfiki had theorized that direct access to the starship computer's vast array of data decryption and search tools, rather than employing them over a connection to the derelict craft's systems, would produce quicker results and without the added threat of somehow triggering some other potentially dangerous process aboard the Raqilan ship. The chief engineer, Chen knew, had taken to heart the earlier, harsh lesson to which they had been subjected, and wanted to avoid any repeats of that episode.

Treating herself to one more stretch before returning to her seat, Chen asked, "How's it coming, anyway?"

"I am continuing my efforts to access what appears to be the main repository of technical information pertaining to the vessel's construction and capabilities," Taurik said, "as well as any information which might pertain to its tactical directives." He looked up from his computer terminal. "I believe it may be helpful to obtain some insight and context into the orders given to Jodis and his crew and the mission they apparently were sent to undertake."

Chen nodded. "I'm still trying to get some background on how this thing was created in the first place." She had been instructed by Commander Worf, acting on direction from Captain Picard, to retrieve any information that might help to locate where the *Arrow* had been built, as well as any historical records to be found within the alien vessel's vast computer data banks. With the revelation from the Raqilan commander, Jodis, that the vessel was—in this time period—in the early stages of its construction, the captain and Commander La Forge had begun to wonder how creating a ship of such immense size and complexity fit with the Raqilan's current level of technology.

"Based on what little we have been able to glean from our sensor scans," Taurik said, "the techniques employed to construct the *Arrow* seem consistent with what I have been able to infer about their future technological prowess. Even the temporal displacement equipment, though perhaps somewhat fanciful when considered alongside the more conventional demonstrations of their research and development abilities, does not appear to be the result of outside influence or aid. All of the components and materials used to fabricate it are consistent with the metals and ores I believe can be found either on the Raqilan home-world or one of the other uninhabited planets or moons within System 3955."

Chen was not convinced. "Yeah, but come on, Taurik. This ship is *gigantic*. I didn't find anything in any of their data files that even hints at a vessel remotely like it. And don't even get me started on the enormous cannon at the heart of this thing."

"The *Arrow*'s primary weapon bears several similari-ties to the ship's other armaments," Taurik countered, "as well as those of Raqilan ships of the era from which they traveled." The Vulcan stopped, as though reconsider-ing what he had just said. "However, you are correct that the antiproton technology appears to be without prece-dent with respect to Raqilan weapons technology. Still, it might be explained as an experimental design, developed specifically for this vessel, which as we all agree was in-tended to inflict destruction on a planetary scale."

"Also, this bit with having only eight people to run the whole show? That's not consistent with how the Raqilan crew their other warships. If anything, they cram too many people into their ships. They don't rely on technol-ogy like we do. They're more like we were a century or two ago, with enough people to run three or four duty shifts around the clock." She frowned. "Something's not adding up here."

Before she could continue her thought, Taurik's work-station emitted a string of almost lyrical tones, and the engineer returned his attention to the cascading streams of information scrolling past on the different screens. One of the monitors had stopped its feed and when she looked over Taurik's shoulder, Chen saw that one line of data had been highlighted and centered on the display.

"What is it?" she asked.

His fingers moving across the console's interface, Taurik replied, "I instructed the computer to alert me in the event certain search arguments resulted in matches from the *Arrow*'s data banks. It would appear one of my parameters was satisfied."

Chen moved to her own workstation. "Hang on. Now that you've isolated the data string, I can help you sort through it." The Vulcan said nothing, his fingers almost a blur as they moved over his console. As she sat at her own station, each of its monitors went blank, erasing the data she had been reviewing and replacing it with an identical message: "Station Deactivated."

"Taurik, what are you doing?"

"I have locked out your access," replied the engineer, "as I have done with everyone else currently attempting to interact with the computer."

Scowling, Chen pushed herself from her chair. "And why exactly in the name of hell did you do that?" When he did not answer, she pressed, "Taurik? Answer me."

"One moment please." He kept his attention on his monitors, eyes moving from screen to screen as he input string after string of commands. It took all of her concentration for Chen to keep up with the flurry of instructions he was feeding to the computer.

"You're locking out an entire sector of core memory," she said. "Why?" Then, seeing that Taurik was moving— not copying—data from the repository they had brought over from the *Arrow*, she began to comprehend what he was doing. "What did you find in there? Taurik, talk to me."

Ignoring her increasingly aggressive questions, the Vulcan continued to work for several more seconds before his station's central monitor cleared and flashed a blinking message: "DATA TRANSFER COMPLETE. SECURITY LOCK-OUT ENABLED."

"What did you do?" Chen asked, realizing as she spoke that her voice had risen in volume and pitch. She cleared her throat in exaggerated fashion as he turned in his seat, then she prompted in a more controlled voice, "Taurik, you're not working and playing well with others right now."

The engineer nodded. "I apologize for my brusque behavior, but I felt that speed was of the essence. As you have discerned, I have isolated a sector in the main computer's core memory and secured it with a fractal encryption code which can only be bypassed with the proper key, which I alone possess." He pressed another series of controls on his console, and Chen watched as her own workstation unlocked and restored to its monitors the streams of information she had been studying.

"You don't think that's going to get somebody's attention?" Chen asked, crossing her arms. "You know, like Commander La Forge? I'm going out on a limb here, but I'm betting the captain won't be too keen on you locking him out of his own ship's computer."

Rising from his chair, Taurik replied, "I will explain myself to the captain and Commander La Forge at a more appropriate time, once our current situation is resolved. In my judgment, decisive action was required before soliciting approval."

"What the hell are you going on about?" Chen said. Then her gaze drifted past him and to his computer station and its blinking message. "Data transfer complete," she read from the screen. "Security lockout enabled. What could possibly be so important that . . ." The rest of her question died on her lips, and she reached up to put a hand to her mouth. "Wait. Taurik, you found something about the future in their files, didn't you? What is it?"

Taurik's expression, as usual, was all but unreadable. "You know I cannot tell you that. I cannot tell anyone, including the captain."

"You just can't keep something like this to yourself, Taurik," Chen said, feeling her unease beginning to rise.

The engineer replied, "I am duty bound not to reveal anything I have seen which may prove disruptive to future events."

Now feeling agitated, Chen snapped, "Why would it matter if you saw something about the Raqilan? We already know where they come from, and what prompted them to come back here. The captain, at this very moment, is working with that Golvonek commander to alter what should be their future, if that maniac Doctor Crusher woke up is any indication." She halted herself, as her mouth was threatening to outpace her mind as she pondered various scenarios. "Come to think of it, what does anything that happens to these two planets matter one way or another to us? If the Federation had been that interested in this area of space, they wouldn't have waited fifty years to send a ship. What does another century matter?"

And then it all clicked.

"Wait. You found something about us, didn't you?" Chen held up her hands. "I don't mean *us* us, but Starfleet, or the Federation, or both. Somehow, in the future, we're involved with either the Raqilan or the Golvonek. That's it, isn't it?"

Taurik replied, "I have already said more than would be considered prudent. However, I will say that I did not study the files, or even review them long enough to note anything which might answer your questions in any meaningful detail."

"Who needs detail?" Chen asked. "I'll take vague generalities."

Shaking his head, Taurik released a small sigh, his first emotional response since his apparent discovery. "You know I cannot divulge such information. I fear that I may already have violated the Temporal Prime Directive. The security lockout is to prevent any further potential breaches, by me or anyone else."

Though she could understand his point, Chen was still perturbed. "Why not just purge the data from the memory banks? Why go to all this other trouble?"

"I need to verify that all related data is included in such a cleanup effort," Taurik replied. "I will do so at the earliest opportunity."

Chen started to make an offer of assistance, but stopped herself. Her friend had already made it clear that he would be keeping to himself whatever it was he had seen in the computer data. In theory, this would minimize possible disruption of future events and the number of investigations this was sure to trigger within the Department of Temporal Investigations, who she knew would soon be receiving some kind of report from Taurik and Captain Picard. "What about the original files, on the *Arrow*?"

"I have already sent an alert to Commander La Forge and Lieutenant Elfiki, warning them of the possible hazards." Once again, the Vulcan's right eyebrow arched. "I trust that their experience and self-discipline will overcome any temptation they may have to view the information."

"Hey," Chen countered, "if I can control myself, I know they can."

His expression unwavering, Taurik replied, "Indeed."

What could he have found? The question rang in Chen's mind. How did Starfleet or the Federation factor into future events with the Raqilan or Golvonek? Perhaps it was the opposite that was true, and it was a lack of such connection or involvement that was the issue. Of course, that line of thinking served only to trigger a host of new questions, and Chen quickly realized she was going to end up going in circles or, worse yet, driving herself crazy as she attempted to ponder all the possibilities.

"Okay," she said after a moment, "I get what you're doing, and why you have to do it. I just wish I could help you. That's all."

Taurik nodded. "Your desire to assist me is appreciated, and under most other circumstances I would welcome the offer."

From behind him, an alert tone sounded from her own workstation, and she looked past him to see that a section of data scrolling on one of her console's screens had stopped and now was highlighted.

"What have we got here?" she asked, returning to her seat. "Maybe I get to violate the Temporal Prime Directive, too." Leaning forward in her chair, she studied the new string of information the computer had flagged. "Okay, maybe not as interesting as your little secret, but at least it's something we can use." She pointed at the screen. "The computer managed to dig out something about the *Arrow*'s construction. There's some kind of facility on a moon orbiting one of the system's uninhabited planets, Landorem. Maybe that's where it was built. Or, will be built."

"Or, perhaps where it is currently being built," Taurik offered.

Chen nodded. "Yeah, that." She shrugged. "I guess there's only one way to find out. Maybe now we can start to get some real answers."

17

Aside from personal combat—real or simulated, though he still preferred the real—there were few activities Worf enjoyed as much as flying. With his present duties, it was a rare occasion that allowed him to take the controls of a shuttlecraft or other smaller vessel, so he took advantage of any opportunity that might present itself. If the flight presented a degree of difficulty that exceeded the usual sort of shuttlecraft journey, so much the better.

Such was the case today.

His fingers moving with practiced ease over the cockpit's main console, Worf guided the shuttlecraft *Siouxsie* out of the path of the oncoming asteroid, watching the mass of rock roll past in the void as the smaller and far more fragile shuttle maneuvered around it.

"That was a little close," said Elfiki from where she sat in the cockpit's copilot seat.

"Perhaps," Worf admitted. Had he allowed the onboard computer to control the craft rather than minding the controls himself, the *Siouxsie* would have altered its course far earlier, giving the asteroid a wide berth, along with the handful of others they had passed since entering the debris field. Like many asteroid belts found in other solar systems, this one was not dense, at least not the region the shuttlecraft currently traversed. Navigating around the hazards the field presented was a routine affair and in truth, the shuttle's onboard navigational and collision avoidance systems coupled with his own skills made it so that the craft was in no real danger. It was this mitigating of risk that might have disappointed him in days past, but age, maturity, and experience had seen to it that Worf was well beyond such youthful imprudence.

This did not mean he could not partake in a bit of occasional fun.

"For some reason," Elfiki said, "I didn't know you liked piloting shuttles."

Worf offered a grunt in reply. "It has always been something I enjoyed. When I was a cadet, I often volunteered to pilot instructors or other personnel to Jupiter or other Academy facilities." From the beginning of his studies, which had included numerous hours spent in flight training and related assignments, he had developed an appreciation for the freedom which could only be obtained by soaring among the clouds or the stars. As an ensign and junior-grade lieutenant, he had been given ample opportunity to strengthen his skills and feed his private indulgence whenever a senior officer needed a pilot for a shuttle or transport.

With no small hint of mischief in her voice, Elfiki asked, "You didn't hit any asteroids during any of those flights, did you, sir?"

"No," replied Worf, "but there is always a first time." Despite the safety features built into the *Siouxsie*'s navigational and helm controls, the geological makeup of the asteroids littering the field was having an effect on the shuttlecraft's sensors, with readings deteriorating in proportion to distance from the ship. For their purposes, scans would be effective enough to guide them through the belt, but Worf had already cut the shuttle's speed even further to lessen the likelihood of being caught off guard by a wayward mass of tumbling rock.

The science officer nodded. "Great. You can just let me off anywhere."

Unperturbed by her gentle humor, he said, "We should be closing on our intended destination."

Tapping a series of controls on her own console, Elfiki reported, "The moon orbiting Landorem is located approximately eleven million kilometers beyond the field's outer boundary." She pointed to one of the sensor displays that the Klingon could see from his seat. "Given the field's relative lack of asteroids, I'm surprised the Raqilan thought it might provide suitable cover. On the other hand, I can also see how the Golvonek thinking that sneaking through or around the field could provide a nice route for a surprise attack."

"Remember that their spaceflight technology is not as advanced as ours," Worf said. "Neither are their sensors. Given the limited number of vessels either side has to expend on interplanetary attacks, it is reasonable to assume they would not take undue risks which might result in the loss of ships." He suspected this was particularly true of the Golvonek, who appeared to have mounted a largely defensive campaign against the apparently more aggressive Raqilan. "At their present technology levels, piloting a ship through the belt would still present a risk. Even with our sensors, if I were to accelerate to maximum speed, the threat to us would increase considerably."

"I'd appreciate it if you didn't do that, sir," Elfiki remarked. "At least, not until we clear the field."

After his private conversation with Jodis, who had informed him that the *Arrow* in the here and now was in the earliest stages of its construction but was unwilling to offer assistance in locating the nascent vessel, Captain Picard had assigned Lieutenants Elfiki and Chen the task of locating its build site. Chen's efforts had been successful in extracting information from the derelict's computer files that seemed to answer this question—data corroborated with earlier *Enterprise* long-range sensor scans of System 3955 in which several of the moons had shown signs of habitation. The readings were inconclusive at this distance, prompting the captain to dispatch Worf and Elfiki in a shuttlecraft bound for the probable location of the *Arrow* as it existed in the present.

Except that the completed Arrow *already exists in the present*, the Klingon mused. *I truly loathe time travel.*

Even setting out on the excursion had required a bit of deception, with Worf and Elfiki departing aboard the *Siouxsie* and warping away from the *Enterprise* on a course that took them out of the Canborek system. Once they had traveled beyond the range of the Golvonek ships' sensors, Worf had altered the shuttlecraft's trajectory so that it could enter the system undetected before proceeding on to their planned destination. The elaborate ruse was necessary to prevent the Golvonek from learning of the *Arrow*'s existence while it still was being constructed. Of course, he also believed that Mynlara or one of her superiors eventually would piece together this odd puzzle and discover the truth behind the weapon ship, thereby thwarting this entire effort at secrecy.

There is nothing to be done about that now, he reminded himself.

A tone from the cockpit's sensor controls made Elfiki reach for the console. She pressed one of the keys on the station's sleek black interface. "We're clear of the field, sir."

"Excellent," said Worf. "Accelerating to full impulse." The relatively short distance separating them from

Landorem and its moon made warp drive impractical, but with the asteroid field now behind them, the *Siouxsie*'s sensor readings would now improve. Altering course, he aligned the shuttle so that the moon was visible through the main viewing port. It was small, gray, and seemingly lifeless, alone among the blackness of space.

After a moment spent studying the scan data being relayed to her console, Elfiki said, "There's definitely a lot of activity on that moon. There's no atmosphere, but the signs of technology are unmistakable, although it's mostly concentrated to one area. I'm picking up what appears to be an artificial construct, but it's much larger than the *Arrow*, along with what's probably a support base and related infrastructure." Then, hunching over her controls, she frowned. "Wait, this . . . something's not right here."

"What is it?" Worf asked.

Elfiki shook her head. "I'm not sure, sir. According to these readings, this ship is a lot further along in its construction than just a simple skeleton or space frame, but that's not even the weirdest part. Our initial scans of the *Arrow*—the one we found, I mean—showed a neutronium composite hull, but that's not what I'm seeing here. The sensors are reading a massive hull that's solid neutronium, with none of the other elements we detected before."

"Are you saying this is not the same craft?"

"Jodis didn't say anything about there being more than one, and we haven't found anything about multiple ships in any of the *Arrow*'s computer files." She pointed to one of her readings. "Look at this, sir. The vessel I'm scanning? It's bigger than the *Arrow*. Not significantly so, but it's definitely longer and wider, and now I'm seeing that its general shape is similar but not identical. This is a different ship, Commander."

Worf said nothing for several moments as the shuttle-craft approached the moon, his attention focused on his own instruments. When a new reading appeared on his console, he straightened in his seat. "We are being scanned," he said. "Low-power sensors, perhaps motion detectors or simple radar, but someone knows we are coming. I am commencing an evasive course." He adjusted the *Siouxsie*'s flight path so that it dropped toward the moon's airless, barren gray-brown surface, the desolate terrain all but filling the forward viewing port as he guided the compact ship into a steep dive. Unlike other models of shuttlecraft, the *McCall* class was designed to fly and maneuver more like a small fighter than actual transport, and this was further reflected in its armaments and defenses.

"I've lost track of their sensor returns," said Elfiki as she hunched over her console. "I think we shook them, at least for the time being." Touching another control and consulting her readings, she pointed toward the viewing port, behind which was a range of dull gray mountains that were growing larger and closer with every passing moment. "The ship should be over that ridge."

Adjusting the shuttle's course, Worf decelerated the *Siouxsie* and maneuvered it over the top of one of the smaller mountains, and as he dropped the shuttle's nose the moon's surface came once more into view. The first thing he noticed was the monstrous, dark gash that had been carved into the dead lunar soil. His initial thought was that it was a natural feature, a canyon created by whatever erosion or earthquake or other upheaval which might have taken place millions or even billions of years earlier, but that notion was quickly dismissed as he noted the straightness and sharpness of the furrow.

Elfiki gasped. "Would you look at that? It's huge. Sensors show it's nearly a thousand meters across and almost nine kilometers long."

In some ways, the trough carved into the lunar surface reminded Worf of the path of destruction wrought by the *Enterprise*-D when its saucer section had crash-landed fifteen years earlier on Veridian III. This trail was wider and deeper, suggesting to the first officer that whatever had caused it had been far larger, contained much more mass, and had not benefitted from a controlled crash but instead plowed unrestrained into the lifeless moon.

Even with the *Siouxsie*'s reduced speed, it took little time to traverse the length of the gouge carved into the arid lunar soil, but well before they reached its far end Worf was able to see structures jutting up from the surface. To him they appeared similar to domes and emergency shelters used by Starfleet personnel and Federation colonists in similar environments or where the atmosphere was poisonous. It was not these that concerned him, however, but rather the very large object around which the structures had been built.

"It can't be," he heard Elfiki say, echoing similar thoughts racing through the Klingon's head as he beheld what could only be the cause of the horrific scar marring the moon's surface. "Look at the size of that thing."

The vessel, if indeed it was a ship, lay nearly half-buried at the end of the colossal trench it had forged with what must have been a harrowing descent from orbit. Though it had amazingly remained in one piece, its hull had fractured in the midst of its death throes with massive fissures visible along its length. Its exterior, dark and mottled, seemed to absorb the sunlight that highlighted the pallid soil surrounding it while reflecting off the metal surfaces of the obviously artificial structures erected around it. Still, Worf was able to make out what appeared to be raised areas, spaced at regular intervals along the broken hull and suggesting to him what might once have been weapons emplacements.

As with the Arrow?

Conical in shape, it was narrowest at its tail end, widening toward its head. Even partially obscured by the dirt and rock it had thrown up as a result of its crash, the crown of the enormous vessel still towered above all but a pair of the nearest buildings, which Worf now saw were little more than elaborate scaffolding, with immense metal skeletons that reminded the Klingon of a construction framework.

"Commander," Elfiki said, her voice low and tentative, "is that what I think it is?"

Having seen two vessels of similar design in his lifetime, Worf knew precisely what the science officer was thinking, and he had no choice but to agree. Without replying to her question, he tapped the communications control on his console.

"*Shuttlecraft* Siouxsie *to* Enterprise."

Looking up from the padd resting in his lap as he sat in his command chair, Picard frowned not only at the note of concern in Commander Worf's voice as his hail was piped through the bridge's intercom system, but also the poor quality of the audio transmission. "*Enterprise* here. What's your status, Number One? Have you found the *Arrow*?"

"*Negative, sir,*" replied his first officer, his words laced with static, "*but, we have found what we think was the Raqilan's template for building it.*"

"What's causing that interference?" Picard asked. "The asteroid field?"

Behind him, Lieutenant Šmrhová said, "Affirmative, sir. The debris contains a variety of mineral ores that are disrupting communications and sensors." After a moment, she added, "Captain, they're sending us a visual feed."

"Patch it through," ordered Picard, setting aside the padd and its engineering status report as he rose from his seat. On the bridge's main viewscreen, the drifting *Arrow* derelict was replaced by images being sent in real time from the shuttlecraft's sensors, depicting the dull gray surface of the moon Worf and Elfiki had been sent to investigate. As with the audio channel, the picture quality of the transmission also was being affected by the asteroid field's disruptive properties. Static and other signs of signal degradation were evident, slicing across the image and causing audible pops and other sound distortion.

"What in the world . . . ?" The rest of Picard's question faded on his lips as he studied the viewscreen. He had expected to see the *Arrow* itself, perhaps in some early stage of construction such as a bare or largely unadorned space frame. He was unprepared for the behemoth now displayed before him. There was no mistaking the monstrosity's silhouette, even as it lay half-buried and wrecked, partially obscured by the rolling hills of displaced lunar soil and stone as it rested within a vast canyon of its own making.

"*Zkurvysyn*," said Šmrhová from behind him. "That's unreal."

Reining in his own shock at the unlikely image on the viewscreen, Picard replied, "I'm afraid it's all too real, Lieutenant."

Planet killer.

Doomsday machine.

Picard was willing to wager that there was not a single cadet at Starfleet Academy who had not read the historical accounts of the first known encounter with such a vessel. Picard himself had presented to his class an oral report on the incident, in which Captain James Kirk and his *Enterprise* had come to the aid of another *Constitution*-class vessel, the *Constellation*, under the command of Commodore Matthew Decker. The *Constellation* had been wrecked by what Kirk's science officer, Commander Spock, had described in his official report as "an automated weapon of immense size and power." Based on observations of the robotic vessel's actions, Spock had determined that its sole purpose was to destroy planets using a fearsome anti-proton weapon and then consume the resulting debris as a fuel source. This rendered the machine autonomous, at least in this regard, so long as it could find planets and other useful spatial bodies to pummel and devour.

"Incredible." The word was almost a whisper. Studying the crashed machine, Picard now saw the ghostly echo of its silhouette in what would become the *Arrow*. The resemblance was subtle, of course, with the Raqilan weapon ship's heritage disguised in its far more angular design, to say nothing of its general form being inverted from that of this wreck which had clearly inspired it. To this point, the *Arrow* had seemed to carry its moniker in reference to its obvious shape.

"The thing's neutronium hull is blocking our sensors," said Lieutenant Elfiki over the open, yet still compromised, communications link, *"but scans of the crash site itself indicate it's been here over one hundred thousand years. It's also a lot smaller than . . . the other one."*

"Of all the things I thought they'd find," Šmrhová said, "this didn't even make the list."

Picard nodded in agreement. "I know I certainly didn't expect to see another one in my lifetime."

After Captain Kirk's defeat of the original machine, a small fleet of ships from Starfleet's Corps of Engineers was required to tow it to a top-secret facility devoted to the storage and study of recovered alien technology. Once consigned to "The Yard," as the research station was commonly known, the machine was studied for a time by a group of Starfleet and Federation civilian scientists, before finally being relocated to what was intended to be its permanent home at a special annex of the Starfleet Museum. That was where the mammoth automaton remained for more than a century, until the Borg had attacked Federation space—a prelude to their all-out and ultimately final invasion—and Picard himself had come up with the odd idea of using it as a possible weapon against the malevolent cybernetic race.

"There's something else, Captain," Elfiki continued as the viewscreen depicted the opaque, cavernous opening that was the mammoth vessel's bow. *"I'm detecting defects in the outer hull, and when I compare my sensor readings to the specs on the original machine recorded during its time at The Yard, I see that the power plant is much smaller and not as powerful."* There was a pause before she added, *"I didn't know they made these things in different sizes."*

"We were under the impression that the original machine was a prototype," Picard replied. "I suppose it's possible that this is an even earlier version of what its builders eventually constructed." The prevailing theory was that the ancient, mysterious, and all but unknown race known only as "the Preservers" had been responsible for creating these drone-like contrivances. The machine defeated by Captain Kirk more than a century earlier and eventually used to thwart the Borg's pre-invasion assault on Federation targets was actually the second such vessel with which Picard and his crew had dealt.

"The machine commanded by Delcara," Worf said over the link. *"It was much larger and more powerful than this one or the vessel we used against the Borg."*

Picard nodded. "Exactly, Number One." It had been nearly twenty years since their encounter with Delcara, the mysterious representative of the Shgin, a race devastated by the Borg hundreds of years before. Consumed by a need to exact vengeance against the Borg for annihilating her people, Delcara spent years attempting to locate a planet killer after learning of their existence from—of all people—Cadet Jean-Luc Picard and his class dissertation on the machine Kirk had fought. Upon finding one of the ancient weapons and learning how to control it, Delcara had unleashed its fury upon the Borg during several successful attacks. Her ultimate plan was to utilize the machine to travel to their homeworld in a bid to destroy the cybernetic race once and for all.

That scheme failed when she attempted to accelerate the machine beyond the maximum threshold for warp speed, and both the planet killer and Delcara vanished, never to be heard from again. According to the prevailing theories with respect to travel at such velocities, it was believed that she and the machine were trapped within some form of infinite loop, occupying all points in the universe at once. What might be the current state of the Federation and its allies—to say nothing of the other races and planets that had suffered at the hands of the Borg in the two decades since Delcara's disappearance—if she had succeeded? Thinking of the numerous worlds and uncounted lives that might have been saved had she not been so blinded by her unquenchable thirst for revenge made Picard shake his head in sadness.

"What else can you tell us about this machine, Lieutenant?"

Elfiki replied, *"Based on our sensor readings, it looks as though its central power plant may have overloaded. I'm picking up signs of damage that aren't consistent with the physical stresses of a simple crash. What's left doesn't look to be much more than a mountain of scrap, sir. If I had to guess, I'd say that the thing suffered some kind of catastrophic systems failure that rendered it incapable of avoiding a crash."*

"It's still pretty impressive," said Šmrhová. Picard turned to her as the security chief gestured toward the screen. "And it's obvious somebody else thought so, too. You have to figure they've been attempting to plunder the wreck for anything useful since they found it."

"We are detecting Raqilan life signs within the structures around the vessel," Worf said, *"though the concentration of neutronium from its hull is obscuring some of our scans."*

Picard crossed his arms. "Have you found any sign of the *Arrow* itself?"

"Not yet, sir," Worf said. *"However, our scans have picked up another concentration of artificial materials on the moon's far side. We were preparing to investigate."* His statement was punctuated by a sharp burst of static that also seemed to affect the visual transmission, which wavered for a moment before returning to its already low-quality state

"It's a given that the Raqilan know you're there, Commander. Make your survey brief, and return to the ship as quickly as possible."

"Acknowledged," replied the Klingon. *"Captain, do you plan to tell Fleet Legate Mynlara about what we've found?"*

"I honestly don't know yet, Number One." His first officer had raised a valid question, and Picard had sensed his unspoken addendum. Would alerting the Golvonek to the *Arrow* in its present state, decades before it would be completed and launched on its mission, constitute a violation of the Prime Directive? Though there were no specific clauses in the regulation for this particular scenario, the decree was broad enough that he could interpret it as he felt appropriate and necessary. In Picard's mind, the current circumstances offered the very definition of "uncharted territory."

Well, Picard reminded himself, *it's the job you wanted.*

18

"Commander, there it is!"

No sooner had the words left Lieutenant Elfiki's mouth and she was pointing through the *Siouxsie*'s viewing port than Worf saw it. The construction facility was cloaked in near total darkness on the moon's far side, away from the Canborek sun and facing into the void of space, but illuminated from within by obvious artificial sources. Its forward section, an elaborate grid of metal beams and other support structures, rested on the moon's surface, extending outward from the depths of a vast cave at the base of an immense mountain. Worf guided the shuttlecraft into hover, holding the shuttlecraft's position so that it remained partially concealed behind the mountain range separating them from their target. Angling the craft so that the viewing port faced the cave entrance, he now saw that cocooned within the convoluted scaffolding was an elongated, tapered skeletal framework. Even though it was decades from completion, the lines of what would become the *Arrow* were evident.

"That tunnel extends several dozen kilometers into the mountainside," Elfiki said. "It's too straight and consistent in its measurements to be a natural formation, and I'm reading other tunnels and chambers extending even farther underground. The Raqilan must've carved it out themselves. The mineral composition of the mountain and surrounding soil shares many characteristics with what we found in the completed *Arrow*, so it's likely the Raqilan processed the raw mineral ore from the tunnels to use in the ship's construction." She blew out her breath. "I'll be damned." Then, as if realizing she had spoken aloud, she added, "I'm sorry, sir. I shouldn't be surprised—or excited—to see this, but it's pretty amazing, and a little bizarre."

Worf shook his head. "Your reaction is understandable, Lieutenant." Seeing the budding spacecraft nestled within the cradle that would nurture it for years to come, he could not help but consider yet again the tangled knots of perception, reality, logic, reason, confusion, and even fantasy, all of which seemed to wrap in and around themselves and one another whenever the topic of time travel was broached. Despite whatever snide comments he might offer on the matter during casual conversation, Worf had always been fascinated with the concept of traveling through time. His later experiences with various aspects of the concept had served to fuel both his interest and his irritation at the incalculable number of variables that always came into play whenever someone or something traveled to a point in the past in a bid to influence future events. Upon learning that the *Arrow* was a device intended for such a purpose, and with the enormity of the mission it had been sent to complete, Worf had spent a great deal of time considering the multitudes of ways Jodis and his crew might affect the time stream. Had the Raqilan given sufficient thought to the myriad ramifications that might ensue as a consequence of the *Arrow* carrying out its assigned task? Even if the weapon ship failed in its mission, its crew still carried with them the ability to affect future history, with no way to foresee the impacts possible as a result of their very presence, let alone any subtle or overt actions they might undertake.

"There's something interfering with our scans," Elfiki reported. "Almost like a scattering field. It's concentrated around the construction site, but I think I can compensate for it." Tapping several controls on her console, she added, "I can filter some of it, sir. Enough to get a decent look."

His attention divided between his controls and the sight beyond the viewing port as he held the *Siouxsie* hovering at a point just above the mountain ridge that acted as a protective barrier for the construction site, Worf eyed the chronometer on his console. They had been here long enough that, despite his precautions, someone should have noticed. "Are you detecting life signs?"

The science officer nodded. "Affirmative, sir. I'm picking up hundreds of Raqilan biosigns in and around the scaffolding and the ship itself. They've got sensors, too, and they know we're here. I just registered their scans." Now aware that time was a factor, Elfiki hunched over her console, and her fingers moved even faster across the controls. After several moments spent studying her sensor data, she gestured toward the viewing port. "It's just the frame, and not even all of that. The tail section looks to be incomplete. However, I'm also getting readings consistent with some of the materials and components from the planet killer."

Worf replied, "They would obviously attempt to reverse engineer some of the components and mechanisms they found inside the machine."

"Right," said Elfiki, "but our scans of the completed *Arrow* showed no such similarities. At least, nothing we were able to recognize. From everything we've seen and when you compare it to what we know about the planet killers, the *Arrow*'s not just a copy. It's a unique craft, engineered from the ground up using the machine more as a guide."

She was right, Worf knew. Their on-site inspection of the *Arrow*'s interior had been enough to demonstrate what the Raqilan had been able to accomplish even with using the wrecked planet killer as a starting reference.

"Perhaps their initial attempts failed, but their study of the machine still was sufficient to drive their own research and development efforts," he said. Unlike the machine, the *Arrow*'s internal systems had been designed and constructed for the benefit of the crew tasked with operating it. While Raqilan scientists and engineers were successful in re-creating some of the machine's propulsion and weapons systems, they had done so in comparably crude form, using materials available to them and operating within the limits of their technology. "Their inability to repair or reproduce the machine's internal mechanisms might explain the major differences in the *Arrow*'s final design."

Elfiki shrugged. "However they did it, there's no arguing that it's still pretty damned impressive." Once more, she pointed toward the viewing port. "Wouldn't it be something to watch them build this thing, knowing how long it'll take and what it will end up being once it's completed? Seeing them work through the technical obstacles and testing their designs?"

"I imagine our entire engineering staff would want to do that," Worf countered.

"Not just the engineers." Elfiki smiled. "I wonder if the need for total secrecy is the major reason the construction will take so long to complete. Ferrying the necessary materials to this location, or mining the raw ores from the moon itself, might attract undue attention from Gol- vonek patrol vessels, if indeed there are such things."

The inkling of something that had bothered him since first hearing about the *Arrow* and its mission started to coalesce in Worf's mind, and he realized what component of the present circumstances seemed not to fit with every- thing else.

"At this point in the conflict," he said, "both the Raqilan and Golvonek homeworlds, though affected by orbital bombardments and other attacks, have not deteri- orated to the point that it makes sense for Raqilan leaders to devise such an outlandish plan to retroactively prevent the war."

Elfiki nodded. "I was thinking about that, too, sir. Maybe at this point, it's just supposed to be a massive weapon, the biggest bat they can come up with for fight- ing back. Just one ship like this, with a weapon powerful enough to destroy an entire planet, would be more than enough to all but guarantee a victory over the Golvonek."

She was interrupted by an alert tone from her console, and she grimaced as she checked the readings. "Sensors are picking up energy signatures coming from points scat- tered around the construction site." Pausing to further study the scan data, the lieutenant added, "They look to be weapons emplacements, sir. Eight of them, and they're all coming online."

Worf said, "Then it is time to leave." Tapping controls to guide the *Siouxsie* into a bank away from the moun- tain, the Klingon felt the shuttlecraft responding to his commands as it angled up and away from the moon's sur- face and back toward space. "Can you ascertain the range of their weapons?"

"Once we leave orbit, we should be fine, sir."

Using the mountain range surrounding the construction site as natural cover, Worf maneuvered the shuttle to block any of the weapons stations from being able to acquire the craft as a target. Once he was satisfied, he increased the *Siouxsie*'s velocity as it arced away from the moon, but the feeling lasted only until another alert tone sounded in the shuttlecraft's cabin.

"Incoming ships," Elfiki said. "Six of them. They look to be Raqilan in design." Her brow furrowed as she studied the sensors readings. "They're small and fast. If I had to guess, sir, I'd say they were some kind of fighter craft, and they look to be loaded for bear. Each ship has six particle cannons. They've got shields, but ours are better."

"Increasing speed," Worf said, his hands already moving to input the necessary commands. He glanced at the small tactical scanner set into the console and noted the *Siouxsie*'s position relative to the moon as well as the six ships. "Activate deflector shields."

"Can't we outrun them?" Elfiki asked.

Worf shook his head. "We can beat them to the asteroid field, but their ships are smaller and more maneuverable than ours." The debris encircling the moon and the planet Landorem offered no clear avenues of escape, so any course back to the *Enterprise* would require him to navigate the shuttlecraft through the debris. Even though the field was not so dense as to pose significant hazards to navigation, the fighters—and their pilots, who presumably had greater experience maneuvering through this area—would have the advantage. "Contact the *Enterprise*. Alert them that we may need assistance."

Elfiki had time only to reach for the communications controls before something slammed into the *Siouxsie*. The entire shuttlecraft seemed to lurch under him, and Worf gripped the console to keep from being thrown from his seat. Even with the shields to absorb the brunt of the attack, the force of the strike was still enough to stress the artificial gravity and inertial damping systems almost to their limit. He lunged for the control that triggered the emergency restraint systems for both his and Elfiki's seats, and Worf felt the harness push out from the recessed compartments in the chair's frame and close around his arms, thighs, and torso.

"They're trying to surround us, sir!" Elfiki snapped as her own harness slipped into place. "If they all gang up on us with the weapons they're carrying, our shields won't hold."

Worf, once again thankful that he had chosen the *McCall*-class shuttle to conduct their investigation, pushed the *Siouxsie* to the top end of its sublight velocity. At the same time, he checked the status of the craft's weapons and saw that its phaser arrays were online, and he instructed the computer to begin scanning for targets.

"We will be in the asteroid field in twenty seconds," he reported, glancing back and forth between his controls and the viewing port. To his right, he caught a glimpse of a fleeting, dull-silver shape disappearing from view as he yet again adjusted the shuttlecraft's course. Elfiki was right. The Raqilan fighters were fast. Perhaps too fast. His fears were strengthened as the *Siouxsie*'s shields were slammed by two quick strikes, the impacts carrying enough power to trigger multiple alarms within the shuttle's cramped cockpit. Only his harness kept Worf from being ejected from his seat, but he ignored the craft's bucking and pitching, noting instead the series of crimson alert indicators beginning to flash on his console.

"Communications are out," Elfiki reported. "We can receive, but I can't open a channel to broadcast. Aft shields are down to forty-six percent. Port impulse engine also has some damage, but is still functional."

Worf ordered, "Route power from nonessential systems to the shields. Can you restore communications?" Glancing ahead through the viewing port, he saw that a handful of asteroids marked the edge of the debris field.

"It looks like an overload, sir," replied the science officer. "I may be able to reroute."

When another salvo rocked the shuttle, Worf decided that was enough. "Stand by," he said, banking the *Siouxsie* to port and away from the oncoming asteroids. The targeting scanner beeped as one of the Raqilan fighters finally fell within its sights, and Worf wasted no time stabbing at the phaser firing control. Twin orange-white streaks spat forth from the shuttlecraft, piercing the void separating it from the smaller fighter. There was no flare of energy, but instead impact blooms as the phasers struck the nimble craft's armored hull before the fighter disappeared out of sight.

"Direct hit, sir," Elfiki said. "I'm picking up damage to its hull and . . . I think . . . its propulsion system." A moment later, she nodded. "Yes, it's definitely dropping back. The other five are still on us, though."

Worf was grateful that the ship with which he had exchanged fire had not been more severely damaged. He did not want to injure or kill any of the Raqilan. Doing so now, with the *Enterprise*—and by extension, the entire Federation—in the earliest stages of communication with both the Raqilan and the Golvonek, would serve only to add even greater stress to an already tenuous situation. Therefore, judicious use of force was more appropriate, at least for the moment. That said, his instinct to engage the remaining fighters was almost overwhelming, but the tactical situation was not in his favor. Five against one, and with the *Siouxsie* already suffering from damage, meant that the situation had been reduced to two possible outcomes: either the shuttlecraft would make its escape, or else the fighters would succeed in capturing it. With a compromised engine, only one of those two results was appearing likely.

There is a third option, he told himself, and the reminder was punctuated by yet another strike against the shuttle's beleaguered deflector shields.

Relying on the tactical scanner to keep him apprised of the *Siouxsie*'s present position, Worf redirected the shuttlecraft back toward the asteroid field and pushed its impulse engines to their limit. As he did so, he noted the warning indicator on his console. "We have damage to propulsion."

"They're closing, sir," Elfiki said. "I'm still working on the communications workaround."

The screen illustrated for Worf what he already knew. Despite all of the speed he might cajole out of the shuttle's compromised engines, the five Raqilan fighters would close the distance before the *Siouxsie* reached the relative safety of the asteroid field. "Divert emergency power to shields and weapons," he ordered, knowing as he did so that he likely was only delaying the inevitable.

There is no dishonor in falling before a superior enemy. The old maxim was one of many he had read and reread all through his childhood as he struggled to retain his Klingon heritage while living at the agricultural colony on Gault with his human foster parents. Like most young Klingons with aspirations of one day becoming a warrior in service to the empire, he had found it difficult to balance the concept with his natural urge to always be the victor in battle. The wisdom to reconcile the two disparate viewpoints had come later, as an adult and after numerous opportunities to put to the test his skills, beliefs, and commitment to the warrior ethos.

But were the Raqilan truly a superior enemy? In numbers, yes, but otherwise? Worf was not convinced that if the odds were different their pursuers would emerge from battle as the victors. Of course, he dismissed that scenario even as he considered it, annoyed with himself for entertaining the thought because it sounded like a feeble attempt to justify the *Siouxsie*'s weaker tactical position.

"Communications status?" Worf asked, the impact from another barrage rocking the shuttle.

Elfiki grunted in obvious frustration. "I'm still trying to reroute. Aft shield generator is out, sir, and two of the ships are trying to maneuver in behind us."

Already pushing the shuttlecraft into a banking, twisting dive, Worf managed to shake loose the pair of Raqilan pursuers, though the tactical scanner showed him that his maneuver had provided only momentary respite. That was confirmed seconds later as yet another particle beam slammed into the *Siouxsie*.

"There goes the port impulse engine," Elfiki reported, fighting with her console in a frantic attempt to mitigate or isolate the damage. "We're also losing power in the starboard system." That much was evident by the strained hum of the engines as they struggled under renewed stress and fading thrust. "There's no way we can outrun them now, sir." A moment later, she added, "I've got partial communications back. Low power, but it's something."

Worf grunted in mounting irritation. "They are closing." Outside the viewing port, he saw the first asteroids as the *Siouxsie* approached the debris field's leading edge. It was a group consisting of one massive asteroid flanked by more than a dozen smaller companions, each of them tumbling as they drifted through the void. Whatever cover they might offer was now beyond reach.

"Commander, we're being hailed." Elfiki stabbed at the intercom controls, and the shuttle's cockpit became awash with static.

"Unidentified vessel, you are trespassing in a region controlled by the Raqilan Military Forces. We have scanned your ship and know it is damaged. You will reduce your speed and cease all attempts at escape, or we will be forced to destroy you. Acknowledge this transmission."

Elfiki frowned. "He called us an unidentified ship. They don't know who we are."

"Not yet," Worf said, "but I cannot imagine their long-range tracking facilities have failed to detect the *Enterprise* or the *Arrow*." He also wondered if the Raqilan military might be monitoring any of the messages Fleet Legate Mynlara was supposed to have been sending to superiors on Uphrel.

"They have to know we're not a threat, right?" Elfiki asked.

The Klingon scowled. "Not anymore." He loathed the very idea of surrendering, but he was convinced that he and Elfiki were in no immediate danger. If their pursuers had wanted to destroy the shuttlecraft, they could now do so with little difficulty. They had to be aware of the *Enterprise*'s presence outside the solar system, and likely wanted as much information as possible. Perhaps Worf could find a way to use that to his and Elfiki's advantage.

"Drop speed to one-quarter impulse and power down our weapons," he ordered, and was greeted by an uncertain nod from Elfiki. "And send a burst transmission to the *Enterprise* with our current position and status."

Elfiki said, "The transmission won't be strong enough to get a response right away."

"It doesn't have to," Worf replied. "It just has to be received. Captain Picard will take it from there." He had no doubt that the captain would be able to navigate the rather troubling wrinkle he and Elfiki were about to introduce to the current situation. Until Picard had a chance to act, he and the science officer would have to exercise patience and discretion in the presence of their new hosts.

Forcing back the feelings of defeat welling up within him, he pressed the control to open the communications channel. "This is Commander Worf aboard the Federation shuttlecraft *Siouxsie*. We are complying with your request. It is not our intention to invite hostile action. We were conducting a peaceful exploration of this area. I regret firing on your vessel, but I did so only in defense of my own ship and crew."

Over the static-filled channel, the disembodied voice replied, *"Your explanations will receive full and fair attention from the appropriate parties."* As he listened to the reply, Worf watched one of the fighter craft move ahead of the *Siouxsie*, taking up position less than two dozen meters off the shuttlecraft's bow. *"You will follow the craft ahead of you. Any deviation from its course will be interpreted as an attempt at escape."*

Feeling his jaw clench, Worf bit off his acknowledgement. "Understood."

19

Except for the beds, the patient ward had been stripped of everything. Every other piece of furniture, along with all of the equipment and supplies stored there, had been relocated. Even the monitors affixed to the beds themselves had been taken, and now the room resembled little more than a holding cell. As Jodis stood before the room's only door, which led out to the medical facility's main work area and was currently closed and locked, he found it an apt comparison.

"How long do you think they will keep us here?" asked Bnira, and Jodis turned to see her crossing the room toward him. Like him, she was dressed in a drab yet form-fitting one-piece garment provided by the human doctor after her staff had found several in the medical section's storage compartment. The clothing possessed no pockets or other means of concealment, and Jodis knew that they had been searched thoroughly before he and the others were allowed to wear them.

"I suspect not for much longer," Jodis replied. "Mynlara will undoubtedly be ordered to tow the ship to one of their bases, but given its size and density, doing so will prove problematic. Eventually, they will realize that the only efficient means of moving it is under its own power, at which time our assistance will be required." The fleet legate had already made plain their status as prisoners, and that the *Poklori gil dara* now was considered seized by the Golvonek military.

Bnira said, "And will we be providing that assistance?" She was making no effort to hide her disdain.

"A fair question," Jodis said, offering a small, sympathetic smile, as he knew Bnira was still mourning the loss of their friends and crewmates. "I confess that I have no answer. At least, not yet." His initial thoughts on the subject were to offer whatever resistance they could muster, but he knew that, ultimately, it would be a futile effort. Given time, Golvonek military and civilian scientists would determine how to gain control of the ship's systems. More interesting to him was the possibility that Raqilan forces of the current time period might try to reclaim the vessel. Of course, knowledge of the *Poklori gil dara* in the present was limited to those involved in the ship's design and construction, the latter of which had only recently begun in earnest, if his calculations were correct. What sort of paradox might that offer, with two such ships now existing in the current time? And as for Jodis and his surviving crew? They were alone here, separated from possible aid not by distance but by time itself.

"We have no allies here," said Bnira. "Except the humans, perhaps."

"Perhaps," Jodis repeated.

"But how do we know the humans did not kill Ehondar and the others?" she asked. "They may have tried to revive them first and failed, or maybe they murdered them."

Jodis frowned. "To what end?" He had been considering their apparent benefactors for some time. The beings who had revived him and Bnira and provided care following their awakening certainly did not present themselves as an enemy. Their every interaction had been peaceful and with the obvious attempt to foster a positive relationship. The leader, Picard, had expressed what Jodis interpreted as genuine regret over their lost comrades, which he attributed to a failure in the cryogenics systems. It was not an implausible explanation, given the duration of the crew's hibernation. To him, Picard seemed to possess wisdom, empathy, and sound judgment, and Jodis felt an implicit desire to trust him. Whether this presented a potential problem as the situation continued to evolve remained to be seen, but for now he was content to see what might happen.

"Even if they are not responsible," Bnira said, "they have been talking with the Golvonek. That makes them untrustworthy."

"Under other circumstances, I would be inclined to agree," Jodis replied, moving to pace the length of the room. It felt good to be moving around again after being asleep for so long. Of course, it amused him to harbor such thoughts, as he recalled no sensation of time's passage while in hibernation. "Still, the more I consider it, the more I come to believe it does not make sense. If we take the humans at their word, they revived us because they thought they were coming to our aid. Given how long we had been asleep, I am rather grateful they are here. If the ship's systems are beginning to succumb to age and neglect despite the best efforts of its builders and the computer, then we likely would have suffered fates similar to Ehondar and the others."

"But what of the Golvonek?" asked Bnira. "They are here, and they will soon be crawling through this ship, learning all its secrets. We cannot allow that."

Jodis nodded. "Agreed, but there is little we can do about that at the moment." What he did not offer was another thought that had been bothering him as they sat in their makeshift cage. His own need to assert some form of control, even while bound to the bed as Picard and Fleet Legate Mynlara questioned him, had caused him to commit a grave error by informing the Golvonek officer of the *Poklori gil dara*'s true origins. It was an inexcusable breach of operational security, though any ramifications likely were minimal. He suspected that Picard and his people, given how much they seemed able to interact with its onboard systems as well as some of the cryptic statements they had made to one another, knew the ship had come from the future. If that was the case, then the human captain seemed to be dealing with the revelation in remarkably stoic fashion. Was it possible these strangers possessed time travel capabilities of their own, or had at least experienced the phenomenon for themselves?

An interesting possibility, Jodis conceded.

"There is a larger concern," Bnira said. "If the Golvonek know where we came from, then they may realize that—at this point in time—the ship is currently under construction. They will go looking for it, and when they find it, they will be able to destroy it. Will that not change the future? What would happen to us?"

Jodis sighed. "If the scientists who oversaw our training are correct, then it will be as though we did not exist." Of course, it was only a theory, one of several they had discussed during countless cycles spent in immersive study attempting to understand the principles of temporal displacement, the alteration or disruption of past events, and their impact on future history. There was no practical knowledge on this subject, given that the earlier temporal relocation experiments had been limited in scope to prevent the very thing the scientists feared might happen. Jodis had always found that aspect of their preparations amusing, given the driving purpose of the *Poklori gil dara*'s mission.

Bnira asked, "So, what do we do?" She gestured around them, indicating the room that was their prison. "We are helpless so long as we remain here."

"We wait," Jodis answered. "Patience, Bnira, is what is now required. Patience, and vigilance. Opportunity may yet present itself."

As if in response to his comments, he heard the sound of the door's locks being disengaged, and he turned as it cycled open to reveal the human captain.

Patience, Jodis reminded himself. *And vigilance.*

For someone who now was a prisoner of the enemy he had sworn to fight, Jodis looked confident to Picard. Like his companion, Jodis seemed to have acclimated to the patient care ward of the *Arrow*'s medical facility, which had been reconfigured to act as a holding area. Golvonek guards now were stationed outside the ward's door as well as outside the medical bay's main entrance. Standing before Picard with hands clasped behind his back, Jodis presented the appearance of someone who was precisely where he wanted to be at that moment.

"Captain," Jodis said, stepping away from his companion, "what can I do for you?"

Standing just inside the doorway, flanked by Lieutenants Konya and Cruzen and with two Golvonek security officers behind them, Picard regarded the Raqilan. "First, you should understand that we've corroborated your claims regarding your mission and this ship with information from your own computer, as well as our own abilities to scan a vessel which has . . ." He paused, glancing over his shoulder at the two Golvonek soldiers who had been assigned by Fleet Legate Mynlara to watch over Jodis and his crew. "As well as our own abilities to verify what you and your vessel experienced."

As he studied Jodis, Picard became convinced that there was more to the Raqilan's story than had been revealed to this point, or even could be substantiated by his crew's review of the *Arrow*'s computer databases. Given their mission, it made sense that Jodis and his people would possess information that would not be recorded, at least not in a computer file that was vulnerable to unauthorized access. In truth, there were dozens of questions Picard wanted to ask of the Raqilan, only some of which pertained to the *Arrow*'s mission.

The captain had been troubled by the report submitted to him by Commander Taurik after the Vulcan engineer had inadvertently accessed information from the *Arrow*'s computer memory banks that provided insight into future events and which may or may not involve Starfleet or the Federation. In keeping with the strictures of the Temporal Prime Directive, Taurik had quarantined all such information and prepared an official statement for the Department of Temporal Investigations. The secretive agency would doubtless take a keen interest not only in the report and the data Taurik had isolated, but also the engineer himself. Having endured his own lengthy debriefings following various time-related anomalies and other odd missions, Picard did not envy the Vulcan. With regulations forbidding him from coercing his junior officer into revealing anything about the information he had seen, the captain could only trust Taurik's assurances that nothing in the weapon ship's computer foretold any danger to the *Enterprise* or its current mission. What happened the moment this incident was concluded, however, would have to remain a total mystery.

"Captain Picard," said one of the Golvonek guards, "You said this was urgent. Fleet Legate Mynlara will not be pleased when she learns I have allowed you access to the prisoners."

"And I also told you to contact Fleet Legate Mynlara and advise her of my intention to speak to them," Picard countered. After his previous discussion with Jodis, he had agreed to the Golvonek officer's request to speak with the Raqilan only with her present, but circumstances had changed and time was of the essence.

To Jodis, he said, "Two of my people have been captured by a Raqilan military patrol while investigating the moon orbiting the planet you call Landorem." He saw the fleeting shift in the Raqilan's expression. Despite his notable self-control, Jodis had been unable to suppress a reaction to the planet's name.

Glancing to the Golvonek guards as though gauging what to say, Jodis replied, "I am unaware of anything of significance there. Still, I am surprised that their ship was not immediately destroyed."

Picard understood why the Raqilan was being careful with his answers. It was likely that the planet killer's crash site as well as the installation where the *Arrow* was being constructed were closely guarded secrets. Conscious of the security considerations as well as the danger of interfering with future events should the Golvonek become aware of the weapon ship, Picard opted to sidestep that matter, at least for the moment. "We received a communication from them which indicated they were being taken into custody."

The message from Commander Worf and Lieutenant Elfiki had come as an encrypted data burst, providing the shuttlecraft *Siouxsie*'s location near the Landorem moon on the far side of the asteroid field at the time it was intercepted by Raqilan military vessels. Worf had reported that they were being escorted to an unknown location, and it had taken all of Picard's self-control not to order the *Enterprise* into the system on an all-out search and rescue mission. Instead, he had opted to send a quartet of sensor buoys which Lieutenant Šmrhová could then use to augment the starship's scans of the moon and surrounding area. Though the buoys had been deployed within moments of receiving Worf's distress call, they had not yet navigated far enough into the system to circumvent the effects of the asteroid field. Staying Picard's hand to this point was that he was not keen on sending in another shuttle or additional personnel without verified reconnaissance of the area, but his reasoned assumption was that had the Raqilan wanted to harm his officers, they would have destroyed the *Siouxsie* rather than capturing it. Despite his desire for restraint, Picard had ordered his security chief to have a tactical team ready to launch at a moment's notice once Worf and Elfiki's location was confirmed.

"Interesting," Jodis said, casting his eyes toward the deck as though pondering this new information. When he looked up again, he once more regarded the Golvonek guards before staring at Picard. "If that is true, then you can be certain the Raqilan military leadership will be most interested in learning all they can from your officers."

Picard nodded, understanding his unspoken meaning. At this point in time, the *Arrow*'s construction would be a secret, with everyone involved operating under strict security protocols, and it would have to be that way for the next several decades in order for the ship to avoid discovery by the Golvonek. In his view, concealing the ship's existence for such a lengthy period of time was nothing short of astounding, but the truth of its construction would likely be revealed in short order.

"Are my people safe?" he asked. "Will they be well treated?"

Jodis's eyes narrowed. "They will be questioned."

"Questioned? Do you mean interrogated? Tortured?" As he posed the questions, Picard watched Jodis's female companion move to stand behind her leader. Though she said nothing, her attention was riveted on him.

"We do not torture prisoners, Captain," Jodis replied. "That said, our interrogation techniques can be quite persuasive. However, your officers will no doubt be something of a curiosity to our people, though I suspect there also will be an element of fear present, as well, given that you are the first beings we have ever encountered from beyond our star system. Our people as well as the Golvonek will have many questions, particularly with respect to your vessel's offensive capabilities."

"I for one hope that a demonstration of those capabilities will not be required," Picard said. "That is not why we are here." His comments elicited a disbelieving expression from Jodis's crewmate, but as before, she remained silent. It was obvious that Jodis alone would speak for them.

"Captain, surely you understand that both my people and the Golvonek will be suspicious about your motives with respect to the other side. Are you colluding with us, or them? Are you inclined to show bias toward them, or us?"

Picard replied, "That is why I have requested an audience with leaders from both your worlds. I have no doubt that your conflict is complex, and I certainly don't presume to tell you how best to resolve it, but my ship and my crew will not become a part of it."

His laughter echoing in the room, Jodis exchanged glances with his companion. "Not become a part of it? Captain, you are already a part of it, and your efforts to revive us have alerted the Golvonek to our presence here. It is likely that the impacts of that are only just now beginning to be felt."

That reality, and its ensuing Prime Directive implications, had troubled Picard from the moment it became clear that the *Arrow* was not simply an abandoned derelict. The situation was now even more muddled and getting more so with each passing moment. Had the *Enterprise* not come across the weapon ship, it was not unrealistic to presume that the massive vessel would have continued to drift for decades before being discovered. Perhaps it would never have been found, at least not by the Golvonek or the Raqilan, before their unrelenting conflict succeeded in destroying both worlds. Was that what was meant to happen? Had the *Arrow* been fated to wander in the void, undisturbed? Its mission an abject failure as the Golvonek and Raqilan obliterated one another?

It really doesn't matter now, does it?

The time for discretion with respect to the Golvonek and the truth behind the *Arrow* was coming to a close, Picard knew, and particularly if Mynlara believed what Jodis had told her about his mission. Even if she doubted the Raqilan, which would be understandable, she still would pass on that information to her superiors. How they might react was anyone's guess, but if the Raqilan of this time period were monitoring those communications, then someone aware of the weapon ship's construction might well be taking action at this moment to protect its secrets.

Picard had been forced to conclude that while such matters likely would be discussed for years once this incident was concluded—regardless of the outcome—such debate and analysis would be put forth by minds far better than that of a simple starship captain. For now, more pressing concerns demanded his attention. The damage had already been done with respect to whatever might be the normal course for the Golvonek and the Raqilan from this point forward, and the only options now left to him involved mitigating that damage and safeguarding his ship and crew.

"We will find a means to reach a mutual understanding," Picard said. The words did not quite sound hollow to his ears, but he could not deny the doubt beginning to manifest itself within. "Fleet Legate Mynlara has told me that your leaders are attempting to forge a peaceful, diplomatic solution. It's obvious that both sides want to end this war. While we cannot ally ourselves against one of your worlds, we can help you to end the hostilities. Help me to do that, Jodis."

The Raqilan replied with another small laugh. "During our training, there were those who put forth the idea that history cannot be changed, that our fates are sealed." He gestured around the room. "If that is true, then will all of this not happen again?"

"If you really believed that," Picard countered, "would

you have accepted command of this vessel and the mission you were given?" Was he sensing some narrow sliver of common ground forming between them?

Jodis smiled. "You are a wise man, Captain. Perhaps there is hope, for all of us."

20

Text on the computer screen was beginning to blur together. Her eyes ached from fatigue, and it required physical effort to keep her head from falling onto her desk. How long had she been sitting here, staring at what was supposed to be her latest status report for her superiors at Directorate Command? Mynlara did not want to look at the chronometer, afraid to see just how little of her scheduled sleep cycle remained before she was to report for her next duty shift.

Command has its rewards, she reminded herself, *but also its price.*

It was not the reports themselves that were tiring, or even time-consuming. As it happened, senior officers within the command hierarchy of the Protective Directorate had neither the time nor the inclination to become mired in missives of great length or specificity. Instead, they tended to delegate the consumption and summarization of lengthier narratives to luckless subordinates. Conversely, those same leaders demanded frequent updates to remain informed about the activities of their field commanders. Therefore, while the substance of the reports she submitted might have decreased as her career progressed, the sheer number of them had proliferated to the point that it seemed Mynlara's every waking moment was devoted to their composition and transmission.

Every waking moment, her exhausted mind repeated

as she pushed herself away from her desk, *and many of the other moments, as well.*

Crossing to the table that served as the dining area in her private quarters aboard the *Calkurizar*, Mynlara refreshed her stein from the decanter of herbal brew provided earlier in the evening by her aide. Though the drink was no longer hot, it still retained much of its flavor. Mustering the energy to return to her desk, she paused to increase the room's lighting. When she had started her work, Mynlara thought the reduced illumination would allow her to relax after the events of the day, but the effect was proving detrimental, as evidenced by her increasing inability to remain focused on the tasks before her. Sleep would provide the restorative result she needed, but for now that was an option that must remain tantalizingly out of reach. As she sipped from the stein, Mynlara sighed while purposely looking away from her bed in the room's far corner, as she knew it would remain empty for some time yet.

She had not made it back to her desk when the shrill chirp of the door alert echoed across the room. Glancing in that direction, she saw the indicator light above the entrance glowing pale orange, signifying the presence of a visitor outside her quarters. Who would be calling on her during her scheduled sleep shift? If there was an emergency or other matter demanding her attention, the duty officer on the *Calkurizar*'s command deck would have contacted her directly through the communications system. So, what was this? With a grunt of minor irritation, Mynlara reached for the intercom control on her desk. The small screen embedded into the panel showed her a visual feed from outside the door, revealing the image of Foctine Vedapir.

Without replying, Mynlara pressed another control and her door opened to admit her second-in-command. As was almost always the case, he and his uniform appeared ready for a formal inspection, despite his having to work for several *linmertu* after the end of his scheduled duty shift. He had not even removed his sidearm, and she knew from experience that were she to inspect the weapon, it would be as immaculate in appearance and function as its wielder.

"You wished to see me, Fleet Legate," he said, pausing just inside the doorway. For the briefest of moments, his eyes shifted to look toward her bed, and Mynlara saw the slight change in his expression. There was a small intake of breath, and she worried if he had come to her quarters with an agenda of his own. Despite his exemplary career, the one potential obstacle to Vedapir's advancement was his occasional misstep with respect to separating professional and personal relationships. Mynlara had almost fallen prey to his charms before rebuffing his overtures and making it clear to him that, since he was her subordinate, a romantic liaison with him was out of the question. To his credit, Vedapir had conducted himself in proper fashion since that incident, with both agreeing to mark it as a shared, passing error in judgment. Thankfully, his fleeting distraction seemed to fade before he returned to her his full attention.

"I am completing my latest status report for Directorate Command," Mynlara said. "You have to wonder what our superiors are thinking. To say that we are dealing with events that are unprecedented seems to be minimizing their significance." Meeting representatives from not one but many civilizations hailing from worlds orbiting distant stars, was nothing short of exhilarating. Despite her best efforts, Mynlara had been unable to keep much of her excitement out of the official report she had already transmitted. At first, she was concerned that her superiors might not believe her account, but the images and scan data she had included with her statement should be more than enough to convince the senior leadership that today had borne witness to a momentous, historic occasion.

"Have you received a reply from Directorate Command?" Vedapir asked.

Mynlara nodded as she directed him to the chair situated next to her desk. "Yes. Naturally, they are very troubled by my report." She had dispatched her initial account soon after her first formal meeting with the human captain and the Raqilan discovered in cryogenic suspension. Balancing the need to observe her orders and duty with respect to the Raqilan battleship and its crew along with the necessity of interacting with Picard was proving quite the challenge. She was struggling against being overwhelmed by the dual pressures, and the guidance she had received from her superiors back on Uphrel had only added to her burden.

After settling into her proffered seat, Vedapir said, "There is much to consider. That the Raqilan have constructed a vessel of such power is troubling enough, but couple that with our first meeting with another interstellar power? The potential for the war to shift against us to the point that victory will be forever out of our reach?" He shook his head. "I would be dishonest if I said that such thoughts did not fill me with great dread."

As she studied her still-warm cup of herbal brew, Mynlara considered and understood the foctine's anxiety. There were aspects of their current situation that unsettled her, as well. "The weapon ship certainly represents a grave threat to our security. If the Raqilan are capable of attacking us from the future, then I fear the war is already lost. Why confront us directly when they can simply circumvent history itself?"

"You do not believe this fantasy Jodis communicated to us?" asked Vedapir, making no attempt to conceal his disdain. "Traveling through time is fodder for children's stories."

Sighing, Mynlara placed her cup on the desk. "Yesterday, I would have agreed with you, but Captain Picard has told me that they are able to verify Jodis's claims. Also, you must admit that the technology we observed aboard the ship is far more advanced than anything we know the Raqilan to employ." She had studied several examples of the systems and equipment harbored aboard the *Poklori gil dara*, and there was no denying that much of what she had seen bore only slight resemblance to technology she knew the Raqilan possessed. The computer interfaces were of particular note, linked as they were to what could only be a sophisticated information management apparatus of far greater ability than anything she had ever seen. As for Picard, the captain had offered to make available evidence collected by his crew which would validate the admittedly odd notion that the vessel had come from the future, at a point in which her people were still at war with the Raqilan, and both worlds had borne the brunt of generations of unremitting conflict.

The idea that hostilities would continue beyond her own projected lifespan and do lasting if not irreversible damage to her planet and those still living upon it threatened to make Mynlara ill. Did it mean the peace negotiations currently under way would prove futile? She presumed there would be further discussions as cycles passed, until one or both sides finally decided that there would never be peace, and all energy and focus would instead be directed toward victory and one civilization's total vanquishing of the other.

Vedapir asked, "Even if such a feat were possible, what would be their ultimate objective?" He gestured toward the wall of Mynlara's quarters and in the general direction of the *Poklori gil dara.* "Destroying Uphrel makes no sense, as the planet itself even now is resource rich. If what Jodis said is true, and they originally traveled back in time to a point before the war began, then such an attack would be further steeped in madness."

"I agree," Mynlara replied. "The very idea seems ridiculous." Though Jodis had not revealed the details of his mission, such an action would not be consistent with Raqilan strategy, which included among its many hallmarks consistency, patience, and efficiency with a pronounced emphasis on avoiding waste of personnel or resources. From the large, more common campaigns waged ship to ship in the void separating their homeworlds to the occasional skirmishes that took place on the system's other planets and moons as each side vied for territory and resources, the Raqilan military prided itself on how it expended such assets in proportion to the objectives achieved. Every weapon, every foot soldier, every last piece of equipment was utilized to its maximum potential for maximum gain, and not simply cast as fodder into the heat of battle.

"What would be the point of obliterating Uphrel," she said, "and particularly doing so at a point a hundred cycles in our past? If that truly was Jodis's mission as a means of somehow preventing the war, then why not travel even further back, to a time before we had settled there?" Even then the idea seemed ridiculous, so what was the Raqilan objective here? The only thing that seemed at all plausible to Mynlara was that the *Poklori gil dara* was meant to be the ultimate deterrent. Had it been sent back to a point before the war's onset? Was it a warning to the Golvonek and possibly also the Raqilan that the conflict in which they soon would embroil themselves would result in the eventual, tragic devastation of two entire worlds? Was it possible that the Raqilan would, in cycles to come, decide that their decision to incite the war was a dreadful mistake to be undone and perhaps even prevented by any means available?

If that were true, then there might be hope for us all. Somehow.

"The only way to know for certain," Vedapir said, "is to interrogate Jodis and his crew, though I suspect getting them to divulge any useful information will take considerable time." Then, his voice lowering, he added, "Assuming the proper conventions are observed, of course."

He did not need to elaborate for Mynlara to understand his veiled reference. Among the many agreements to which Golvonek and Raqilan leaders had agreed to with respect to the conduct of war were several pacts regarding the treatment of prisoners. Indeed, the rules had raised no small amount of cynical commentary among the military ranks, in that diplomats seemed able to agree on anything that prolonged the conflict, but nothing that might bring about its end. Both sides had pledged that the handing of prisoners as well as other noncombatants and civilians always would be carried out with utmost dignity and benevolence. For the most part, those guidelines had been observed, with violators punished in accordance with the penalties established for such behavior.

"You and I have discussed this before," Mynlara said. "There is no place for anything other than the 'proper conventions.' Even after everything that has happened, the Raqilan understand that, as well." Mynlara supported the prisoner accords, believing that such acts of consensus communicated a deeper desire to seek the ultimate, peaceful end to the war, even if both sides seemed incapable of finding further common ground. Though she carried out her duties and obeyed her superiors in keeping with her oath as an officer, there were occasions when she found herself outraged at the apparent unwillingness of military and civilian leadership to reach a final, lasting peace between the two worlds.

Vedapir clasped his hands and rested them in his lap. "Still, we now face most unusual circumstances."

"If we abandon our principles at the first sign of adversity," Mynlara countered, "then they are not principles worth upholding. That would seem especially so now, given that we have been contacted by beings from other worlds."

"About that," Vedapir said. "What are you going to do about the newcomers? Do you believe their captain can be trusted?"

It was a fair question, Mynlara knew, and one she would expect him to ask. "He has presented himself as one deserving of such trust. Our probes of their vessel tell us that if he had wanted to destroy our ships, he could have done so with little effort."

"But will he ally himself with us, or the Raqilan?" Vedapir asked. Before she could answer, he held up a hand. "I know that he has said his people are prohibited from interfering with the affairs of worlds that are not their own, but they are here, are they not?" Again, he gestured toward the wall and the direction of the *Poklori gil dara*. "They have already rendered aid to the Raqilan. What more can we expect from them?"

Mynlara replied, "They assisted Jodis and his crew before understanding our conflict. Picard understands at least some of the complexities of our conflict, and I see in his eyes the struggle he wages within himself as he attempts to avoid taking sides." She had only her observations and interaction with Picard to guide her, but her instincts told her that the human was a man of principles and integrity. His request to address leaders of both Uphrel and Henlona only served to strengthen her feelings of trust for him.

"I can appreciate the strain you must be under," Vedapir said. "You are here, far away from our home, forced to make judgments and decisions without guidance from higher authority. There are any number of questions and decisions weighing on you, and it would be difficult to find fault with how you have comported yourself throughout this affair. However, I would be remiss in my duty if I did not ask whether you have considered a strategy for taking control of the Federation ship, should circumstances require us to do so."

"That is why you are here," replied Mynlara as she shifted in her seat. "You are not the only one who has considered such a course of action. With so much at stake we cannot afford to leave anything to chance." She wanted to believe that Picard would keep to his word and not interfere with Golvonek military affairs or her attempts to secure the weapon ship, but what if his stance changed? What if he decided to return the vessel to the Raqilan? "If we do not control the weapon ship, then it must be destroyed, or else we risk it being turned against us as was its original intent. If only we could know for certain."

Vedapir leaned back. "These are trying times, after all."

Pushing herself from her chair, Mynlara began pacing the width of her quarters. "Trying times. How often has that term been used to justify actions we know to be regrettable, if not reprehensible?" Despite the Golvonek having fought a largely defensive war throughout the generations, there had been occasions when bold, aggressive, and lamentable action was taken to thwart Raqilan attacks or other plots that might have resulted in devastating loss of life. Mynlara had undertaken such deeds more than once. They had been necessary, she knew, but that knowledge had done little to ease her remorse at what war had forced her to do, and the memories of those acts would haunt her for the rest of her life. For that more than any other reason and like so many other Golvonek and Raqilan, as well, Mynlara wanted peace for both worlds. If Jodis was being truthful about the future that awaited them, then to desire otherwise was to invite eventual extinction.

"Picard has said or done nothing to indicate he might turn against us. Also, have you considered that their presence here might be a good thing for all of us? He has said he is willing to speak to our leadership. If he could bring both sides together, he might just be the impetus needed to rededicate ourselves to the peace process." After a lifetime in service to her planet and the war, the very notion of it no longer permeating every aspect of her people's very existence seemed as much fantasy as the idea of a massive weapon from the future traveling through time to erase her world from history itself.

"What has the leadership said?" Vedapir asked.

Mynlara sighed. "Directorate Command has expressed concerns about the outsiders, and they want both the *Poklori gil dara* and the *Enterprise* secured. I have received orders to see to this as soon as possible. The weapon ship is a deterrent, no matter who controls it. As we speak, reinforcements are on their way from Uphrel. Once they arrive, we will take full control of the weapon ship, and use it to commandeer the *Enterprise*."

Saying nothing for a brief interval, Vedapir seemed to be studying her. Then he said, "I believe this to be a wise course of action. As you have already stated, there is far too much at stake for us not to act to protect our people."

During his time aboard the *Calkurizar*, Vedapir had distinguished himself as an officer capable of handling any task or decision he faced, and Mynlara had come to rely on him as her most trusted confidant. Principled and driven, he had never been afraid to express a viewpoint even if it meant disagreeing with her. Though he observed all military protocol in the presence of subordinates, he long ago had earned the right to speak in blunt fashion whenever they conversed in private, where he had no reservations about arguing with her if circumstances demanded it. This direct, honest manner had been one of the qualities she respected in him, more so because when such conversations did occur, more often than not he succeeded in convincing her that his position was the correct one. He would, in her estimation, make a fine fleet legate when his time came for promotion, and she had made notations to that effect in several of his evaluations.

After another pause, Vedapir said, "You seem uncomfortable with these orders."

"My comfort is of no consequence," Mynlara snapped. "I will carry out my orders, but that does not mean I support what I have been directed to do. Picard has extended the hand of friendship, and we will smack it away in a clumsy attempt to plunder his ship and its finite resources. Is that what we have become? Bandits and looters?" Staring at the door leading from her quarters, she shook her head. "No. That is not who or what we are."

You have no choice, she reminded herself. Duty demanded nothing less.

These are trying times, after all.

21

Worf's first impression of the room in which he and Lieutenant Elfiki stood was that the air was stale. He was certain he could taste the metallic tinge permeating what likely was an atmosphere subjected to uncounted iterations of recycling and scrubbing of pollutants. How long had the environmental systems of this station been in operation? Years, perhaps decades, he thought.

"They didn't exactly roll out the red carpet for us, did they?" asked Elfiki.

Worf replied, "I suspect they do not receive many visitors." Escorted by the Raqilan fighters, he and Elfiki had piloted the *Siouxsie* back to the moon that was home to the weapon ship's construction site. They had guided the shuttlecraft to a larger installation that sensors showed to have been built on the lunar surface as well as extending underground and into a nearby mountain range. The landing pad on which they had come to rest had descended into a subterranean hangar, where the Starfleet officers were met by a team of Raqilan soldiers wearing equipment harnesses and helmets and wielding formidable-looking rifles. Under guard, Worf and Elfiki were taken deeper into the complex, where they were searched before being deposited in this bare, uninviting room. Throughout the process, the soldiers had treated their charges with respect if not outright courtesy, though the looks on their faces told Worf that they likely were operating under strict orders regarding the handling of their new prisoners.

"This place reminds me of one those remote observation outposts along the Neutral Zone," Elfiki said. "All tunnels and narrow passageways carved into the rock." Worf saw her rub her upper arms as though warding off a chill. "I never liked those places."

Recalling from her personnel record that the science officer had served on such an outpost as an early assignment following her graduation from Starfleet Academy, Worf said, "My understanding is that you requested a posting to one of those stations."

Elfiki nodded. "I thought it would be a way to get an interesting perspective on the real state of relations between the Federation and the Romulans. It was after the Dominion War, but before that business with Shinzon. Still, our alliance had pretty much run its course by then, and the situation seemed like it was changing every day. At one point, I was sure a fleet of warbirds would run right over us, but the diplomats always found a way to keep things from escalating." Looking around the room in which they had been deposited, she added, "Of course, after being stuck inside an oversized tin can for months on end, there were times when an attack might've been welcome. Still, so much of our joint history is tied to that buffer between us. Some of those outposts have been there for two hundred years." She made a show of sniffing the air. "This place smells about the same, now that I think about it."

They had been standing alone in the dingy room for the past several minutes, and Worf had detected no signs of surveillance. The only possibilities came from what looked to be a ventilation grate in the ceiling and what appeared to be a communications grille embedded in the wall near the room's only entrance. There were no visible controls on the unit, and the room itself was devoid of furniture or any other items that one might use as a weapon. Worf and Elfiki had been relieved of their phasers, and their hosts also had taken the Klingon's baldric. The first officer took momentary comfort from the look on the Raqilan guard's face upon being told that any mistreatment of the cherished vestment would result in Worf becoming, as he had put it, "irritated." Conversely, both officers had been allowed to keep their combadges when the Raqilan guard in charge of their escort detail and search realized that the devices also functioned as translators. Beguiled by this wondrous technology, the guard had run off to tell his superiors that they would be able to speak directly with the "outsiders."

After a few moments spent in silent investigation of the room, Elfiki had made her way to the door when she took an abrupt step back from the entrance. "Commander, someone's coming." Worf also heard muffled footfalls on the metal deck plating of the corridor outside the room, and he moved to stand alongside the science officer. When the door opened, it was to reveal two Raqilan sentries, both males—so far as Worf could discern under their helmets and body armor—and each carrying an imposing-looking rifle of the sort he had seen carried by other soldiers during their capture. The guards stepped through the doorway and assumed flanking positions to either side of the entrance, leaving it clear to admit another Raqilan. This one, also a male, was dressed in a more formal uniform that to Worf suggested an officer. A charcoal gray ensemble, it was highlighted by a single silver stripe running down each sleeve from shoulder to cuff, and an assortment of multicolored diamonds adorned his chest, just below his high, stiff collar. The uniform's dull color served to highlight its wearer's lavender skin. Despite what Worf guessed to be a significant effort on his part to maintain his composure, the Raqilan's eyes betrayed his surprise upon getting his first look at the strange beings standing before him.

"Remarkable," said the new arrival, nodding in open appreciation. "I am Sasel Pitrotha, commander of this facility. I must confess that I did not at first believe the reports relayed to me upon your capture, but there can be no denying that you most certainly are not Golvonek, or Raqilan, for that matter."

Recognizing Pitrotha's title from the briefing provided by T'Ryssa Chen regarding Raqilan military rank structure and remembering that "sasel" was an approximate counterpart to a Starfleet captain, Worf offered a formal bow of his head. "I am Commander Worf, first officer of the Federation *Starship Enterprise*." He gestured to Elfiki. "This is Lieutenant Elfiki, my science officer. I wish to apologize once again for firing on your vessels, sir. I assure you that it was in self-defense, and we regret any damage or injury our actions may have caused."

Pitrotha actually shrugged. "Your reaction to attack was understandable. I would have expected nothing less from anyone else in your position."

Something about the way the reply was phrased gave Worf momentary pause. He had spent enough time battling diplomats—literally and figuratively—to recognize the beginnings of a verbal trap when he heard one. It was obvious to him that Pitrotha had entered the room with his mind made up so far as whatever fate awaited Worf and Elfiki, and now he was spending a few minutes playing with his prisoners, likely for his own amusement.

"We are new to this region of space," said the Klingon,

deciding to see where an attempt at dialogue might lead. "We represent an interplanetary cooperative of many worlds and civilizations comprising many billions of diverse beings, who have joined together for the betterment of all our members. Our mission is to make contact with other advanced societies and hopefully establish peaceful relations and perhaps even alliances."

Pitrotha nodded. "Yes, and yet we find you trespassing in our space, spying on our installations. Is this how your people extend the hand of friendship?"

"We weren't spying," Elfiki snapped, then cleared her throat as Worf cast a warning glance in her direction. "It was not our intention to spy. Our scans detected the presence of life on this moon, and we came to investigate." Though she was telling the truth in the strictest sense, Worf knew that her statement, delivered in defense of Pitrotha's accusation, left several openings for someone keen enough to recognize and exploit them.

Pitrotha appeared to be such a person.

"Investigating signs of life?" he asked. "And when your scanners revealed to you the presence of such life on our moon, what did you do? Did you make any attempt at communication, in keeping with your mandate to form 'peaceful relations' with the 'advanced civilizations' you find during your 'investigation' of other people's sovereign territory?" He smiled, but it was not a pleasant expression. "No, of course you did not. Instead, you chose to turn and flee at the first sign of detection. These are not the actions of friends, or those who wish to be friends."

Clasping his hands behind his back, he began to walk around the room. Worf did not so much as move his eyes to track the Raqilan's movements, listening instead to the sounds of his boots on the deck as he paced behind the

Klingon and Elfiki. Even with the guards and their rifles trained on him, Worf felt his muscles tensing as he waited for Pitrotha to make what would be the fatal mistake of attacking him. Two seconds later, the officer moved back into his field of vision, his expression fixed and neutral.

"Your Federation sounds like an impressive collective, and it is obvious that your technology is extraordinary, as well. Our technicians have already set to inspecting your craft, and the early status reports are rather illuminating."

Worf had expected the *Siouxsie* to be subjected to such scrutiny, and Elfiki had taken the precaution of locking out and encrypting access to the shuttlecraft's onboard systems. He knew that those measures would not prevent Raqilan soldiers or engineers from boarding the shuttle or even cutting through the hull to inspect elements of the propulsion or weapons systems, but denying them the computer would at least hamper such efforts.

Lieutenant Elfiki, however, could not resist one small ploy.

"You might want to tell your technicians that I armed the shuttle's self-destruct mechanism prior to your taking us into custody. It'd be a damned shame if one of them accidentally triggered it."

When Pitrotha laughed, it echoed off the room's smooth metal bulkheads. "I admire your poise, outsider, though I suspect you are being less than truthful with me. Rest assured that my people are quite good at what they do, and I have every confidence that they will detect and disable any triggers or traps you may have left for them." He eyed Worf as he continued to pace. "I also find it hard to believe that you would destroy your most likely means of escape, which brings me to another point of discussion. Where is the rest of your clan? Where is the larger, more powerful vessel you must have at your disposal?"

Seeing no sense or advantage in lying about something he guessed Pitrotha already knew, Worf replied, "Our ship is holding station outside your solar system. We dispatched a distress message prior to our capture, and you can be certain our captain will not hesitate to launch a rescue mission."

"Yes," Pitrotha said, "one of our deep space tracking stations has identified the presence of your ships beyond our system's outer boundary. We are attempting to investigate further, but it appears Golvonek forces have gotten there first."

It took Worf an extra second to realize that the Raqilan officer had referred to more than just the *Enterprise*. Was he operating under the impression that the *Arrow* was an alien vessel, rather than the very ship undergoing construction elsewhere on this moon? If this was the case, then his small verbal gaffe had provided Worf with a valuable clue about the level of long-range scanning technology available to the Raqilan military. Of course, there was at this particular moment precious little he could do with that information. Schooling his features to show no outward reaction, he wondered without looking in her direction if Elfiki also had noted the slip.

When Worf said nothing, the Raqilan officer smiled again. "So, you now understand my dilemma, yes? Here you are, strangers, possessing what looks to be remarkable technology, and you apparently have allied yourselves with our sworn enemies. What am I to do here?"

"We haven't allied with anyone," Elfiki countered. "The Golvonek came out to us. It's not our fault they're more on the ball than you are." Pitrotha frowned at the unfamiliar expression, but the science officer did not elaborate.

Instead, Worf said, "She speaks the truth. We were first contacted by Golvonek vessels while still outside your system. I assume they somehow detected us with scanning technology similar to your own."

"You say you are not allies of the Golvonek," replied Pitrotha. When he stepped forward as though attempting to intimidate him, Worf very nearly lashed out just from reflex. Only force of will kept him rooted in place as his captor moved to stand just within arm's reach. "Does that mean you would consider joining with my people?"

Worf shook his head. "No. We are forbidden from taking sides in conflicts such as yours. My captain has relayed the same information to the Golvonek representatives who intercepted our ship. He has offered to appear before leaders of both worlds, if all parties agree that it assists in what I understand to be ongoing peace negotiations."

Again, Pitrotha laughed, starting to pace once more. "Those negotiations have been ongoing since I was a child. I suspect that the current iteration will yield results no better than previous attempts. However, like many who have served our people for the vast portion of our lives, we would welcome the announcement that our services were no longer required. I have children of my own, Commander, one of whom I have not seen since her birth. If your captain, or anyone else, can say or do something which might bring an end to our war, I and countless others welcome it." When his circuit of the room brought him once more face-to-face with Worf, he stopped, and the Klingon saw that his eyes seemed haunted by futility.

"Until that day comes," the Raqilan continued, "I

have my duty, which includes protecting my people from spies and saboteurs, and those who would assist spies and saboteurs."

For the first time, Worf raised his voice. "We have told you we were not spying, and neither were we intending sabotage. If your technicians are of any worth, they already will have discovered that the weapons aboard our shuttle were more than sufficient to inflict significant damage had we wished to do so." He leaned closer, though Pitrotha did not retreat. "And the weapons on our ship are far more powerful."

Whatever response Pitrotha might have offered was interrupted by the door behind him opening to admit another Raqilan soldier. Unlike the detail already standing post at the doorway, the new arrival did not carry a rifle but instead a sidearm in a holster along his left hip. In his hand was an oval-shaped metallic object that reminded Worf of a padd.

"Sasel Pitrotha," said the soldier, "I apologize for disturbing you, but we have received a new message from Central Operations, and we were instructed to inform you immediately."

Without replying, Pitrotha extended his hand and took the tablet from his subordinate, angling it so that Worf and Elfiki could not make out whatever was displayed on its surface. Worf watched the Raqilan's expression change as he reviewed whatever he had been given, and after a moment he looked up from the device and his gazed fixed on the Klingon.

"This is not possible." Turning to his subordinate, Pitrotha asked, "Is this verified?"

The soldier nodded. "Yes, Sasel. Central Operations reports that they examined the communications signals twice and verified our decoding procedures. They are already preparing to dispatch ships to that location."

"But how can this be?" Returning the tablet to the soldier, Pitrotha looked once more to Worf. "Why did you not tell me about . . . about the *other vessel?*"

"We assumed you were already aware of it," Worf replied, "just as you knew about our own ship."

Elfiki added, "We detected it drifting in open space and changed course to investigate. When we discovered survivors aboard, we attempted to render assistance. It was only then that the Golvonek found us. As you can imagine, they were pretty surprised to see the ship, too."

From his evident confusion, it was obvious to Worf that Pitrotha, as a mid- or lower-level officer in the Raqilan military and likely having no direct involvement with the *Arrow*'s construction, also had no knowledge of the real reason for its existence. For him, and perhaps most of the Raqilan living in the here and now, the massive vessel presented an anomaly.

"Prepare a proper holding cell for them," Pitrotha said after a moment, and there was no mistaking the uncertainty in his voice. "I will inform Central Operations and request instructions. I have no doubt they will want to speak with our guests." It was clear to Worf that the Raqilan had no idea what to make of the information he had been given, and now he was struggling to maintain his bearing in the presence of his prisoners. Pitrotha and the guards left and the door closed behind them, leaving Worf and Elfiki in the room, at which time Elfiki released an audible breath and shook her head.

"At least that wasn't weird, right?" Looking to Worf, she said, "Did you catch what he said about them not being able to confirm what their sensors were showing them?"

Worf nodded. "I did. The messenger also mentioned using message decoding protocols, which means they likely intercepted communications sent by Fleet Legate Mynlara."

"This situation is getting crazier by the minute, sir."

"I suspect that our value as prisoners has just increased," Worf replied. "Now that the Raqilan know about the *Enterprise* and the *Arrow*, there will be considerable effort to secure the weapon ship. If the Golvonek have learned its true purpose, then they likely will make every effort to prevent that from happening. We may quickly find ourselves in the middle of rapidly escalating hostilities."

Elfiki had been walking around the room, her hand brushing against the smooth surface of the dull metal bulkheads. "Where does that leave us, sir?"

Studying their surroundings, Worf grunted in irritation. "We must remain patient. Perhaps an opportunity for escape will present itself."

For now, they would wait.

Worf hated waiting.

22

"It feels like it's getting awfully crowded out there."

Picard nodded in agreement at Aneta Šmrhová's observation. "Indeed." He stood before the main viewscreen, watching the six Golvonek vessels as they moved into position around the *Arrow*. The image on the viewer had been shifted so that he now was able to see the entire length of the weapon ship, with the Golvonek cruisers maneuvering around it. The three smaller vessels commanded by Fleet Legate Mynlara, already in orbit around the *Arrow*, also were adjusting their positions to allow their larger counterparts to assume this new formation.

"I've scanned the new arrivals, sir," said Šmrhová, standing at the tactical station behind Picard. "From what I can tell, they don't have any sort of tractor beam systems, but I am reading what looks to be a series of grappling arms and magnetic couplers, deployed from the center of each vessel and overseen by a central control point." She shrugged. "They're sort of a cross between the old *Ptolemy*-class ships Starfleet used to use for towing space-based starbases or outpost stations and ancient tugboats used to guide larger sea vessels in and out of harbors and ports. That is, in the sense that it took several ships to maneuver something that big."

Sitting at the flight controller station, Lieutenant Joanna Faur gestured toward the viewscreen. "I think that qualifies."

"Right you are, Lieutenant." Studying the new, larger ships as they continued to settle into position around the *Arrow*, Picard noted that they did not look at all like combat ships, or even exploration vessels. Stout and utilitarian in design, their hulls were swathed in manipulator arms, maneuvering thrusters, and modules whose functions which escaped him, as well as control and observation ports which likely allowed crew members direct line of sight to any number of operations taking place outside the ship. These were ships meant for hard, demanding work, concerned more with function over form, and it was this distinct lack of refinement that in turn gave the vessels a sense of elegance Picard found intriguing.

"Are you detecting any indications that they may be launching transports?"

Behind him, Šmrhová replied, "No, sir, and none of the vessels are showing any active weapons. So far, everything seems to be in accordance with what Fleet Legate Mynlara told us."

"Maintain scans," Picard said, "and get an update from Lieutenant Chen. I want to know when she and the rest of the away team will be finished and on their way back."

The security chief nodded. "Aye, sir."

With Jodis and his colleague, Bnira, on hand to offer insight into the *Arrow*'s onboard systems, Picard had made the decision to detach Chen and other *Enterprise* personnel from the situation and allow Mynlara's people to take over. The two Raqilan were of course being coerced to assist their Golvonek captors, and while it was a situation that unsettled Picard, there was precious little he could do about it. Fleet Legate Mynlara had declared the *Arrow*'s revived crew as prisoners of war, at which time regulations and treaties between the two sides stipulated that such prisoners were obliged to obey all lawful orders put to them. While they could not—in theory—be compelled to participate in actions that might bring harm to their comrades, readying a captured vessel for safe transport to an enemy base seemed to fall within the parameters of compliance. On the other hand, the Raqilan also were obliged and expected to use any available means to attempt escape, which could include sabotage of the *Arrow* or its key systems. Therefore, Picard knew that Jodis and Bnira were at this moment operating under heavy guard. Meanwhile, the captain had ordered his ship and crew to detach themselves from the situation, and he remained hopeful that both Golvonek and Raqilan leaders would accept his offer of a joint meeting to discuss how the Federation might offer assistance to both sides and perhaps find a way to end the war.

Politics, he mused. *Didn't I come all this way to get away from that sort of thing?*

Turning from the viewscreen, Picard clasped his hands behind his back and began a slow circuit of the *Enterprise* bridge, proceeding past the port-side workstations until he was standing beside Šmrhová. Resting his right hand along the top edge of her tactical console, he asked in a low voice, "Have you had any luck with the sensor buoys?"

"No, sir," replied the lieutenant, frowning. "I've still got a lock on all four of them, and they've mapped about sixty percent of the moon's surface, including the *Arrow*'s construction site as well as where Commander Worf and Lieutenant Elfiki found the crashed planet killer. I've also found two installations of decent size, which look to comprise modules and structures both on the surface and belowground, but the moon's mineral composition is interfering with sensor scans for anything more than fifty meters or so below the surface. The readings show life-forms at both those locations, but things get more muddled the deeper we scan. If the away team's even on that moon, they're probably in one of the underground complexes."

Tapping his fingers on the tactical console's edge, Picard released a small sigh. "Damn." He glanced once more to the viewscreen and the *Arrow*, which now was surrounded by the Golvonek towing vessels. "Is your response team ready to go if the buoys report anything useful?"

Šmrhová replied. "Yes, sir. We've got a shuttle prepped in the main shuttlebay." She paused before adding, "With your permission, Captain, I'd like to lead the team when the time comes."

"No," Picard said. "With Commander Worf missing and Lieutenant Konya seeing to the away team over on the *Arrow*, I need you where you are." Noting the hint of disappointment in her eyes, he added, "I appreciate you wanting to lead from the front, Lieutenant. In fact, I'm tempted to lead the team myself, but part of being a leader is knowing your proper place. For us, that place is here." He offered a small smile. "Such are the burdens of command."

Drawing a deep breath, Šmrhová nodded. "I understand, sir." As Picard began to move away, she added, "I'm sorry, Captain. It's just that I've never been comfortable sending other people into harm's way while I coordinate or oversee them from a distance. I know it's supposed to be one of those things you eventually get used to, but I guess I'm just not there yet."

"That concern never goes away, Lieutenant," Picard

said, warming to the subject. Mentoring junior officers was one of the more rewarding aspects of command, and one he had always embraced. "At least, it shouldn't. It's a reminder that the people in your charge are not simply resources to be exploited or squandered. Let that concern guide you when you're required to send them into danger."

"Does it ever get easier?"

Picard shook his head. "Never, and nor should it. That, too, is a burden of command."

A series of beeps sounded from her console, and Šmrhová reached for the station and tapped several controls. "Long-range sensors are detecting the approach of several vessels, sir, outbound from System 3955. Eight in total, and they're not Golvonek, or at least they're not consistent with the Golvonek ships we've seen so far." She entered more commands and waited for the console to relay new information before adding, "They have to be Raqilan."

Turning in her seat, Faur asked, "Well, that wasn't entirely unexpected, was it?"

"I'm actually surprised it took them this long," replied Picard, moving away from the tactical station and toward his chair. "Open a hailing frequency, Lieutenant. We may as well get the preliminaries out of the way."

After several seconds, the security chief replied, "Captain, they're not responding to our hails. I can verify that they're receiving. They're just not answering." Without being asked, she adjusted the main viewscreen's image so that it now displayed what essentially was an armada of vessels, traveling in tight, precise formation.

Not liking the possibilities the image and Šmrhová's news conjured, Picard settled into his chair. "What else can you tell me about the ships?"

Šmrhová replied, "They're all armed with particle weapons, but like the Golvonek I'm only seeing heavy armor plating, rather than deflector shield generators. Those ships are made for fighting up close, sir. Their armor looks like it could withstand anything less than full phasers, and even then it'd have to be a sustained strike."

"Estimated time to arrival?" Picard asked. Leaning forward in his seat, he rubbed his chin as he studied the eight ships on the screen.

"At their current speed, just over sixteen minutes," said the security chief.

"Open a channel," Picard said, rising once more to his feet. "Attention, Raqilan vessels. This is Captain Jean-Luc Picard of the Federation *Starship Enterprise*. We have detected your approach and wish to open a dialogue with your leader. Our presence here is peaceful, and we have already rendered assistance to the ship we found drifting beyond your star system. We intend no aggressive action toward you or the Golvonek. Please respond." Waiting in silence for a moment, he turned to Šmrhová, who shook her head.

"No response, sir."

Picard frowned. "Send that at regular intervals, Lieutenant. If nothing else, we may annoy them into replying."

It's time to go home.

As it had at least a dozen times in the last half hour, the thought teased T'Ryssa Chen. Standing near the ramp leading into shuttlecraft *Jefferies*'s passenger and cargo section, she watched as transporter beams coalesced around six *Enterprise* away team members standing on the field-deployable transporter pad. The shimmering white energy beams enveloped the officers before fading from existence, leaving her standing alone in the *Arrow*'s massive landing bay.

Almost alone.

"Hey, you want to make yourself useful?"

Smiling at the familiar and quite welcome voice, Chen turned to see Tamala Harstad and Beverly Crusher, each carrying two equipment cases and flanked by Lieutenants Rennan Konya and Kirsten Cruzen as they crossed the landing bay toward her. The security officers also carried equipment satchels, having earlier returned their phaser rifles to the shuttlecraft's weapons locker in favor of the standard sidearms holstered on their hips.

"Is that all of it?" Chen asked, stepping away from the *Jefferies* and extending a hand so that she might relieve Harstad of one of her cases.

"We're it," she replied. "Everything and everyone else should be back on the *Enterprise* by now."

Having overseen the return of the away team and its equipment back to the ship, Chen nodded in agreement. The remainder of the engineering team that had been assisting the Golvonek boarding party with readying the *Arrow* for towing had already returned to the *Enterprise*, leaving just the five of them standing here in the docking bay. "All that's left is the transporter gear, and we can get out of here." With Konya and Cruzen to help her, the portable transporter pad and its support equipment could be broken down and stored aboard the shuttle in less than twenty minutes.

After notifying the *Enterprise* that she and her four companions were all who remained from the away teams and that they would be departing the *Arrow* within a half hour, and as the pair of security officers moved into the shuttlecraft to stow their gear, Chen looked to Crusher. "How are Jodis and Bnira?"

The doctor scowled. "Medically speaking, they're fine. There's nothing more I can do for them." She shook her head. "I can only imagine what they must be feeling, separated from loved ones and friends, and prisoners on top of that. We know from past experience that when someone goes through something like this, there's an acclimation period. The people we've encountered who've endured it have all handled it in different ways, but there's still an adjustment to their new life. Jodis and Bnira haven't had a chance to begin that process, and now this." Sighing, Crusher reached up to rub her forehead. "I just wish there was something more we could do."

"Maybe after all this settles down," said Chen, "and after the captain's had a chance to talk to the leaders from both sides, we can offer to help." Ascending the *Jefferies*'s ramp, she stacked the equipment case with the others. "It's a sure bet neither the Raqilan nor the Golvonek have any experience with this sort of thing." She knew enough about the effects of temporal displacement, as a consequence of either time travel or prolonged hibernation. In each of the cases she had studied—several of them having been encountered by various members of the *Enterprise* crew—the person who had undergone the ordeal had taken considerable time before finally coming to terms with living in another era. While most had settled into rewarding lives, a few had been far less accepting of their new reality.

"What were they supposed to do?" asked Cruzen as she emerged from the shuttle and stepped down the ramp. "I mean, from what we know, they weren't supposed to go back to their own time after they accomplished their mission, right? So, what then? Go back to Henlona and be hailed as heroes? How long do you think it would've taken the Raqilan to accept the truth of what Jodis and his people had done?"

Standing inside the shuttle's cargo area, Konya said, "I just want to know how they were supposed to live with themselves. Destroying an entire planet and its population? I don't care how well trained or indoctrinated you are. That takes a special kind of emotional detachment."

"More like insanity," Cruzen countered.

Chen said, "We have no idea what they went through as part of their preparation. For all we know, they were totally brainwashed." She grimaced at that unpleasant thought.

"It's possible," Crusher said, handing Konya the second of her equipment cases. "The only way to know for sure would be to conduct a full brain scan on them and see if we could detect any anomalies, but for that I'd need to run tests on another subject as a comparison."

Harstad snorted. "I guess we could fly to the Raqilan homeworld and ask?"

"Yeah, we'll get right on that." Chen was moving toward the portable transporter pad when movement from across the landing bay caught her attention and she looked up to see a number of Golvonek soldiers marching across the deck in their direction. Each of them—ten, she counted—wore helmets and equipment harnesses and were armed with the rifles she had seen members of the guard detail carrying. None of them, Chen decided, looked at all happy.

From where he still stood in the *Jefferies*'s open hatchway, Konya said in a soft voice, "Doctors." He gestured for Crusher and Harstad to join him, but by then one of the guards was motioning toward them with his weapon.

The rest of the group was beginning to fan out, forming a line as they approached the shuttlecraft.

"Aw, damn," Cruzen said. "What's this about?"

The answer to her question came when one of the Golvonek soldiers took aim and fired at them. A harsh crimson bolt of energy spat from his rifle and slammed into the shuttle's hull, sending Konya ducking into the craft and the rest of the away team scrambling for cover.

"Hey!" Chen shouted, dropping to one knee as her hand fumbled for the phaser on her hip. She had only just pulled the weapon from its holster and brought it up to aim toward the soldiers when another phaser report whined in her ears. Konya, crouching inside the *Jefferies*'s open hatch, had fired and his first shot caught one of the lead soldiers in his chest, sending the Golvonek slumping to the deck. To her left, Chen saw Cruzen, phaser also in hand, maneuvering around the shuttle's nose as another Golvonek rifle fired and a second energy bolt punched the *Jefferies*'s hull. Using her own phaser to provide covering fire, Crusher was pushing Harstad up the shuttle's ramp. Chen, realizing for the first time that she was the only member of the away team without protection or concealment, pushed herself to her feet and ran for the ramp. Another rifle blast chewed into the deck plating in front of her, halting her in her tracks.

"Put down your weapons!" someone barked, and Chen looked over her shoulder to see one of the Golvonek standing behind his companions and pointing in her direction. Also aimed at her were the rifles of five soldiers, who were walking shoulder to shoulder as they advanced on her. This, Chen decided, did not look good. At *all*.

"Lieutenant!" Konya shouted, drawing fire from two more soldiers for his effort. Ducking back into the shuttlecraft, he gestured toward Chen. "They're jamming our communications!" Anything else he might have said was drowned out by another rifle blast, this one catching the security officer and spinning him around as he fell back into the *Jefferies*.

"Rennan!" Chen shouted, but then caught sight of Harstad lunging across the shuttle's passenger compartment to where Konya had sprawled across several equipment cases.

"Put down your weapons!" the voice repeated, calling out across the open landing bay. "The warning will not be repeated!" When Chen looked in that direction, it was to see three of the soldiers training their rifles on her. Holding her hands up and away from her body, she allowed her phaser to drop from her right hand. It fell to the deck, clattering across the metal plating at her feet. She remained still as the soldiers closed the distance between them, each of them aiming their weapons at her head. Try as she might, Chen was unable to keep from looking at the muzzle of the closest rifle, which now was mere centimeters from her face.

"What the hell do you think you're doing?" she asked, making no effort to quell the anger and shock in her voice. From the corner of her eye, she could see Harstad kneeling over the very much unmoving form of Rennan Konya.

If he's . . . if they've . . . I will kill them all.

Walking up behind the trio of soldiers was the Golvonek Chen had spotted moments earlier, the one who appeared to be directing the movements of his colleagues. She recognized him as Fleet Legate Mynlara's second-in-command, Foctine Vedapir. The Golvonek carried himself with the self-assurance one would expect from someone who knew they were in complete control of the situation.

"From this moment forward," Vedapir said without greeting or preamble, "you will do precisely as you are instructed, or you will die."

23

Even before the Golvonek spoke, Jodis could sense his growing annoyance, though he did not care.

"How much longer?" the soldier asked from where he floated behind Jodis and Bnira at the entrance to the *Poklori gil dara*'s cockpit. His voice was tense, as though he was speaking through gritted teeth. That was understandable, Jodis thought, given the Golvonek's apparent age and probable lack of experience. His uniform insignia marked him as a tanzal, a low-level officer typically given responsibility for a moderate number of lower-ranking conscripted subordinates. He had not offered his name, and Jodis suspected that his assignments to this point likely had been the sort that had kept him from combat or indeed any form of direct engagement with the Raqilan, and this might well be his first encounter with an enemy prisoner.

Keeping his tone even and without looking up from his console, Jodis replied, "I am not certain. It has been some time since we last operated these controls, and there has been significant deterioration in various shipboard systems. It requires us to find alternative means of activating and coordinating certain processes." In truth, it seemed to him as though it were mere *linmertu* since he had last operated his station. Though he and his crew had been instructed to expect a degree of disorientation with respect to their individual perceptions of the passage of time, it still was an odd sensation for him to be here with the knowledge that he and the others had slept for more than sixty cycles.

As for the ship itself, Jodis was both surprised and impressed at how well it had functioned during its crew's prolonged hibernation.

Not in all respects, of course.

There had been some notable degradation in certain processes, the most tragic of which was the loss of six members of his crew. How or why he and Bnira had been spared the fate of their companions was a question that would not be answered without a thorough examination of the computer logs, though Jodis believed that neither he nor Bnira would ever get to conduct such an investigation. That did not concern him so much as denying that chance to those Golvonek military and civilian scientists who likely were anticipating the opportunity to tear apart the *Poklori gil dara* and harvest its many secrets.

"Foctine Vedapir ordered this task to be completed over a *linmert* ago," said the tanzal. "I suspect that if I report your lack of progress, he will believe you are acting in deliberate fashion to delay or hinder our preparations."

Jodis opted to turn in his seat so that he might face the soldier. He also noted the Golvonek's two companions, lower-ranking soldiers wearing helmets, who were maintaining station near the entrance to the tunnel connecting the control deck with the rest of the ship, each holding a rifle in one hand while using their other to hold themselves steady in the cockpit's null gravity environment. In fact, all three of them were struggling to keep from drifting around the cramped room while focusing their attention on their charges. It was the precise effect Jodis had wanted when he told their superior officer, Vedapir, that he and Bnira needed access to the control deck to carry out the necessary steps to ready the *Poklori gil dara* for towing to a Golvonek military base. Watching the soldiers and their clumsy movements, Jodis could not resist a small smile. "He might well be correct. Perhaps you should inform Fleet Legate Mynlara, instead, as it appears she has more patience than Vedapir."

The comment produced the expected and desired reaction, as the tanzal drew his sidearm and pointed it at Jodis.

"Why do you test me? Do you not value your life?"

Ignoring the weapon's muzzle looming in his vision, Jodis instead fixed his gaze on its wielder. "If your commander wanted us dead, we would already have been executed, and I will wager that she will be quite unhappy if you kill us before we complete our task." The weapon was close enough that Jodis was able to note its power level was set to a non-lethal selection, though at this proximity even the reduced effect could prove injurious or even fatal. Still, it was enough to confirm his suspicions regarding the tanzal's orders regarding his and Bnira's treatment, thereby granting him a bit of latitude.

He gestured around the cockpit. "Perhaps I am mistaken, but I do not believe you have yet had the opportunity to familiarize yourself with the operations of this vessel. If I am wrong, then feel free to shoot me and carry on in my stead. Otherwise, leave us to our work."

The tanzal scowled, and he pushed his weapon's muzzle farther forward, and for a brief moment, Jodis believed the young officer might well kill him. Then he pulled back the weapon, the rushed, jerky movement enough to push him off-balance in the gravity-free environment before he steadied himself with his other hand on a nearby console.

"Work quickly, Raqilan," he said, returning his side-arm to its holster. "My patience nears its end."

Instead of acknowledging the tanzal, Jodis turned to Bnira, who was seated in her usual place at the workstation above him and to his left. "The drive system should be enabled by this point." Automated systems overseen by the ship's computer had managed to effect repairs to the pulse drive, though Jodis had instructed Bnira to keep this information from their captors for as long as possible.

Without turning from her console, she nodded. "It is not at full power, but it will be sufficient to assist the tow ships." Her eyes met his and Jodis noted the fleeting look she gave him, acknowledging her role in their hastily improvised ruse.

It had been determined, either by Fleet Legate Mynlara or her second-in-command, Foctine Vedapir, that the six vessels dispatched to guide the *Poklori gil dara* to an as-yet-unidentified Golvonek military installation would by themselves prove insufficient for the task. Therefore, the weapon ship's own drive system was to be activated to assist with maneuvering it into the Canborek system and its ultimate destination. Jodis of course had refused to cooperate with this endeavor, but that largely was a pretense. In truth, he needed the ship's systems activated and operating at their best capacity if he was to put into motion the plan he was formulating, and he hoped that resisting Foctine Vedapir's demands would provide cover for his real intentions, at least for a short while.

After that, it would not matter.

"Transfer the computer to passive mode," Jodis said.

Bnira shifted in her seat before glancing down at him. "Acknowledged."

Looking over his shoulder to the tanzal, Jodis added,

"After all, it would be most unfortunate if the ship interpreted your vessels' presence as a threat and destroyed them. I might find the guilt stemming from such a tragedy too much to bear."

The Golvonek officer's eyes narrowed in mounting irritation, and his hand moved once more for his weapon though he did not draw it. "I do not find your commentary amusing."

"Assuming we both live through the day, I will endeavor to do better."

Bnira turned in her seat. "Jodis, the computer's passive mode has been activated."

"Excellent. Our work here is nearly completed." By design, the measure was reserved for situations where large-scale or broad-spectrum upgrades or repairs were to be made to the ship's onboard systems. To facilitate such tasks, the onboard computer and its extensive network of monitoring and oversight software needed to be removed from its normal autonomous operating mode so that engineers and technicians could have free rein to service individual systems or components without the computer's central operations core attempting to compensate for gaps in its network. According to the supposed experts who had trained Jodis and his crew in the maintenance of the computer and its peripheral hardware and software, attempting to carry out such extensive modifications to the existing framework without first disabling its self-governing protocols could—in extreme cases—be interpreted by the ship as sabotage. At the time, Jodis had considered such a design ridiculous in concept and execution, even allowing for the heightened security and secrecy surrounding the *Poklori gil dara*. Now, however, he had come to appreciate the odd foresight possessed by the vessel's creators.

"So," said the tanzal, "we are finished here?"

Disabling his lap restraints, Jodis pushed himself from his seat and twisted his body in the null gravity so that he faced the officer. "Nearly. A single task remains." He pointed to the console the Golvonek was using to maintain his position in the cockpit. "The weapons station must now be disabled, so that the defensive systems will not activate when your vessels maneuver into their final positions and latch onto our hull for towing."

The tanzal held up his hand. "Do you really expect me to allow you access to this vessel's weapons? Surely you do not consider me to be so dull-witted."

"It is not as if I can press a single button and destroy your ships," Jodis replied. "Even if that were possible, your vessels are certainly built to withstand a moderate level of punishment, are they not? Or, is propaganda the only thing the Golvonek military can produce with any quality?"

Again, his words had the anticipated effect, as the tanzal glared at him and pointed a finger at his chest. "You will tell me the proper controls and sequences, and I will deactivate the weapons, and if you are deceiving me, I will know, and I *will* kill you."

"Of course you will," Jodis said, noting as he spoke that the two soldiers positioned at the hatchway had renewed their interest in covering him with their rifles, though neither could hold their weapons with both hands, as they each needed one to steady themselves. "Very well, Tanzal. Follow my instructions precisely." He proceeded to direct the Golvonek through entering several command sequences to the console, each of which evoked a response from the station in the form of a blinking light or an indicator going dark. After entering the last command, the officer pointed to one status reading.

"This says the console is standing by for a commit instruction."

Jodis nodded. "Everything is now set." He pointed to a green control at the center of the console. "That is the execute control."

The tanzal pressed the indicated button, at which time a web of blue-white energy erupted from the console, wrapping itself around his arm and traveling upward to envelop the rest of his body. He shrieked in pain, jerking and twitching as the electrical shock coursed over him. The strike was over as quickly as it had begun, with the console shutting down in direct response to the deliberate overload Jodis had programmed for that station. Now freed, the tanzal shoved himself away from the station, his sudden, abrupt movement rolling his body into a spin. His feet struck the nearby bulkhead, pushing him back in the opposite reaction and into the guard who had lunged forward to render assistance. The soldier's inexperience with gravity-free maneuvering betrayed him, and he had to fumble for a handhold.

That was when Jodis struck.

Using the back of his chair as a platform, he launched himself forward, hands out ahead of him and balled into fists. His aim was true and he struck the tanzal in the face, sending the officer spinning backward until his head slammed into the bulkhead. Jodis's momentum carried him through the attack and into the soldier who had come to the tanzal's aid, and he lashed out with another fist. Experience and training allowed him to quickly arrest his movement in the null gravity and reorient himself thanks to a nearby handhold. In his peripheral vision, he saw the second guard scrambling to help, raising his rifle in search of a target. Before he could bring up his weapon, Bnira was on him, pushing down from her station and wedging him beneath the underside of a nearby console. Using one hand to steady herself on the workstation, she pummeled him with her other fist.

Another punch rendered the tanzal unconscious, and Jodis wasted no time retrieving the Golvonek's sidearm from its holster. Verifying the pistol's power setting, he aimed it at the nearer soldier and fired. The weapon's report was almost deafening in the cramped control deck as a bright bolt of energy struck the guard in his back, sending him tumbling across the cockpit. His rifle sailed from his hand and Bnira retrieved it, swinging it like a club and catching the remaining soldier across his face. The guard grunted in pain and blood spurted from his nose, discharging a cloud of globules around him. Jodis shot him with the pistol and his body spun in reaction from the impact before he crashed into the far bulkhead.

"You did not kill them?" Bnira asked, still spinning after clubbing the other soldier. Reaching for an adjacent console, she stabilized herself.

Jodis shook his head. "No." He held up the pistol. "It was set only to disable."

Her expression one of relief, Bnira reached up to wipe perspiration from her face. "We do not have much time."

"We will not require much," Jodis replied as he removed the tanzal's weapon belt and affixed it around his own waist. "I have already activated most of the key sequences." Returning the pistol to its holster, he pushed himself to his station and settled back into his seat. "Once I engage the final protocols, the computer will carry out the remaining instructions. After that, it will be too late for anyone to do anything."

Since his revival, he had given much thought to their original mission and the requirement or even desire to continue when it had become apparent that their objective was out of reach, separated by time from him and Bnira. The temporal displacement engine was beyond their ability to repair, which meant they were stranded in this time period, regardless of whatever other choices they might make. In the present, the war was already inflicting lasting damage to Uphrel and Henlona, with the Raqilan and Golvonek civilizations plunging headlong toward oblivion. Still, radical action might be sufficient to salvage the situation, and give both worlds a chance at healing and lasting peace.

Or, perhaps the threat would remain. As Picard had earlier intimated, completed and operational *Poklori gil dara*, even in its compromised state, presented a tempting prize to both sides, and the element of surprise Jodis and his crew would have enjoyed if the original mission had proceeded according to plan was gone. There would be no dramatic statement to announce the vessel's presence and scare all parties into seeking all means to end the war. Such a declaration was still possible, of course, even if a new means of delivery was required.

Regardless, Jodis had decided that now was the time for sending that message.

"You know they will try to stop us, Jodis," said Bnira. "They will have no choice."

Jodis nodded. "They can try, but they will fail."

Let us begin.

24

There were now entirely too many ships in this area of space, Picard decided.

Pacing a circle around the *Enterprise* bridge's perimeter stations, he studied the formation of Raqilan ships displayed on the main viewscreen. Eight vessels, each of them seemingly identical to one another while bearing only the slightest resemblance to the ships Fleet Legate Mynlara commanded. Unlike the Golvonek vessels that were wide and angular, these new arrivals appeared more utilitarian in design. Dual cylindrical hulls connected to squat, rectangular units with superstructures projecting atop and below the main sections. Picard noted the openings at the front of both cylinders and a multitude of components and other features mounted along each ship's center hull area. Something about their construction made him think the additional framework extending from the ships' main hulls might be components retrofitted to the vessels' original configuration. As with their Golvonek counterparts, the exterior of these ships featured dark hull plating and a distinct lack of external illumination. The ships, he concluded, were not at all attractive, but he supposed that they did not need to be, given their primary purpose.

"Sensors are picking up groups of smaller ships docked inside each of the vessels, Captain," reported Aneta Šmrhová from her tactical station. "Though the larger ships are carrying some impressive weapons, I think they must be carrier-type vessels, meant to deploy groups of smaller fighter craft."

Picard paused as he came abreast of the main viewscreen, his gaze fixed on the eight Raqilan craft. He expected them to break formation as they drew closer in an attempt to assert some sort of dominance over the Golvonek vessels already keeping station around the *Arrow*, but, to his surprise and relief, they remained on course and maintained their speed, offering no outward signs of aggression.

"Are their weapons armed?" he asked.

Šmrhová shook her head. "Nothing I can detect, sir."

Seated at the conn station, Lieutenant Joanna Faur said, "It's as if they're going out of their way to be nice."

"Not unreasonable," Picard replied. "After all, we have something they want and don't want the Golvonek to get their hands on, but whoever's commanding those ships likely has orders to be on their best behavior when communicating with us."

"I should know in a heartbeat if they try anything, and our own weapons should be enough to get us out of a jam, if necessary." The security chief gestured toward the viewscreen. "I'm not saying I'd want a long, drawn-out fight, but we should be able to smack their noses if we have to."

Picard allowed a small smile. "Agreed. Maintain yellow alert until further notice, but be ready with shields and weapons at my order." He hoped that the *Enterprise*'s presence would be enough to keep the commanders on both sides from taking any sort of undue action toward their counterparts, but he wanted to be ready in case the situation soured.

Turning from the viewscreen, he directed his attention to Faur at the conn station. "Lieutenant, lay in an evasive course away from the middle of this. If for some reason the Raqilan or Golvonek decided they're no longer interested in playing 'nice,' as you put it, I'm going to want some breathing room in very short order."

Faur nodded. "Aye, Captain."

An indicator tone sounded from Šmrhová's console, and she reported, "Captain, we're being hailed by one of the Raqilan ships."

Finally, Picard thought. "On screen, Lieutenant."

The image of the ships hovering around the *Arrow* was replaced by that of a Raqilan female standing at the center of a large control room. Unlike the military officers with their stark uniforms standing behind her or manning workstations in the background, she affected the air of a politician or other dignitary. Whereas the soldiers' expressions were all but unreadable, hers was warm and welcoming as she stood with her hands clasped before her. Still, Picard's instincts told him her smile was somewhat less than sincere.

Definitely a politician, he decided.

"Captain Jean-Luc Picard of the Starship Enterprise," she said, parroting his introduction from the message Lieutenant Šmrhová had been broadcasting since sensors had first detected the Raqilan ships, *"I am Envoy Dnovlat, representing the people of Henlona. It is my supreme honor to speak with you on this day on behalf of all Raqilan."*

Stepping toward the viewscreen, Picard replied, "The honor is mine, Envoy. I bring you greetings from the United Federation of Planets, with whom we hope your people will want to foster peaceful and mutually beneficial relations."

"*We are aware of your declared mission of peaceful explo-ration, Captain, and I must admit to being awed at the pros-pect of undertaking a task of such noble purpose. Of course, we also understand that you know of our ongoing conflict with the Golvonek people.*"

"Indeed we do," Picard replied. "As I've previously told the Golvonek's representative, it is not our desire or in-tention to interfere with your affairs, and we cannot take sides in your conflict. Our original mission called for us to determine whether making direct contact with either of your governments was appropriate." It was interesting to him that the Raqilan had admitted to knowing about the *Enterprise*'s mission and reason for being here. She had just confirmed that at least some of the communications between Fleet Legate Mynlara and her superiors had been monitored by Raqilan assets. What else had they learned?

"*I have been informed of this, as well,*" Dnovlat said. Her expression faded a bit and she stepped forward, her image growing in the viewscreen. "*In fact, I have heard it firsthand, from two of your most impressive representatives.*"

She motioned to someone out of view, and a moment later Picard was forced to withhold an audible sigh of relief as Commander Worf and Lieutenant Dina Elfiki walked into the frame.

"Mister Worf," he said. "Lieutenant Elfiki. It's good to see you both. I trust you're all right?" Both officers looked to be in excellent condition, with no visible signs of mis-treatment, though Picard suspected the shuttlecraft and their individual equipment were at this very moment ob-jects of intense scrutiny.

The Klingon nodded. "*Yes, Captain. We have been treated quite well.*"

"That's good to hear," Picard said. "Envoy Dnovlat,

I thank you for returning my people safely to me." He directed a brief glance to Lieutenant Šmrhová. "Number One, we'll see about getting you back aboard ship in short order, once we're finished here." Another glance to the security chief was rewarded with her giving him a brief nod, the silent communication enough to tell him that she had interpreted his comments as he had hoped, and now had transporter locks on Worf and Elfiki.

Moving so that she once more stood at the center of the viewscreen image, Dnovlat extended her hands toward Picard. *"As you have already suggested, Captain, we do still have matters to discuss. First and foremost, there is the fact that you and your crew have taken it upon yourselves to insinuate yourselves into our affairs."*

And there it is, Picard thought.

"If you are referring to the derelict vessel, Envoy, our discovering it was as unexpected as it was accidental, and when we detected signs of life aboard, we only investigated to render assistance."

"Yes, that," Dnovlat said, and to Picard it was obvious from her tone that she had been waiting for him to broach the topic of the *Arrow*. *"As you can imagine, this presents some problems for us. My advisors are most concerned at this breaching of security and trespassing. After all, the* Poklori gil dara *is a military vessel."*

Clasping his hands behind his back, Picard replied, "Envoy, I think we both know that the situation is not quite so simple. There are . . . variables . . . to be considered with respect to the ship, as well as the reasons for being where we found it, would you agree?"

"Certainly, but there is another matter: this business with the Golvonek taking ownership of the Poklori gil dara *as a seized military asset."* Dnovlat's expression hardened. *"Un-*

derstand, Captain, that we do not recognize their claim, and we intend to do everything in our power to see that the vessel does not remain in their hands."

Picard said, "This appears to be a matter which could benefit from mediation, Envoy. I have already been requested by the Golvonek to speak to leaders from both your worlds, and I would accept such an invitation if you or your superiors agreed to participate. It's my understanding that both sides seek an end to this conflict. Perhaps this is an opportunity to explore such a possibility, and I would be privileged to assist in any way I can."

From the tactical station, Šmrhová said, "Captain, we're being hailed by Fleet Legate Mynlara's ship."

"On screen, Lieutenant," Picard replied. "Split the image." If there was going to be any attempt at speaking to both parties, he figured now was as good a time as any to begin that process. He could only hope that Dnovlat and Mynlara would see things his way.

There's only one way to find out.

On the viewscreen, the display shifted so that Dnovlat occupied its left side, with its other half dominated by an image of Fleet Legate Mynlara.

"Captain," the Golvonek began without greetings or other preamble, *"we have been monitoring your communications with the Raqilan envoy."*

"Forgive me," said Dnovlat, *"but I am not in the habit of dealing directly with military officers, regardless of their station. Fleet Legate Mynlara, you are to remove all Golvonek from the* Poklori gil dara *at once, or we will be forced to view your actions as hostile."*

Stepping closer to the screen, Picard held up a hand. "Envoy Dnovlat, please. Let us not be too hasty."

"View our actions as hostile?" snapped Mynlara. *"Has that not been your way throughout this war? In your eyes, our very existence is a hostile action."*

The Raqilan emissary bristled. *"I will not be lectured to by an underling."*

"Envoy," Picard said, employing his firm, command voice. "Fleet Legate, this is getting us nowhere. Surely there is a way for the three of us to speak with one another in a civilized manner."

Mynlara held up a closed fist. *"My orders are clear, Captain. The Raqilan ship was a derelict, discovered in open space. We were here first, and we therefore claim it for the Golvonek. That it also carries a weapon capable of annihilating my people cannot be ignored, as we certainly cannot risk it being employed against us."*

Drawing a long, slow breath, Picard said, "Envoy Dnovlat, her concerns are valid. Given the threat the ship represents, perhaps this situation can spur renewed negotiations. I believe this is a unique opportunity to make significant strides toward the goal of lasting peace."

"There can be no negotiations so long as the Golvonek insist on stealing our property," Dnovlat replied.

Undeterred, Mynlara glowered out from the screen. *"And I cannot surrender what may well be the instrument of our obliteration."*

"Then I see no need for further discussion." Dnovlat pointed an accusatory finger toward the screen. *"Captain Picard, I regret that the historic occasion of our first meeting must be under such circumstances, but as you can plainly see, we are at an impasse. My ship commanders are under orders to secure or destroy the* Poklori gil dara *at all costs."* She motioned once more to someone Picard could not see, but then two Raqilan soldiers stepped into view, each

brandishing weapons as they moved to take up positions flanking Worf and Elfiki.

"Envoy, what are you doing?"

Dnovlat replied, *"I am ensuring your cooperation in this matter, Captain. I apologize for this action, but I cannot allow you to interfere with our mission."*

"And I cannot allow you to threaten my people." Picard waved a hand toward Šmrhová. "Now, Lieutenant."

"Aye, sir," replied the security chief, and Picard watched the viewscreen as columns of sparkling white energy showered Worf and Elfiki. It took just seconds for the transporter system to claim them, the officers disappearing before the eyes of Dnovlat, her soldiers, and everyone else on the screen before materializing at the front of the bridge.

"Welcome aboard, Number One," Picard said as the beams faded. "And you, Lieutenant."

From the viewscreen, Dnovlat's voice was almost a shout. *"How did you do that?"*

"We have a multitude of tools and technology at our disposal, Envoy. Now, I implore you to demonstrate restraint. Surely there is common ground to be found here. You may well be squandering a singular opportunity to bring your people and the Golvonek together."

"They have had generations to do so, Captain," Mynlara countered. *"It was they who started this war, and if they had wanted to end it, they could have at any time. Nothing will change. This monstrosity they have constructed only affirms their desire to conquer us once and for all. If you want the ship, Raqilan, you will have to fight for it."*

Dnovlat's eyes narrowed. *"So it shall be."*

"Captain!" Šmrhová called out. "Sensors are picking

up weapons activating on both sets of ships, and I'm detecting energy signatures from a significant number of the smaller craft stored aboard the Raqilan vessels."

"Raise shields," Picard ordered. To Dnovlat and Mynlara, he said, "I still have people aboard that ship, who are in the process of leaving." For that matter, where was the away team? Lieutenant Chen had reported their expected departure some time ago. Had it already been longer than a half hour since her last check-in? What was the delay? "I must now warn both of you that I *will not* tolerate any action taken against them."

"If you are unwilling to recognize our property rights, Captain," Dnovlat said, *"then my government may be forced to view you as colluding with our enemy. If your people are aboard that vessel, they will be treated as prisoners of war."*

"Envoy Dnovlat," Picard began, but it was too late, as the Raqilan diplomat had severed the communication, leaving only Mynlara staring out from the viewscreen. "Fleet Legate," he said, "there's still a chance to keep this situation from escalating."

The Golvonek's expression was almost one of resignation. *"I truly wish there was something else I could do, Captain, but the time for negotiation has passed. We have no choice but to defend ourselves."* She, too, ended the communication and her image vanished to be replaced by the *Arrow* and the Golvonek ships positioned around it.

"Sir," Šmrhová called out, "the Raqilan ships are launching their fighters."

"Go to red alert," Worf ordered, having wasted no time resuming his duties as he and Elfiki proceeded to their stations. "All weapons to ready status."

Turning from the viewscreen, Picard crossed to his

command chair. "Conn, move us away from the *Arrow*. And where the hell is the away team?"

"I've been attempting to contact them, sir," Šmrhová replied, "but I'm not getting any response. I'm not even able to tell if they're receiving my messages. There's some kind of disruption field emanating from inside the *Arrow*, but I can't pinpoint the source."

Picard settled into his seat. "Can you scan for their life signs?" The lack of communication was troubling. Had the away team run into trouble with the Golvonek detachment working to secure the *Arrow*? With the situation around the weapon ship deteriorating by the second, his options for regaining contact or even sending a rescue party after Beverly and the others were dwindling in rapid fashion.

"Already trying to do that," said the security chief, "but the ship's armor is still an issue with our sensors, even after our attempts to reconfigure." A moment later, she added, "The Golvonek tow vessels are moving away from the *Arrow*, and the other ships are maneuvering into a defensive formation."

"Bridge to engineering," Picard said. "Mister La Forge, we need more power to the sensors to scan for the away team on the *Arrow*."

Through the bridge's intercom system, the chief engineer replied, *"On it, Captain. I can't make any promises, though."*

On the viewscreen, Picard watched as the first wave of Raqilan fighters engaged one of the Golvonek tow ships. Streaks of red-white energy bolts, fired in groups of four or more, lanced across open space and slammed into the hull of the larger, lumbering vessel. Brief explosions erupted across the ship's surface as outer plating was breached and atmosphere lost even as its pilot attempted to move it out of the line of fire. Weapons placements along its length flared to life, spewing energy beams after its attackers.

"The fighters are too fast and maneuverable," said Worf from his seat to Picard's right.

"It appears so," the captain replied. "Conn, keep us out of the fray. Lieutenant Šmrhová, any luck locating the away team?"

"Negative, sir. The farther we get from the *Arrow*, the more muddied our scans become. If Commander La Forge can't find a workaround, the only way we may have to find them is to get closer." A moment later, she added, "A group of the fighters are changing course and maneuvering away from the fight. I think they're trying to intercept us."

"Unwise," Worf said.

On the screen, the image shifted to show six Raqilan fighters approaching. Traveling at first in a tight formation, the small vessels broke away from one another and began spreading their configuration in what Picard guessed was an enveloping maneuver designed to catch the *Enterprise* in a crossfire.

"Ready phasers," he ordered. "Target their propulsion and fire when ready."

Acknowledging the order, the lieutenant released a barrage of phaser strikes at the incoming ships. Two beams struck the closest vessel and its immediate reaction was to change course and maneuver out of the viewscreen's frame. Another of the ships released a barrage of weapons fire that flared against the *Enterprise*'s forward deflector shields as the fighter darted past. The other ships in the formation all changed course and began moving away.

"Shields are holding steady," Šmrhová reported. "The ship I hit is showing damage to its main propulsion systems and is on a course back to one of the Raqilan carrier ships. The other fighters are breaking off and returning to the main group."

Worf asked, "Were they testing us?"

"It would seem so," replied Picard, tapping his fingers on the arm of his chair. As he watched the battle—such as it was—unfolding on the viewscreen, he noted that both the Raqilan and Golvonek vessels were moving away from the immense weapon ship, likely in a bid to gain more maneuvering room, but it did give him an idea. "If we could get close enough, we could launch a shuttle over to the *Arrow*."

Looking up from the console next to his own chair, Worf said, "Captain, the portable transporter pad Commander La Forge set up aboard the *Arrow* is still online. I request permission to lead a team over there."

Šmrhová added, "The response team I had on standby for a mission to go after Commander Worf and Lieutenant Elfiki is still ready to go, sir."

"Good," Picard said. "Lieutenant Faur, plot an evasive course back to the *Arrow* that will get us within transporter range just long enough for the team to beam over. I'll want to be in and out of there as quickly as possible." Then, recalling his earlier conversation with the security chief, he added, "You will lead that team, Lieutenant Šmrhová. Make your preparations and be ready to transport once we're in position. Bring back our people." He looked to Worf. "I could use an experienced hand at tactical, Number One."

Though he looked at first as though he might protest the change in orders, the first officer's expression softened just enough to convey that he grasped Picard's implicit meaning. With the faintest hint of a smile breaking through his warrior's façade, Worf nodded. "Aye, sir."

Šmrhová stepped away from the console as he moved to relieve her. "Understood, Captain," she said. "And thank you."

"Be ready for anything," Picard said. "I suspect there will be at least a few people over there who aren't expecting guests."

25

"I told you to stay seated."

Beverly Crusher glared at the Golvonek soldier and the rifle he aimed at her, leveling the most severe expression she could muster.

"If you were going to kill me, you'd have done it already." She had to raise her voice to be heard over the steady thrum of the *Arrow*'s main power generators, which reverberated over every exposed surface throughout what Geordi La Forge earlier had told her was the giant ship's central engineering section. She hooked a thumb over her shoulder to where Lieutenant Rennan Konya sat on the deck. "He has a head injury and needs treatment I can't provide without my medical kit from the shuttle. If you don't let me help him, his symptoms will only get worse."

Though the Golvonek weapons had been set to stunning force during the brief, intense shootout in the landing bay, after being hit Konya had struck his head on one of the equipment containers stored inside the *Jefferies*. The Betazoid now sported a sizable gash in his forehead, which was deep enough to cause Crusher concern. His speech and movements also seemed to be somewhat slowed, leading her to believe that he was suffering from a concussion. She and Tamala Harstad had done their best to stop the wound's bleeding using pieces of material stripped from their uniforms, but Crusher knew that time was of the essence so far as treating whatever other damage may have been inflicted. For his part, Konya appeared to be holding his own, but bravado and physical stamina would only take the security officer so far before his condition worsened.

The Golvonek soldier, obviously young, inexperienced, and of low rank or position, seemed almost like a child wearing a parent's uniform, with his equipment harness and helmet seeming at least one size too large for his frame. He appeared to struggle with the dilemma Crusher had given him. He gestured toward her with the muzzle of his rifle. "Step back, and stay with your companions. I will seek instructions."

"Seek them quickly," Crusher admonished, holding her hands away from her body and stepping back from the soldier. Behind her, Konya sat next to Harstad on the deck, resting with their backs against the warm metal bulkhead. Lieutenant Kirsten Cruzen stood to Konya's right with her back against the same wall, arms folded across her chest. From the way the security officer's eyes moved, Crusher could tell she was continuing to study the engineering section—everything from equipment to consoles to storage lockers and the Golvonek soldiers scattered about the chamber—searching for any weakness or oversight she might exploit. She had remained silent since their arrival here, dividing her attention between her concern for Konya and finding some way to gain an upper hand against their captors.

"How are you feeling, Lieutenant?" Crusher asked, kneeling beside Konya.

His complexion pale and with sweat running down his face, he frowned and shrugged. "I've been better, Doctor." He reached up to touch the crude bandage Crusher had improvised from another section of material stripped from the blue uniform shirt under her tunic, and she noted how the area covering his wound was moist and dark.

"We're going to change that dressing in a minute," she said, nodding to Harstad, who began shrugging out of her own tunic to sacrifice a portion of her shirt's remaining sleeve.

"It's damned hot in here," said Harstad as she set to work.

Crusher nodded. "This is pretty much the belly of the beast." She glanced around the room, noting that its layout was exactly as La Forge had described it. Everything around them seemed designed and constructed around the *Arrow*'s primary particle cannon, the presence of which was denoted by the section of curved bulkhead running the length of the chamber and—she knew—continuing in both directions from end to end, drawing energy from the vessel's immense engines and channeling it through the array at its bow. The weapon was enormous, and even shielded as it was from view, its power was palpable. Though she had seen a visual record of the cannon's test against a moon, Crusher shuddered at the thought of what such a device might do to an inhabited planet. This, in turn, conjured thoughts of the immense planet killer machines from which the *Arrow*'s builders had drawn their inspiration. Such weapons served only one purpose: annihilation.

And where are we? Standing helpless in the heart of one.

"I'm telling you, I don't understand all of this!"

The shouted words drew Crusher's attention to where, across the chamber, Lieutenant T'Ryssa Chen was working at the main five-sided control tower occupying the center of the room, her every move tracked by the watchful eyes of another armed Golvonek soldier. Two more stood near the hatch leading out of the section, blocking that obvious avenue of possible escape.

"You will tell me what Jodis is doing," said the soldier confronting the engineer, gesturing with his rifle to the console. "My superiors demand a status update."

"Then tell them to come down here and look this over for themselves," countered Chen, waving toward the workstation. "I've only been studying this stuff for a couple of days. It'll take me months to figure it all out, and that's *without* you waving that thing in my face. So, why don't you cut me some slack here, okay?"

The soldier scowled. "You speak gibberish, like a child."

"And you sound like a Klingon with acute constipation." Chen threw up her hands in apparent exasperation. "What are we even doing down here, anyway? Don't you have Jodis and Bnira to help you do whatever it is you're trying to do? You know that when our captain finds out you've kidnapped us, he's not going to be very happy, right?"

The soldier grunted in growing irritation. "I do not care about your captain. If you cannot tell me what Jodis is doing, then you are of no further use to us."

"All right, all right." Shaking her head, Chen moved back to the console, and Crusher saw her cast another sidelong look at the guard as she did so. "I thought the Golvonek were supposed to be the civilized ones, oppressed and hounded by the mean old Raqilan who couldn't leave you well enough alone?" If the soldier replied, Crusher could not hear it.

"I know I was out of it for a while," Konya said in a low voice, "but what are we supposed to be doing down here, anyway?"

Cruzen replied, "They've got Jodis and Bnira up on the bridge, activating and configuring various onboard systems so that they can either tow the *Arrow* somewhere, or at least have it move under its own power while being escorted. Since they have no way of knowing what Jodis and Bnira are doing, they want Chen to watchdog whatever's happening topside."

"And I guess that's not working out as well as everybody hoped," said Harstad.

Grimacing as he shifted his body in an attempt to make himself more comfortable, Konya said, "I tried contacting the *Enterprise* when the shooting started, but they were jamming comm. Did anybody have better luck?"

"No," Crusher replied, glancing in the direction of the guard she had confronted and who was still watching them. His rifle's barrel pointed at the deck, but his attention remained focused on the away team. "But it won't be long before they realize we're overdue." Their phasers had of course been confiscated along with Crusher's and Harstad's tricorders by the Golvonek soldiers who had taken them into custody. Though the team had been allowed to keep their combadges for their translation abilities, contacting the *Enterprise* was not an option at the moment thanks to the Golvonek's continued disruption of all transmissions to and from the *Arrow*. "When we don't check in or respond when they call, or they figure our comms have been jammed, the captain will send someone to get us."

"The problem is that someone had to authorize these guys to hold us," said Konya. "If that someone is Mynlara, then she might be getting set to ambush the *Enterprise*." He looked around the room. "We need to find a way to warn them."

"Yeah," said Cruzen. "I've been thinking the same thing."

"Uh-oh." Konya smiled. "I know that tone. Somebody's going to get hurt."

Crusher eyed the security officers. "Don't you two go doing anything stupid."

"Never." Cruzen shifted her stance, lifting her left leg so that the bottom of her foot rested against the bulkhead. "I'm just waiting for the right opportunity to present itself."

Harstad asked, "What if the right opportunity never comes?"

"Then we'll have to make one up."

Footsteps behind her made Crusher turn to see one of the guards who had been standing watch near the hatch walking in their direction. He carried his rifle cradled in the crook of his right arm so that its barrel pointed at the floor ahead of him. With his free left hand, he pointed to Crusher.

"You. Come with me."

"Where?" asked the doctor.

Instead of replying, the soldier glared at her from beneath the lip of his helmet before pointing toward Chen. Crusher crossed the deck to where the lieutenant was hunched over one console, and she saw from the look on her face that while she was trying to remain composed, something was worrying her.

"T'Ryssa," she said as she moved to stand next to the younger woman. "What is it?"

Pointing to the adjacent stations, Chen replied, "There's so much happening at once I can't keep track of it all. I need some extra help." She directed Crusher to the adjacent workstation and the doctor spent several moments familiarizing herself with its various screens and indicators. With Chen guiding her, she was able to begin rattling off various readings, watching the controlled torrent of information scrolling across the different monitors.

"Something's happening," Chen said after another minute, her voice so low that Crusher almost missed it. "There's a lot of power being routed to the main engines; more than should be needed for a simple tow or escort." The lieutenant was silent for several seconds before moving between the two stations and when she looked up, Crusher saw the lieutenant cast a furtive glance in her guard's direction. When she spoke again, Crusher had to strain to hear her.

"He's also been directing power to weapons. He's doing a good job of hiding it, even from me, but I was watching it happen in real time. It's been pretty quiet for the past several minutes, but something's definitely not right here."

"What do you mean?" Crusher asked.

"There was a lot of activity early on, but now everything's holding steady, as though they were done up there, but I don't think so. I picked up a localized power surge a few minutes ago from one of the stations on the command deck, and since then all of the readings have been holding steady. Nothing new seems to be turning up, and I've been faking my answers to our friend with the gun."

"You're sure?"

Nodding, Chen replied, "I've been crawling around inside this system for the past couple of days. I have a pretty good handle on how it works. I'm just playing dumb for the guards. Trust me, something big is about to happen."

Crusher frowned, uncertain what any of this might mean. Was Jodis planning sabotage, and if so, for what purpose? With just himself and Bnira, he was grossly outnumbered even by the small force of Golvonek soldiers scattered across the *Arrow*.

"What are you doing?"

The soldier's barked question made her flinch, and Crusher turned to see him walking toward them, his rifle aimed in their direction.

"I asked you . . ."

The rest of the guard's sentence was lost amid the abrupt blaring of an alarm echoing through the chamber just as the room's illumination as well as every control station began flickering in rapid sequence. Each console emitting its own series of alert indicators only added to the escalating frenzy, and Crusher and Chen stepped back from their console as it too started flashing and whining.

"Is it supposed to do that?" Crusher shouted above the din. She felt a hand on her shoulder before she was pushed aside and the soldier guarding them grabbed a handful of Chen's uniform tunic and pulled her closer.

"What is happening?"

"I don't know!" replied the lieutenant. "It's some kind of power fluctuation. I don't know what caused it."

"You are lying!" the guard snapped, pushing Chen away and bringing up his rifle, but before he could aim it a ball of angry red energy slammed into his side, spinning him around and into the nearby console. Crusher and Chen both ducked toward the workstation, dropping to the deck as a second shot rang out above the alarms. Another crimson bolt zipped across the room, striking one of the soldiers near the door and throwing him against the bulkhead behind him. Searching for the source, Crusher turned to see Rennan Konya, kneeling next to Harstad and brandishing the rifle he had taken from the soldier lying prone on the deck before him. Konya fired the weapon again, chasing after the other soldier near the door, who had lunged for cover.

Scanning the area where the away team had been held, Crusher saw no sign of Cruzen. Where the hell had she gone?

Something red and hot drove into the console above her face and she cried out in shock, dropping to the floor and covering her head as sparks and what felt like bits of shrapnel peppered her uniform. From the corner of her eye, she saw the Golvonek soldier closing toward them at the same time she sensed Chen scrambling away from her, pushing herself to her feet and raising her hands. The guard shifted his aim, and Crusher saw the fear and hatred in the young Golvonek's eyes as he leveled his weapon at the lieutenant.

Then Kirsten Cruzen appeared from the shadows surrounding the central tower, dropping toward the deck behind the soldier and swinging her right leg. She caught the guard behind his knees, sweeping his legs out from under him and sending him crashing to the floor. Already moving, Cruzen rolled to her feet and kicked at her opponent's head just as he was trying to regain his footing. She caught the lip of his helmet and snapped back his head, and with an audible grunt of pain, the guard fell once more to the deck. When he tried to get up again, another shot from Konya dropped him for good. Wasting no time, Cruzen sprinted to retrieve the guard's fallen rifle. As though she had been handling such a weapon all her life, the security officer brought it to her shoulder and spun toward the exit, looking for the remaining Golvonek soldier.

"He's still in here!" Chen said, having returned to the central control tower. Her hands moved in rapid fashion over the console. "All of the doors are still sealed!" She pressed another set of controls and the alarms stopped, plunging the room into a sudden, merciful silence except for the omnipresent thrum of the *Arrow*'s engines.

"Rennan, sweep left," Cruzen called out. She moved away from Crusher and Chen, keeping her back to the curved bulkhead protecting this section of the *Arrow*'s primary weapon. Crusher watched Konya direct Harstad toward her and Chen before he moved to his left, with the two security officers implementing a rapid search of the immense room for their lone remaining adversary.

Konya, moving along the room's far side, suddenly turned and waved frantically in Harstad's direction. "Doctor!" he shouted, dropping his rifle and dashing across the open deck toward her. As he closed the distance between them, Crusher caught sight of something small and dark bouncing along the floor. Harstad saw it, too, and started running away just as Konya tackled her and pushed her down, sending them both sliding toward a nearby workstation.

"Get down!" Chen yelled, and Crusher felt the lieutenant grab her arm before yanking her toward the floor just as a white flash erupted in the middle of the room, accompanied by a deep resounding thump. She curled into a ball, closing her eyes to protect them against the flash, and over the sound of the blast, she heard bits of metal or some other substance spattering across the console above her head. When that faded, all that was left was someone crying out in pain, followed by more weapons fire from somewhere behind her.

"Doctor, are you all right?" she heard over the ringing in her ears, and she looked up to see Chen staring down at her and offering a hand.

Allowing the lieutenant to pull her to her feet, Crusher looked to where she had seen Harstad and Konya just before the explosion and gasped when her eyes fell on two prone figures lying on the far side of the central tower.

"No," Chen whispered, taking off across the deck toward them. "Rennan! Doctor Harstad!"

Crusher followed, only partly worried about another explosion or being shot by the remaining Golvonek soldier, but she ignored that thought as she focused on Harstad and Konya. Reaching them first, Chen knelt between them, and as Crusher drew closer she saw that they both were moving, albeit slowly, and there was blood on both of their uniforms.

"Check Konya," she heard Harstad say, and her pain was evident by the strain in her voice. Crusher noted the nasty gash on her right leg, which Chen was already attempting to treat. In contrast, Konya was in much worse shape. He lay on his side, his back covered with numerous bloody tears and cuts, confirming Crusher's guess that he had borne the brunt of the blast while protecting Harstad with his body. Though he was conscious, his reaction was little more than a series of moans and slurred words she could not understand.

"I need my kit from the shuttle," she snapped, unfastening her uniform tunic and removing her blue shirt so that she could press it against Konya's back. "He's already going into shock, and I have no idea how bad his injuries are." Once she had him lying on his side, she looked to Harstad as she closed her tunic. "How's she?"

Chen, her attention fixed on Konya, nevertheless was able to reply, "Some minor cuts, but I think she'll be okay. What about Rennan?"

"Working on it." Hearing footsteps, Crusher shifted around to see Cruzen jogging toward them and brandishing not one but two Golvonek rifles.

"I got the last one." Her eyes widened in surprise and worry as she caught sight of Konya and Harstad. "Oh, no."

"What was that explosion?" Crusher asked, dividing her attention between Cruzen and her patient. "Some kind of grenade?"

"Looks like it." Dropping to one knee beside Konya, Cruzen said, "It sprayed shrapnel, but the equipment took most of the damage."

Chen gestured toward the central tower, which now featured all manner of holes, tears, blown monitors, and darkened consoles. "If they hadn't gotten that thing between them and the blast, they'd probably be dead."

"We need to get them out of here," Cruzen said. "Back to the shuttle and the *Enterprise*."

Crusher shook her head. "I don't want to move him until I can check all of his injuries." She grunted in frustration. "I need my damned tricorder."

"I'll get it and whatever else you need from the shuttle," Cruzen said.

Chen said, "You can't go alone."

Holding up one of the rifles she had appropriated, Cruzen replied, "I've got company." She patted Konya on his shoulder. "I'll be right back," she said, more to him than anyone else. Rising to her feet, she nodded to Crusher. "Hang tight, Doctor."

After leaving the other rifle with Chen, the security officer jogged from the room on her way to the landing bay, leaving Crusher and the engineer to tend to their wounded crewmates. Using a portion of her own uniform shirt, Chen was able to dress Harstad's leg wound to Crusher's satisfaction. She then moved back to the central tower. The side opposite the blast had escaped damage, and that set of consoles was still functional.

"Damn that Jodis," said the lieutenant. "He's even smarter and sneakier than I thought."

"What?" Crusher asked, still tending to Konya, who continued to mumble incoherently under his breath.

"He's locked out the computer," replied Chen, "and brought the main drive up to full power. I'm also seeing that he's charged all of the ship's weapons." She paused, then turned from the console. "Including the main cannon."

"Are you serious?" Harstad said, and Crusher heard the weakness in her voice. Though she was not as badly wounded as Konya, she still was suffering disorientation from the grenade.

"Any idea what Jodis might be doing?" Crusher asked.

Chen shook her head. "Whatever it is, I think he's planning to make a lot of noise when he does it."

26

Of course the Golvonek had posted guards at the docking bay. Kirsten Cruzen would have been disappointed if they had not.

At the far end of a utility corridor that branched from the main passageways running the length of the *Arrow*, Cruzen hunkered near the bulkhead at the T-intersection and studied the scene at the walkway's far end. Two soldiers stood flanking the reinforced hatch leading to the weapon ship's landing bay. Each of them, like all of the other rank-and-file troops she had seen, wore helmets and equipment harnesses over dark uniforms. While both soldiers possessed pulse rifles like the one Cruzen had liberated on the engineering deck, only one carried his weapon in a manner that would allow him to bring it to bear in rapid fashion. His companion's rifle was propped against the bulkhead behind him while he worked to adjust something on his harness. The two of them were mumbling something, but it was soft enough and too far away for her combadge to render a translation.

Not that it really matters, Cruzen thought, *or that I care*. She had no chronometer, but she knew it had been nearly five minutes since she had left Doctor Crusher and the others in the *Arrow*'s engineering section. Though she was only trained as a field medic, she could tell from the extent of his injuries that Rennan Konya needed more attention than Crusher's medical kit could provide. His condition needed to be stabilized so that he could be transported back to the *Enterprise* for more extensive treatment, and that meant getting past the two soldiers at the far end of this hallway by any means necessary.

Verifying that the power level of her purloined rifle was fixed on a nonlethal setting, Cruzen rose from her crouch and lifted the weapon to her shoulder as she stepped into the corridor. At the passage's opposite end, the soldier still carrying his rifle only noticed her after she had already centered him in her sights and was pressing the firing stud. The weapon bucked against her shoulder as it belched forth a ball of roiling crimson energy, which zipped the length of the passageway and struck the Golvonek in his chest before he could make a move. The strike pushed him back against the bulkhead, and he was unconscious before he even began sliding to the floor.

"Don't!" Cruzen barked, shifting her rifle to cover the second soldier, who froze in the act of reaching for his weapon. It remained untouched, still leaning against the bulkhead as the Golvonek spread his arms and held them out to show that they were empty. As she approached him, she gestured for him to move away from his rifle.

"How did you escape?" he asked.

Cruzen frowned. "We were smarter than your friends. Now, you want to prove to me you're smarter than they are? Answer my questions and do what you're told." She nodded toward the hatch leading to the landing bay. "How many more of you are inside?" The soldier hesitated enough to tip her that he was hoping to deceive her, at which point she stepped forward and put her rifle's muzzle to his face. "Don't screw with me. My friend's hurt and needs medical attention, which means I have to get what I need from our shuttle. If he dies because you kept me here playing games, then I'm personally going to dropkick your ass out the nearest airlock. Do we understand each other?"

While it was obvious that not everything she said was clear to him, the soldier nevertheless seemed to grasp her overall meaning and had the good sense to nod rather than offer up any displays of misplaced bravado. Instead, his eyes shifted nervously between her and the hatch before he replied, "There are two guards."

"Tell me you're not lying to me," Cruzen said, her tone hardening, and she jabbed the rifle's muzzle forward an extra few centimeters to emphasize her point. "Make me believe there's not more than two, and that you're not hoping the other ones will catch me when I walk through that door."

The soldier shook his head. "I am not lying to you."

He then made the mistake of making a grab for her rifle.

Anticipating such a move all along, Cruzen was ready for the sudden attempt. The guard was fast—his right hand darting for the weapon's barrel—but she still managed to step backward, pulling the rifle away from his reach as his hand closed around nothing.

"Nice try," she said before she fired. The weapon's energy bolt punched the soldier and threw him against the bulkhead, and he sagged insensate to the floor. "Idiot."

After verifying that both soldiers were only unconscious, Cruzen removed the power cells from both of their rifles as she had taught herself to do after a hurried inspection of the weapon she had acquired down. She also relieved one of the soldiers of his sidearm, unzipping the top half of her black uniform tunic and tucking the weapon along her left side. Only when she was done searching the guards' uniforms for anything else of potential use did she notice the odd new device which had been installed over the hatch's control pad. The technology was at odds with everything else she had seen aboard the *Arrow*, and she surmised that it was some sort of lock-defeating mechanism installed by one of the Golvonek. It possessed a small display screen and a pair of oversized buttons, one of which was depressed. On a hunch, Cruzen pressed the other control, and as it engaged, its companion popped out before the hatch released a pneumatic hiss and began cycling open.

"Here we go," she said, raising the rifle in her hands and aiming it ahead of her as she stepped through the hatchway. The landing bay's interior appeared to be in much the same condition as when she had last seen it, with the notable exception of the Golvonek soldier who wasted no time shooting at her. Throwing herself toward a stack of cargo containers as the soldier fired, Cruzen rolled and winced in momentary pain as her shoulder struck the unyielding metal deck plating. She came up on one knee behind the closest of the containers and pulled up her rifle, searching for her attacker, who now also was moving for cover to her left. Cruzen heard him shout something before she detected movement to her right and saw a second Golvonek scrambling in response to her sudden arrival. He was slow and had been caught in the open and so made an easy target for Cruzen, who sent him tumbling stunned to the deck with a single well-aimed shot.

Then she heard another shout from somewhere straight ahead, and knew the guard outside the hatch had been lying.

Bastard.

How many more were in here? Searching the spacious compartment, she saw no other signs of movement, and from her current position, she noted the distance between her and the *Jefferies*. The shuttlecraft sat where the away team had left it, the rear hatch leading into its passenger and cargo area still open, and Cruzen saw that at least some of the equipment stored aboard the craft had been ransacked. To its left she spied the field transporter pad and its accompanying portable control console, which still appeared to be activated. It was a possible means of escape, to be sure, but perhaps also a way to summon reinforcements from the *Enterprise*. She was certain that Captain Picard considered the away team overdue by now and likely was scanning for them and attempting to make contact.

A blast of weapons fire striking the cargo container made her flinch, and Cruzen ducked back behind it. The shot had come from her left, but more from her flank than ahead of her, which meant that the first Golvonek she had encountered was on the move. This much was confirmed when another shot hammered the container, and she had to scramble forward to keep from being exposed. Her movements carried her around the oversized box's nearest corner and that's when she caught sight of the third soldier maneuvering in her direction. He was using the *Jefferies* itself as cover, keeping the shuttlecraft between them as he advanced, and Cruzen realized he had given her an opening to exploit.

Lunging from her hiding place, she jogged for the shuttle, keeping it in front of her and using it to conceal her own advance across the open deck while at the same time using the cargo container to shield her back. If this was going to work, she would need to capitalize on being out of her opponents' sight for these few precious seconds. Cruzen sidestepped to her right, aiming her rifle down the shuttlecraft's starboard side just as the Golvonek stepped into view. He was unprepared for the sudden sight of her standing right in front of him when she fired. The rifle's energy bolt struck him and tossed him backward where he collapsed in an unmoving heap on the deck.

Cruzen heard running footsteps behind her but she was already moving, sprinting for the *Jefferies*'s bow and imagining she felt a white hot target between her shoulder blades. She ducked around the shuttlecraft just as the first shot struck its hull and kept moving, sliding around its front and stopped as she reached its port side. Listening to the sound of approaching footsteps, she smiled to herself as she realized the Golvonek was attempting his own version of the maneuver she had just used on his companion. Her smile faded when a metallic disc bounced into view and skittered across the deck.

Oh, shit!

She lost her grip on her rifle as she threw herself back around the shuttlecraft's angled nose just before the explosion came. It was close enough to shake the *Jefferies,* and Cruzen heard shrapnel peppering its hull, but the shuttlecraft had proven a worthy shield, protecting her from the blast. Her ears still ringing, she pushed herself to her feet and darted back the way she had come, gambling that the third—and hopefully last—Golvonek soldier would be moving forward to inspect the results of his grenade. She had run the length of the shuttle's port side and was almost at the rear hatch when the guard stepped into view. Cruzen had but a fraction of a second to realize that her adversary was female before lowering her shoulder and driving it into the Golvonek's chest.

Caught by surprise, the soldier released a grunt of shock and pain as Cruzen plowed into her, pushing both of them toward the deck. Cruzen lashed out with a free hand, swiping the guard's rifle from her hands and sending it sliding across the floor away from them. The soldier was already recovering, rolling away from Cruzen and trying to regain her footing, but the security officer got there first. She struck the Golvonek's chin with the top of her booted foot, the kick driving the guard's head up and back. Her opponent again fell back to the deck, giving Cruzen enough time to draw from inside her tunic the pistol she had taken from the guard outside. With no time to check its power setting, she leveled the weapon and fired, and the pistol bucked in her hand as it released the compact ball of flaring scarlet energy. The soldier gasped in renewed surprise and crumpled to the deck, and Cruzen stepped forward, aiming the pistol at her opponent's chest. A quick look verified the guard was still breathing, and Cruzen allowed a small sigh of relief when she confirmed that the weapon had been set to a stunning force.

After first verifying that there at least appeared to be no other Golvonek lurking in the landing bay's shadows, Cruzen boarded the *Jefferies* and inspected its cockpit console. As far as she could determine, everything looked functional. She tapped a command sequence into one control pad to unlock the rest of the station, at which point all its displays, indicators, and interfaces flared to life.

"Now we're talking," she said to herself, settling into the pilot's seat. "Well, not really," she added, eyeing one scan reading which showed that whatever the Golvonek were using to jam communications frequencies, it was still in operation. Contacting the *Enterprise*—for the moment at least—was not an option.

"No time to worry about it," she said, relocking the console and pushing away from the seat. Moving to a storage locker along the shuttle's bulkhead, she keyed its security code and the door opened, giving her access not only to a medical kit for Doctor Crusher, but also spare hand phasers, of which she availed herself of four. Cruzen dropped three of the weapons into a satchel that she then slung over her shoulder before she holstered the remaining phaser on her left hip.

Guess we're doing this the hard way.

27

"Stay awake, Rennan. That's an order."

Despite his condition, Rennan Konya still managed a weak smile as he lay on the deck in the *Arrow*'s engineering section, his head resting in T'Ryssa Chen's lap as she caressed the side of his face. A large patch on the makeshift bandage covering the gash on his head, a piece torn from the sleeve of Chen's blue uniform shirt, was dark with Konya's blood, but a quick inspection had told her that the bleeding had all but stopped. The same was true for the wounds across the Betazoid's back, which Doctor Crusher had checked a few moments earlier. Still, Konya had lost a lot of blood and his skin was pale and cold. Crusher, using her medical tricorder that Chen had found along with their phasers and other confiscated belongings, had been able to determine that his injuries were serious enough that treatment in the *Enterprise*'s sickbay was fast becoming critical. Even without medical equipment of her own, Chen was able to check Konya's pulse with her fingers pressed to his neck, and she found it racing. He was teetering on the dangerous edge of shock. By her calculations, it had been just under fifteen minutes since Kirsten Cruzen had set off for the landing bay to retrieve a medical kit from the *Jefferies*. What was taking her so long? Had she run into trouble?

"To hell with what I said earlier," said Crusher as she knelt next to Konya and placed her hand on his forehead. "We need to get him to the shuttle, now." Shifting her position, she turned to face Tamala Harstad. "How about you? Think you can make it to the landing bay?"

The younger doctor nodded. "You bet."

"I can carry him," Chen said.

The doctor eyed her skeptically. "You're sure?"

Chen nodded. "I'm half Vulcan, remember? I can at least get him to the shuttle." Though she lacked the physical strength and stamina of a full Vulcan, she still was stronger than the average human. She figured that carrying Konya across her shoulders would allow her to make the transit to the landing bay. "Here's hoping the Golvonek haven't sabotaged the shuttle."

"I'm never going to hear the end of this," said Konya, slurring the words. "Am I?"

"I certainly hope not," Chen said. She waited until Crusher checked his improvised bandages, before shifting him to help her get him to his feet. Then she heard from the far end of the room the sound of the hatch leading from the engineering section cycling open. When she turned to look in that direction, it was in time to see a half dozen Golvonek soldiers moving into the chamber. Each of them carried pulse rifles and the group was spreading out as they entered the room.

"Not this again," said Harstad. Both Chen and Crusher were drawing their phasers when a new voice roared, echoing off the metal bulkheads.

"Stop where you are! Surrender your weapons!"

Chen recognized the voice as belonging to Foctine Vedapir, the Golvonek officer who had presided over their capture in the *Arrow*'s landing bay. *Aw, damn it all to hell.*

As members of his detail collected phasers from the away team, Chen watched Vedapir crossing the engineering chamber's open deck, shaking his head in obvious disapproval while his gaze moved to each of the Golvonek soldiers Konya and Cruzen had dispatched.

"Under normal circumstances," he said after moving to stand before Chen, "I would order you taken to one of our detention cells, where you would answer for the crimes of assaulting my men and interfering with our mission."

"Assaulting your men?" Crusher snapped, and Chen glanced over her shoulder to see the doctor glowering at Vedapir. "Are you kidding? You attacked *us*, remember?" Instead of replying, the foctine's expression clouded with annoyance and he started to step in her direction, but Chen slid over and blocked his path.

"Not a good idea," she said, tapping her chest with a finger. "I'm in charge, so I'm responsible for these people. You deal with me." Though she did her best to project confidence, she still felt her stomach heave as anxiety gripped her.

Behind her, Chen heard Crusher say in a soft voice, "Lieutenant."

"Fine," Vedapir said, leaning close. "If they do anything else which displeases me, I will kill you."

So, they still need us alive, Chen mused. While that was comforting, it did little to settle the knot of worry twisting in her gut.

Pointing to Chen, Vedapir looked to one of his guards. "Bring her."

"Where are you taking her?" Konya asked. His voice was still weak, but Chen still was able to hear the defiance and even warning in his tone.

The foctine ignored the question, but instead turned and walked toward the central control tower and its array of consoles. With a push from one of the soldiers behind her, Chen followed the Golvonek officer until she stood next to one of the workstations that had escaped damage. "The main computer no longer allows access via any of the stations or monitors. Tell me why."

Though she already knew the answer to Vedapir's query, Chen made a show of studying the console and the readings depicted on its various monitors and indicators. "If I understand this correctly, a security lockout has been enabled." Jodis obviously had done something while working on the *Arrow*'s bridge. She had been able to follow most of his steps, but her lack of familiarity with some aspects of the ship's complex network of systems was still hindering her efforts.

"I know this," replied Vedapir, waving at the station. "Tell me how to counteract what has been done."

Chen shrugged. "I don't know. I'll have to study this some more before I can figure something out." Her statement was almost a lie, but there was just enough truth behind her words to make her feel as though she had avoided breaking yet another Vulcan sacrament with respect to personal conduct.

Not yet, anyway.

His eyes narrowing, the Golvonek stepped closer to Chen. "That is unacceptable. If you cannot assist me, then I will conclude that you are working in league with Jodis, and you will be arrested and tried as spies."

Before she could respond to the accusation, a metallic chirp sounded from something on Vedapir's uniform belt, and he reached into a pouch along his left hip to retrieve what Chen recognized as a communications device.

"What is it?" he growled into the unit.

"Foctine Vedapir, this is Tanzal Singen. We have swept the forward part of the vessel and there is no sign of the prisoners."

Vedapir's irritation flared, and for an instant Chen thought he might crush the communicator. "How is that possible? There are only so many avenues of escape from that area." He closed his eyes, drawing a deep breath before continuing, "Begin a sweep from the forward-most section and search back toward the rear. Overlook nothing, no matter how improbable a hiding place it might be. I want them found. Have all guards stationed at junctions and key areas report with current status, and do so at five *linzat* intervals." Without waiting for a reply, he tapped a control and returned the unit to its belt pouch.

"Jodis is obviously attempting sabotage," he said to Chen before once more pointing to the control consoles. "Tell me how he is doing this, and what his targets might be."

"If it's sabotage," Chen replied, "then the obvious targets are propulsion, life-support, weapons, and the computer that controls it all." She pointed to the console. "Looks to me like he's got the computer, so the rest of it is just a matter of time, right?"

For the first time, Vedapir displayed genuine anger. "I grow tired of your words, outsider." When he moved forward this time, Chen saw his hand raising as though to strike.

I don't think so.

One quick step placed her within arm's reach of the Golvonek, and Chen thrust the heel of her hand up and into his chin. It was with unqualified satisfaction that she felt his head jerk in response to the sudden strike before he staggered backward. She could have opted for a nerve pinch, of course, but she decided this would send a more effective message to Vedapir and his guards, hurt more, and make her feel better.

"T'Ryss!" Konya shouted, and from the corner of her eye Chen saw him pushing himself to his feet in a noble yet futile effort to help her. The guards between her and the rest of the away team now were turning toward her, their rifles swinging in her direction, but she did not care. Vedapir was still on his feet, which irritated her more than she wanted to admit.

So hit him harder.

Even as she moved toward him, intending to attack again before the Golvonek could respond, he was drawing his sidearm from the holster on his hip. Chen calculated the distance between them and the time left for her to reach him before he could fire the weapon, and realized she was about to come up on the bad end of that equation.

Whoops.

Vedapir had raised his pistol to shoot when something shrieked from above and behind Chen just before a bright red ball of energy punched the foctine in the chest. It was followed by other reports and Chen flinched, dropping to one knee and raising her arms to cover her head. She saw the Golvonek soldiers dropping one by one to the floor, each of them struck by weapons fire raining down from . . . where?

As sudden as the unexpected attack had been, it ended with the same abruptness, the echoes from the energy bolts already fading. Chen turned toward the source of the fire and saw Jodis and Bnira standing at different points along one of the catwalks suspended above the curved bulkhead protecting this room's section of the *Arrow*'s primary particle cannon. The two Raqilan both carried Golvonek pulse rifles and were moving the muzzles left to right and back again as they searched for any remaining threats.

"Do not be alarmed," Jodis said, his voice echoing off the chamber's bare metal walls. "We have no quarrel with you, but we will not hesitate to act if you attempt to interfere with us."

Moving to stand with Konya and Harstad, Chen and Crusher watched as Jodis and Bnira descended a ladder connecting the catwalk. The two Raqilan took a moment to disarm the Golvonek guards, and Chen watched as Jodis verified that each of the soldiers was unconscious.

"Secure them in the storage room," Jodis said, then gestured to the away team. "They can move them there. See to it that none of them are harmed."

It was an unusual order, Chen thought, given the circumstances. Jodis obviously was a well-trained soldier, himself. Why would he not simply eliminate the Golvonek rather than dealing with prisoners and the problems they might cause?

While Bnira covered the away team with her rifle, Jodis, cradling his own weapon in his left arm, made his way to the central tower and began tapping a rapid-fire sequence of controls. The complex string of instructions was almost too fast for Chen to follow.

"There is extensive damage to the control systems," he said after a moment, and Chen noted how he eyed the destroyed sections of the control tower with disapproval. "I am having to make adjustments to compensate."

Bnira asked, "Should we relocate to a different part of the ship?"

"I have already locked out the other access points prior to routing everything here," Jodis replied. "It would take too much time to rework the configurations, and we would have to deal with the Golvonek." After entering more commands to the console, he added, "I have secured this section, and everything we need is here." In response to his actions came a telltale flickering of the overhead lighting as a low, ominous hum began to fill the room.

"What is that?" Crusher asked, looking around for the source of the new sound.

Chen frowned, listening to the warbling, muffled drone. A renewed sense of apprehension gripped her as she realized what she was hearing.

"It's the particle cannon," she said. "He's bringing the main weapon online." It took her an extra moment, straining to make out the readings on the control console, to confirm her statement, and more. "Wait. He's activating everything. He already charged all of the weapons, remember? Now he's powering up the propulsion system." She noted that among the systems now online was the warp drive. Fear began to grip her as she conjured various possibilities, and she looked to Bnira. "What are you doing?"

The Raqilan did not move, and the muzzle of her rifle did not waver. "We are completing our mission."

Well, sure. That makes a warped sort of sense.

"You can't be serious. What's the point of going through with it now? You missed your target by decades, and the time travel equipment is hopelessly wrecked. You're stuck here, in this time period. What good is it to go after Uphrel now? You won't achieve your objective, which—by the way—involves the murder of millions of innocent people no matter when you decide to do it. That's insane just by itself, and still is, but now you won't even be doing it for the original reasons." Chen expected

Bnira to argue with her, or to somehow put her in her place and tell her that she had no hope of understanding the complexities of this age-old conflict, but the Raqilan said nothing. She remained silent, keeping her rifle trained on the away team.

Behind Chen, Konya said, "For the record, I think you and Jodis are both out of your damned minds."

Looking past Bnira, Chen watched as Jodis continued to enter commands to the console. Something about what he was doing did not seem right, and it took her an extra moment to comprehend what she was seeing.

"Damn it," she said, turning to exchange glances first with her shipmates. "He's not just targeting the Golvonek ships. He's going after *everything.*"

28

Red alert indicators flashed at every bridge station, and the audible alarm wailed loud enough to make Picard wince. Before he could order it silenced, Worf already was tapping a control on his console to terminate the klaxon.

Standing just behind the conn and ops stations, Picard studied the *Arrow* and noted the presence of new lights and other power sources activating all along its massive hull. Where before it had appeared dark and lifeless, now it seemed to pulse with new vitality and purpose. A sleeping leviathan was rousing from slumber.

"Report."

"All of the *Arrow*'s weapons are activating, sir," replied Worf from where he now manned the tactical station. "They appear to still be in standby mode, but sensors are detecting the ship's targeting scanners have been enabled. Also, its main propulsion system is increasing to full power, and readings also show activation of its maneuvering thrusters."

Seated at the conn station, Lieutenant Joanna Faur asked, "Where do they think they're going to go?"

"Any luck getting through to Doctor Crusher or the others?" Picard asked.

Worf replied, "Negative. Still no response on any frequency, and I am detecting what appears to be a moderate-level jamming field. I am attempting to compensate."

Sitting next to Faur at the ops station, Glinn Dygan

said, "Captain, the Golvonek ships are breaking formation and appear to be taking evasive action."

Picard frowned. "Are they attempting simple escape, or
engaging the Raqilan ships?"

"Neither, sir," replied the Cardassian. "It would appear
they are regrouping, possibly in preparation for defensive
action against the *Arrow*."

On the viewscreen, Picard watched as all of the Golvonek towing vessels, still being harassed by the Raqilan
fighter craft and even heavier weapons fire from the larger
support vessels, began to distance themselves from the
Arrow. As for the Raqilan ships, they seemed content to
press their attack, paying the former derelict no heed as
they continued their strafing runs.

"The Raqilan certainly seem to have no problem with
this latest development," Worf said.

"What the hell is going on over there?" Picard asked.
Had Mynlara ordered her people to deploy the *Arrow*
against the Raqilan? Or, was it possible that Jodis and his
shipmate, Bnira, had somehow acquired control of the
weapon ship? Given what would have to be an extensive
knowledge of the vessel and its every operation, Picard
considered it more than reasonable that even two people
possessing such expertise could seize the vessel from their
Golvonek captors.

Worf reported, "Captain, we are being hailed by Fleet
Legate Mynlara."

"On screen."

The Golvonek's visage filled the image, her expression
one of near panic. *"Captain Picard, you must help us!"*

"I don't understand," Picard said, maintaining his
composure. "You told us that you were taking control of
the ship."

"The vessel is not under our control!" Mynlara snapped. *"Our desire was only to move the ship to one of our bases, but Jodis has somehow seized it. He is the one responsible for these new attacks, both on my ships as well as those of the Raqilan."*

Picard stepped toward the screen. "I still have people on that ship, Fleet Legate. Where are they? Does Jodis have them?"

Shaking her head, Mynlara replied, *"I do not know."*

"Captain," Worf called out, "the *Arrow* has just disabled two more Raqilan ships, as well as another of the Golvonek tow vessels."

"Can you not see that we require your assistance?" Mynlara's voice was rising, almost with every word. *"One of my ships is functioning on emergency power. Its life-support systems will not be able to sustain its crew."*

"Assuming Jodis is in control of the ship," Picard said, "why has he not destroyed your ships? It's certainly within his power to do so."

Mynlara's eyes narrowed. *"How am I to understand what thoughts drive someone like Jodis? It seems apparent to me that his mental faculties are defective, perhaps as a consequence of his long hibernation."*

Before Picard could respond, Worf said, "Captain, the *Arrow* is getting under way, and sensors are detecting its targeting systems are active. Power readings are increasing across the ship, with definite surges in the weapons systems."

"They're going on the offensive," Picard said, turning from the screen. "We'll have to continue this discussion later, Fleet Legate." He gestured for the communication to be severed even as the Golvonek was preparing to protest. The Golvonek's image disappeared from the viewscreen, replaced once more by the *Arrow*. "Conn, increase our distance, and maintain full power to the shields."

Lieutenant Faur was in the midst of acknowledging the order when the captain saw the first barrage of weapons fire explode from ports along the *Arrow*'s port hull. Streaks of red-white energy lanced forth from multiple locations, crossing space and seeking targets with deadly precision. On the viewscreen, three Raqilan ships were struck in rapid succession, the impacts tearing into each vessel's hull as they scrambled to maneuver out of the line of fire.

Why the Raqilan ships? Even as the question formed in his mind, Picard watched new salvos reach across space, tracking after the Golvonek tug ships and inflicting similar damage as they, too, attempted to flee.

"What are they doing?" Turning to Worf, Picard said, "Open a channel to the *Arrow*, Number One."

The Klingon nodded. "Aye, sir."

Waiting for acknowledgment that the frequency had been enabled, Picard once more approached the main viewscreen. "Jodis, this is Captain Picard aboard the *Enterprise*. Your attack on the Raqilan and Golvonek vessels is unprovoked and unnecessary. I urge you to reconsider this course of action, and I request to speak with my people who are still aboard your ship."

"They *are* receiving us, Captain," Worf reported.

"Sir!" Faur called out. The lieutenant was pointing at the screen, and Picard looked up to see the *Arrow*'s course shifting, pulses of energy visible along its flank as maneuvering thrusters flared to life. The vessel moved with a grace and speed that belied its size, continuing to unleash weapons fire from multiple points as it pivoted on its axis.

Worf said, "Sensors show its primary particle weapon is online, and I am reading indications of scanners locking on to multiple targets." A second later, he added, "Including us."

"Conn, keep us out of its path," Picard said, returning to his command chair. "Number One, ready phasers and target any of those weapons ports you can." He had not wanted to take direct action against the *Arrow*, but Jodis was leaving him with precious few options.

"Aye, sir," replied Worf. "Still no response to our hails."

The *Arrow* fired yet again, unleashing another volley of blasts from various particle cannons, each seeking a different target and scoring hits on both Raqilan and Golvonek vessels. The Raqilan fighters and their support craft now were turning tail, seeking escape, while the Golvonek tugs, far slower and less maneuverable, were no match for the weapon ship's tracking systems. Those ships better able to defend themselves were turning toward the attack, breaking formation and firing on the *Arrow* in a series of rapid hit-and-run strikes.

"Their counterattacks are having an effect," reported Glinn Dygan. "Sensors are showing widespread damage across the *Arrow*'s surface, along with some weapons ports and other components."

Worf added, "There are definite power fluctuations, sir, as well as what appear to be attempts to reroute. It could be the onboard computer working to compensate."

How much damage could an attack of this sort inflict? While it had been determined that the *Arrow* might be susceptible to injury after any prolonged battle, Picard reasoned that the odds still were in its favor to disable or destroy most if not all of the vessels around it.

"I am reading a new energy surge," said Dygan. The Cardassian turned in his seat. "It's the primary cannon, Captain."

Picard directed his gaze to the viewscreen in time to see the array mounted at the *Arrow*'s forward edge flaring to life, its emitter glowing with the fury of a sun before a wide beam of focused energy erupted from the cannon, streaking across space and washing over the closest of the Golvonek vessels. He braced himself, expecting to see the tug obliterated by the beam's force, but the ship's destruction never came. The effects were still severe, with the ship lurching and spiraling away as it succumbed to the weapon's force.

"According to these readings," Worf said, "the cannon is not operating at full capacity."

Was it a deliberate choice, or merely the result of damage to the weapons system? Picard had no way to know that, of course, but the onscreen evidence of the particle cannon's power was obvious, even if it was operating in a compromised state.

"What's the status of that ship?"

"Widespread overloads and system cutouts," replied the first officer. "Propulsion is offline, and life-support appears to be operating from auxiliary power sources. The ship has begun transmitting what I believe to be a distress signal."

"Captain," Faur said, "they're firing again."

On the viewscreen, the *Arrow* had selected another target, this one a Raqilan carrier. As before, the particle cannon's immense beam lashed out, its energy enveloping the retreating vessel and disrupting its flight path. Picard saw the ship's engine ports flicker and darken along with other light sources along its hull or emanating from portholes.

"And you're saying the weapon isn't firing at full power?" Picard asked.

Worf nodded. "It appears that way, Captain."

"Notify the transporter room that we're moving into position. Make sure Lieutenant Šmrhová and her team are ready to beam over." Picard decided that he no longer had the luxury of waiting for the right time to risk dispatching his rescue team. "Lieutenant Faur, maneuver us to within transporter range." If all went according to the plan he was conjuring even as he spoke, the *Enterprise* would only be that close to the *Arrow* for a handful of seconds. "Guide us clear the moment the away team is on board. Mister Worf, you'll handle the transport."

Both officers acknowledged the orders and Picard watched as Faur tapped a hurried sequence of commands to her console. The image on the viewscreen shifted as the *Enterprise* changed direction until the *Arrow* once more was in view. Pulsing with life, the immense vessel was executing yet another in an ongoing series of pivots and turns. Its primary particle cannon and its array of smaller armaments spit crimson fury in all directions as it continued firing at any Raqilan or Golvonek ship reckless enough to still be within weapons range. For the first time since the battle began, Picard felt the deck shudder in response to the starship weathering an assault on its own defenses.

"Shields are holding," Worf reported. "We have entered transporter range. Dropping shields and energizing now."

Picard counted to himself the seconds he knew were needed to complete the transport cycle, each one a seeming eternity with the ship's shields down. Ticking off the last one, he ordered, "Shields up. Conn, get us out of here." As he issued the command, he saw the *Arrow* rotating yet again, and this time the gargantuan ship's nose was turning toward the screen.

"Away team is aboard the ship," Worf noted. "Sensors are picking up an increase in the power levels to the *Arrow*'s primary weapon."

Picard felt his grip tighten on the arms of his chair. "Evasive maneuvers, *now!*"

The deck disappeared from beneath Geordi La Forge's feet.

It was only for a second, and the shift was perhaps only a handful of centimeters, but the effect was sufficient to send the engineer stumbling across the deck and flailing for any sort of handhold. His feet found purchase on the flooring and he stumbled and all but fell into the railing encircling the *Enterprise*'s warp core. Matters were not helped by the sudden dousing of nearly every illumination source within the engineering section, and La Forge heard members of his staff reacting to what could only be a brutal attack on the starship. The very hull of the ship seemed to howl as it absorbed the brunt of whatever had just hit it, and adding to the chaos was the wail of a red alert siren that succeeded in drowning out every other sound in the room.

As quickly as it had been extinguished, the main lighting returned as did most of the active status monitors and control stations arrayed around the cavernous chamber.

"Everybody okay?" he called out, and received a chorus of assurances that beyond a few hard falls, which in time would produce nasty welts and bruises, no one had been injured.

Doctor Crusher's going to be busy tomorrow, La Forge mused. *Assuming we all make it to tomorrow.* The errant thought made him think of Tamala Harstad, who at last report was one of the few remaining away team members still on board the *Arrow*. The team had been overdue to return to the *Enterprise* even before the current situation had erupted, and now the chief engineer knew he had to place aside his personal concerns and focus on the issues at hand. From the looks of one set of status monitors on a nearby workstation, those issues were many and increasing by the minute.

"Bridge to engineering," rumbled the voice of Worf through the intercom system. *"Damage report."*

Moving toward the master systems display table, the freestanding workstation positioned between the warp core and the engineering section's main entrance, La Forge called out, "Whatever that last attack was, it smacked us around pretty good. We're still assessing everything."

"The Arrow *fired its primary particle cannon,"* replied the Klingon.

La Forge scowled. "Yeah, well, don't let it do that again." He glanced up to where Lieutenant Commander Taurik had taken up station on the other side of the table. Since returning to the *Enterprise*, it was the first time the chief engineer had seen his assistant following the bombshell revelation that the Vulcan had come across potentially hazardous information about the future that was the *Arrow*'s point of origin. A list of regulations longer than La Forge's arm had required Taurik to sequester himself until such time as he completed a detailed report for the Department of Temporal Investigations. The contents of that report were not allowed to be shared with anyone else on board, including La Forge and even Captain Picard himself, and Taurik also had created a protected archive within the *Enterprise*'s main computer for storing the potentially volatile information retrieved from the *Arrow*.

Given time, La Forge could defeat the encryption guarding that archive, but he knew doing so might cost him his career and perhaps even result in incarceration. Of course, all of that paled when compared to the potential for altering the course of future events.

So, don't do that, and focus on your job.

As he studied the master display, which depicted a computer-generated dorsal schematic of the *Enterprise*, La Forge saw entirely too many areas of the ship highlighted in red for his comfort. "What's the story, Taurik?"

The Vulcan engineer said, "There are power outages throughout the ship. Backup systems are activating in most cases, but several processes will require rerouting." The long fingers on both of his hands were moving at a rapid pace across the table's interface. "I am dispatching repair teams to those locations. Deflector shield generators overloaded and are resetting, though I predict they will only return to seventy-eight-percent capacity."

"Weapons are offline," Worf said over the speaker, *"as is flight control. Those are the top priority."*

"We're on it," said La Forge, looking to where Taurik was directing his attention to one section of the table's display. "We've still got warp drive, for whatever that's worth."

Worf replied, *"The* Arrow *is breaking off its attacks and is setting course into the Canborek system."*

Why would it be doing that?

Before the engineer could ask the question aloud, realization struck him. "You've got to be kidding."

"Mister La Forge," said the voice of Captain Picard, *"it's looking as though Jodis might be setting the* Arrow *on course for Uphrel with the intention of carrying out its original mission. How extensive is the damage to flight control?"*

Taurik replied, "We will be unable to maneuver the ship at impulse speeds until the problem is corrected. Warp travel is possible, though of course not recommended."

Stepping around the table, La Forge began tapping another set of controls. "We're trying to work around the problem, Captain, but it's going to take some time." It was growing more difficult to maintain his concentration on the tasks before him. If Jodis had regained control of the weapon ship, what had become of Tamala and the rest of the away team? It took every scrap of self-discipline he possessed for La Forge to resist asking that question of the captain. Instead, he said, "Sir, I don't know that we can put up much of a fight against that thing. You saw what one shot did to us."

"Then we'll just have to stay out of its way," Picard replied, *"but we have to do something. Several of the Raqilan and Golvonek vessels have been disabled, and the truth is that they simply don't possess the firepower to defeat the* Arrow.*"*

Across the table from La Forge, Taurik was listening to the captain's report and raised one eyebrow. "Why would Jodis attack Raqilan ships?"

"He targeted anything within range, basically clearing a path for the Arrow. *Geordi, I can't sit here while he destroys an entire planet. Noble intentions notwithstanding, this situation is our fault, and the* Enterprise *is the only thing standing in Jodis's way."*

"How much time do we have?" La Forge asked, dividing his attention between the workstation readout he was using to prioritize resources for the repair work and directing Taurik and damage control teams to where they could do the most good in the least amount of time. Glancing up from the table, he saw members of his staff climbing ladders and crawling into access conduits, swarming over the engineering room and adjacent sections as they set to various assignments. Other teams, tool kits and satchels in hand, were heading for the hatch and out to other areas of the ship currently demanding attention, and he knew his people here were being supplemented by repair teams from all over the ship.

"*The* Arrow *is moving into the Canborek system at warp two point one,*" Worf answered. "*At their present speed, they could be orbiting Uphrel within thirty minutes.*"

Looking at the swaths of red bathing the display table's ship diagram, La Forge blew out his breath and shook his head. "Okay, Taurik. Let's get to work."

"Acknowledged," replied the Vulcan, retrieving a padd from the display table and setting off to direct other members of the engineering staff.

All of the needed repairs could be made, given sufficient time, but under the present circumstances, it was going to take a miracle to get the *Enterprise* back into the fight.

I just hope we haven't run out of those.

29

Aneta Šmrhová saw the Golvonek soldier before he saw her.

That's just your bad luck, thought the security chief as she aimed and fired her phaser rifle in a single smooth, rapid motion up the dimly lit corridor. The Golvonek had no chance to react before the stun beam enveloped him, and he collapsed against a bulkhead before sliding unconscious to the floor.

"Nice shooting, Lieutenant," remarked Ensign Eli Chapman, one of the recent additions to the *Enterprise*'s security detachment.

Behind Chapman, Lieutenant T'Sona said, "Lieutenant Šmrhová's marksmanship scores are among the highest for the crew."

"No kidding," added Ensign Bryan Regnis, keeping his voice low. "Whatever you do, Chapman, don't let her sucker you into a bet. She'll have your lunch. And your dinner." The detachment's resident sharpshooter, even Regnis had been hard-pressed to match Šmrhová's scores. "Are you sure you weren't a sniper in a previous life, or something?"

"Okay, enough," Šmrhová said. "I'll whip you on the phaser range later. Let's keep moving." Despite the situation and its plethora of unknowns, she was confident in her abilities and those of her team to accomplish the mission given to her by Captain Picard. After having to stand by while sending subordinates into harm's way, she now felt useful as she led the effort to rescue the away team. Though the captain would never say as much aloud, Šmrhová knew that in addition to being worried for the safety of anyone under his command, he also harbored an obvious personal concern for Doctor Crusher. Duty and professionalism saw to it that Picard almost never permitted his own feelings to take precedence over a mission, but that did not mean he was immune to such conflicting thoughts. How he managed to compartmentalize such turmoil, Šmrhová would never understand.

"Do you hear that?" asked Lieutenant Jarata Beyn, the last of the three security officers Šmrhová had elected to bring with her. The brawny Bajoran was cradling a phaser rifle in the crook of his right arm and holding a tricorder that looked like a toy in his oversized hand. "This thing's main power plant is increasing its output."

The omnipresent thrum of the *Arrow*'s massive engines had been a constant companion from the moment they had materialized on the portable transporter room in the weapon ship's landing bay. Even now, as they moved deeper into the giant vessel's inner compartments, the sound of its power plant resonated across every surface, with frequent spikes in tone and pitch as energy was routed to weapons, propulsion, and other critical systems. After being asleep for decades, the ship had been brought back to life, presumably to fulfill its lone, appalling purpose. The idea that such a vessel existed for no other reason than to destroy an entire civilization was something that she had considered largely in the abstract sense: a theory to be discussed and debated. From a tactical standpoint, she could understand the reasons for such a weapon, but the very notion of targeting millions if not billions of noncombatants to secure a military objective sickened her.

We can't let that happen.

Šmrhová was aware that Captain Picard had been wrestling with the Prime Directive implications of interfering in the conflict between the Raqilan and Golvonek, but to her the matter had been decided the instant the *Arrow* had unleashed its weapons against the *Enterprise*. Now it was a matter of survival for the starship, and the admirals, diplomats, and historians could argue about it later.

Which is why I'll probably never be an admiral, or a diplomat, or even an historian.

Šmrhová was okay with that.

"Lieutenant," said Ensign Regnis, who was pointing toward a dark lump on the deck ahead of them. "Another soldier."

"How many is that, now?" Šmrhová asked. "Six?"

Upon their arrival in the landing bay, the first thing to greet her and her rescue team was the trio of unconscious Golvonek soldiers strewn around the shuttlecraft *Jefferies*, the interior of which appeared to have been rifled if not outright looted. With no way to know what had happened here and still lacking the ability to contact any of the missing away team, Šmrhová had assigned the fifth and sixth members of her group to remain with the shuttle and secure any remaining equipment. Guiding them was her tricorder and the internal schematics of the *Arrow* provided by Commander La Forge after his team's initial surveys of the colossal weapon ship. It had not taken long before her scans had pinpointed human, Betazoid, and Vulcan life signs. One human as well as nearly two dozen Golvonek biosigns were scattered across the ship, with the human not all that far from her team's present location. Along the way, they had found the half dozen other Golvonek soldiers, all unconscious, leading Šmrhová to believe that at least one member of the wayward away team was clashing with the aliens for reasons as yet unknown.

As for what she presumed was the rest of the team, they along with two Raqilan life signs were concentrated in or near the *Arrow*'s engineering section.

So that's where we're going.

"Whatever's jamming communications is still active," reported Jarata, studying his tricorder. "If we can get into the computer system, we might be able to take care of that."

Šmrhová shook her head, her gaze still fixed on her own tricorder. "We know where the away team is. We'll just concentrate on that." Adjusting one control to better tune the device's scans, she added, "I've got a human life sign heading in our direction, and he or she has a tricorder, too." Whoever it was, they were coming at them at a rapid pace, the bio signature growing sharper with each passing second. Also clearing from the haze of distortion affecting the quality of the tricorder's scans as a result of the *Arrow*'s armored hull were at least five other life signs, all Golvonek. "Company."

"I hear them," said T'Sona, and when Šmrhová eyed her the Vulcan gestured with her phaser rifle toward the length of passageway that lay ahead of them. Three dozen meters away, the corridor was intersected by another tunnel running transverse to the larger conduit. Within seconds, Šmrhová heard the sounds of rapid footsteps, growing louder.

"Take cover," she ordered, and the team moved to crouch along the bulkheads to either side of the corridor, trying to conceal themselves using the shadows cast by the dim lighting. As Šmrhová raised her phaser rifle to her shoulder and sighted down its length, a figure dashed into the intersection and turned toward her, cloaked in partial shadow. She saw the familiar silhouette of someone dressed in a Starfleet uniform, carrying an equipment satchel while wielding a hand phaser and a tricorder. Shoulder-length dark hair gave away the runner's identity as Šmrhová recognized Lieutenant Kirsten Cruzen.

"Hello, fan club!" Cruzen snapped as she came abreast of Šmrhová, turned, and dropped to kneel beside the security chief. Her breathing somewhat labored from what Šmrhová assumed was a protracted dash through the *Arrow*'s bowels with pursuers dogging her every step of the way, she offered a tired smile. "I brought some friends."

Other running footsteps from the crossing corridor were coming closer, and Cruzen did not wait for any order to fire as the first dark figure emerged into the intersection. The orange beam of her phaser illuminated the hallway as it struck what Šmrhová recognized as a Golvonek soldier. He or she—it was impossible to tell with the uniform, helmet, and other equipment—was spun around and fell to the deck just as a second soldier appeared in the passageway. Šmrhová fired her own weapon, dropping her target. Voices called out from around the corner, the remaining soldiers taking obvious heed of their companions' misfortune.

"Don't give them a chance to regroup," Cruzen cautioned, rising from her crouch and moving up the corridor toward the intersection. Before Šmrhová could utter the first word of protest, the security officer was halfway to the junction. Then something appeared from around the corner. It was small and close to the floor, and Šmrhová realized it was one of the Golvonek, peering out into the corridor to search for threats. Only a portion of his helmeted head was visible, but Cruzen saw it and lowered her phaser toward it. She never had the chance to fire before another beam flashed in the corridor and passed over Šmrhová's shoulder to strike the Golvonek's head. Using the confusion as cover, Cruzen advanced to the intersection and fired into the other corridor. Another weapon sounded in the passageway, and Šmrhová saw the pulse of red energy strike a bulkhead above and behind Cruzen, but then the hall was silent and the lieutenant was backstepping into view, searching for other targets.

"All clear," she called out.

Shifting her position, Šmrhová saw Ensign Regnis lying in a prone position on the deck, his phaser rifle still aimed up the corridor. His had been the shot that had taken the concealed Golvonek. "Nice shooting," she said.

"Thanks," replied the ensign as he pushed himself to his feet.

The team regrouped at the junction, where Cruzen stood surveying the results of the brief skirmish. Catching Šmrhová's gaze, she smiled again. "I've been trying to out-maneuver these goons for fifteen minutes. I was hoping if I led them this way, you'd be ready for them."

"So it's you who's been leaving a trail of bodies behind you?" asked Regnis.

"They're all stunned," Cruzen said, "not that they'd return the courtesy if the situation was reversed." She explained the methods used to subdue the away team, including the nasty-sounding device that had injured Rennan Konya and Tamala Harstad.

"How many more of them are aboard?" asked Lieutenant Jarata.

Cruzen shook her head. "No idea, but right now that doesn't matter." She grabbed the strap of the satchel slung over her shoulder. "We need to get to the engineering deck. Konya's hurt pretty bad, and we have to get him back to the *Enterprise*."

"That might be a problem," Šmrhová replied, explaining in rapid fashion the state of the battle between the *Arrow* and both the Raqilan and Golvonek ships as well as the *Enterprise*. "I don't know what happened after we beamed over."

"Then we'll fly him out of here on the *Jefferies* and take our chances," Cruzen said. "But we can't waste any more time talking about this, Lieutenant."

She was right, Šmrhová knew. *Focus on the mission.*

"Okay, then," she said, stepping to the front of the group and leading the way to the *Arrow*'s engineering deck. "Let's do this."

T'Ryssa Chen grew more agitated with each moment. She stood next to Beverly Crusher and the remainder of the away team, all under the watchful eye of Bnira. Jodis was immersed in the rush of information being relayed to the control console's various monitors and indicators, all of which seemed to have increased their output as the *Arrow* continued to carry out its attacks. The illumination from all of the displays made his lavender skin seem almost pale, and to Chen he appeared like a ghost, which seemed oddly fitting given how he and Bnira had—in a manner of speaking—been resurrected.

"I think you've proved your point," Chen said after Jodis had halted the ship's weapons and turned his attention instead to propulsion and flight control. He ignored her commentary, of course, instead maintaining his attention on those consoles that still were active on the engineering deck's damaged central control tower. After what from Chen's vantage point appeared to be a devastating attack on the *Enterprise*, Jodis had tracked and fired on several more Raqilan and Golvonek vessels before moving the *Arrow* away from the skirmish. The weapon ship had been following whatever course Jodis directed for twenty minutes, and though she only was able to read portions of Raqilan written text, Chen still was able to interpret some of the labeling on monitors depicting what appeared to be navigational charts. She also noted the large number of alert messages and indicators highlighting many of the control tower's remaining functional displays. Despite the *Arrow*'s obvious advantage over the *Enterprise* as well as the Golvonek and even Raqilan vessels, the weapon ship still had sustained significant damage during the brief firefight.

"What's he doing?" Crusher asked, kneeling next to Rennan Konya.

Chen replied, "From what I can tell, he's definitely put us on a course into the Canborek system. I can't make out the exact destination from any of the charts he has visible, but do we really need to guess where we're going?" She directed her gaze to Bnira. "You're really going through with this?"

"Be quiet," warned the female Raqilan. Based on how she held the pulse rifle she was using to guard the away team, Chen had no doubts Bnira knew how to employ the weapon.

"Or what?" Chen asked. "Your boss over there said he didn't want to hurt us, so long as we didn't get in his way. Are you going to shoot me for being annoying?"

Bnira's eyes narrowed. "I am considering it."

"I get that a lot." Turning from her, Chen looked to the unconscious Konya as Crusher rested her hand on his forehead. On Konya's opposite side, Harstad sat with her back propped against the bulkhead, doing her best to assist Crusher.

"How is he?" Chen asked. The Betazoid security officer's condition seemed to have stabilized, but the doctor's concern had not lessened. Despite the crude initial aid techniques she had been able to administer, Konya still required more attention than Crusher could provide without better resources.

"Not good," replied the doctor. "We need that medical kit."

"I know that your companion is en route back here," said another voice, and Chen looked over her shoulder to see Jodis walking toward them. "If you continue to cooperate, she will be allowed to return and help you with your injured friends."

Chen studied the Raqilan's face, searching for signs of deception, but found none. "Just like that?"

It appeared to take an extra moment for Jodis to comprehend the meaning of her question before he nodded. "Yes. As I said before, I have no quarrel with you, and there is nothing you can do now to stop us." He nodded back to the central control tower. "I have locked out computer access from every interface on the ship except that one. It is commendable that you were able to make so much progress circumventing our security measures, but there will be no more of that. From this point forward, only Bnira or I can interact with the ship's systems."

"What of the damage?" asked Bnira.

As though annoyed to discuss such subjects in front of their prisoners, Jodis said, "It has been mitigated. It will not interfere with our mission."

"What mission?" Crusher asked. "What's left to do?

It should be obvious by now that the Golvonek can't stand up to this ship. You've already won whatever battle you're looking for. Surely, the Golvonek will realize this if they haven't already. I can't imagine their government won't be begging to talk with your leaders about ending the war once and for all, so what's the point of continuing?"

Rather than appearing to take satisfaction from his apparent command of the current situation, Jodis instead looked to Chen like someone weary of conflict. "The only battle I am interested in is the one I can prevent. To that end, I have no quarrel with the Golvonek, either."

"What battle?" Harstad asked, glaring at him. "You'd think Mynlara would be sending messages back to her planet right now, telling them you're on your way to blow them up. If that doesn't get them to the negotiating table, I don't know what will."

Jodis smiled. "You actually believe my intention is to blow up Uphrel?"

"Isn't that the whole point of all of this?" Chen asked, waving her hands to indicate the room and, by extension, the *Arrow* itself. "The whole crazy plan to send you back in time to end the war before it even starts?"

"I concede that may have been someone's idea," Jodis replied, before allowing his gaze to drift from hers as though recalling a memory. "Or, rather, it will be someone's idea in the future, but that was not the *Poklori gil dara*'s original mission. That bit of frantic, desperate inspiration came much later, when it became obvious that time, lack of vision, and simple arrogance had seen to it that the Raqilan were destined to lose the war, no matter who historians in generations to come might declare the victor."

"What are you saying?" Crusher asked. "That this ship was built to only be a deterrent?"

Bnira replied, "That was its original intent. The *Poklori gil dara* was to be the ultimate, final weapon constructed by either side for our war, its supremacy never to be challenged; and once the war ended? It would remain on patrol, always ready to take up arms against anyone who challenged the truce both sides would inevitably embrace."

"Peace through superior firepower," Chen remarked.

"Exactly," replied Jodis, shaking his head. "It was a ridiculous plan: deploying incredible, untested technology created by trying to mimic weapons and other systems purloined from an alien race. We were banking the future of our civilization on the promise *Poklori gil dara* offered, motivated as we were by sheer desperation. According to analysts and other experts, we were losing the war. It had been predicted that the Golvonek would win as a consequence of simple attrition, possessing as they did more ships and people to fly to them, along with a wider availability of more plentiful resources. Facing this, we had been devoting everything we had into what many believed to be an anxious, final gambit. If the scheme failed, it likely would signal the eventual defeat of our people at the hands of the Golvonek."

Chen asked, "If that was the case, then why the time travel element? It's our understanding that the basic idea was to go back and prevent the war in some manner, and avoid all the bloodshed, loss of live, and damage to both planets."

"That is basically correct," Jodis said, stepping back to the control tower. "As you have learned, our war has not been a constant source of conflict for all these generations.

There were periods of truce, if not outright peace. Government leaders and diplomats spent inordinate amounts of time attempting to reach lasting agreements, but something always disrupted those negotiations, and we would find ourselves back where we had begun.

"The idea of traveling through time was introduced by a small group of radical scientists. Until that point, they had toiled in near obscurity, fielding outrageous theories and making bold claims about the concept's feasibility. Somehow, they managed to acquire the attentions of someone in the Raqilan senior military leadership, where the idea took hold. It was an audacious plan, to be sure, and perhaps if all had gone as conceived, it might well have been successful."

"Except that your people didn't count on this ship's crew being traitors."

The statement was out of her mouth before Chen could even stop it. Standing here, watching Jodis work, reviewing his cryptic statements and the actions he had taken to this point, she had found a thread weaving through it all, and in one moment, it all made sense.

With an expression of genuine admiration, Jodis nodded in her direction. "In a manner of speaking, you are correct."

"You've been working for the Golvonek all this time?" Crusher asked, her brow furrowing in disbelief.

"Myself, Bnira, and our dear friend Ehondar. We are—or will be—members of a group of Raqilan dissidents working with the Golvonek to end the war. We were many, scattered all through our civilian government and military structure. When word of the *Poklori gil dara*'s construction became known, and later the mission for which it was being built, an effort was put in motion to recruit and train specialists who could then be inserted into the project. The effort took many cycles and required great patience on the part of all involved, most especially those of us who might end up actually working on the ship. We worked in isolation and secrecy, each not knowing who among us might be part of the resistance movement. Only when the three of us were selected along with the others for the ship's crew did we know who our allies were."

"All that time," Harstad said, "all that secrecy, and they never knew about the spies working among them?"

"I am certain they at least suspected such an effort," Jodis replied, "but we were never discovered. We maintained our secrets throughout our training, even as the ship neared the end of its construction. At the time, the goal was simply to seize control of the vessel and deliver it to the Golvonek leadership. Once we learned of the mission to travel to the past, things changed."

Chen nodded in understanding. "The Golvonek saw the advantage in such a mission."

"Correct," Jodis said. "Not everyone, of course, but even the Golvonek have their extremist voices, calling for more aggressive action against the Raqilan. For the most part, they had fought a defensive war, launching offensives against enemy targets only when it served to protect Golvonek interests, rather than the simple securing of territory or resources. This, however, was different. Now, some within Golvonek leadership circles were demanding more forceful responses to the Raqilan threat. Despite a brave façade, for the purposes of leading the populace, in private the Golvonek leadership was all but paralyzed by fear. How does a leader go about telling his people that they might be wiped from existence by a colossal weapon sent through time to destroy their planet generations before they were born?"

"You can't," Crusher said, "not without triggering a mass panic."

"And you certainly do not communicate to the people your own scheme to use such a weapon against your enemy; to employ the very horrific tactics your adversary would use against you. We continued our training and final preparations as the ship was readied for launch. We would travel to the past, and seek to end the war before it could engulf both our peoples."

Shaking her head in disbelief, Chen said, "You're going to destroy your own planet?" Could it possibly be true? All this time, Jodis had intended to turn the *Arrow* on those who had built it? "Are you insane?"

Jodis did not answer, his attention once more on the workstation. When a tone emitted from one of the consoles, he smiled again. "Your captain is most persistent."

"Talk to him, Jodis," Crusher pleaded. "If anyone can help you figure out a peaceful solution to all of this, it's Captain Picard."

Turning from the tower, Jodis said, "From our brief conversations, I have grasped that your captain is virtuous and principled. I regret firing on your ship, but I could not afford to let him interfere with what we must do here."

"Just talk to him," Chen said. "Tell him what you want. Let him at least try to help. You can't possibly want to actually do this."

Bnira said, "Such staunch devotion." She looked to Jodis. "Perhaps we should listen to him."

"Perhaps," Jodis said, his fingers moving across the console. "However, he will first listen to us. They will all listen to us."

30

Time was running out.

Picard tapped the arms of his command chair, studying on the bridge viewscreen the *Arrow* as it moved through space. In the distance but growing closer with each passing moment was the green-brown world Henlona. The weapon ship had proceeded on its course through the Canborek system with only token resistance from Raqilan ships. Sensors showed that others were coming, traveling inbound from patrol routes or other assignments in a last-ditch effort to save their home planet from annihilation. Within minutes, a hastily assembled fleet of warships would be converging on the *Arrow*. Would it arrive in time?

Will it matter if they do?

"The vessel is slowing," reported Worf, who still stood at the tactical station behind Picard's left shoulder. "Sensors are detecting a targeting scanner in operation, aimed at the planet." After a pause, he said, "Correction. The scanner appears to be targeting the planet's moon."

"What about the particle cannon?" Picard asked.

The first officer replied, "It is active and at increased power levels."

"Conn, time to intercept?"

Seated in front of him, Lieutenant Joanna Faur replied, "Three minutes, twelve seconds, captain. Flight control systems are all working normally."

Picard offered up a brief message of thanks to the

prowess of Geordi La Forge and his engineering staff, who had managed to restore the *Enterprise*'s damaged or compromised navigation systems and give the starship a chance to chase the *Arrow*. "What about weapons?"

"Commander La Forge reports those systems should be online within five minutes."

It would be close. The *Enterprise* would arrive on scene unable to defend itself, with the *Arrow* settling into whatever final positioning it required to bring its primary weapon to bear on Henlona. Could he bluff Jodis long enough to buy his engineers the extra minutes they needed to extract yet another miracle from wherever they conjured such things?

"Captain," Worf said, "the *Arrow* definitely is targeting the moon, and I'm detecting a power spike from the primary weapon."

"Is the moon inhabited?" asked Picard, dreading the answer.

The Klingon replied, "Sensors show signs of habitation, both on the surface and underground, with approximately two hundred thousand life-forms."

"Hail them again," Picard snapped. Why would Jodis be targeting his own people? It made no sense. "Engineering, I need weapons *now*." The *Enterprise* was the only thing standing between the *Arrow* and the moon with its defenseless inhabitants, but he knew they still were too far out of range.

Faur pointed to the viewscreen. "They're firing!"

The *Arrow*'s forward edge glowed red before the beam surged forward. Without being asked, Worf adjusted the screen's image to show a pale brown orb hanging in space just as the particle beam struck it. The display was clear enough for Picard to see soil and rock pushed outward in all directions as the energy beam drilled into the moon's surface. He gripped the arms of his chair, bracing himself to watch the moon's destruction along with the poor souls who called it home.

"Wait," Worf said. "The energy readings are indicating tectonic disruption, but the effects are not on a scale sufficient to destroy the moon." Seconds later, he added, "I am detecting seismic disturbances, but that is all."

"Earthquakes?" Picard asked. On the screen, the particle beam faded, leaving behind an immense, dark hole bored into the moon's surface. "It's not possible that he miscalculated." Rising from his chair, he nodded as he comprehended what he had just witnessed. "It was a demonstration."

"The particle cannon is acquiring a new target," Worf said. "It's Henlona, sir, and now I am picking up a wideband broadcast message. It is being directed at the planet and transmitted on multiple frequencies."

"Let's see it," Picard said. On the screen, the *Arrow* disappeared, replaced by a close-up image of Jodis. The Raqilan's face was unreadable, though there was a glint of determination in his eyes.

"People of Henlona, I am Jodis. Like my parents before me and theirs, as well, I have spent my entire adult life in service to the Raqilan. When I first joined our military, it was my sincere desire that I be the last of my family ever to fight in a war. When I was given command of this vessel, I saw in it an opportunity to make my dream into reality."

"The message is being transmitted toward the Golvonek homeworld, as well," Worf reported, "though they will not receive it for nearly thirty minutes."

"This ship, as originally envisioned, was a means of ending our war. In many cycles still to come, it will be seen as a

tool with which to forge a lasting peace between our peoples. Of course, peace extracted under threat of obliteration is something less than an ideal for which we should strive. It is a testament to how far the war will push all of us, that such a measure is seen as not only necessary, but also desirable. You must understand that, from where I have come, the war has lingered for far longer than you now know it. Both Henlona and the planet of our enemy have suffered the brunt of unremitting conflict. We have reached a point where we survive merely to fight. Our attempts at peace have failed, and if we were to reach some final truce, it would not matter, for we will have succeeded in destroying that for which we have fought so long and with such obsession." Jodis paused, his expression turning somber. *"Even in the future, generations from now, we still do not know who might win our war, but the truth is that neither side will emerge victorious. We have doomed ourselves to eventual extinction."*

"Captain," said Glinn Dygan from the ops station, "sensors are picking up the approach of thirteen vessels. They all appear to be of Raqilan design, sir. Based on their defenses, I would classify them as battleships of some sort."

"Analysis, Mister Worf," Picard ordered. "Are they powerful enough to take on the *Arrow*?" He held out little hope that the fight might actually destroy the weapon ship, but any sort of delay or distraction might prove useful.

The first officer replied, "From a technological standpoint, they are no match, but given sufficient time, they may be able to mount a successful counterattack."

"What you now see before you is the manifestation of a single, final, frantic attempt to secure victory," Jodis continued. *"Of course, such triumph, attained in the far-off future,*

would be hollow. The only way such a feat could truly have meaning is if there is a civilization to benefit from the accomplishment. As that would be all but impossible, given the unrelenting nature of the war as it will continue in cycles to come, there remained but two options: fight until there was nothing left, or somehow find a way to avoid war altogether. This ship, the Poklori gil dara, is the means by which the second option can be achieved."

He paused, looking down at something not visible on the screen, and Picard noted that sadness seemed now to grip him.

"What you now see before you, this ship and the weapon I now control, is what the Golvonek were meant to see. It is the last thing they were supposed to see before I carried out my orders to destroy their planet." Once more, he stopped, and this time, he shook his head. "Do you understand how callous one must become to justify obliterating an entire civilization—a world teeming with innocents who have no idea what the future holds—to prevent a war which will end up devouring us all? And yet, here I stand, my hands ready to deploy a weapon of unparalled power, on the very people who gave birth to this monstrosity. Our people, yours and mine. We are responsible for this abomination. Think about that for a time, while I consider my next action."

Without warning, the transmission ended and Jodis's visage disappeared, replaced again by the Arrow, in the distance but now much closer than it had been just moments earlier.

"He's quite the attention-getter," observed Faur.

"Captain," Worf said, "we are being hailed by one of the Raqilan ships. It is Envoy Dnovlat."

"I can only imagine what she wants to talk about," Picard said. "On screen." The moment the frequency was opened and before he could formulate any sort of greeting, the female Raqilan was standing so close to the visual pickup that he thought she might actually crawl through the viewscreen and onto the bridge.

"Captain Picard! You must help us! Surely you see that Jodis has lost all reasonable measure of sanity?"

Dnovlat moved aside, revealing Fleet Legate Mynlara, much to Picard's surprise. *"Captain, I agree with the envoy. While the Golvonek obviously do not want the weapon used against us, neither are we prepared to see it utilized against the Raqilan. That is madness. If Jodis will not listen to reason, then the ship must be destroyed."* She turned to Dnovlat. *"The envoy saw to it that my crew was rescued from our crippled vessel. It was an act of compassion that only serves as proof that we can work together to overcome our differences and stop this war, before we travel too far down the path of mutual destruction."*

"The fleet legate gives me more credit than I deserve. It was vessels under her command that began assisting damaged Raqilan ships first, Captain."

Picard nodded. "So, it seems you now have a common foe. What will you do if and when you vanquish your shared enemy?"

"I cannot speak for my leadership, Captain," replied Dnovlat, *"but if this incident does not provide the proper motivation to seek a permanent truce, then perhaps we are beyond redemption and Jodis should do as he so desires, but I have to believe we have a chance to finally make the correct choices, for all our people. Jodis is about to rob us of that opportunity."*

Stepping closer to the screen, Picard replied, "Envoy, I believe that neither you nor I possess the firepower necessary to disable that vessel, let alone destroy it. Besides, based on what I observed, it seems to me that Jodis is in total command of his faculties."

"*So, do you believe Jodis capable of carrying out his threat?*" asked Mynlara.

"At this point," Picard said, "I believe that only Jodis can answer that question."

"*Engineering to bridge*," said the voice of Geordi La Forge, interrupting the conversation. "*Captain, weapons control has been restored. You've got everything at your command.*"

Buoyed by the news, Picard replied, "Excellent work, Commander. Stand by, as the next few minutes may be . . . interesting. Bridge out." Looking over his shoulder to Worf, he said, "Number One, ready all phasers and quantum torpedoes. Conn, maneuver us between the *Arrow* and the planet."

"*Captain, what are you doing?*" asked Dnovlat.

"Whatever I can, Envoy."

Would it be enough?

The question taunted Picard.

"Wait!"

The hatch leading onto the engineering deck opened, and T'Ryssa Chen had only enough time to recognize Lieutenant Kirsten Cruzen lunging through the doorway before she threw up her hands, hoping to head off another firefight in the room.

"Don't shoot!"

Cruzen, to her credit, did not fire the phaser that she had aimed at Jodis. Behind her, Lieutenant Aneta Šmrhová and a team of *Enterprise* security officers, each of them brandishing phaser rifles, entered the room and fanned out, forming a wedge with Cruzen at its center.

Jodis, like Bnira, had taken the wiser course of holding his own weapon with its barrel raised toward the overhead, his free hand visible to the new arrivals. "I do not wish to fight you."

"That's great," Šmrhová said, gesturing with her phaser rifle. "Prove it to me by dropping those weapons."

As Lieutenant T'Sona and Ensign Regnis collected the surrendered pulse rifles, Cruzen moved toward Doctor Crusher and the wounded Rennan Konya and Tamala Harstad, removing the satchel she had slung over her left shoulder and handing it to Crusher. "How's Rennan?"

Taking the satchel and opening it, Crusher was relieved to see the medical kit Cruzen had retrieved from the shuttlecraft. "He's holding steady, but we need to get him to the *Enterprise*."

"Jodis and Bnira are getting set to destroy their own planet," Chen replied. "We're waiting to see if he goes through with it." She gestured toward the Raqilan. "I don't think even he knows what he's going to do."

"Of course I know," Jodis replied. Keeping his hands raised in deference to the pair of phaser rifles, Šmrhová's and Ensign Chapman's, still trained on him, he gestured toward the central tower and the image of Henlona displayed upon one of its monitors. "Do you actually believe I want to exterminate my entire civilization?"

"You were ready to do that to the Golvonek, weren't you?" asked Šmrhová.

"Oh, right," Chen said. "That's another new development. These guys are working for the Golvonek. Or they were, or will be." She sighed. "*Whatever*."

"Spies?" Cruzen asked. "Traitors?"

"We are not traitors," Bnira replied. "We are sympathizers. There were many of us who wanted to end the war and achieve peace for everyone, not betray our own people."

Šmrhová's expression illustrated her skepticism. "This whole time, you've been . . . what, exactly? Waiting for the right moment to tell us all of this?"

"We have been prisoners since the moment of our revival," Jodis said. "We did not know whom to trust, and therefore could not take the chance of the ship falling into the wrong hands. That is still a concern, but we have taken steps to prevent or at least minimize that possibility."

Chen said, "I don't think the people down on your planet are buying your story. It might have something to do with you pointing that big giant gun at them." She waved in the direction of the particle cannon. "It's just a guess, though."

"Fool," Jodis said. "Do you honestly believe we plan to murder our entire world? Do you think us so evil?"

From where she knelt next to Konya, holding a tricorder she had taken from the medical kit, Crusher said, "Based on the events of the past hour or so, you're not showing us much to make us think any differently."

"It was necessary to maintain an illusion," Jodis said, pointing to the monitors on the central tower. "As we speak, leaders from around my planet are attempting to make contact, begging me not to fire." He walked toward the console, tapping one of the displays with a finger. "Do you see this? It is programmed to monitor communications to and from Henlona, and it is already receiving transmissions from one of the Raqilan ships. Fleet Legate Mynlara is aboard that ship, pleading with our leadership to make a new overture toward peace with the Golvonek. In time, both governments will be desperate to talk with one another."

"Okay, then you've made your point," Chen said. "So, dial back the aggression, and give them the time to work it out for themselves."

Jodis shook his head. "Not yet. We must remain here, ready to carry out the threat, until our leaders take action."

Cruzen asked, "What's to stop them from doing just enough to appease you so that you'll stand down? Then they arrest you, seize the ship, and pick up where they left off by turning it on the Golvonek. You have to know someone's thinking about that down there, right?"

"There will be no seizing this vessel," Bnira replied. "We have taken steps to prevent that. No one will be able to use the ship for their own agenda."

"Why don't I like the way that sounds?" Chen asked.

A new alert tone sounded from the console, and Jodis turned to study it, his features clouding with renewed irritation. "Your captain. Again."

"What's he done now?" asked Crusher.

"He has maneuvered your ship into position ahead of us," Jodis replied. "I admire his bravery and principles."

Chen considered this new development. What did the captain hope to gain by using the *Enterprise* as a shield against the *Arrow*? One strike from the ship's particle cannon at full strength likely would be more than enough to destroy the starship. "He doesn't know you're basically trying to bluff your own people as well as the Golvonek. If you don't tell him what's going on, he's liable to fire everything he has at you."

"I cannot contact him," Jodis said. "Our communications would almost certainly be intercepted by the Raqilan military, and our ruse would be exposed."

"Look, I really don't care about any of this," Crusher

said, closing her tricorder and pointing to Konya. "We need to get Rennan back to our ship, now, and to do that we need to get him to the landing bay."

"No problem, Doctor," said Lieutenant Jarata Beyn. The muscular Bajoran handed his phaser rifle to Ensign Chapman and stepped toward Crusher, Konya, and Harstad. "I can carry him."

"Carefully," Crusher warned. "He's in pretty bad shape."

Jarata smiled. "Worry not, Doctor. I'll treat him as though he was my baby nephew."

"There are still elements of the Golvonek security detachment scattered across the ship," Jodis said. "They will attempt to stop you."

"That's what we're for," replied Šmrhová.

Another alert tone pinged from the central tower, more ominous than any of the other indicators Chen had heard from the *Arrow*'s various shipboard systems.

"What is that?" she asked. She could tell from the way Jodis was frantically tapping at the console that something unexpected—or worse—was happening.

"The computer has enabled a new protocol, one with which I am unfamiliar."

Stepping toward the tower, Chen eyed the workstation. "You're kidding, right? What kind of protocol are we talking about?"

"I do not know." Jodis did not look away from the monitors, his fingers sweeping across the console with a practiced speed and dexterity.

Chen pointed to one monitor. "There. What's that?" Following her guidance, Jodis highlighted a portion of computer-generated text. She leaned closer, and frowned. "Is that a security program of some sort?"

"It appears so."

Moving to stand on Jodis's opposite side, Bnira studied the monitors. "Jodis, that is a contingency protocol, but I don't recognize it."

"That is because it is not a standard component of the ship's computer," Jodis said. After entering more commands to the console, he gestured to another monitor. "This procedure was executed from a clandestine partition installed in the central computer core. It was not intended for us, but rather for the computer itself." He looked to Chen. "Another of the automated processes overseeing ship functions."

"And what does it do?" Chen asked.

Bnira replied, "Its mandate is to carry out our mission as though the crew was dead, incapacitated, or otherwise unable to function."

"You can't be serious," Crusher said. Chen glanced in her direction and saw the doctor standing with Cruzen, Harstad, and Jarata, the latter cradling the wounded Konya in his oversized arms.

"I am afraid so," Jodis answered, his gaze still fixed on the instruments. "I am attempting to circumvent the process, but it was designed to defeat such measures."

"What are you saying?" Cruzen asked. "Tell me you're not saying what I think you're saying. You're saying the computer's going to fire the cannon at the planet anyway?"

In response to the lieutenant's query, another status monitor flared to life, illuminated by rapidly changing Raqilanscript in what Chen recognized was a numeric sequence.

"That's what he's saying." Chen pointed to the monitor. "And that's a countdown."

31

———

Seated at one of the computer terminals in the *Enterprise*'s engineering section, Taurik waited for the starship's systems to complete their connections. Despite the obvious differences in technology between the ship's main computer and that of the *Arrow*, interaction on a limited level was possible thanks to the interface process created by Lieutenant Dina Elfiki. That protocol already had served Doctor Crusher and her medical team during their efforts to revive Jodis and his crew from hibernation, and Taurik now hoped it would aid him in being able to convince the *Arrow*'s computer not to undertake a horrific action.

"You should be tied in now, Taurik," said the voice of Lieutenant T'Ryssa Chen over the intercom system. The communications jamming effect had been neutralized aboard the *Arrow*, and Taurik found himself pleased to hear his friend's voice.

"The connection is complete," Taurik said after a moment.

"There we go," added Commander La Forge, who stood behind him and watched as Taurik worked. When Chen's call for aid had come over the communications channel, the chief engineer had wasted no time putting his assistant to work. Despite his own formidable skills, La Forge was deferring to Taurik's superior computer expertise while standing ready to help.

Studying the new strings of data that had coalesced

on the workstation's monitor, Taurik said, "This encryption scheme is inconsistent with the rest of the software installed to the *Arrow*'s main computer. I recognize none of the embedded keys or signatures."

"Yeah," Chen replied, *"tell me about it. Whatever this is, it's a completely different animal, and whoever installed it knew what they were doing. I've been through the central core three or four times by now, and I never even saw the partition where this thing was hiding."*

"Understandable, as it likely was designed to avoid detection." Taurik scrolled through columns of Raqilan computer text, seeing nothing that appeared to be of any use in circumventing the security measures encoded to this new algorithm. "It is a remarkable example of programming."

"You can admire it later," Chen replied. *"Any ideas on how to beat it?"*

Taurik said, "Not yet. This may take some time."

"I don't think it's going to wait around."

Leaning closer to the workstation, La Forge said, "You're saying that even Jodis doesn't have a way to get around this thing?"

"Jodis didn't even know about it until it was triggered, and it's wired into everything. He thinks someone in their resistance cell had it implanted as a failsafe in case he and his crew changed their minds at the moment of truth, or something. It's like a whole other master control protocol designed to replace the main operating system in the event of . . . whatever pisses it off, I guess."

"That may be the key." Seeing segments of the programming code that looked promising, Taurik highlighted and isolated those sections from the rest of the stream. "However, I am hampered somewhat, as part of the system's defense mechanism is to guard against remote intrusion. I am encountering numerous obstacles the deeper I penetrate into the software."

Chen's grunt of irritation filtered through the intercom. *"I was wondering about that. I don't think I can stop that, so just do the best you can. If you see something, you can always guide me as I go after it directly from here."*

"Very well," Taurik replied. His primary concern was not that he and Chen, working with Jodis and Bnira, would not be able to defeat the computer protocols, but that they would fail to do so in time to prevent the *Arrow*'s particle cannon from destroying the Raqilan homeworld. He wondered if the people down on the planet knew or had been told of the current predicament. Logic suggested that notifying the populace of its own imminent extinction might lead to mass panic and a breakdown of civilization, government, and social services, but perhaps their culture and customs called for a gathering of family and other close friends when a death was at hand.

None of that is of any consequence just now, Taurik reminded himself.

"Engineering to bridge," said La Forge. "Captain, we're having trouble circumventing the *Arrow*'s computer lockouts. I don't know if we can get this done in time."

"Keep working, Commander," replied Captain Picard over the speaker. *"If you're unable to defeat the security, I'll have to take more direct action."*

"Such action may not be prudent, sir," Taurik said. "According to my analysis, part of this measure's protection scheme is direct access to shipboard scanners and defenses. It has registered the *Enterprise*'s presence within weapons range."

"We know. Worf is tracking its energy output, and I suspect it will react the instant we attempt to lock our weapons, but we're about to be left with no choice. The Raqilan fleet has taken up position around the ship, as well."

"Jodis and Bnira have been able to counter its attempts to engage," Chen said, "but I don't know how much longer they can keep that up."

From the corner of his eye, Taurik saw La Forge lean toward the console again. "There," he said, pointing to one portion of the computer scrawl. "What's that right there?"

Seeing what the commander had spotted, Taurik nodded in approval. "Yes, that may be it. Lieutenant Chen, I believe we have an access point to the encrypted subroutines."

"I'm all ears," Chen replied. Then, because it was her, she added, "That's right, I said it."

"Part of the scheme's design is dependent upon it being able to infiltrate the rest of the computer network through ordinary processes, including low-level protocols which, while not critical, are still required throughout the rest of the system to facilitate operation."

"Right. It's supposed to blend in."

"Precisely. Because of this feature, it should be possible to infiltrate the protected routines using a similar method, only in reverse. This will not work if we attempt it through any of the major processes such as weapons or navigation or life support, but we may be able to exploit something far more mundane and perhaps overlooked."

La Forge said, "Like trying to get into a house through a crack in the foundation."

Pausing to ponder the comparison, Taurik replied, "An inexact analogy, but sufficient for our purposes." After another moment spend studying the computer data, he added, "This will still take time, perhaps more time than we have."

"Then we're out of options," Picard said. *"Lieutenant Chen, warn the others."*

New alarms wailed throughout the engineering deck, and T'Ryssa Chen felt the ship shuddering around her. Even here, with nearly half the ship's length between where she stood and the *Arrow*'s forward edge, the effects of the *Enterprise*'s renewed attack on the weapon ship could be felt.

"Multiple strikes forward," reported Bnira, standing next to Jodis at the central tower's other remaining and still functional workstation. "There is massive damage to the particle cannon and surrounding hull sections."

"Can it still fire?" Chen asked.

His eyes studying the cascading streams of data scrolling across multiple monitors, Jodis shook his head. "No, but it is still drawing energy from the power plant." He pointed to one of the displays. "The encrypted protocols are executing some other measure."

"What's left?" Chen studied the data, looking for some clue. When she saw it, she reached out to tap one of the display screens. "Right there. Look. It's targeting something on the planet's surface."

Bnira replied, "That is the largest city on our world, at least in this time. That region accounts for nearly twelve percent of the entire population."

"Okay, but what does it matter if the particle cannon is

out of commission?" asked Lieutenant Cruzen. After dispatching the rest of the away team as well as Šmrhová and her rescue team back to the *Arrow*'s landing bay, she had remained, unwilling to leave Chen alone with the Raqilan as she worked to assist Jodis and Bnira.

Chen saw another reading on the monitor devoted to the ship's navigation, and then everything made total, horrific sense. "Oh, damn."

"The protocol is attempting to enter a course toward the planet's surface," Jodis said, "with the intention of using the ship as a projectile."

Chen called out, "Taurik, are you seeing this?"

"Affirmative," replied the Vulcan. *"Captain Picard reports the other Raqilan ships are moving to intercept."*

"They will not be able to stop us," Jodis said.

"This is Captain Picard. Lieutenant Chen, I want all of our people off that ship right now. Jodis, if you can't alter your course, then we'll have no choice but to fire."

Jodis replied, "Captain, their ships will be unable to inflict enough damage to prevent the ship from following this trajectory. We have to stop it here."

From the monitors, Chen saw the navigation system already laying in the new coordinates, and she heard the renewed thrum of the *Arrow*'s engines as it pushed the weapon ship forward. Studying the monitors with the computer text, she said, "Taurik, your idea of infiltrating the secured protocols; can we use that to interfere with the navigation system?"

"Perhaps, but the ship will still be little more than an armed explosive with an active trigger. Unless or until we can completely override those processes, the ship is an imminent threat, and that is without considering the possibility

that the secured routines do not contain measures to defeat our efforts."

"Always the optimist." Looking to Jodis, Chen said, "We need to find a place to dispose of this thing that's away from, well, everything."

Jodis nodded, and for the first time since the current crisis began, he smiled. "There is just such a suitable location."

"Assuming our infiltration is successful," Taurik said, *"we will need to monitor the process and be ready to make adjustments. That will require manual oversight and action."*

Jodis said, "Understood. I will remain here to assist with the procedure." Turning from the console, he said to Bnira, "Retrieve Foctine Vedapir, and tell him to send a shipwide broadcast to his people to evacuate immediately." To Chen, he said, "You should go, as well."

"But I can help," Chen protested.

Over the still-open communications frequency, Captain Picard's voice was unyielding. *"Lieutenant, get to the landing bay for return to the* Enterprise."

"Captain, it will take three of us to cover everything," Chen said. "Navigation, propulsion, and just keeping the damned computer off our asses while we work. We can get where it needs to be, lock in its final course, and then get the hell out of here."

There was a pause, and she knew the captain was weighing whatever paltry options might be left to him. When he responded, his tone was softer. *"Very well, Lieutenant, but stay only as long as absolutely necessary."*

"Request permission to remain with Chen, sir," said Cruzen. "She may need my help."

Picard replied, *"Permission granted, Lieutenant. The away team is preparing to depart the* Arrow *aboard the shuttlecraft, but the portable transporter pad is still in the landing bay, and we're locked on to its signal. The Enterprise will remain in transporter range for as long as necessary.*

"It's nice to be loved, sir," Chen said. "We'll continue to feed updates as appropriate."

"Keep this channel open."

Turning to Jodis, Cruzen asked, "Okay, now what?"

32

Beverly Crusher placed the hypospray against Rennan Konya's neck and heard the pneumatic hiss as it discharged its medication into the lieutenant's bloodstream. Within seconds, his eyes fluttered and opened, and he turned his head upon noticing Crusher sitting next to him.

"Where am I?" he asked, his words slow and slurred.

Crusher said, "On the *Jefferies*. We're getting ready to head back to the *Enterprise*."

Frowning, Konya raised his head to look around, and she watched him take in their surroundings. He was lying on one of the couches in the rear of the shuttlecraft's passenger area. The compartment was packed with equipment and members of the away team as well as Lieutenant Šmrhová's security detail. "There are a lot more people here than I remember. What did I miss?"

"A lot, my friend," said Lieutenant Jarata Beyn, sitting on the couch next to Konya's head. "It's been a rather exciting couple of hours."

"What?" Konya, still weakened from his injuries, failed in his attempt to push himself from the couch and let his head fall back against the cushion. "Did something heavy fall on me? I hurt everywhere."

"I've treated the worst of your injuries," Crusher said, "at least enough to get us back to the ship. You'll be fine once we get you to sickbay." After treating the wounds he had sustained from the Golvonek grenade blast, she had opted against using the portable transporter pad to return Konya to the *Enterprise*. T'Ryssa Chen had warned that the *Arrow*, operating as it was under the protected contingency protocol that was fighting to assume total control of the ship, it might attempt to fire on the *Enterprise* as it drew to within transporter range. The *Jefferies* was the safer option for the away team's extraction, so everyone had piled into the compact craft.

"Great," Konya said. "I can use the rest." Reaching up with one hand, he touched the dermal patch Crusher had placed on his forehead as a replacement for the crude bandages she and Harstad had used. "How's Doctor Harstad?"

"I'm fine, Lieutenant," she replied, sitting near his feet. "My leg's going to be sore for a couple of days, but I'll live."

"How'd I even get down here, anyway?"

Jarata patted his shoulder. "You're welcome."

The mock expression of annoyance and shame was enough to tell Crusher that Konya was feeling somewhat better. "Oh, wow. Moose? You're going to make me pay for that, aren't you?"

"Indeed I am," replied the muscled Bajoran. "And not for nothing, but I think you might want to talk to the doctor about a better diet. I suggest more fruits and salads."

A small, dry laugh escaped Konya's lips, and he squeezed his eyes shut. "Don't make me do that. Well, at least I avoided having Chen carry me." That made him open his eyes, and he turned his head, looking about the shuttle's interior. "Wait, where is she?"

Crusher gave him a shortened account of the events that had transpired after his injuries, but it was when she got to the part about Chen remaining behind to help Jodis and Bnira that the Betazoid found new strength. He pushed himself from the couch, wincing with every move but ignoring his own discomfort.

"We can't leave Trys alone back there," he snapped, gritting his teeth in obvious pain as he bit off each word.

Crusher placed her hands on his shoulders, stopping him from standing. "Cruzen's with her, Rennan. Jodis and Bnira need her help to steer the ship to a safe location."

Footsteps on the *Jefferies*'s boarding ramp made Crusher look to see Lieutenants Šmrhová and T'Sona making their way through the open rear hatch.

"That's it," Šmrhová said, handing her phaser rifle to T'Sona for return to the shuttle's storage locker. "Everybody's aboard. We can button up and get out of here."

"What about Chen and Cruzen?" Konya asked. "Hell, what about the Golvonek?"

Looking out through the hatch, Crusher saw several Golvonek soldiers and other personnel, all of them readying their own transport craft for departure. She had heard the warning broadcast over the *Arrow*'s internal communications system by Foctine Vedapir, alerting everyone aboard the weapon ship to depart at once. No one had given the away team or the *Jefferies* a second glance in their haste to flee.

"They're evacuating, just like us," she said. "Chen and Cruzen will use the transporter pad once they're finished helping Jodis and Bnira."

Konya replied, "I hate that plan."

"You're in no condition to help, Lieutenant," Šmrhová said. "Now lie there and let Doctor Crusher take care of you. I didn't come all this way just to have you die on me."

"I'm not going to die." Konya gestured toward Crusher. "She already made sure of that."

Šmrhová, her expression flat, did not hesitate. "Then I'll kill you if you don't behave."

The remark drew another pained laugh from the Betazoid, who raised a hand in weak surrender. "All right, you win." Shifting his gaze to Crusher, he said, "Tell me whatever they're doing up there isn't dangerous or stupid."

Crusher laid a hand on Konya's arm. "Relax, Rennan. Chen knows what she's doing." As she tried to reassure him, her own thoughts to turned to T'Ryssa Chen and Kirsten Cruzen.

Don't you two make a liar out of me.

"This may have been a bad idea."

Chen felt beads of sweat running down her torso beneath her uniform. For the fourth time in thirty minutes, she renewed her attempts to outwit the invasive program worming its way through every facet of the *Arrow*'s computer network. She now understood how its computer design, intended to assist a minimal crew with managing all of the vessel's automated processes, was working against her.

"Whoever wrote this code was a damned genius," she said, "and one twisted son of a bitch." She paused to wipe perspiration from her brow, feeling the dampness of her uniform sleeve. Once more, she set to creating on the fly a new protocol to deflect the malicious software's latest, relentless efforts to seize total control of the system.

"I do not believe the creator of this protocol has been born yet," remarked Bnira.

"Not really important right now," said Kirsten Cruzen,

from where she stood next to Chen. Looking around the room, the security officer shook her head. "I feel about as useless as a tuxedo at a Betazoid wedding."

Chen could not help the chuckle her friend's comment prompted. "I can't wait to tell Konya that one."

"What is a tuxedo?" Bnira asked.

"Later."

Like Chen and Jodis, Bnira had been devoting her full attention to fighting the contingency program, using whatever openings Chen could provide to maintain the *Arrow*'s present course away from the planet Henlona and across the Canborek system toward its new target. Glancing to one screen, Chen noted that their escorts, thirteen Raqilan warships and the *Enterprise*, were maintaining their positions all around the weapon ship, having traveled with it from the Raqilan homeworld. During the transit from Henlona, Chen and Jodis had been forced to engineer a workaround when the override program had momentarily taken control of the *Arrow*'s weapons and fired on one of the Raqilan ships.

Another alarm sounded from one of the screens, and Chen noted the message relayed by the computer that another weapon port now was offline.

"That's fifteen, Lieutenant," said Captain Picard over her combadge's open frequency. *"We're continuing our attacks."* After the persistent program had been circumvented yet again, and with the weapon ship's defensive field generators taken offline by Jodis, the escort fleet and the *Enterprise* had taken the opportunity to disable or destroy several of the *Arrow*'s weapon ports. Outwitting the protocol was proving more and more difficult, however, as it had begun replicating itself and depositing self-sufficient subroutines throughout the computer system,

each one branching out and snatching control of other automated processes without the need for direct oversight from the main program.

"At least twenty-two of the ports are operating under independent control, Captain," Chen warned. "I'm trying to find a way to grab them back, but it's taking time." She had realized that this new ploy was deliberate on the program's part, diverting her efforts to neutralize the core processes and return total control of the vessel to Jodis.

"I have isolated the process overseeing the particle cannon's power nodes," said the Raqilan, his attention focused on his own console, "though I do not know how long it will endure before the protocol makes another attempt to commandeer that part of the system. It is an impressive construct."

Chen grunted in irritation. "That's one way to put it." As far as she had been able to determine, the contingency protocol, along with being able to take over the ship's function in the event of the crew's incapacitation or death, also had been designed as a means of guaranteeing the *Arrow* carried out her mission even if Jodis or the others decided not to follow their orders. "Someone in your resistance movement is one cold bastard."

"I do not understand your statement," Jodis replied, "but if you mean that they were misguided when they decided on including this measure, I am forced to agree with you."

"Desperate times, I suppose," Chen said. Though she could not condone even the idea of an act as heinous as genocide, she at least thought she might understand those who may have viewed such a tactic as necessary. After generations of incessant conflict and the promise of societal upheaval as both sides eventually succumbed to the ravages of war inflicted upon their worlds and their civilizations, Chen imagined more than a few Raqilan and Golvonek able to justify the *Arrow* and its peculiar mission to prevent the war from happening at all. In some ways, it reminded her of the decisions with which Starfleet—and Captain Picard in particular—had wrestled when it seemed all but certain that the Borg would overrun the Alpha Quadrant and destroy the Federation. As she had then, Chen now tried to understand and even sympathize with the stresses faced by these people who had known nothing but generations of war.

No, she decided. *It's still insane.*

An alert tone sounded on Bnira's console, and she said, "Jodis, we are approaching outer orbital perimeter."

"Good," Jodis replied. "Enter the final coordinates to navigational control." He swept his hand across one of his station's interfaces, and one of the larger monitors shifted to show a pale gray moon. The lifeless orb filled the screen, its image enhanced so that Chen could make out craters and other terrain features.

"Captain," Cruzen said, "has the base been evacuated?"

Picard replied, *"Yes. The last transport departed just moments ago, and our sensors have verified no life-forms within the projected blast radius. You're all clear, Lieutenant."*

"Coordinates locked into navigation," Bnira reported, and Chen noted on one of the displays that the target of the *Arrow*'s new—and final—course now was visible on the screen. Illuminated by the brilliant Canborek sun, the Landorem moon's arid gray soil surrounding the mountain served to highlight the network of metal support structures enclosing the skeletal framework of . . . the *Arrow*. Even from this distance far above the surface of the moon, it was easy for Chen to discern the weapon ship in its embryonic state of construction.

"Well, that's just weird to look at." Chen knew she should not be surprised to see the nascent vessel, its construction decades away from completion, but the sight only reinforced the bizarre nature of this entire affair and to what lengths the Raqilan had gone—or would go—in pursuit of total victory over the Golvonek.

"You should probably know that the Raqilan government is none too pleased with this course of action," Picard said, breaking Chen from her reverie.

Cruzen replied, "I'm guessing the alternative's a bit less agreeable."

"That seems to be the consensus. I was worried that the Raqilan might try to interfere once they realized where you were heading, but their ships are keeping their distance."

Chen said, "In a couple of minutes, it won't matter." Like the captain, she also had been worried that the Raqilan might be spurred by the realization that they were about to lose the weapon which their military promised would bring about an end to the war. She had anticipated some measure of resistance, if nothing else than to force Jodis to select another location for disposing of the *Arrow*. On the other hand, she had admired the audacity of his choice, which was just so perfect on so many levels. Of course, she supposed there might be temporal ramifications to consider, such as the apparent paradox of using the completed version of the weapon ship to destroy its earlier, burgeoning self. How would the supposed rules of time travel view such a thing?

When this is all over, somebody at the Department of Temporal Investigations is going to have an aneurysm.

"It is time," Jodis said. "Bnira, execute the new course."

It might have been Chen's imagination, but she was certain she felt the *Arrow* groan in protest as the ship changed its trajectory to assume its new heading. "How much time?"

"Less than ten *linzatu*. If we leave now, that should be sufficient time to abandon ship."

Chen made the calculation and conversion in her head. They had just over six minutes before the *Arrow* completed its descent from orbit and plummeted into the lunar surface. It would be close, but if they ran full out, they should be able to get to the landing bay with time to spare. "Did you get that, *Enterprise*?"

"*Affirmative,*" replied Commander Worf. "*Proceed to the extraction point, Lieutenant.*"

"Aye, sir." No sooner had she replied than Chen saw another alert flash on her console, and her breath caught in her throat as she saw what was happening. "Damn it!"

"*What is it, Lieutenant?*" asked Picard.

Biting back the growing need to utter profanities or punch something, Chen said, "It's the contingency protocol, sir. It's trying to infiltrate the propulsion and navigation systems."

"Navigation control just deleted the coordinates," Bnira added, hunched once more over her console. "I need to enter them again."

Jodis said, "It will do no good." He pointed to another monitor, the one Chen recognized as displaying the current status of the propulsion and navigation systems. "The protocol is attempting to circumvent the remote guidance systems. Without that, the ship will not maintain course to target."

"You're saying it could abort?" Cruzen asked.

"Possibly," Jodis replied. "It might even be able to prevent the crash." He turned from the workstation, his gaze locking with hers. "The process must be overseen manually."

It took an extra second for the implications of his statement to register, and when it did Chen felt her mouth drop open. "Wait. You can't . . . ?"

"There is no other option," Bnira said, turning to Jodis. "We will need to stay."

Jodis pointed for the door. "But you must go. Bnira and I can do this."

"What about getting off the ship?" Cruzen asked.

"Once we are certain the process cannot be aborted," Jodis replied, "we will follow you to the landing bay, but we cannot ask you to remain. You have already done enough, and this is our responsibility." He reached over and placed a hand on Chen's shoulder. "Like your captain, you are of noble character. If all of your people are of similar quality, then the Raqilan and Golvonek have made exceptional new friends today."

There was a finality to his words that made Chen uneasy, and she felt moisture forming at the corners of her eyes. "Jodis," she began.

"It is time," he replied, his voice quiet as he nodded toward the door. "Go."

33

On the viewscreen was perhaps one of the most surreal scenes to which Picard had ever borne witness. Angled toward the Landorem moon, the *Arrow* was accelerating as it began its descent. Its massive aft engines glowed white with the energy they produced to send the weapon ship to its doom. Picard imagined the image as similar to that of a foundering oceangoing vessel, its bow disappearing beneath the waves as its stern rose into the air before the entire ship slipped into a watery grave.

"Time to impact?"

"Four minutes twenty seconds at its current rate of acceleration," reported Worf. The first officer had moved from the tactical console and resumed his normal station in the seat to the right of Picard's command chair. "Sir, the main shuttlebay reports that the *Jefferies* has arrived, and Doctor Crusher is on her way to sickbay with the injured away team members."

"What about Chen and Cruzen?"

"They are en route to the *Arrow*'s landing bay."

Nodding in approval, Picard said, "Are transporters locked on?"

"Affirmative, sir," Worf replied. "They are standing by the moment Chen and Cruzen reach the pad."

What was taking so damned long? The seconds seemed to crawl, each one taking an eternity. "Jodis, this is Captain Picard, can you hear me?"

"*I hear you,*" replied the Raqilan. "*We are maintain-*

*ing course and speed, but we are still fighting the contingency
protocol.*" He did not say anything else, and neither was
that necessary. Picard had known from the moment Jodis
explained the dilemma what it would mean for him and
Bnira.

"I understand."

"*Captain,*" Jodis said, "*I have a request of you.*"

"What is it?"

"*Talk to our people, the Raqilan and the Golvonek. Convince them to seek peace. What has happened today—what
almost happened today, and what was supposed to happen—
should be more than sufficient to demonstrate the futility of
continuing as we have. There must be change, and it must
start today. Tell them, and make them understand.*"

Feeling his throat tighten, Picard nodded. "I will tell
them, Jodis. You have my word."

"*It was an honor to know you, Captain, if only briefly. May
your journeys continue to be safe and rewarding. Farewell.*"

There was a beep as the connection closed, leaving
Picard to stare at the viewscreen and the *Arrow*, plunging
headlong toward the moon.

"Impact in three minutes," said Worf.

It would feel like three centuries, Picard knew.

Where the hell are Chen and Cruzen?

"Where the hell is the landing bay?"

Sprinting down the corridor, Chen glanced over her
shoulder at Cruzen, who was keeping pace but looking
flushed. The security officer's breath also was sounding a
bit labored, and Chen was reminded that her friend had
already been through quite a lot to this point.

"This way," she said, pointing to her right as they
neared another intersection. What had started out as

a simple dash from the *Arrow*'s engineering deck to its landing bay using as a guide the internal schematic contained in Cruzen's tricorder had become a great deal more complicated. Sealed hatches were their biggest obstacle, as different sections of the ship, directed by whatever independent computer processes oversaw such things, automatically prepared the vessel for what it likely was registering as an imminent collision. Such emergency action schemes obviously included a loss of internal atmosphere as one potential risk, and as such, the ship's numerous compartments were being sealed off as a protective measure against hull ruptures.

That's going to be the least of this beast's problems in about three minutes.

All around them as they ran, Chen heard the hull vibrating and objecting to the increasing stresses being placed upon it. Now likely caught by the moon's gravity, there would be almost no chance of the *Arrow* emerging from its descent. It either would hit its target or else break apart and scatter its remnants across the lifeless lunar soil. She doubted that even the insidious programming built into the ship's computer could do anything to change that looming reality.

Rounding the turn in the passageway, Chen stopped short of dashing straight into yet another sealed hatch. This one was larger and looked more formidable than the others they had encountered, yet appeared to be just as locked. "Whoops."

"Damn it!" Cruzen snapped. Even as Chen tried pulling on the door's recessed handle and found it sealed, the security officer retrieved her tricorder from the holster on her hip. Activating the unit, she used it to scan the control pad set into the bulkhead next to the hatch. This was the third time they had been forced to deal with a sealed hatch, but the algorithms Commander La Forge had provided following his team's initial survey of the ship had come in handy.

"The landing bay should be just down this corridor," Chen said.

Looking up from the tricorder as she worked while regaining her breath, Cruzen eyed Chen. "You're not even winded."

"Thank my cursed Vulcan constitution."

"I need to get one of those." Aiming her tricorder at the control pad, Cruzen executed the signal that should have unlocked the hatch. Instead, nothing happened.

"Uh-oh," said Chen.

"Shit. Something's different." Cruzen attempted the sequence a second time, but achieved the same result. "The damned computer must be overriding the locks or something."

Chen looked around the hallway but saw no alternatives for bypassing the hatch. "Not for nothing, but we've got about two minutes."

"Thanks." When the unlock sequence failed for a third time, Cruzen tossed aside the tricorder and drew her phaser. "To hell with this."

Holding up a hand, Chen said, "Whoa, hang on. It'll take too long to cut through." She rapped the hatch with her knuckles. "They're reinforced pressure doors, remember?"

"Yeah, I remember." Cruzen tapped the phaser's power setting and Chen saw its level indicator increase to maximum. "You might want to find cover."

"What if that doesn't work?" Chen asked, watching Cruzen finish setting the phaser to overload before jamming the weapon into the door's latch.

Grabbing Chen by her arm and pulling her along as she ran back to the intersection and rounded the turn, Cruzen said, "It'll work."

"How do you know?"

"Because if it doesn't, we're screwed."

Both women dropped to the deck and covered their heads with their hands just seconds before the phaser detonated, the concussion from its explosion radiating down the narrow corridor. Chen felt the rush of displaced air on her exposed skin as her ears popped, which was followed by a ringing sensation as the blast faded.

"Let's go!" Cruzen said, dragging Chen to her feet before they both ran back to the junction. Turning the corner, Chen was relieved to see a gaping hole where most of the hatch had been. Scorch marks defaced what was left of the pressure door, and the floor, bulkheads, and ceiling were peppered with rents and tears from shrapnel. Beyond the newly created opening, the *Arrow*'s landing bay beckoned.

"Hot damn." Cruzen clapped Chen on the shoulder. "We're out of here."

Chen tapped her combadge as they entered the bay. "*Enterprise*, we're here. Stand by for transport."

"*Acknowledged,*" replied Captain Picard. "*All due haste, Lieutenant.*"

"That's captain-speak for haul ass," Cruzen said, leading the way into the landing bay. The Golvonek transport ships Chen had seen earlier were gone, as was the *Jefferies*. All that remained where the shuttlecraft once had sat was the very welcome sight of the field transporter pad. Without ceremony, Cruzen and Chen dashed onto the portable platform.

"*Enterprise*, beam us out!"

Over her communicator, Chen heard Picard bark, *"Transporter room, beam them directly to the bridge!"*

There was nowhere to go. There was nothing left to do except wait.

Jodis stood before the console, watching the image of the Landorem moon's surface loom ever closer. Gravity had trapped the *Poklori gil dara* in its implacable grip. There would be no reprieve, and no chance of the computer or its contingency protocol to assert final control. He had calculated the time required to traverse the distance separating the engineering deck from the landing bay or even one of the emergency escape vehicles and concluded that either destination was beyond reach. The end, he suspected, would come quickly and without pain. He would not suffer, and neither would Bnira. Rather than fear, he instead felt relief, and he took comfort in knowing that when death claimed him, he would not be alone.

He felt Bnira take his hand in hers, holding it tightly and pulling him toward her. Her body pressed against his as her other arm wrapped around his waist. When he turned his head, their eyes met, and in hers Jodis saw no panic or worry, but instead only peace.

"This is but one stage of being." Bnira glanced toward the screen, her smile never wavering as she returned her gaze to his.

Jodis said nothing, unwilling to detract from her calm resolve. Unlike Bnira and other members of the crew, Jodis had never believed in an afterlife, but at this moment, he understood the serenity others seemed to find in accepting such possibilities.

"I have no regrets," Bnira said, reaching up to stroke the side of his face.

Jodis smiled. "Neither do I." Despite the impediments time and fate had seen fit to place before them, he and his crew had accomplished their mission, at least in some respects. He could take solice in that, and also in the knowledge that those who had followed him and Bnira—Ehondar, but also the others, who had never known the true nature of what Jodis had set out to do—had not died in vain. He trusted the human, Picard, to see to that.

To the side of the monitor displaying the moon as it filled the screen and drew ever closer, a smaller indicator cycled through remaining moments, dwindling toward nothingness. For the last time, he turned to Bnira, who clutched his face in her hands and pulled his forehead to hers.

"I hope yours is the first face I see."

Jodis smiled. "I look forward to that."

Despite preparing himself for the sight, Picard still flinched as *Armageddon's Arrow*—the *Poklori gil dara*—plunged like a tremendous spear into the moon's surface. As planned to exacting degree by Jodis, the weapon ship struck the construction site of its past self almost dead center, the entire installation disappearing in a flash of light and energy. The blast wave expanded outward in seconds, washing over the dead gray soil and consuming everything within its radius. Without an atmosphere to sustain it, the detonation was snuffed out almost instantly, leaving behind an expanding cloud of dirt and ash thrust away from the surface.

"Damn," said Lieutenant Dina Elfiki, turning from her science station and watching the scene with wide, disbelieving eyes. Her reaction was mimicked by nearly everyone else on the bridge, and even Picard felt himself moved by what had just taken place.

Standing near the bridge viewscreen where they had been materialized, Lieutenants T'Ryssa Chen and Kirsten Cruzen stared at the unsettling imagery. Chen was the first to react, and when she turned from the screen, Picard saw the tears running freely down her cheeks.

"It's good to have you back," the captain said, his voice low and quiet.

Chen nodded, but said nothing, her gaze shifting between him and the viewscreen. Where the installation had been seconds earlier now was nothing but an enormous crater. Part of the mountain forming one end of the construction base had collapsed, with mammoth pieces of rock falling into the crater.

"Sensors show it was an overload of the ship's engines and the power plant for the particle cannon," reported Lieutenant Šmrhová, who had resumed her duties at the tactical station after returning with the away team. "I also picked up secondary detonations of materials inside the mountain. The result was total obliteration of the build site."

Picard asked, "So, there's nothing at all left of the *Arrow*?"

"There's debris and other residue, but the blast pretty much wiped out everything." Šmrhová shook her head. "Whatever's left of the artificial structures are in the crater."

Worf said, "Captain, we are receiving an incoming hail from Envoy Dnovlat, as well as the commander of the Raqilan fleet. They seem eager to speak to you."

"I can imagine," Picard said. Had the events of the day sparked new motivation in the envoy and by extension the Raqilan government? What of the Golvonek? Surely, knowing the fate their world had avoided would renew their own desire to seek peace? Though buoyed by some of the initial reactions from Dnovlat and Mynlara, he remained cautious in his optimism. The captain hoped this was but the first of the steps necessary to bring the Raqilan and the Golvonek once more—and perhaps for the final time—to the negotiating table. "Notify the envoy that I'd welcome the opportunity to speak with her, once we have stabilized our situation here."

Without turning from the screen, Cruzen asked, "What about Jodis and Bnira?"

A new wave of sadness threatened to rush forth, but Picard forced himself to maintain his composure. "They stayed aboard."

"They never hesitated," said Chen, "never once thought about abandoning ship. They knew all along."

"Yes," Picard said. "They knew." He was certain that the fleet of Raqilan ships that had assumed orbit around the moon had observed the *Arrow*'s end. It was likely that images of the weapon ship's final moments already were being transmitted back to Henlora and perhaps Uphrel, as well. Within hours, every Raqilan and Golvonek would know what had happened here today. He hoped that was the case.

I will personally see to that.

34

———

Just as she was sure would happen, T'Ryssa Chen's mood brightened the moment she entered sickbay and saw Rennan Konya sitting up in bed.

"Well, look who it is," Konya said, smiling upon seeing her walk into the room. "Talk about your welcome sights."

Crossing the patient ward to stand next to his bed, she reached out and placed a hand on Konya's arm. "How are you feeling?"

"Like ten credits," replied the security officer without missing a beat. "Doctor Crusher patched me up, good as new. There aren't even any scars, even though I asked her to leave me just one." He offered a mock frown. "I even told her I'd let her pick her favorite."

Chen rolled her eyes. "You're an idiot. You know that, right?" Despite his silly comments, it was wonderful to see him more like his old self. "You had us worried there, for a while." She looked across the ward to where Tamala Harstad also sat on a bed, though unlike Konya she was dressed not in a patient's pajamas but instead casual civilian attire. "What about you, Doctor?"

Harstad replied, "I'll be fine. There was some ligament damage from the shrapnel, but Doctor Tropp made short work of it. I'll be back to full duty in a day or two." Nodding toward Konya, she added, "I opted against trophy scars, though."

"Coward," said Konya, his eyes narrowing in the mischievous manner he summoned all too infrequently, but which Chen had noticed was on the increase even before this mission. Before she could remark on that, the doors opened again, this time to admit Commanders Worf and La Forge.

"There she is," said the chief engineer, his face brightening upon seeing Harstad.

"Here I am," replied the doctor. "Where have you been?"

"Fixing the ship."

"It's always something."

La Forge gestured to Worf. "Like having to repair and clean up the shuttlecraft other people leave with the aliens who capture them."

The Klingon's expression remained fixed. "The *Siouxsie* was returned reasonably intact."

"Yeah, but not for their lack of trying," replied La Forge, and it required physical effort for Chen not to laugh at the glare Worf directed at him. Following the *Arrow*'s destruction, the Raqilan had returned the *Siouxsie* to the *Enterprise*, but it was evident that their engineers had attempted to access the shuttlecraft's systems. The security lockout programmed by Lieutenant Elfiki into its onboard computer had thwarted those efforts, but repairing the damage the craft had sustained during its encounter with Raqilan patrol ships would keep La Forge and his team busy for the next few days.

"The damage was as unavoidable as it is regrettable," said Worf. "However, if I am not mistaken, all of the shuttlecraft were due for scheduled maintenance anyway."

La Forge offered an expression of mock annoyance. "Yeah, that makes it all better." He moved to Harstad's bed and she shifted her position so the pair could greet each other with a warm embrace that made Chen smile.

"Lieutenant Konya," said Worf as he moved to stand at the foot of the bed, "it is good to see you recovered from your injuries. Your actions aboard the *Arrow* were noteworthy, and I am pleased to inform you that I have submitted a request for commendation to Captain Picard."

"Thank you, sir," Konya replied, and Chen noted how he now sat a bit straighter in the bed. "I appreciate that."

Turning to Chen, the Klingon said, "I have made a similar request on your behalf, Lieutenant. Your actions were well above the requirements of duty, in keeping with the finest traditions of Starfleet officers." For the first time, he smiled. "And with the heart of a warrior."

Surprised by the news but also the unexpected compliment, Chen felt a surge of embarrassment. "Thank you, Commander. I don't know what to say."

"I will notify the captain of your response," said Worf. "I am sure he will take great pleasure from that."

"Wow," Konya said, unable to stifle a laugh as he reached to tap Chen on her arm. "Maybe you should ask Doctor Tropp for an analgesic cream or something to treat that burn."

Appearing satisfied with himself, Worf turned and walked away without another word, leaving Chen once more alone with Konya.

"Is it me, or is he getting funnier?" Konya asked.

Chen replied, "It's you." Looking around to see if anyone else might be within earshot, she turned back to Konya reached for his hand. "Listen, about before."

"Before what?"

"Don't make me smack you," Chen said, grinning.

"You know what I mean. Before, on the *Arrow*. You, me, the apology."

"Oh, right," Konya said, drawing out his response. "That. I seem to recall suggesting we might discuss it later."

Chen nodded. "Well, it's later." With everything that had happened, she had not had time to process their brief encounter on the *Arrow*. Like anything else not pertaining to the matters at hand, she had pushed aside those feelings, forcing them into their own little sealed compartment in the back of her mind until she could revisit them without distraction. Now, it seemed, was the right time.

Squeezing her hand, Konya smiled. "Look, I know I sprang that on you, but I meant what I said. I'm sorry about everything. No matter what, Trys, you're my friend." He paused, his gaze shifting to the sheet covering him from the waist down. "When I heard you were staying behind to help Jodis and Bnira, I was scared." Bringing over his free hand, he rested it atop hers. "Scared I'd never see you again, and worried that I'd never get a chance to make things right between us." As if sensing her hesitation, he added, "I'm not asking for anything. I'll respect whatever you tell me, and I promise that we're still friends, no matter what else might happen."

Feeling the warmth of his hands on hers, Chen said nothing. Instead, she leaned toward him and kissed him. They held the kiss for several seconds before Chen pulled back, her eyes meeting his.

"I'm not sure I understood you," said Konya, his expression deadpan.

This time, Chen did smack him, playfully and on the arm. "Idiot."

"Hey, you two," said Harstad. "Let's keep it professional here."

Chen and Konya looked over to see that the doctor had risen from her bed, and Commander La Forge now was escorting her to the door.

"Wait," Konya said, "you got released?"

"Good behavior," replied Harstad, "which means you'll be here for a while yet. I've been given bed rest for a couple of days before I return to duty." She nodded to La Forge. "So he gets to wait on me hand and foot until then. Doctor's orders."

"I'm regretting this already," La Forge said.

Konya said, "Thanks for taking care of me on that ship, Doc. I owe you one."

"Oh, no," replied Harstad. "You saved my life over there. We're even. You just take care of yourself, and you'll be back to regular duty in no time."

"Maybe I'll ask for some of that bed rest." The lieutenant smiled, nudging Chen with one finger. "I just need somebody for that waiting on hand and foot thing."

Chen slapped him again. Harder this time.

"Captain Picard, I cannot thank you enough for all you have done on behalf of the Raqilan people. We eagerly await your address to our peace delegation, and feel that with your guidance and wisdom, we finally will achieve the peace which has eluded us for so long."

Sitting at the desk in his ready room, Picard studied the image of Envoy Dnovlat on his desktop monitor. Unlike during their previous conversations, the Raqilan diplomat was brimming with enthusiasm, which she allowed to penetrate her otherwise composed, even detached façade. Her unfiltered emotion was contagious, and Picard found himself smiling in response.

"The honor will be mine, Envoy. I have already received authorization to meet with your delegation, and our Federation Council anticipates a constructive dialogue. Perhaps it will be the first step toward a longer, cooperative relationship between all our peoples." Though the *Enterprise* was scheduled to continue with its exploration mission, Starfleet Command had approved his request for a brief extension of their time in the Canborek system. As Admiral Akaar had put it, there was much to be gained by establishing formal relations with the Raqilan and the Golvonek, the first potential Federation allies in the Odyssean Pass.

"*That is my hope, as well, Captain.*" She paused, her expression softening. "*If I have one regret, it is that Jodis and Bnira cannot be with us.*"

Picard nodded. "They will be there, at least in some sense, as the dream they held for peace is shared by many Raqilan and Golvonek. Pursuing that dream honors their memory."

"*They are being called 'Ambassadors of Destiny' in some circles,*" Dnovlat replied. "*It seems an apt title. With your help, we will see their dream realized.*" Something or someone off screen made her turn, and after a moment, she returned her attention to Picard. "*I am afraid that duty summons me, Captain. I look forward to meeting you in person and perhaps sharing with you some of the delicacies of our people.*"

"I would welcome that, Envoy, and the opportunity to return the favor."

"*Farewell, Captain.*"

With the communication finished, Picard sighed, relishing the end of the long day he and his crew had endured. There still was much work to be done, of course, aboard ship as well as with the Raqilan and the Golvonek,

but soon the *Enterprise* would be off again, ready to encounter what might be waiting out among the stars.

Exiting his ready room, he stepped onto the bridge
to find Commander Worf standing in front of the center seat, reviewing something on a padd. Upon noticing
Picard's arrival, Worf nodded in his direction. "Captain."

Seeing Taurik standing near the aft starboard turbolift
alcove, his hands clasped behind his back, Picard said to
Worf, "Number One, you have the bridge." He walked
toward Taurik. "Commander."

"You wanted to see me, sir," replied the Vulcan.

Picard gestured for Taurik to accompany him into the
turbolift. After directing the car to his quarters, he turned
to face the engineer. "It seems we have matters of great
sensitivity to discuss, Commander."

Nodding, Taurik replied, "Indeed. In accordance with
the Temporal Prime Directive, I have completed a detailed report for transmission to the Department of Temporal Investigations. I am ready to dispatch that report on
your order, sir."

"Is there anything in there you can tell me?" Picard
asked, hearing the whine of the turbolift as it slowed its
descent before moving horizontally.

"No, sir. Per regulations and after careful consideration, I have determined that there is nothing with which
I am at liberty to discuss with you. The only thing I can
offer is my assurance that with the Raqilan weapon ship
destroyed, there is very little likelihood of this information being discovered or accessed by anyone else. I have
compartmentalized and encrypted the data to which I
was exposed, and it has been placed in a secure archive
within the main computer. That archive is accessible only
to me via voice authorization and a fractal encryption key,

which I will provide upon order to Temporal Investigations agents when they arrive to retrieve it. I believe I have acted in the best interests of Federation security and the well-being of the *Enterprise*, its crew, and you, Captain."

Picard smiled at the engineer's resolve. "I have no doubt about that, Commander." He could not deny his desire to hear more, especially anything that might pertain to future events involving the Federation. He also was intrigued by more straightforward information, such as the factors that were considered by Raqilan civilian and military leaders before making the decision to construct the *Arrow* in the first place. Despite his own feelings, Picard knew that Taurik was doing the proper thing by isolating himself with the knowledge he had obtained.

"Have you informed Starfleet Command about the wrecked planet-destroying machine?" Taurik asked.

"Yes. A science team will be dispatched to examine it and perhaps even collect the remains for transport to one of our research facilities, as was done with the original machine. I suspect this discovery will make some small group of scientists very happy." With the loss of the original planet killer during one of Starfleet's final confrontations with the Borg, Starfleet research specialists had been without any examples of the ancient alien technology. There would be much celebration when it was learned that another, possibly older version of the device had been found.

Taurik was silent until the turbolift began to slow, at which time he said, "Computer, hold turbolift." In response to his command, the car halted its horizontal motion. Taurik waited for that before returning his attention to Picard.

"Captain, I must admit to a certain degree of trepidation regarding the knowledge I possess with regard to future events. It will be . . . agreeable . . . to discuss this with Temporal Investigations, but I am troubled about how they may react and what that might mean for my status aboard the *Enterprise.*"

It was not an unreasonable concern, Picard knew. It was likely that DTI agents would submit Taurik to extensive debriefing sessions with an aim of learning from the Vulcan every scrap of information he had seen. They also would expend considerable effort studying the information to which he had gone to great lengths to quarantine, with special attention paid to any information pertaining to the *Arrow's* temporal displacement technology. Based on what he understood of the department's voluminous rules and procedures for handling temporal violations of any sort, there was no way to predict any lasting repercussions to Taurik.

"Whatever happens, Commander, you have my full confidence and unwavering trust. Your integrity is beyond reproach, and I will support you to the utmost of my ability."

Taurik's right eyebrow arched. "Thank you, Captain. Your trust is most gratifying."

After releasing the turbolift and excusing the engineer to carry on with his evening plans, Picard made his way to his quarters. The doors were still parting when a small ball of energy leaped from the sofa at the center of the main room and rocketed toward him.

"Papa!" said René, bounding across the room to take his father's hand. "Look! Mommy's home."

Picard smiled at Beverly, who had found a comfortable place sprawled across the sofa. "Welcome home." He had been looking forward to this all evening. The events of the past days had seen fit to keep both of them focused on their duties, and then there was poor René, who seemed none the worse for wear following an extended stay with Hailan Casmir and his staff in the *Enterprise*'s childcare facility. Just seeing his son was enough to alleviate the stresses of the just concluded mission.

Not bothering to move from the sofa, Beverly said, "It's good to be home."

Though she and the away team had been back aboard the *Enterprise* for several hours, she had been engrossed in patient care and he had been dealing with the aftermath of the *Arrow*'s destruction. As such, this was the first time they had spoken to each other since her return. "Are you all right?"

"Just tired," Beverly replied. "Nothing a week's worth of sleep won't cure."

"I like the sound of that," Picard said, taking a seat on the sofa near Beverly's head and allowing René to climb into his lap.

Reaching up to place a hand on his leg, Beverly said, "I don't remember exploration being this exhausting. Is it going to be this way from now on?"

"It's not supposed to be," Picard replied as René shifted to a comfortable position before reaching for a book lying on the end table to his right. "The excitement of finding out what happens next is supposed to make us forget all about that."

"What happens next, Papa?" René asked.

Picard smiled. "That's a good question, and there's only one way to find out. We have to go and look for ourselves, don't we?"

"Then let's go."

"See what I mean?" Beverly chuckled. "Exhausting."

Unable to resist teasing her, Picard said, "Of course, I suppose the simple explanation is that we're just getting—"

"Do not finish that sentence." A moment later, she asked, "I was thinking about a hot bath and a glass of wine. What about you?"

"He's going to read!" René beamed, handing Picard the book he had retrieved. For his part, Picard was eager to lose himself in the pages of a book—any book—if only for a short while. That he could share one of his most treasured pursuits with his son made the activity all the more special. Already he could feel the pressures of command slipping away, allowing him a few precious moments of respite. They would return, of course, but not just yet. René would see to that.

Recognizing the tome his son had given him, Picard could not help the wry grin he directed to his wife.

"The one with the aliens," René said. "They crashed on Earth a long time ago, and it was a big secret. Read it, Papa."

Rolling her eyes, Beverly threw up her hands in mock surrender. "I'm leaving now." She headed for the master bedroom, leaving Picard and René alone on the couch. The boy shifted his position again as he tapped the book's cover, anxious to continue their shared adventure.

"What happens next, Papa?"

ACKNOWLEDGMENTS

Thanks very much to my editors at Pocket Books, who called on me to continue the adventures of Captain Picard and the *Enterprise*-E after the events of *The Fall*. One of the things I hoped to see after that miniseries was a return to exploration that is a hallmark of *Star Trek*, and when I was writing *Peaceable Kingdoms* I did my best to leave as clean a slate as possible for the next writer to take the baton for this new chapter in the story of *Star Trek: The Next Generation*. I had no idea at the time that I would be that writer, or else I might've set up things a bit differently. I mean, who doesn't want to see Picard and the gang on vacation, solving a murder mystery on some resort planet before heading off to seek out new life and civilizations, am I right?

Hello? Bueller?

Thanks also to the incomparable Doug Drexler, whose artwork graces the cover of this book. In recent years, Mr. Drexler has created some truly beautiful art for *Star Trek* novels and calendars, including my personal favorite from the *Star Trek: Vanguard* novel series, *Open Secrets*. That said, I think he may have outdone himself this time. He showed me a rough version just as I was looking for that last little bit of juice to finish the manuscript. It was the perfect motivation to help me reach the finish line. You truly are a steely-eyed missile man, Mr. D!

I would be remiss in my duties if I did not offer a sincere salute and tip of my hat to renowned science fiction author Norman Spinrad. If you're reading this part of the book first, then I won't spoil it for you as to why I feel compelled to thank him for his inspiration.

Finally, dear reader, I offer my sincere appreciation for your continuing support of my work. I am very fortunate to do what I do, you are a big reason for that, and I remind myself of that fact each and every day. Thank you!

ABOUT THE AUTHOR

Dayton Ward has been modified to fit this medium, to write in the space allotted, and has been edited for content. Reader discretion is advised.

Visit Dayton on the web at www.daytonward.com.